GOOFY FOOT

David Daniel 1945-

Thomas Dunne Books | St. Martin's Minotaur
New York

Thomas Dunne Books.
An imprint of St. Martin's Press.

www.minotaurbooks.com

Library of Congress Cataloging-in-Publication Data

Daniel, David.
    Goofy foot : an Alex Rasmussen mystery / David Daniel.
        p.   cm.
    ISBN 0-312-32349-2
    1. Rasmussen, Alex (Fictitious character)—Fiction.   2. Private
investigators—Massachusetts—Lowell—Fiction.   3. Lowell
(Mass.)—Fiction.   I. Title.

PS3554.A5383G66 2004
813'.54—dc22

                                                2003058550

10   9   8   7   6   5   4   3   2

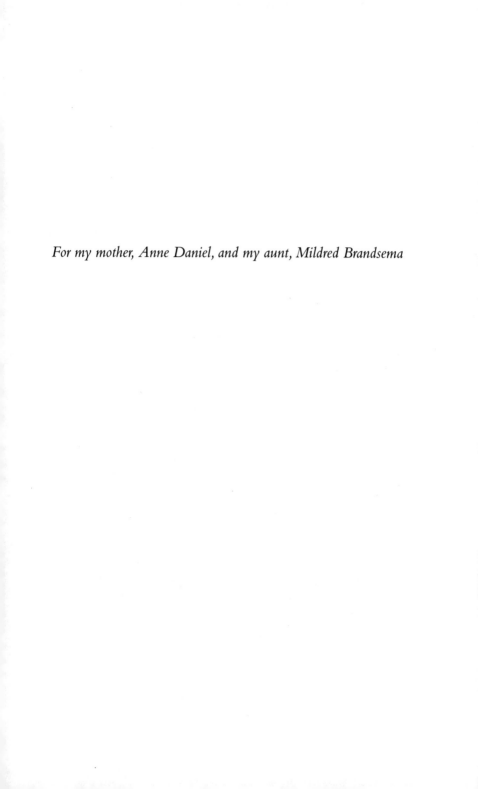

For my mother, Anne Daniel, and my aunt, Mildred Brandsema

Acknowledgments

Thanks to Ruth Cavin, Daniel Kotler, and James Evans at Thomas Dunne Books/St. Martin's Press, and to Erika Schmid, Tim Trask, and David Bergquist. Thanks, too, to *The Offering* (spring 2002), edited by Anthony Szczesiul, and the Whistler House Museum of Art: Poets and Painters series, where portions of this novel first appeared.

GOOFY
FOOT

1

I looked up and saw the old guy standing in my office doorway, pulling a sawed-off shotgun out of a brown paper bag. He was wild-eyed, winded from the three-flight climb. The bag was the long, thin kind that hero sandwiches come in. He tossed it aside and stepped toward my desk, where my morning coffee steamed in the cup. "You're Mr. Rasmussen . . ."

"Whoa!" I threw my hands high.

"I'm gonna give it to you!"

My heart was banging off the tin ceiling. "Hold on."

"It's gotta be now!"

The ugly snout of the shotgun glared at me in the June sunlight sliced by the venetian blinds—maybe the last sunlight I'd ever see. It was double-barrel, big-gauge, and this close it was like looking into the Ted Williams Tunnel. If it went off, I was pâté.

"Mr. Rasmussen—"

He knew my name. I tried to run the flushed mug. The loser in a bitter divorce case I'd done investigative work for? An insurance cheat I'd outed? A face in the crowd?

And that's when I recognized him.

He worked in the pizza shop around the corner. Tony's, what

else? A nice old fellow, I'd always figured. So he'd cracked. Standing in the Bessemer blast of the pizza oven, one too many customers saying "Hold the anchovies," and he'd wigged and come through the building at 10 Kearney Square—the Fairburn Building, if you take your irony straight—looking for people to shoot on sight. Another mad dog fizzing with rage, needing someone to blame. Except nobody else was around. The city golf tournament was on, and there wasn't a businessman, accountant, or lawyer to be found; they were all out whooping it up at Mount Pleasant or at Vesper. Not private eyes, though. There was one working, and this old guy had found him.

"Look—" I was still scrambling for a life ring.

I heard the siren then—had been hearing it for the past minute, wailing somewhere. It was on Merrimack Street now, just outside, but rather than calm me, it was a razor strop across the raw edge of my nerves. Would the old guy get me before the cops could get him? He stepped closer, pushing the office door shut behind him. He said, "It ain't working no more, Mr. Rasmussen."

I blinked.

"I was cleaning the vent over the oven. I found it on top the ceiling." I noticed now that the weapon was rust-spotted. "One of them dropped ceilings," he said. "A gun I don't know where it come from, and it's lying up there. You're some kind of cop, ain't you? I don't like guns. Guns scare me. I brung it for you to get rid of it."

I wanted to hug him. He'd found the old gun and it had spooked him and he didn't know what to do about it, so he'd stuck the barrel in a paper bag and gone around the corner because he'd once seen the gold lettering on my third-floor window—ALEX RASMUSSEN, PRIVATE INVESTIGATIONS—except someone had spotted him and punched 911. Carrying an unlicensed firearm, even in a sandwich bag, was a one-year mandatory in Massachusetts. And if this seemed silly, stranger things had happened. I couldn't see the scared old guy coping with prison. Or me losing my ability to earn a living. I heard stealthy footsteps in the corridor. I looked around and grabbed an idea. Maybe it'd play. Or maybe it would get us both cells at Concord.

"Give me that," I said. "Quick."

I yanked open the coat closet and stood the shotgun in the dark back corner, behind my trench coat and a vacuum cleaner. I grabbed the vac's flex hose and twisted the black plastic tube off the end. I kicked the closet door shut. I heard the outer door to my waiting room rattle open. I had the eighteen-inch-long tube on the desk as the inner office door flew open and a uniform edged in in a crouch, his 9-mm two-handed in front of him. He was nobody from my days on the job—the faces kept getting younger. He was panting, too: nerves, probably, or the climb. He knew the moves, though. Hands choking the thick rubber grip of the nine, arms twitching the piece this way and that, finger on the trigger. His tension rang off the metal file cabinets. "Where is it?"

"Down, boy!" I said. "Where's what?"

"The weapon."

"Bottom drawer. What's going on?"

"Don't move." With his left hand he brought his walkie-talkie to his mouth. "Okay, I'm here on the third floor, suite three-one-five."

"I'm coming up," said a second voice. "The elevator working?"

The cop looked at me. "The elevator work?"

"Not since before Clinton."

"No," he told the other voice. The voice swore and signed off.

"Okay, lay the weapon on the desk," the cop ordered.

I unlocked and opened the drawer carefully. I reached past the fifth of Wild Turkey—a gift from a client—and hoisted the .38 Smith & Wesson by the trigger guard and set it on the linoleum desktop. "It's legal," I said.

"The other, I'm talking. Shotgun." The nine ratcheted toward my visitor. "Someone saw you come up the block hauling steel."

"Hauling steel?" I said. "Where'd you get that? Creative writing class?"

The nine leaped my way. "Knock off the crap. What's your name?"

I told him.

"You?"

The old guy couldn't get a name out. He looked ready to jump from his skin. "He wouldn't know a Glock from a glockenspiel," I said. "What is this?"

"It's in a bag," the cop said.

"A paper bag?" I let out a breath that I hoped sounded like recognition and relief. "Three minutes ago?" I lifted the plastic pipe, and I retrieved the bag. The rest was easy: my old pal had borrowed my carpet sweeper and forgot to return the attachment, until now. The cop used his walkie-talkie and nixed backup. To justify the hike, I supposed, he asked to see paper for the .38. I was happy to oblige. He lamped the carry permit and my investigator's license, both neat and up-to-date, and looked as relieved as we were.

"How come you're not out at the tournament with the rest of the city?" I asked him when he'd holstered his heater. "You're missing the tee-offs."

"I might ask you the same."

"And give crime a holiday?"

When the cop was gone, the old guy clamped my right hand in a damp double handshake. "I knew you was the one to come to."

"I'm him," I said, my voice finally down in the range where it belonged.

"You take care of the gun, eh? I don't want."

"Okay. I'll take care of it."

He was still pumping my hand. "You come by. Vito—that's me—I make you a pizza, special. Whatever you like. You like anchovies?"

I didn't say a word.

When he'd gone, too, I locked the outer door. I'd had enough company for one morning. I brought the sawed-off out of hiding. It was a Parker Brothers, according to the name etched on the housing; not the board-game makers, I guessed, though it wasn't a gun name I'd ever heard of. It was twelve-gauge, ugly as sin and as empty as my safe-deposit box. Termites had been working on giving it a pistol grip. Under the dust and corrosion, I could make out some scrollwork, but the piece was in dire need of oil and blueing. I tried to remember what the pizza joint had been before it was Tony's and came up with a string of grease pits. If the shotgun was wanted in some old crime, I'd check it out quietly with a sergeant I knew on the force. If it was clean, I'd take it home for dismantling and disposal. Or maybe the hawk shop downstairs would give me ten bucks for it as a curio. For now, it could rust in peace in the closet. As I shut the door, the telephone rang.

"Mr. Rasmussen?" It was a woman asking this time. She had a nice voice, refined and a little uncertain. "Do you—I know it sounds crazy—my name's Mrs. Jensen, by the way. Paula Jensen. Do you make house calls?"

"Where to, Mrs. Jensen?"

"I'm in Apple Valley. Would it be possible to have someone come out?"

"What's the nature of the business?"

"My daughter may be missing."

"You're not sure?"

"Well, I know where she is . . . or who she's with, at least. I just haven't heard from them in a few days. I know it's probably nothing. Still . . ."

"How old is your daughter?"

"Sixteen."

I could have pressed on with smart questions—Who was she with? Where?—could have told her to start at the beginning, but I was still shaky from my face-to-face with guns. Besides, voices sometimes told you things about the people they belonged to. Paula Jensen's told me she was trying to mask real worry. "What's your address?" I asked.

2

Apple Valley is fifteen minutes west of Lowell. Lauren and I used to go there for autumn drives to pick Macs and Red Delicious, but Lauren was ex, living in Florida, and acres of orchards and fields had been felled, plowed under, paved over—no connection. Even the old stonewalls, those fossil symbols of Yankee practicality, weren't inviolable. The past was being dismantled to make way for housing developments and express malls and new roads for fossil-fuel guzzlers. Even so, Apple Valley seemed a world away from Lowell as I got off 495 and headed through the town center. My four-year-old black Probe GT had been payment in a barter deal I'd worked out with a fellow called Honest Abe—at least, that's what it said on his marquee, complete with red, white and blue propellers spinning in the breeze. HONEST ABE'S PRE-OWNED WHEELS. I hadn't taken the 8-ball shift knob off the 5-speed yet. I was starting to like it.

I found the address Paula Jensen had given me—a large home ringed with lawn and oak woods, in one of the newer subdivisions—and pulled into the driveway. Eleven-A.M. sunshine was slow-cooking the asphalt in front of a three-car garage as I climbed out. I peered into the nearest bay and saw a Blazer parked there, along with a ride-on mower almost as big as the Chevy. At the front door I pressed the bell and heard it chime inside with a rich *bing bong* that I could never hear without conjuring up the tag line of a certain cosmetics giant—talk about the power of advertising. But I didn't get a chance to use the line, or any line. No one answered. I wandered around the side where there was a stockade fence. Through the cracks I saw the aquamarine glimmer of a swimming pool. On a patio adjacent to the pool, a woman stood at a gas grill. I used the gate.

"Mrs. Jensen?"

She swung around in surprise and let out a breath. "Oh, I didn't hear you."

"Sorry," I said.

"Are you from Mr. Rasmussen's office?"

I had to grin. "The one and only."

She wiped her hands on a chef's towel and shook my hand. "You got here quickly." The nice voice from the telephone fit her. She was small and pretty, with delicate features, her shoulder-length, sun-streaked brown hair tied back in a loose ponytail, a fine mist of freckles across her cheeks. Her eyes were the shade of her faded denim shorts. "I'm just getting a light lunch ready. Ross is coming home early, for a change—he likes to dine al fresco."

With that setting, I would, too. "Tell me about your daughter," I said.

We took chairs at a wrought-iron table. Under the umbrella the temperature was a pleasant eighty.

"Shel—that's Michelle—went to California to be with her dad. She goes every summer. Except this year, Ben—that's her dad—arranged to drive back across the country with her and rent a house down on the South Shore of Boston for a week."

"And Ross is . . . ?"

"My husband." She blushed becomingly beneath her tan. "Current husband. Ben Nickerson was my ex—*is* my ex. Oh my, am I being silly?"

"No, I just want to get the details right. Please go on."

"I guess they had fun driving cross-country, from what little I could get from Shel. Now they've been here for several days. In Standish. Only I haven't heard from them since the day before yesterday."

"Is that unusual?"

"Not really, but she—"

A portable phone chirped nearby. "Excuse me." She answered it, listened for a few seconds, then lowered the phone and held it against her chest. "I'll be right with you," she told me. "It isn't her."

I stepped away to give her space. I adjusted the gas flame, futzed at grilling chicken a moment with a long fork, the way I'd seen a chef on TV do, then wandered to the pool, where an inflated vinyl alligator floated in one corner. I went over to peer through a back door into the garage. In the bay adjacent to the Blazer a lot of toys were spread on the floor: a doll's house, a small-size girl's bicycle, a Barbie Corvette.

Paula Jensen had slipped into the house, and now she reappeared. She had a kind of awkward grace when she moved. She handed me a framed photograph. "This is Michelle."

I looked at a pretty girl standing before a fireplace hung with Christmas stockings, wearing an I-really-don't-want-to-be-here smile. Her eyes seemed wary and wise. "You said she's sixteen?"

"Well, that was taken last winter. I don't have anything really recent."

"You've tried calling where she's staying?"

"And get no answer. She tends to turn off her cell phone when I call. I even drove to Standish last evening to see if they were at the beach house Ben rented, but they weren't. I talked to the police. When I didn't hear anything this morning—I don't know, maybe I'm overreacting. Ross thinks I am. I'd be all freaked out if I didn't know she was with Ben."

"What did the police say?"

"They told me I could fill out a report, though the policeman said it might be premature—given her age and the fact that she's with her dad."

"Is there someplace else they might've gone? Other family members in the area?"

"No, none. I suppose they could've driven to the Cape, though

Ben hates the traffic this time of year. He went the last time he was here, and it depressed him for days. He still has a Patti Page image of Cape Cod. Maybe they went out fishing. They both love the ocean—though if it was an overnight trip, I hope they'd have told me."

"Is it possible to take a look at Michelle's room?"

"Search it, you mean?"

"Look at it. It could give us an idea of where she might've gone."

"Well . . . I don't like to invade her privacy, but—"

She lowered the grill flame further and we went inside. The house was spacious and cool. She led me up carpeted stairs. Her daughter's bedroom was dim, the blinds drawn to the sills, and had a faint smell of oft-worn clothes, though when I put on a light I saw it was actually pretty neat for a teenager's room. The bed was made, there was a computer on a desk, and a field hockey stick and a tennis racket were collecting dust in one corner. The walls were papered with rock posters. A few were of bands that my generation had liked and that hadn't done an interesting thing artistically since. Most of the posters, however, showed recent musicians, bony-chested guys with wraparound tattoos and more hair than a beauty salon. A CD player sat on a bedside table. I poked a button, and music came from the speakers. The jewel case depicted a scaly half-human figure nailed spread-eagle to a boulder, its head, hands and clawed feet forming the points of a star. Blood was running down the boulder. There was a small child in the foreground, gazing at the figure. *Nihilistic Angels* was the title of the CD, by a group called Satan Bugg. I set the case aside and shut off the player. The music didn't bear comment.

"Does she use the Internet a lot?"

"Doing papers for school, mostly. We've got a house hookup downstairs, but Shel isn't much interested. She's a rather indifferent student. Katie, on the other hand . . ."

I glanced at her.

"I'm sorry—Katie is my other daughter. Ross's and mine. She's eight. Her room is through there."

I opened a door to the adjoining room and poked my head in.

The room was sunlit and had shelves overflowing with stuffed animals and books. The wall posters were of horses in misty meadows and *Lord of the Rings* characters. "Katie's at day camp this summer," Paula Jensen offered at my elbow. I drew the door shut, and we went back out to the landing. "Well?"

"Unless your husband's on the charcoal diet, we'd better get downstairs."

She managed to save the chicken and put it into a covered dish. "How old was Michelle when you and your former husband divorced?" I asked.

"She was five."

"What's her bond with him like?"

"It's good. Especially in the past few years. She looks forward to seeing him each summer."

"What about before the past few years?"

"Mmm . . . it was okay. You know, an adjustment."

"Does she get along with your husband?"

"With Ross?" She looked surprised. "Just fine."

"And with you?"

"Like any sixteen-year-old girl and her mother, I guess. Why?"

"Has Ross been married before?"

"No. Mr. Rasmussen, I'm not sure what—"

"Mrs. Jensen, I'm willing to look into this for you, but the more you can tell me, the better chance I'll have. I need something to go on."

"Like what?"

"Information. Like, there are a lot of toys—upstairs and in the garage—but Michelle's pile definitely seems smaller. And no recent photo?"

"We did have a family shot taken." Her brow creased with uncertainty. "It may be in Ross's office."

Seeing that she wasn't going to run with the ball, I trudged on. "Sometimes . . . a busy man, with his own child and a stepchild—"

I broke off as her chin tightened and, unexpectedly, her eyes filled. When she'd blinked back the tears, she managed a blurry smile. "Actually, that was Ross who called before. He's been working day and night on a big case, and the client had Red Sox tickets, so they were going to go. I was hoping he'd get here so you two could meet. He knows more about this sort of thing."

"About missing children?"

"About investigations. He's an attorney."

"Does he know you called me?"

She shook her head. "I did it on my own."

"What's his take on this?"

"He agrees with the police, thinks it could be just Ben being irresponsible. He'd definitely say that getting outside help was premature."

"Could it be?"

She drew a breath and sighed. "Ben hasn't always been the most reliable person. Can I . . . can I think about this for a little bit, Mr. Rasmussen? I'll pay you for your time."

"No need. Call it a free consultation. And call me Alex."

She smiled gratefully. She glanced at the food. "This won't keep. Have you eaten yet? You haven't. Stay," she said, then added apologetically, "It's nothing fancy."

It was when your idea of gourmet food was a hot dog at the lunch counter at Wal-Mart. We sat at the wrought-iron table overlooking the pool and the woods beyond the stockade fence. There were lettuce and tomatoes and a cold potato salad, which she served with the chicken on plates painted like slices of watermelon. She poured lemonade. I asked her to describe her daughter. I learned that Michelle's hair was dyed black now, worn short, and that she had a pierced eyebrow, which sometimes sported a silver ring.

The food was good, and I ate a second helping. Between chews I asked about her husband. She told me the name of his firm, which I recognized as a top-flight outfit known for corporate and civil law. "He works hard. Too hard, maybe, but try to tell him that." She mustered a grin. "He'll make partner. We've been married nine years and have Katie. She's bright, and Ross loves her, but he's . . ." She sighed. "So busy. His way of showing his love is to buy her things. With Shel . . . it's been tough on both sides, right from the start. They've kept a distance. Shel spends a lot of time in her own head."

"Listening to Satan Bugg?"

"Awful, isn't it? It's so angry-sounding. But it's probably no worse than what we listened to."

"Like hell it isn't," I said.

"No, you're right."

We talked some more. As I got ready to go, she grew anxious again. "Ross just naturally isn't as concerned as I am over this. He says it's only been a day and a half. He thinks I'm being paranoid. Maybe I am a bit, I don't know. I do know Ben, and I don't think he'd pull any kind of stunt."

"Was there a custody dispute?"

"Not really. We were living in San Diego at the time. We both wanted what would be best for Shel. Ben wanted us to live near enough so he could see her regularly, but once Ross and I got married and we were going to come back here, Ben briefly made an issue of it. I think that was only because he felt threatened. Ross can be pretty aggressive. But once things were inevitable, Ben accepted it. He's actually been good. He comes east every other summer, and Michelle goes out there alternate years. He's a marine biologist, so he likes taking her to the coast."

"Is her last name the same as his?"

"Nickerson, yes." The note of concern in her voice was unmistakable. "I don't know if I should tell you this . . ."

"Then maybe you should."

"Well . . . I woke last night at some god-awful hour, and I sat up in bed and—" She caught a breath. "And just below the threshold of actually *speaking* it, I thought, 'he's dead.' "

" 'He' being your ex?"

"I don't know. I'm not sure what I meant, only that it felt real. I'm pretty intuitive. I think it's this left-hand, right-brain thing. Ross told me it was just anxiety leaking out." She smiled feebly. "What do you think?"

"If you hire me, you're getting an investigator, not a shrink. With missing a person, you never know, but I've had some luck finding people. Of course, if it is anything more serious, it's a matter for the police."

She nodded. "I know."

"But you don't have to worry about getting my approval. If she were my daughter, I'd be doing the same thing."

She seemed relieved. "Have you got children?"

"No."

"A wife?" She caught herself. "That's none of my business. It just came out."

I knew it had. The answer—yes—almost just came out. "It's been two years. I'm divorced."

"I'm sorry."

"Me, too. Well, if you want, I can drive down to Standish and have a look around."

"I'd like that. How soon?"

"Right now, if you like."

"Yes. Do you want me to go along? Or call ahead at least? I've spoken with the police down there."

"I'll figure out an approach. I've got an eye patch and a wax nose that work sometimes for undercover work." She smiled uncertainly a moment before seeing that I was kidding. "It's a small town," I said. "Could I borrow that photograph you showed me? And have you got one of your ex?"

Ben she didn't have, but she got me two of Michelle: the wary kid with wise eyes in both.

"Do you know what kind of car Nickerson is driving?"

"It's a dark blue Grand Cherokee, with tinted glass. It'll have California plates."

I told her what I charged and about the retainer fee. In the kitchen she plucked a pen from the bouquet of pencils and pens in a jar on the counter. "Whom shall I make the check out to?"

"Mass Electric, Blue Cross Blue Shield. My landlord." I smiled. "Just write it to me; I'll fend off the others." I gave her my card and pointed out the spelling change. The "Rassmusen" on the card was supposed to be one *s* the first time, two the second.

"Is that on purpose?" she asked.

"Dyslexic printer. His math's fine, though. If you hear anything in the meantime, the phone number's right."

She walked me back out to my car. "I feel better," she said. "I couldn't bear just sitting. I feel like I've taken some action." She gave me a look of shy gratitude and shook my hand, and for an instant, before she let go, I had the idea she didn't want to.

"I'll be in touch in a few hours," I said. "And for the record, I'm a leftie, too."

She waved as I drove off. Going toward the highway, I thought about a recent conversation I'd had with my office neighbor, Fred Meecham, Esq. He'd said I needed more exposure. A squib in the yellow pages wasn't sufficient anymore. Why didn't I put an ad in the *Sun* or buy some time on the local cable TV channel, he said. He said things were slow, maybe there were people out there who only needed a little prompting to come out of the closet with mysteries they wanted solved. It could be money well spent, he said. Could I do my own voiceover? I asked. Or get a plane to pull a sign over the stadium where Lowell's Red Sox farm team played? He was serious, he said. I asked him how come *he* didn't run an ad; there were attorneys who did, and he didn't seem that busy lately either. He got flustered and snorted that it would be unprofessional. Now, looping onto 495, I composed ad copy. "P.I.: House Calls, Grills Tended, Master of Disguise, Right-Brain Thinker." It had possibilities galore.

3

The distance between Lowell and Standish was sixty-five miles, and about forty years. Located on the South Shore of Boston, north of the Cape, it was what you'd expect. It was an All-American town, according to the sign as you entered, and a Crime Watch community, and the Rotary met Tuesdays at noon at Dimitri's. It was a tidy town center with white-spired Congregational and Unitarian churches and a sun-bleached row of shops arranged around the wedge of the colonial cemetery and town green, complete with old cannons, a bandstand and a moss-flecked granite cistern brimming with pink geraniums. Everything seemed to repose behind picket fences and under the graceful fans of what might be the last American elm trees anywhere. At the end of the road, where Sea Street met Atlantic Avenue, sat a few restaurants, a realtor and a bottled-goods store. Beyond lay the ocean. A rock jetty went out at an angle, serving as a breakwater so that boats could moor inside its protective arm. And they did; the blue water was dotted with sailboats and cruisers of every description. Log onto the *Yankee* magazine Web site, keyword "quaint."

In truth, Standish was pretty in the afternoon light. I opened the car windows to the aromas of the ocean, mowed grass and honeysuckle. A knot of teenagers was standing on a corner in front of a rustic drugstore that had big jars of colored water on display in the window. Was one of the kids Michelle Nickerson? It had been a long time since I was sixteen. I don't think I liked it much: too little to do and too many people telling me how to do it. I still didn't like the last part. Which is probably why I didn't miss wearing a uniform.

The Standish Police HQ was in an old wood-frame structure that said "Municipal Hall" above the columned entrance. There was a pair of spanking new Crown Victoria prowlers parked in front. Sometimes you can go in under the radar, but the town seemed small, and time was a factor—I didn't want to waste any of it being cute. I stepped into a lobby of deep shadows and varnish and the waxy smell I associated with schoolrooms of my childhood. The building also housed the board of selectmen, tax assessor's office, and shellfish warden, with a sign in the form of a large hand, index finger extended, pointing up a stairway for these latter. In Lowell, the hand would be palm open.

On a glass-enclosed bulletin board were instructions on CPR for drowning victims, a Lyme-disease alert, and a photocopied "Missing" flyer with a picture of a slightly cross-eyed Maine coon cat (there was a five-dollar reward).

Unlike a lot of towns that had gone to bulletproof glass and intercoms as a firewall between the public and public servants, here the door swung open in welcome when I turned the knob. The big windows, which formerly would have required a hooked pole to open, had been refitted with energy-efficient panes that kept the air-conditioning in. A young officer in a short-sleeve khaki uniform was sitting before a computer screen the size of a sports-bar TV. The equipment was a lot better than when I'd been a cop, but the hunt-and-peck hadn't changed. He hopped up at once and came over. "Can I help you, sir?"

"I'm looking for Chief Decastro."

"*Del*castro," he corrected. "With an *l*."

"Noted. Is he in?"

"May I ask the nature of your business, sir?"

I told him. Just then, the door rattled behind me. I opened it for another cop, who came in balancing a cardboard tray of take-out coffee cups. "Thanks," he said. He was even younger than the typist, with a boyish blond crew cut and crisp uniform. His mustache seemed to be an attempt to make him look old enough to carry handcuffs and the 9-mm on his belt. The cops seemed to grow green as willows in Standish. He set the coffee tray on the counter. "Jeez, Ferry," the speed typist hissed, "took you long enough."

"No snickerdoodle decaf fresh," Ferry said. "Fran had to brew some. I know you're easing off the high-test, and I didn't figure you wanted non-fat gingerbread latte."

The typist took two of the sealed cups, one of which he set beside his keyboard, and carried the other into the office at the rear. The cups said "The Storm Warning" on them. When he returned, he said, "Sir, if you come with me, the chief will see you."

Delcastro, at least, looked old enough to shave. In fact, his cheeks already had the blue ghost of what would be full shadow come five o'clock. I guessed him to be my age. He had intense dark eyes and a stubborn face, which bore the imprint of his years. His black hair was clipped short and starting to fade to gray at the temples. His arms were suntanned and thick, though he wasn't fat. No piercings, tattoos or visible scars, if it matters. I introduced myself and handed him my investigator's license. Though he tried to mask it, I saw him frown as he studied it. As he began to jot something on a pad, I scanned the office. A big curtained window at his back faced the town green. The walls held the usual cop clutter: framed photos showing our hero at various phases of his illustrious career; citations from a grateful citizenry; assorted insignia from other law enforcement jurisdictions—cops never seemed to outgrow the Boy Scout yen to collect badges. When Chief Delcastro handed my license back, I told him why I was there. He nodded. "I didn't think she seemed all that satisfied. Sit down."

He stepped outside the office a moment and soon reappeared, shutting the door behind him, and took his seat. "I'll tell you the same thing I told Mrs. Jensen. I said if she wants to fill out a missing persons report, I'll file it, and we'll go from there."

"She had the feeling you were discouraging her from that."

"The kid's a teenager; been gone, what, a day?"

"Almost two now. There's the girl's father, also."

"Exactly. Who gets to see his kid, what, a few weeks in a year? If I spent my time looking for every teen that hasn't called a parent or who comes from a broken—excuse me, a *blended* family—I'd be doing nothing else. Have you got kids?"

"No."

Delcastro shifted his weight carefully on the chair and folded his arms. They were more than just thick; muscles moved in them. Gyms cranked out body boys (and girls) these days like link sausage, but I knew they hadn't in his era. A lot of cops his age were wearing bellies bigger than their pension. Some of them, though, still believed in courtesy. I said, "I just wanted to check in with you."

"Look, my town's ready to explode." He glanced out the window, so I did, too. Midmorning traffic flowed past the town green where a group of teens—probably the same ones I'd seen in front of the drugstore—were lazily kicking a little leather sack around, trying to keep it in the air. Did Delcastro think it was a bomb?

"I've got a summer population that triples," he said, "budget restraints that make running full-tilt through Labor Day a juggling act. I've got traffic and beach parties, and at least once every summer someone misses the turn on Sea Street and cracks into the historic marker. I've got the power-squadron types—with more horsepower than brainpower, some of them—turns out I have to winch them off a sandbar. And then there's heatstroke and sunburns and some backyard gourmet three sheets to the wind spritzes lighter fluid on himself and sautés his weenie."

"And don't forget the great white shark," I said.

He rolled a dark blue gaze my way. "Now you listen to me, hotshot!"

I said, "I recall reading about some town in California that made news by declaring itself a nuclear-safe zone, officially banning the dropping of atomic bombs on the place. Why don't you decree this a trouble-free town, so everyone will breathe easier? You've got a full plate, okay; that's the cop business. But keep perspective. It's seasonal. In my town, trouble is round the year. My guess is you signed on for it. In at least some of those photos there you're smiling."

"You're out of line, buster. And way off your turf. Lowell, for Christ's sake. I thought they put that in a museum."

I readied another salvo, but suddenly I heard us: a pair of dogs with our ruffs up. I almost laughed—would have, but I hadn't sniffed out a sense of humor yet. Despite the modern trappings, there seemed to be a small-town tint of rough justice about the place. Instead, I sighed and sat back. I even gave him a bone. "Yeah, sorry," I said contritely. "I know what you're saying. I wore a uniform for eight years."

"Why didn't I guess? Ex-cops either open barrooms or hang out a PI shingle. Why'd you leave?"

A veteran cop could smell a phony story a mile away, especially one coming from a private op, whom he'd view as a natural threat anyway. But I didn't care to have Delcastro inquiring into my past too deeply, so I kept it simple. "I thought I'd see what it's like to fetch my own coffee."

His grunt seemed to imply I'd chosen wrong but wasn't worth his hassling. "Anything doing?"

I shrugged. "I get by."

He appeared to accept it. We'd stepped off on the wrong foot; it happened sometimes, despite my winsome persona. I understood turf. But now I guess we'd bonded—at least, as much as we were likely to. He pried the plastic lid off his coffee cup and sniffed, probably making sure it wasn't candy-flavored. "Want some of this? It's black and usually pretty decent." I declined, and he took a sip. "Okay, so your client is worried because she hasn't heard from her daughter. Does she think the girl was taken by a stranger?"

"She's pretty sure the girl and her father are together," I admitted.

"But it's not a domestic abduction?"

"She doesn't think Nickerson would pull anything like that."

"What then?"

"That's what I hope to find out. I understand that Nickerson grew up here?"

"Yeah, long time gone, though."

"Have you seen him since he's been back?"

"I didn't even know he was here until the Jensen woman told

me. He's renting a place out at Cliff Beach for the week, been here since Saturday. He's welcome, but if he's got the notion to come back and stir up trouble, I'll make damn sure he doesn't."

The response puzzled me. I was thinking of Paula Jensen's depiction of her ex-husband, and the ideas didn't jibe. "Is there reason to expect he would make trouble?"

Delcastro sipped his coffee, maybe debating how much to tell. "He was okay in his time. Brain boy, science-fair type. He did have at least one brush with this department."

I waited.

"Trespassing, I think."

"Arrested?"

"I'm not even sure. It was ages ago. But my coffee's going cold, and so is this conversation. Anything else you wanted?"

"I just wanted to check in."

We eyed each other a moment, cop to cop, then we both stood. He waved me over to the big window. He nodded at the old slate headstones at one corner of the green. "Those are the original English settlers of Standish . . . they date from the sixteen hundreds. My own people were here a hundred years later—Portuguese whalers. Now we've got new blood, too. I like this place. It's a community that works. Open-town-meeting government, good people."

I waited for the pitch, but he'd evidently made it. "Well, you've checked in. Take a look around and then go tell the kid's mother the offer remains open. I still like the logical explanation that the pair are together and will turn up in a day or so. But any official request, I'll take it dead serious."

"Fair enough," I said.

"But I don't want funny going on in my town, you follow me?"

"No funny," I said. He accompanied me to his door. "I would like to drive out to the beach house that Nickerson's renting. I have the address."

"*Ferry,*" he called.

The blond crew-cut coffee gofer hopped up.

"Let Mr. Rasmussen here follow you out to Cliff Beach."

"That's not necessary," I said.

"Yeah, it is," Delcastro said. "I don't have all day to draw you a map, or come haul you out of the sand if your Probe gets stuck."

"Ouch."

4

"Did I come up clean?" I said to officer Ferry as we walked outside together.

"Sorry?"

"On your computer." Delcastro had obviously given him my P.I. license number to run.

"Yes, sir. It's a small town. The chief likes to keep track of things."

I said I understood, and he seemed relieved. He was a good-looking youth, neatly attired in his uniform, which was maybe a tad busier with paraphernalia than it needed to be, but he wore it well, along with the faint scent of English Leather. I said if he was coming back this way, why didn't I ride along with him, and he said fine.

The cruiser was one of the Crown Vics, loaded with electronic gear and still wearing the new-car smell that's not supposed to be that healthy. The Lowell cruisers were just as carcinogenic, though with cigarette smoke and funk. Outside the town center the road wound past a couple of take-out seafood places, a package store, a small market, a florist and a movie house named the Strand. "I bet you kissed your share of young ladies in the balcony there," I said.

Ferry blushed again.

"This is nice. It's quiet here, I imagine. Crime wise."

"It is, but it's changing. Like everywhere."

I envisioned a rash of magazine thefts from doctors' waiting rooms. He said, "Just last week someone rifled all the machines over at the Wash Tub coin-op laundry. And we've had reports of Ecstasy being used out at the Beachcomber."

"What about kidnapping?"

Ferry's head swiveled around fast, his expression shocked. "No."

"Just raising an ugly specter," I said. I let the image fade away in silence, then said, "Chief Delcastro is a friendly fellow."

"Yes, sir. He's a pro."

I guess they'd quit teaching irony in high school. Possibly you didn't need it to get along in quaint towns, or maybe Delcastro was only that way with me.

"His family goes way back in town here. He's the only one who wasn't a fisherman. He's been on the job awhile. Me, this is my second summer. I'm still in college."

"Criminal justice?"

"Yes, sir, but I've got plenty to learn."

I liked the fact that he recognized it; it was the beginning of wisdom. Too many wannabes, jazzed up on TV cop shows, thought they knew it all, and when the pressure came down, they squawked and ran. There was no cutting to a beer commercial in a real crisis. Though maybe young Ferry would never have to find out. I said, "Do you know Ben Nickerson?"

"No, sir. Who is he?"

"A fellow who used to live here. I'm trying to locate him and his teenage daughter." I gave him the abridged version of my quest. He listened, nodding. The Ford had the big Interceptor package, and I kept waiting for him to put the pedal down now that we'd reached an empty coast road, but he drove as cautiously as a library trustee. We passed a stretch of small weathered houses and then salt marsh. Delcastro hadn't been kidding about finding the beach. To the left, beyond a sagging wind fence, lay a small rocky cove. Out by the point stood homes bigger than what we'd seen. On the sandy shoulder sat a handful of cars and vans. I could see several dark forms in the water, and for a moment I thought they were seals, then I realized they were people in wet suits sitting on surfboards.

"Soakers," Ferry said.

"I haven't shot a curl in a long time—not *ever*, for that matter. Translation?"

"There's a break off the point out there where the locals hang. If the wind and tide are right, it'll sometimes be three feet. Mostly though, it's mush, but surfers are optimists—the only people I know who pray for rough weather."

Just then, one of the prayerful broke from the throng and started to paddle ahead of a coming wave. Ferry slowed the car to a stop. The surfer dug hard for a moment, then, in one fluid motion, he was up. He wasn't in a wet suit like the others: he was wearing a T-shirt and cutoff jeans, his hair flying like a damp rag as he gained speed—but he was the only one riding. The direct distance to the shore wasn't long—maybe forty yards—and the wave wasn't that big, but the surfer broke to the left on a sharp angle and worked the wave, cutting back and forth in a zigzag motion. He finished in a froth of white water a few yards from the rocky shore. Ferry gave a low whistle. "It figures," he said. "Red Dog."

"A friend of yours?"

"No, sir, but he's the man. If a duck took off from a millpond, he could catch a curl off the ripples. Give him something decent, he shreds." There was a note of grudging admiration in his voice as he put the Ford in gear.

We meandered for a bit, the sea cut off from view by grassy dunes, then the road looped, and there was a stretch of five homes along a secluded beach. They sat atop thick pilings that rose from the sand and held the houses aloft, presumably above the menace of storm surge. Ferry drew the cruiser into the parking area behind the second house down. I got out, broken clamshells crunching under my feet. A realtor's rental sign stood among the patch of beach roses that flanked the walkway to the door. A thin crust of sand had drifted across the path and was combed in windrows. I went up three wooden steps to the door and knocked. When I got no answer, I put my hands to one of the sidelight panels and peered in, but curtains made it hard to see much. I walked around the side and gazed at the ocean. Above the strip of sandy beach, seagulls were giving full voice to their evident approval of life in Standish.

I went down the steps to the deck. As I was about to climb, I was startled to see a man standing on the beach twenty feet below, peering up at me. In the sunlight, his hair looked on fire. He started up the beach toward me.

"Hi, there," he said, stepping into the deck shadow.

"Hi." It wasn't Ben Nickerson. Out of the sun, the man's hair was a froth of white curls. He was on the short side, five-six or so, wiry, with a tanned, good-looking face and sunglasses. He wore deck shoes and summer slacks and a blue oxford shirt with a little embroidered emblem on the breast pocket that looked like a row of pine trees.

"I'm Ted Rand." He motioned with his head. "The last house down is mine."

I introduced myself, and we shook hands. "Welcome to God's little acre, Alex." His smile was warm, and amiable wrinkles fanned around his sunglasses. "I'm just out for a constitutional. I didn't know today was the changing of the guard. Saturday's usually the day new folks come."

"Actually, I'm looking for the people who've rented the place this week."

"Ben Nickerson?"

"You know Ben?"

"Well, from years ago, when he wasn't much bigger than this." He held a palm waist high. "He grew up here. He's been living out on the other coast. Traitor." He chuckled. "Ben's done well, I gather."

"He's a marine biologist," I said, wanting to establish that I was legit by being in the know. "Has he been around?"

"I saw Ben just once, to say hi to. In town. I've hoped to get by for a chat and a beer, but it's a busy season. I'm not out here much. You a friend?"

"I know his former wife," I said and let it go at that; I didn't see a point in broadcasting my business too widely yet. "Was he with anyone when you saw him?"

"I thought so, but I'm not sure."

"Do you recall what day that was?"

Rand removed his sunglasses and let them dangle on a neck strap. His eyes were bright and blue, nested under thick eyebrows. "It must've been the day he arrived. Saturday, I think, yes. Are you staying in town?"

"No, I just stopped by to see if he was here." I didn't know if Rand had spotted the police cruiser out front.

"Well, if you see Ben, you give him my best . . . Alex, right? I may get by for that beer yet." He tipped an imaginary hat. "And you enjoy your visit." He put on his sunglasses and set off down the beach with a perky stride.

I went around to the street side where Officer Ferry was standing by his car, his face tipped toward the sun. People here seemed to use the sun like a battery, to recharge themselves. "Any luck?" he asked.

"Just trying to get the lay of things."

I copied the real estate agency's name into my notebook and then wrote, "Please call me" on the back of one of my cards and pushed it under the front door. When we were in the car, I said, "I ran into a fellow on the beach. Ted Rand?"

"Ah, right. He owns one of the houses along here. Mr. Rand's a big wheel in Standish. Awfully nice fellow."

Back in the center, Ferry dropped me at my car. "Good luck, sir," he called. Perhaps it was my imagination, but as he rolled off, I thought he was memorizing me in his rearview mirror—maybe to run in his database.

I checked the local phone book on the chance that Nickerson had family in the area, but there were no listings. I tried directory assistance and learned the same thing. I walked over to the waterfront. By asking, I learned there were two local shops that ran fishing charters for day parties and a third place that rented boats. I checked all three, showing the more recent of the two photographs Paula Jensen had lent me. No one knew or had seen Ben and Michelle Nickerson. I picked up a copy of the local paper, a weekly with yesterday's date, and paged through it while I sat on a bench overlooking the harbor. I learned that there was a franks 'n' bean supper planned for the upcoming Saturday night, that the Masque Players were performing *Spoon River Anthology* at the Unitarian church parish hall and that Annabelle Potter was recovering nicely, thank you, after an emergency appendectomy. The big story was that the Point Pines eighteen-hole golf course and luxury homes development was on schedule. My last stop was the real estate office.

A suntanned man in a madras plaid sports coat and an elaborate comb-over was talking on the phone. He glanced up as I entered. "You're kidding," he said quietly, eyeing me without acknowledgment before going back into his dimension. "You are kidding." It was his part in the conversation, every ten seconds or so. I looked around.

The walls displayed photos of local sale properties. The lowest home price I could see was close to half a million dollars, and not much house at that. On a table along one wall was a scale model of the development project that I'd just read about, Point Pines. It ran along an outlying neck of ocean-front land. For the houses directly on either the ocean or the golf greens, the price tags had plenty of zeroes. It didn't seem hard for a realtor with hustle to make the Zillion Dollar Club in this town.

"You're kidding," the man in plaid said again. Finally he got to say, "That crumb. Well, let me know." He unglued the phone from his ear and hung up. He shook his head a moment, then looked my way. "Help you?"

"I'm interested in a rental place out at Cliff Beach."

"For next year?" He fingered his scalp gingerly, checking on his carefully lacquered do, and walked over.

"I want to talk about this year."

He drew air through his teeth. "Whoo. You're kind of late. Everything's long booked. Occasionally there's a cancellation, but I wouldn't count on it. You could try the old Cape Way Motor Lodge just outside of town. They usually have vacancies, if you don't mind Spartan."

The phone rang, and he excused himself to get it. When he came back, I said, "Actually, I'm interested in one of the houses that's already been rented. Ben Nickerson and his daughter are staying there."

The names didn't shake loose any memories. I told him where

the house was, and he nodded. I showed him the photographs of Michelle Nickerson. He said he was sorry but he hadn't dealt with that rental. The telephone interrupted us again. Why is it they never answer the phone till you go there in person, and then they don't *stop* answering? He returned with his undivided attention. "Rentals, you were saying. Mitzi Dineen is the one to talk to. She's our rental superstar."

"Is she in?"

He squinted toward a magnetic board beyond the desks, where little metal squares bore people's names—Megan, Mitzi, Rosemary and Andy—and an hour-by-hour time line on one side. Using my detecting skills I judged this fellow to be Andy. Bingo. "Andy Royce," he revealed. "Commercial solutions are my bailiwick. Mitzi's out with a client now, due back at three-thirty. Can I have her call you?"

"I'll try again." I took a card and thanked him. I gestured toward the scale-model homes on the golf course. "That's quite an operation."

"Right out on Shawmut Point. Phase-one homes are due for completion in a few weeks," he said politely. Having sized me up already, he didn't waste his time trying to pitch a sale. "Have a splendid day."

5

It was going on 6 P.M. when I got back to Apple Valley and shook the traffic tension from my limbs. I found Paula Jensen on her patio again, grilling a medley of summer vegetables this time. Her light brown hair was combed out now, hanging full to her shoulders. Her surface was backyard casual, but her movements were tense, and I sensed she was holding on, damming back her anxieties about her daughter. She was glad to see me. I filled her in on what I'd learned.

"It's true," she admitted. "Chief Delcastro did say I could fill out a missing persons report, but he certainly didn't encourage it. He said not much time has gone by and that since there's no reason to think Michelle was abducted, it made sense to wait. I think he's convinced I'm overreacting. Maybe I am. She's under no requirement to check in with me every day. Still . . ."

"Delcastro said your ex had a scrape down there when he was growing up."

She frowned. "Ben did?"

"That's what he said. Trespassing."

"I never heard anything about that."

What had Delcastro called Nickerson? Brain Boy? "Has your ex-husband been in any trouble lately? Or ever?"

"Trouble? No." She sounded slightly defensive, as if she took it as an attack on her taste in men—or maybe it made her that much more edgy about her daughter's absence. "What kind of trouble?"

"Any kind. I'm just fishing."

"No. He's a respectable businessman."

"I thought he was a biologist?"

"That's the business. He supplies marine specimens to research labs. I helped him get it started, back when we were married. He's built it up over the years. He's got clients across the country."

"When is your daughter due back officially?"

"So you're taking the police chief's view?"

"I'm casting my bread upon the waters. It's supposed to be why you hired me."

She sighed. "Sorry. Shel is due back Saturday. I hoped she'd have called today. I did try her several times while you were gone. Though, to tell you the truth, I'm feeling a bit relieved. At least there isn't some obvious problem, or you'd have heard. Wouldn't you?"

"It is a pretty small town."

"I'm still hoping this is just a dumb mix-up. I pray it is."

We went into the kitchen, where she poured us some lemonade into tall glasses. A salmon steak was marinating in a dish on the center island. I wondered if her husband was still at the Sox game. I'd caught a couple of innings on my way back, until the roof dropped on the starter and they were burning through their bullpen almost as fast as the government was using up Social Security. I sat on a stool. "How did you and your ex meet?" I asked.

"I was a college sophomore at the time, undecided about a major, though I was considering nursing. In my family, you became a teacher, a nurse, or a nun. Nun was out." She grinned and promptly blushed. "I was taking a bio course to fulfill a requirement. One day the instructor crammed the class into cars for a field trip. Groan. My idea of wildlife was 'Where's the party?' I rode in this old van with the lab assistant, but when we got there, a marsh someplace north of Boston, and he had waded into it, his excitement was so . . . out there. He was like a kid sharing his birthday toys. I actually got enthusiastic about bio. At semester's end I'd earned a decent grade and got a request from the lab assistant for a date."

"Ben?"

"Yep. And I accepted."

"Romantic."

"Unmitigated disaster. He spilled popcorn, tried the whole movie to inch his hand around my shoulders. He never quite made it before a wicked attack of pins and needles felled him. When he finally dropped me at the dorm, I think we were both relieved. But I liked him. He was shy, and good-looking in this sort of intent, brooding way. So I took a chance, and next time I saw him I said, 'Take me to the salt marsh.' He did. He'd brought an extra pair of hip boots and a net. He pointed out things I'd never even thought about. Like how, in an ecosystem, everything there has a purpose. And he knew all the Latin names. *Echinoderms, Mollusca* . . . I still remember. The date was as wonderful as the movie date had been bad."

"That line really worked, huh? 'Take me to the marsh.' I'll have to try it. And brush up on my Latin. Would you say 'crustaceans' or *'crustacea'*?"

Smiling, Paula Jensen slid onto a stool across from me. "I think the hip boots were a nice touch," she said.

"Most guys try to make do with rubbers."

We laughed, with the result of her relaxing a little. I did, too. She poured more lemonade for us. "Later Ben got a teaching fellowship at Scripps, so we got married and went to San Diego together. I was twenty-one. I taught third grade, and he did research and taught. Eventually, he started his business and got away from teaching. There were hassles with the business, but it got off the ground—that's what he does now—and then Michelle came along, and we were a family."

It sounded nice in her telling. "What happened?" I asked.

She smiled, a trifle sadly. "I don't know. When things are going good, people sometimes do things to mess it all up for themselves. Does that make sense?"

"I'm widely known for it."

She gave me a look, and I had an idea she wanted me to go on. I might have said that she could ask Lauren, who was living in Florida at last check. I didn't. "As the business grew successful," she resumed, "the money—which is something neither of us had ever had—became important to Ben. He liked fancy things. Clothes, a sailboat, nice vacation trips. But none of it seemed to make him very happy. I think he should've gone back to teaching. That's where he was most truly alive. I still think of that man wading in the salt marsh." She stopped, and I saw her eyes were shiny. We drank lemonade in silence.

On the corner a stubby green-and-white school bus, with CAMP ESTES lettered on the side in red, drew to curb and began popping out small kids like a gaudy reptile giving birth. "Katie's home," Paula said, peering out the window. "They went hiking today." In a moment, one of the kids came dashing across the lawn toward the house, two long sandy-blonde pigtails flying from the back of a blue baseball cap. Paula hesitated and added, "I haven't told her anything about hiring you."

"Hi, Mom." Kate Jensen slung a daypack onto a counter stool and gave her mother a brief hug. She was a freckled string bean with the decided look of a kid who could outrun most of the boys in her class—and in a few years would have to. Her legs were tanned, her shorts and T-shirt grass-stained. She favored her mother in the bonny blue eyes and full-mouth department.

"Hi, Bug. How was camp?"

"Great. Dad home yet?"

"Not yet. He went to the Red Sox game."

"Good."

"This is Mr. Rasmussen."

The girl gave me a fleeting Harriet the Spy glance, and I had the feeling she digested me, from my dusty brogues to the loose knot of the tie in my damp shirt collar. "When he does get home," she said, "I hope he's got over being pissed."

"What did I tell you about your language?"

"I know. But did he call you about the juice I spilled on the way to camp this morning? That little cup-holder thingy in his car is majorly messed up. I tried to put the juice box in it, but it tipped.

I thought he was gonna barf bricks. He said the thing was ergonomically designed and I'd neutralized it. I told him car engineers aren't eight-year-olds. Is there any more lemonade?"

When Kate Jensen had poured herself some and gone out to change clothes, her mother shot me a look of frustration and pride. "Ergonomically designed?" I said. "Don't ask me to spell it."

Paula smiled. "She's a reader, devours books. She calls them word sandwiches."

"That's a healthy diet."

She took our empty glasses to the sink, businesslike now. I pulled out my notebook. "Is there anything else I should know about your ex?"

She considered this a moment. "Ben used to talk about coming back east and buying a place on the Cape. The business was doing okay . . . but *we* weren't. Maybe the idea of returning here was one of those last-ditch efforts you make to try to fend off the inevitable. You know how people do. Anyhow, we never made it. We both wanted what's best for Michelle, so neither of us made a battle over custody in the divorce. We share it."

"What brought him back this time?"

"A chance to introduce Shel to his past, I think . . . his hometown. He wants her to know her roots. In some ways, he's never let go of the idea of coming back. He subscribes to the Standish weekly paper, has it mailed to him in California."

Beyond the picture window I saw a dark blue Audi sedan wheel into the driveway. "Here's Ross," Paula said, rising. I got up, too. "We talked on the phone again, and I did tell him I'd retained you."

Good. I didn't like surprises. At the door, a tall man in a gray suit set aside his briefcase and bent and pecked his wife's cheek. Ross Jensen was athletic-looking and handsome. His tie, like mine, was loose, but his shirt collar wasn't wilted, nor his suit rumpled—mine would need Botox injections to get the wrinkles out. "How was the game?" his wife asked.

"They got shelled. I left after the stretch." He glanced past her. "Whose car is that in the driveway?"

I was standing in the living room. I raised my hand and pled no contest.

"Ross, this is Mr. Rasmussen."

"Oh, yeah." He glanced my way. "It doesn't leak oil, does it? I just had the driveway seal-coated."

Certainly no one was making a fuss over me. "Not to worry," I said. "It *burns* every drop of oil it can get."

He gave it what it deserved. "I'll be with you in a few minutes."

The Jensens excused themselves and went into another part of the house. I wandered through the kitchen entrance to the garage. Katie was there, listening to a Discman through headphones and trying to tighten the kickstand of her bicycle. She wasn't having much luck with a pair of pliers. I got her attention, and she lowered the headphones around her neck. I showed her that a better approach was to turn the bike upside down, which we did. On the workbench, I found a can of WD-40 and a Crescent wrench. I sprayed the kickstand fastener and let her adjust the wrench. She applied it to the nut, and with a twist it came loose. "Cool," she said.

"What are you listening to?"

"A CD."

"Satan Bugg?"

She made a face. "They blow chunks."

"Does your sister know you think that?"

She ventured a small grin. "I tell her, but she'll just have to outgrow them on her own. I'm listening to an audio book. *The Lion, the Witch and the Wardrobe.*"

"Have you read all the *Chronicles*?"

She shrugged. "Three times." She looked at me. "Are you supposed to find Shel?" At my surprised expression, she said, "Mom found you in the phone book. She left it open on the counter with your name circled."

So much for keeping family secrets. "That's the general idea," I admitted.

"And what'll you do? Bring her back here?"

"She lives here, no?"

"Shel should stay where she is."

"Do you know where she is?"

"*Wherever,* I mean. She ought to stay there. Maybe she'll get a better deal than she gets here."

Moving with care, I set the bike back on its wheels. With equal care, I said, "She doesn't get a good deal here?"

Katie regarded me as if the question was stupid. "No, it's just that—"

Ross Jensen appeared. He had changed into chinos and a green V-neck sweater with a local country club's name monogrammed in gold on the right chest. He gave me a look and scrubbed Jenny's head. "I'll play with you in a little while, Champ. Get yourself some lemonade."

"I already had some. I want to have a stand and make a sign and sell lemonade. Can I?"

"No one will stop. People are on their way home now."

"Tomorrow, then. If it's a really hot day?"

"You've got camp."

"I could skip one time."

"People are too busy for lemonade stands. Besides, how much would you sell it for?"

"I don't know. Ten cents a cup. No, twenty-five."

"You'd lose your shirt. You need to think about it. Put together a business plan and we'll talk further. Maybe next weekend."

She brightened. "I can do it?"

"We'll see."

She set the Discman on the workbench and pulled on a bike helmet. When she'd rolled out into the driveway and toward the empty street, Jensen watched her a moment, then turned to me. "What do you think about this whole thing, Rasmussen?"

"Twenty-five cents a cup sounds pretty good."

He frowned. "My stepdaughter's being gone. What's your take on it?"

Attorneys were always more comfortable asking questions than answering them. I didn't rush to respond. I hauled out my dog-eared notebook. "She isn't where you think she should be, and you haven't heard from her in a couple days. I can understand your worry."

"Did Paula mention Michelle's little vanishing act this past winter?"

She hadn't, but then there were a lot of things no one was mentioning.

"Just an overnight to Lowell," he said. "She snuck out to a concert, and she and some others ended up getting picked up by the police afterward. No charges were filed, except against the ringleader, because he was older. For loitering."

"When was this?"

"February. Paula was down with the flu, so I retrieved Michelle. I told her if she's going to run away, it makes more sense to go south. Or do it in warm weather."

"You think that's what happened now?"

"I hope she learned her lesson. I grounded her hard for that little stunt." He frowned. "Paula told you about her ex?"

"Ben Nickerson."

"I haven't liked him from day one. Or I haven't warmed up to him, put it that way. Maybe it's just the scientist thing. His head is always in the clouds."

"Yet he's a successful businessman."

"Did my wife tell you that?"

"I got that idea."

"Well, I'm not sure how successful he really is. He approached me about borrowing some money for his business—presented it as an investment opportunity."

"When?"

"Six months ago or so. He said he was planning to expand his on-line business. When I pressed him for specifics, he didn't offer much. I told him I was going to pass. That's the last I heard."

"You didn't check it out?"

"For what? Do you know how busy I am?" He grimaced. "We did pay for Michelle's airfare out there this time, and the rental on the house down there in Standish, but he's going to reimburse that. Look, does he figure in this?"

"You brought him up. What's your sense?"

"I couldn't say. I don't think he's a criminal. Leave it at that."

I had the feeling that Jensen wasn't going to be as generous with information or his time as even his wife had been. I followed him out to the driveway, where the Audi was parked.

"Nice ride," I said.

He bent and stuck his head in the window and inhaled. "Smell that."

I put my head inside and sniffed, too. It smelled a lot more expensive than Officer Ferry's Crown Vic; forget any comparison to my heap. "The Moroccan leather?" I said. "Or the burled oak?"

"Mango Breeze. Spilled this morning." He walked me toward my Ford. "My firm works with private investigators on occasion, Rasmussen." I thought he was going to run some names by me, but he didn't. "I'd have gone with one of them—they're a known quantity—only I don't like them being privy to my personal business. I checked on you. Your outfit's pretty small."

"Just me," I admitted. "But I think the selection of magazines in my waiting room can hold its own against Pinkerton's."

"I want to be sure you're not going to take my wife for a ride."

"There might be some ops around who'll make like cabbies and take the long way, to keep the meter running. I don't personally know any. I don't even know that many cabbies who do it."

"Your faith in the honesty of your fellow man is touching."

"I don't spend a lot of time gilding it. We've all got to swim in the same waters."

"Okay. Paula seems to have formed a favorable impression of you very quickly. Of course, she hasn't really got any basis of comparison. But she tends to be right about people pretty often, I'll give her that. So what's your sense?"

"Standish isn't a big town, and folks seem to know each other. I spoke with someone this afternoon who saw Nickerson the day he arrived. It's reasonable to assume others have seen them. If he and your stepdaughter are there, they shouldn't be hard to locate. If not, I ought to be able to get a line on where they've gone. Usually these are connect-the-dots cases. I've got Michelle's photograph—actually, Mrs. Jensen said you might have a more recent family shot at your office."

He frowned. "I'll check."

"I'll go back first thing tomorrow. If I'm getting somewhere, I'd probably stay overnight in a motel. And I recommend that you file a report with the police down there."

He shot me an interrogating glance. "I don't think that it's indicated yet."

"It can't hurt."

"It might." Reading my surprised expression, he went on, "My firm is wrapping up a sensitive litigation this week. I can't go into it except to say that any publicity, for me or the firm, could cause a setback. A missing persons report is bound to become news, especially in a small town. And then the Boston papers get it? No. It isn't the kind of notice one wants. It could make a parent seem . . . careless."

It wouldn't have been my take, but it wasn't for me to tell him what he should do.

"Understand, I'm not against filing a report," he went on in more measured fashion, "but I'm not convinced that it's needed yet. I still believe that my stepdaughter and Nickerson just haven't been in touch."

"Do you think it's possible that Michelle did a fade on her own?"

His smooth brow beetled. "I'm not ready to rule out anything. My stepdaughter has a pretty strong will. She's at a stage where she feels a need to assert her independence."

He made it sound like a character flaw. "I'd like to look into Nickerson's background a little."

"That's okay with me. All of this is. I just don't want to see my name in the papers."

I nodded. "If it does get there, it won't be through me."

"Okay, Rasmussen, your price is competitive. Let's give it two more days, shall we? I expect results. I'll approve the motel idea if you think it makes sense." He fished a little leather card case from his pocket and took out a card. He borrowed my pen and circled something on it and handed the card to me. The words were in raised black letters on the crisp ecru foolscap: his name, along with "Randolph, Blinkman & Bearse, Attorneys at Law," and assorted phone and fax numbers, and e-mail and Web addresses. One number was circled. "If you need to reach me, you can call me at that confidential number."

His handshake was as dry as a salt cod. When I'd backed my car out, he walked over to check for oil drips. I guess I was clean; as I wheeled away, he was squatting, pinching a dandelion that had invaded the lawn; then he rose and went through his garage to his dinner.

I got back to Lowell, where the average car is nine years old and probably costs just as much to insure as this year's model in Apple Valley—though nine years didn't sound bad in a city where many of the landmarks go back two hundred. It was the best light of day, ambering across the Merrimack River, burnishing the granite and the brick of the old mills. They were the big-boned remains of what life had been long ago when their ilk stretched for a full mile on the rolling river and along its miles of branching canals, all of the mills going three shifts, a noisy, dusty warp and woof processing thousands of bales of cotton and wool a day, producing over two million yards of cloth a week, textiles that helped clothe a nation. A museum, Chief Delcastro had called it, and it was that, and a state and national park; but more than those things it was a city with a stubborn pride in work, holding its own in a tough world. Cloth had been something you could lay your hands on at the end of the day. Not like now. Now it was all bits and bytes and information at warp speed.

I was in the information business, too. From my office I called the Lowell police headquarters and asked for Sergeant Ed St. Onge. We'd been together in the Major Crimes Bureau when I was a cop and had kept a connection since. They tracked him down. Before I could utter a word, he said, "Is this about your vacuum cleaner?"

It took me a moment to realize what he was referring to. "I'm in awe of your prescience."

"When your name turns up on any police notepad, it gets attention."

A few years back, Lowell had gone an entire year without a single homicide: some kind of record, which had the U.S. Attorney General in town, pumping hands and talking tough. But it was where all records end up—in a book, collecting dust. There'd been a hatful of murders in town in the past month, with arrests running a few sizes behind, and the *Sun* editorialized about Dodge City. I mentioned this.

"It isn't me watching," St. Onge said. "Droney's the one who keeps tabs on you."

Droney, Captain Francis X., aka the Ogre, had been the foot behind the bum's rush when I left the cops. "How is he these days?"

"Tread light around him. No lie. He's still got a few teeth. Sharp ones."

I acknowledged it. And since Ed had raised the topic of the corroded shotgun standing in my coat closet, I asked him if there were any cold cases in the city where a sawed-off had been used in the commission of a crime but was never found. To his knowledge there were none.

"The case could be very old," I said. "The shotgun is."

"Want to tell me more?"

You could take the Fifth with St. Onge, but it would show poor judgment to lie. I gave him the story. "You're lucky you didn't end up shot by the patrol officer and become a martyr to misapplied deadly force."

"Then the city could give me the funeral it's been planning for years."

He let it lie. "Parker Brothers, huh? Don't they make Monopoly?"

I said I thought it was a different outfit. He said he'd check and let me know. "If it's clean, you can bring it in here and we'll dispose of it."

"You still drop them in Boston Harbor?"

"Something like that."

"No, thanks, I'll dismantle it all by myself."

"Be careful you don't get your nose caught in the pliers. And now that you've got your vacuum cleaner back, maybe you ought to use it. Last time I was up in that flea bin, the dust bunnies looked like tumbleweeds."

"Before you go—the reason I called—there was a case of a runaway kid, an overnighter, apparently, picked up with a group of other juveniles here last February. One may have been charged as an adult."

"For?"

"Loitering."

"Ha, that's almost refreshing."

I gave him Michelle Nickerson's name.

"Let me get this right. You want me to open official files for unofficial business."

"Please," I said.

In the pause, I could hear his ire ticking, like a car that's been run hard on a bad road. But he knew that favors didn't run only one way. He sighed and said he'd get back to me. The phone rang almost as soon as I hung up. It was Paula Jensen.

"I talked it over with Ross," she said. "Instead of you staying in a motel, we'd like to offer you the beach house."

"Where your ex is supposed to be?" I asked.

"We've already paid for the week, and there's lots of room. Then you'd know right away if they returned."

"When they came stumbling home to find Goldilocks."

"I'm sorry. I don't mean to tell you how to do your job. If you'd prefer a motel—"

"Mrs. Jensen—"

"Paula, please. I'm probably keeping you from other cases."

"Paula, I could tell you I've got a staff of associates going twenty-four seven to handle the caseload here at my corporate towers. The truth is the agency is me, a telephone, and that Ford out there. As for caseload, that's hyperbole. I've got two or three ongoing insurance investigations, none of them more pressing than Christmas shopping right now. I'm available. You've paid me. I'm going to try to locate your daughter. And the truth is, it would be convenient to stay at the beach house if it's not a bother."

"It's not at all."

"I'll go down first thing in the morning."

"Thank you for being honest with me and for not guilt-tripping me."

"I did, though," I said. "Now how are you going to feel firing me?"

I liked hearing her laugh. Something told me she hadn't been doing it much lately. She said she'd call the realtor, Mitzi Dineen, and make the arrangements. In the meantime, maybe Ben and Shelly would show up and none of this would be necessary. I said I hoped so.

As I got ready to go, my neighbor from the suite down the hall stopped by. In his way, Fred Meecham, and his Mount Holyoke graduate paralegal, Courtney, gave the building a tincture of class it had no right to expect any longer. Its heyday had been a hundred years ago. Now, with the likes of Acme Telephone Sales, a smoking-cessation hypnotist, World Wide Pawn, and assorted other two-bit operations, including yours truly, an ambulance chaser would have fit right in; but Meecham wasn't that. He was a hardworking, bright, reasonably honest attorney, whose specialty, like mine, was anything that came through the door. Occasionally he even threw work my way, though Courtney was on top of most of it. We'd been neighbors on the third floor for years, and yet, in all that time of breathing the same dusty air, sharing the same washroom down the hall, we had never become buddies. Never would. He possessed a bit too much of the city booster, I-care-what-people-think spirit—but I liked him. Lately he was on this kick to advertise—*my* services, not his. In his view, advertising was for the kind of lawyer who used fall-down artists, but a PI on the other hand . . . Maybe he thought more business rolling my way would roll more business his way. Maybe he was a genuine altruist, and it pained him to hear the silence of my telephone and not see a line outside my waiting room. Whatever the case, I liked him fine.

"Hey," he said. He was ruddy from an afternoon at the city golf tournament.

"Who won?" I asked.

"It's not like that. There're two more days of rounds. The final round is on Friday. You should come out with me."

"I'll let you know next week."

He came in. "Have you been sitting here since this morning?"

Rather than replay my exciting day, I shrugged. He started out and then turned. "I'm telling you, an ad in the newspaper, maybe a

TV spot, you could get clients. Have you given any thought to what I said about marketing?"

"Some. How about a big pointing hand in the lobby: 'Mysteries solved, three floors up'? Or billboards on the Connector: 'Dial R for Rasmussen.' " He scowled and headed for his office. "Too Hitchcocky?" I called after him.

I stopped by the Copper Kettle for the bar smorgasbord and some familiar faces, but all the talk was of par and shots under. I got some pickled eggs and kielbasa—the Exxon special—and took them in a plastic container to my apartment, where I cracked open a beer and settled in to watch Gary Cooper and Patricia Neal in *The Fountainhead* on PBS.

6

On Wednesday I was up early and packed two days' worth of clothes and essentials. I took my cue from people I'd seen in Standish yesterday—chinos and cotton shirts, a sport coat and a summer-weight suit, and some ties—and left to get ahead of the rush hour. I needn't have bothered. I didn't clock sixty until I got past the Needham flats.

The young police officer named Ferry was on duty, sipping his coffee, cinnamon spice, if my nose was right, though his English Leather was in the mix, too. He told me that as far as he knew, neither Ben Nickerson nor his daughter had shown up yet. I drove out to the beach house and confirmed it. My card was still under the door from yesterday. I left it there. Paula Jensen had said she'd make the rental arrangement, so I trusted her on that. An AT&T van was parked across the street, and a lineman—who turned out to be a linewoman, was on the pole. I called up to her and asked if she'd noticed any vehicles at the house; she hadn't.

I drove a few towns farther south to Plymouth Harbor and, starting there, worked my way back through Duxbury, Marshfield and Scituate. Going on a profile I'd built of Nickerson's interests, I visited the local PDs, charter fishing places, the whale-watch services and whatever few small-boat rental places still did business. I talked to harbormasters, yacht clubbers and wait-staff. I spoke with a cranberry grower, a lifeguard, and a woman in Pilgrim garb. No one knew anything helpful. I showed the photographs of Michelle Nickerson to kids of her age, one of whom wore a Satan Bugg T-shirt, which I commented on. It didn't forge any bond; the youth just seemed dismayed that I'd ever heard of the band.

I made a phone call to Mitzi Dineen, the realtor I'd tried to see yesterday. I dropped Paula Jensen's name and left word that I'd be at the beach house at 2 P.M. I also kept an eye out for a blue Grand Cherokee with California plates. At ten minutes to two I got back to the house on Cliff Beach. My card remained tucked under the door, so I retrieved it. I poked around outside, looking for something I hadn't even thought to look for earlier: signs of forcible entry. I saw none. I went and leaned against my car.

At 2 P.M. sharp, a green Saab wagon with an "I ♥ Standish" bumper sticker wheeled into the parking area and braked with a shushing of crushed clamshells. A suntanned middle-aged woman in a tropical-flower–print dress bustled out. "Hi, Mr. Rasmussen? Here I am." Grinning, she thrust a hand at me. "Mitzi Dineen." She had blonde-streaked hair cut in a youthful fashion. She was fifty, trying to look thirty and splitting the difference. "So you're the lucky one! Mrs. Jensen called and explained that you'd be using the place for a few days. Mr. Nickerson hasn't returned?"

"Apparently not."

"You're gonna love it here. Everyone does. Everyone." She sounded insistent about it, as if I'd picked up the wrong idea somehow and needed to be set straight. "Standish is the best location on the South Shore. One of the best anywheres!"

You can take them out of South Boston, but the accent stays and stays. "You're gonna absolutely positively adore it." She dug in a wicker pocketbook and produced a ring of keys that would've given a jail warden penal envy. "Here we go."

We stepped into a summer home with shiny wood floors, drapery-drawn windows and modest furnishings. "We're in the family room," she said with a little Vanna White twirl. "There's the Atlantic out there. What do you think so far?"

"I absolutely positively adore it."

She gave me the tour.

"Did you see Ben Nickerson and his daughter when they came?" I asked when we got downstairs again and she paused for breath.

"What? Oh. I spoke with him by phone, actually. He called from California. He sounded excited to be coming. I was out on caravan the morning they arrived, so I left a key. Once people settle in, I'm invisible unless they need me. I did tell Vin that Mr. Nickerson would be here. I always do that, just to keep him in the loop. It's an added safety service, no extra charge."

"Vin?"

"Police Chief Delcastro. He's 'Vin' to us locals. He's a native. There aren't all that many. Sadly, a lot of them can no longer afford the taxes and have to move elsewhere." Her sympathy seemed as genuine as a crocodile's. "We get people from all over who move to town. 'Wash-ashores.' Goodness, I'm one!" She laughed.

"Delcastro knew Ben Nickerson from before, I gather."

"Years ago, yes. That's another nice thing about the town—have you got a family, Mr. Rasmussen? Kids?"

"Not at the moment."

"Well. It is a very safe town with good public services. And the schools are tops. We're back in the kitchen now." The woman liked to announce where she was and what she was doing, I guess in case it was happening so fast that my head was awhirl. She brimmed with perkiness—almost too much for the house, which had a closed-up feel, almost without any sign of recent habitation. She tugged a cord and opened draperies on the large sliding-glass door. Beyond was a deck overlooking the beach. Wanting fresh air, I slid open the door. The cries of seagulls drifted in, along with the smells of burning charcoal, and of the ocean itself. It was slightly cooler here than inland. I walked to the railing and looked down onto the strip of clean sand. Only a few people were in evidence, most of them parked on blankets, catching rays.

"What did I tell you?" Mitzi Dineen beamed at my side.

"You sure did." I beamed back. We went inside and she went on extolling the virtues of Standish, but I was peering about, looking for some enlarged understanding of where Ben and Michelle Nickerson might be. I wasn't offended when the realtor apologized that she had to be running off to another appointment. She tugged a key from her ring and gave it to me. "The beach comes with the rental. The one rule here is, relax and enjoy! And if you fall in love with us and want to stay . . . Well, I'm off." She trilled a laugh all the way to the Saab.

Alone, I brought my suitcase in and took my own tour. The house was what you'd expect: durable appliances and housewares, decorator touches, an assortment of books and board games for rainy days, but the overall effect was of a temple for beach worshipers. Skylights and big windows let the light pour in. There wasn't much that didn't seem to belong. Some condiments and tubs of Chinese take-out in the fridge. On a kitchen counter was a fishbowl, but I didn't see any fish in the water, only a small snail shell in the sand at the bottom. In an upstairs closet hung a black satin jacket. I took it out. "Satan Bugg—Playing for Your Soul Tour" was printed on the back in red, along with the band's pentagram logo. The tour cities were all West Coast venues. Was it Michelle Nickerson's? In a wastebasket, amid some balled local newspapers, I found a roach with purple lipstick on it. Had the teenager smoked it? For people who supposedly had been here for several days, the Nickersons hadn't left much of themselves. Was it possible they'd taken their things and gone on a side trip? The jacket, though, seemed to deny it. If it was Michelle's—the size was right—and she was such a fan of the group, would she leave it behind if she didn't intend to return?

"Eagle eye has landed," I said when Paula Jensen answered the phone.

"Anything?" she asked right off.

Which told me she hadn't heard a word. I took forty seconds and filled her in on my day so far. I held off on the roach for the moment. She said that the Standish police had faxed her a missing persons form to complete, which she was doing now and was going to fax it back. She said the jacket sounded like her daughter's.

"Does she wear purple lipstick?"

"I've never seen her. Black, sometimes. Why?"

"Just curious." No need to air my vague wonderings about her daughter's smoking dope. "You spoke to Delcastro for the first time when?" I asked.

"The day before yesterday."

"How did he react to learn Ben was in Standish?"

"He seemed matter-of-fact about it. He did give me the impression that he thought I was being premature about this."

We talked a minute more and agreed to be in touch immediately if either of us learned anything. I thanked her again for arranging the use of the house. Back in Standish center, I noted there were lots of vehicles with out-of-state plates. Still, if Nickerson's Jeep was around, it shouldn't be too hard to spot. I walked around in the heat shimmer, looking, when someone said, "Hi, there."

It was the young cop again, Ferry. He was on a foot patrol. Beneath the mesh front of his blue baseball cap, his brow glistened. I asked him if he'd recommend someplace for a late lunch. Before he could say, a gray van with "Point Pines Development" and a pine-tree logo painted on the door in red and green went past.

"That's the outfit building the new golf course out on Shawmut Point," Ferry told me. "Eventually, it'll also include that whole stretch out there on the breakwater—a new marina, shops, restaurants."

"I can't wait that long. I'm hungry now."

"Dimitri's is good," he said seriously. "Though that's best in the evening. Try the Storm Warning, right over there." He indicated a small wooden building near the base of the jetty, by a big rusted anchor.

"The name's no commentary on the food, I trust?"

"No, sir. It's just a—" This time he caught on and grinned.

The wait-staff wore yellow oilskin hats, and the menus were carved on oar blades, but the food was good anyway. As I ate a clam roll, I noticed a person standing alone far out on the granite jetty where Point Pines would evidently transfigure the town. Something in his stillness as he stood gazing at the horizon under the flat of his hand, drew me. After a few moments, he went down the far side of the jetty and was gone.

After eating, I scanned the square for a public booth, but I might as well have looked for a white whale. I got my cellular phone from the car and called the Coast Guard station in Scituate Harbor. An efficient-sounding guardsman told me my call was being recorded and took my questions. "No, sir, no one by those names has been rescued, and there've been no accidents reported at all in the past forty-eight hours. Are you reporting them overdue or missing, sir?"

Was I? "No, I just wanted to be sure. Thanks for your help."

"We're here to serve, sir. Thank you."

I called the Lowell Police Department and asked for Ed St. Onge. "Who's this?" a woman asked sharply.

"John Updike," I said.

"The baseball player? Oh, sorry, I didn't realize you knew Ed. He's not in right now. Take a message?"

"No, thanks." If Francis X. Droney was as interested in my doings as St. Onge had hinted, I wasn't going to make it easy. I said I'd try again.

The woman cleared her throat. "If I may ask, how's your season going, John?"

"Read my latest and see." I hung up, dug out my notebook, and called the number for Ben Nickerson's marine supply company. It would be noon in California. After a few rings, a machine picked up. A man's recorded voice said, "South Coastal Marine Supply will be closed for vacation until July twentieth. Leave a message and we'll get back to you." I left my name and phone number and asked Ben Nickerson to call me about a personal matter.

I headed back to the beach house to see if Nickerson and his daughter had returned. If they had, I was going to take the afternoon off and walk the beach. Some of the women in town were looking good in their suntans. My social life of late had been about as hot as Norma Desmond's. Of course, I didn't have the wax museum to play in or Erich von Stroheim at my beck and call. Still, that was okay. Lowell's Red Sox farm team was playing pretty good ball, and a night in the stadium with a hot dog and a beer was my speed. The Spinners didn't win any more games than their parent club, but then the players weren't earning twice the GNP of Pakistan, either. But all of that was moot; the Nickersons hadn't returned.

I remembered Ted Rand, whom I'd met yesterday. Officer Ferry had said Rand was a player in Standish. Perhaps his knowledge of the town might shed some light I could use. I walked down to the last house, a weathered cedar affair built on pilings. There was a handicap ramp leading to a side door. The inner door was open, just an aluminum screen door in place, and a television set playing loudly within. I knocked.

Down on the beach, a few bathers were poking toes into the water. Other people lay sprawled in the sun, working on their tans. It was the only work anyone seemed devoted to. I knocked again. Under the sounds of a detergent commercial I heard a faint creak and a noise that sounded like slithering. Despite the warmth, a shiver went down my spine. I leaned close to peer through the screen and was startled to see somebody sitting in there, a foot from the screen. "Sorry," I said, recovering. "Is this where Ted Rand lives?"

"Yes? What is it?" the person demanded through a rusty pipe. Man or woman, I couldn't tell.

"My name is Alex Rasmussen. I met Ted yesterday afternoon."

The figure loomed nearer, coming into partial light, and I saw now that it was a woman. The rubber tires of her wheelchair bumped the screen door. "Teddy ain't here."

Years of confinement had atrophied her. The flesh on her face sagged. Limp white hair danced around her head like a hula skirt. A thin sour odor came from within the house, despite the TV announcer's claims about springtime freshness. "Well, that's okay. Just tell him—"

"He's dead."

That stopped me. Images from Hitchcock rose in my mind. I stood staring through the screen at the fuzzy image, as if it too were just another plot twist. "You can come in if you want to."

I didn't want to. Something about the sallow old woman sitting in her dark house with the TV at full volume unnerved me, made me want to run down the beach and plunge into the cold water, as if a contagion might exist in there, or worse: as if I might find the body of Ted Rand lying in the flickering light of a daytime rerun, seized in the grimace of a chest-clutching knife attack. But that was just heebie-jeebies. I'd seen Rand alive and well not twenty-four hours ago. I opened the screen door and stepped in. The woman rolled her chair backward. "Come on, I don't bite." I followed her through a short entryway into a large kitchen full of modern appliances and felt rationality reassert itself. It wasn't the Bates Motel.

The old woman used a remote control and shut off the sound, leaving on the picture. *Bay Watch.* I dragged my eyes back to her. Her arms were puffy, with a lot of sunspots, giving the effect of nutmeg sprinkled on an egg custard that had cooled and curdled. Between the hem of a faded housedress and tattered slippers, burst veins mapped her lower legs. What did I expect? She looked ninety. Her eyes were the only things that seemed to have life in the pudding body. They met mine: sharp and wild as a hawk's. I gave my name.

"Huh?" she demanded.

I said it louder.

"There's coffee," she said.

"No, thanks, I only wanted to—"

"I just made it. Go on."

It seemed to be a ticket for admission. I chose a sturdy white mug with a blue sailboat on the side and half-filled it. I gestured with the pot. She shook her head. "One cup a day's all I get anymore, and I drunk it already. I just like the smell. Pills are my potion these days." I took in the counter and its bewildering array of medications in brown plastic vials. "Doctor says I've got a kidney stone the size of Plymouth Rock. He says he could blast it with some kind of beam, and I say no, sir. I don't want no beam inside me, and I sure don't want to pass it, neither."

I set the cup aside. The sharp old eyes watched me. "You're a rough-looking thing," the woman said. "You'd be about Teddy's age. Older, actually. You didn't go to school with him, did you?"

"Ted Rand?" I was confused.

"What?"

"No, I didn't go to school with him."

"You know Teddy?"

Taking a new tack, I said, "There's a man and his daughter staying two houses down. Ben and Michelle Nickerson. Did you happen to meet them?"

"He was in that silly little war down in . . . wherever it was. With the pineapple-face drug dealer."

"Ben Nickerson was?"

"Noriega. Wasn't he the one?"

"I mean, was Ben Nickerson in the service?"

"Teddy. Did you play football with him?"

Back to that. "No," I said.

The woman nodded, but I had my doubts she meant it. David Hasselhoff had rescued a young beauty in a thong and was giving her mouth-to-mouth; he seemed to be having a lot more fun at the beach than I was. Before I could rephrase my question, the old woman said, "Teddy's dead." The tape loop was about to start again. Her mind was a time machine, with the lever set on yesterday. I sat a moment more, feeling the one gulp of coffee roil in my stomach, then I thanked her and got out of there. She called after me: "There's answers to our questions."

I stopped and moved partway back. "Which questions, ma'am?"

She fixed me with her hawk stare. "All of them."

7

As I walked back along the beach, I heard music coming from the rented house where I was staying. It sounded like the noise I'd heard yesterday morning on the CD player in Michelle Nickerson's bedroom. I climbed the deck steps on swift feet and slipped open the screen slider. Someone was in the house. There were keys and a pair of sunglasses on top of a large book on the counter that hadn't been there before. I went in. A woman was sitting at the table. It was Paula Jensen. She didn't hear me. In front of her was a portable CD player, and beside that the black satin Satan Bugg jacket. Becoming aware of me, she hopped up with a little cry and snapped off the CD player.

"I seem to make a habit of startling you," I said.

"I didn't know where you were." She reddened slightly. "Anything?"

"Not yet. Are you okay?" She looked a little frayed.

"I decided to drop off the missing persons form myself, then I came here. I was thinking the music might help me learn something."

"Did it?"

"It gave me a headache. I'm too keyed up. I keep trying Michelle's cell phone, but I get the 'no service' message."

"You said she turns it off."

"I'm hoping that's what it is."

"You want some aspirin?"

"It'll go away. I just want to know that my daughter is safe."

We both sat down. "Is your husband okay with the missing persons report?"

"He just doesn't want us to be the couple on the six-o'clock news, looking like deer caught in the headlights of a truck."

I nodded, but for reasons of my own. When a disappearance reached the level of TV news, it usually didn't bode well for anyone, though I didn't say this. "Chief Delcastro isn't likely to broadcast it."

"What's your sense of him?" she asked. "Can he help?"

"He seems overprotective of his town. I feel like my pant cuffs get wet every time I talk to him. But he strikes me as efficient." I nodded at the jacket. "Is that familiar?"

She drew it to her. "It's definitely Shel's. Ben got it for her in California." I could hear a pull of hope in her words, counteracting the worry in her face. "Have you found anything else?"

I told her what I'd been doing. I wished it were more. When I'd told her about the pale old woman I'd just spoken with, she said, "Teddy Rand. Why's that familiar?" She thought a moment but shook her head. She took me up on the offer of a painkiller, and we found some Advil. Paula picked up the large book that lay on the counter. On the pebbled gray cover I read the name *The Torch*.

"It's Ben's high school yearbook. I had it in storage at home. I thought you might find it helpful." She paged it open to a senior class portrait of Benjamin Nickerson. Dark, probing eyes peered out through wire-rim glasses, and wings of lank dark hair were parted over a studious brow. Paula stared at it too, as if it were a mirror that reflected the past. Nickerson's list of school activities was brief: key club, biology club and band. I tried to picture him a few years later courting a pretty college coed like Paula, but it was a stretch. Of course, I hadn't seen him in hip boots.

"The photo *is* dated," she said.

"Even so, the book might point me to some people in town who would know him."

"Oh, I hope so." She gave me a grateful look, though I hadn't done much to earn it so far. I asked if she'd eaten yet, but she said she should be getting back home. "In case Shel calls there. And I need to be there when Katie gets home from camp."

"How's her business plan for the lemonade stand coming?"

Her smile was welcome. "She's already done a spreadsheet."

I walked her to the door. "By the way—" She pointed to the fishbowl on the table. "That's probably Ben's."

"A seashell?"

"Come here."

We bent to the bowl. Paula put her hand on my arm, a tender natural gesture, as we both peered close. "There," she said excitedly, "see it?" Tiny pink claws appeared under the edge of the shell. "A hermit crab. It'll live in there until it outgrows the snail shell and has to find another."

"It won't find many in there," I said.

"Michelle will get one for—" She broke off.

Her eyes swept mine for an instant, and they were frightened. I wondered if she was having one of her intuitions. Gently I gripped her shoulder. "Are you all right?" She made her face tight and nodded. "Will you be okay to drive?"

"I'm fine now, really." And she did appear to pull herself together. "I was going to say that I bet Ben found this and gave it to her as a project. He can't resist teaching." She smiled into my eyes for a moment, as if some bond was being strengthened between us. We walked outside together.

After she had gone, I locked up and went to my car. As I opened the door, I saw a little yellow sticky note on the window. "Wuz in the area. J" it read, written in green ink with a little smiley face. I puzzled that a moment but got no flash of inspiration. I pressed the note onto a page of my pocket notebook and drove back into town.

Delcastro had said that Standish jumps from four thousand year-round souls to three times that in the summer. A good number of them appeared to be out and about as I parked near the center. Over at the town common a small ring of kids were kicking around a little leather sack, as I'd seen them doing yesterday. I wandered over and paused to watch. They were a slope-shouldered crew, with baggy clothes and sparse little goatees sprouting from their youthful chins. Several were wearing T-shirts with the names of rock bands on them. When their momentum broke, I asked about the game, and they said it was called Haki Sack. I showed them the photos of Michelle Nickerson, and they shook their heads, polite but not very curious about who she was or why I was asking. "What about night action?" I said. "Is there any place where you go to hang out?"

"The Beachcomber," said one kid.

"Yeah," another agreed, "the Beachcomber's a chill."

"What is it?"

"An under-twenty-one club. It's on the coast road just outside town." They gave me directions.

I thanked them. I started away, but then turned. "Resolve an issue for me. What's with Satan Bugg?"

"They bite," one kid said at once.

"You bite," another kid told him. "They're cool."

"*Were* cool. They're teeny-bop music."

"Well . . . maybe."

"They're definitely not Creed."

"Or Tool," said a third.

They started off on a riff about groups I'd never heard of. I waved thanks. The logical thing to do would be to buy a tape of the band and decide for myself. Unfortunately, the Ford's player had a cassette stuck in the deck from a previous owner. Honest Al had taken the car in trade the very day I got it, so I took it as is. I had no idea what the tape was, and I hadn't found time yet to get it surgically removed. But music wasn't my main concern right now.

Standish was terra incognita, but I had the sense that it was small enough that someone had to know something. Ben Nickerson wasn't a total outsider or a wash-ashore either. I set course for the Storm Warning. At the take-out window, people were getting fried clams and ice cream. As I ordered coffee, someone behind me said, "Hello again."

It was the ubiquitous patrolman Ferry. He touched the visor of his baseball cap in an informal salute. "Can I buy you coffee?" I asked.

"No, sir, not necessary. We're well cared for here."

The waitress, a pretty dark-haired woman of about thirty, whose name tag said "Fran," smiled from under the yellow oilskin hat. "Don't be fooled by him," she told me. "At the end of the month we send the department a bill."

She bent to serve other customers, and I asked Ferry, "What can you tell me about Teddy Rand?"

"Not Ted?"

"Start with who's who."

He tucked his traffic ticket pad into a compartment on his multi-purpose belt, and we wandered over to a picnic table set up for the convenience of patrons. "They're father and son," he explained. "Ted Rand is our number one citizen, I guess you could say. Not that anyone actually does, but it's true. He runs Point Pines Development."

"That's his baby, huh?"

"He's very generous. Teddy's his son. TJ, they used to call him, for Ted, Junior I suppose."

"Is Teddy Rand dead?" I was thinking of the old woman's mantra.

"Well, not literally. He was a great athlete at Standish High, and smart. He was supposed to go to the Ivy League; instead he joined the Marines and went down to Panama. When he got hurt, Mr. Rand and his wife took it really hard."

"Is she the old woman that lives on the beach?"

"That'd be Mr. Rand's mother. Mr. Rand owns that house she's in. That's where he and his wife used to live. I think the shock of TJ getting wracked up did something to their marriage."

"What happened to him?"

"TJ? I don't know the details. If you want the story, who to talk to is Chet Van Owen."

I put the name in my notebook.

"He and TJ were tight. Big local jocks—they were both *Patriot*

Ledger All-Scholastic in football. He's the one who got Teddy Rand messed up for good."

That sobered me, and reminded me of what I was after. "Would Van Owen know Ben Nickerson?"

"The guy you're looking for?" Ferry lifted off his cap and scrubbed at his crew cut. "You got me there. Maybe, I guess. They'd be about the same age, and this was a small town then."

"Where would I find this Van Owen?"

"You saw him yesterday. The guy who was surfing. Red Dog." He glanced toward the common. "There won't be any waves today."

"You can tell that?"

He pointed. "Flag." It hung limp on the pole. "Plus some of those kids would be in the water if there was surf."

"Is everyone around here a surfer?"

"It's hard to grow up here and not at least dabble. And that's where it ends with most of us. There're a lot of boards collecting dust in toolsheds and garages. Not Red Dog's, though. He's the best surfer around here ever. Hell of a football player, too," Ferry said admiringly. "When he played linebacker he'd be all over the quarterback before he could set his fingers on the laces. But what he really loved was riding waves. He's good enough he could've made the California pro scene. You could check the sporting-goods store over at the Hanover Mall—he works there sometimes."

The walkie-talkie on Ferry's belt squawked, and he picked it up.

I glanced again toward the common and saw the small knots of kids hanging out. It seemed a lot less work than a job, or paddling a surfboard around in cold water. Ferry listened to a message about some debris reportedly in the road somewhere, and he said he would check it out. He belted his walkie-talkie.

"Last thing," I said. "When you told me that Ted Rand has been generous, what did you mean?"

"Point Pines has made him a lot of money. The rec center across the common came from his donations. Some of the high-tech gear in the station, too. He even worked out something with the dealership that supplies his company with vehicles, and they donate the Crown Vics."

As if on cue, one of the new Fords rolled to a stop at the curb.

A shaggy-haired, square-jawed cop sat at the wheel. The sunlight hitting his mirror sunglasses made them gleam like headlights. From the passenger side, Vin Delcastro got out. Ferry, whose back was to the curb and hadn't seen them arrive, turned now as the door closed. Seeing the chief, he hopped to his feet.

"You like hanging around, enjoying yourself, officer?" Delcastro said. "Want me to get you some ice cream?"

Ferry flushed under his tan.

"My fault, Chief," I said. "I was bracing him."

"I should've guessed. Go on," he told Ferry, who sputtered apologies and moved off to resume his foot beat. To me, Delcastro said, "You find out what you need to know?"

"Little by little."

"Well, Mrs. Jensen dropped off a missing persons report, so I guess we'll be doing your job for free. You can collect your bill and go on back to Lawrence."

"Lowell," I said.

"Show me the difference. Big dead cities on a big dead river."

He was goading me; it was part of the territorial thing. I didn't snarl. "Can I buy you a latte?" I asked.

He ignored it. "Or maybe you like being on vacation here, out of the rat race."

"This is a quaint spot," I admitted.

With nothing to push against, he let the attitude go. He gazed around, as if to confirm that I was right. Beyond the breakwater, a fleet of small boats with colorful sails was billowing seaward, obviously finding more wind than the town flag was. Seagulls soared and dived for the sheer pleasure of it. "Well, it's a free country. But don't be bothering my patrol people when they have a job to do. You got questions, Rasmussen, run them my way."

He headed back to the car. The cop at the wheel was watching me, had been the whole time, his big arm on the windowsill. I couldn't see his eyes behind the mirrors of his sunglasses. It was fine with me.

8

I drove out to Route 3 and down one exit to the Hanover Mall. The Wide World of Sporting Goods was a supermarket for jocks and jockettes. I found the windsurfing and surfboards section without a road map. It was full of fluorescent shorts and hats, wet suits and sandals. Except for one board on display, there wasn't a surfboard in sight. Nor was the music coming from ceiling speakers the Beach Boys. It sounded closer to the stuff Michelle Nickerson listened to. A few other customers milled around eyeballing merchandise. Hanging on the wall behind the sales counter was a section of old shipworm-eaten plank, charred on the ends and painted with a curling wave and the logo Ride a Legend. Amid the Formica, stainless steel and fluorescence, it looked as out of place as a lizard in a candy dish. A slim salesclerk drifted my way. She wore tiny amber-tint eyeglasses and a tie-dyed T-shirt that clung to her thin chest. She could have been eighteen or thirty. "Help you?"

"Is Chet Van Owen around?"

"Chet?" Her eyebrows arched.

"I was told he works here."

"Red Dog, yeah. He's not on now."

"Do you know when he will be? Or where I might find him?"

"He's probably at Coast Guard."

"Where?"

"Down the Cape."

"He's in the Coast Guard?"

"It's a beach. He surfs there."

"Oh. Any idea when he'll be back?"

"When the wind stops. When the spirit moves him." She had a cute, spacey grin. "When he realizes he's an old man in a kids' game and he's crossed the line from poverty to destitution. It's random." She shrugged her lean shoulders and consulted a sheet of paper taped to the wall. "He's *scheduled* to work tomorrow evening, but I'm not promising, and you shouldn't hold your breath. Excuse me one sec?" She stepped over to assist a woman with a lot of brassy blonde hair who was looking at sunglasses, but she said she was just browsing. The clerk came back to me. As if a glimmer from a customer-service briefing occurred to her, she said, "Is there anything *I* can help you with?"

"I'm looking for someone Van Owen may have known—a guy who grew up in Standish. Ben Nickerson."

"Mmm, can't help you there. You want to like leave a message for Red Dog?"

Not convinced he'd get it, I wrote the address of the beach house on the back of one of my cards, along with the message: "Would like to talk to you about Ben Nickerson." The girl said she was likely to misplace it; why didn't I put it right on Red Dog's workbench. She led me through a door underneath the charred wood plank into a back room, more shed than showroom, with a high industrial ceiling and a concrete floor. The air was raw with the smell of fiberglass resin. Along the outer wall, surfboards stood in vertical rows. There must've been forty of them in different shapes and sizes. Nearby, across a pair of sawhorses, lay a surfboard in the process of being repaired or built. On the deck of the board was a sun face with rays coming off and the name Sunshine Superman.

"It's hot, huh? I don't surf," the clerk said, "but if I did, I'd want that puppy."

"Do you make them here?"

"All those are factory stock." She dismissed the vertical boards with a wave. "These custom sticks, though—that's what Red Dog does." She stepped over to several sleek white boards. "He used to have his own shop, but it burned down, so he works here now. *When* he works." She sighed. "I'm not knocking him. He's a wave slave, what can I tell you?" Her tone had the same grudging admiration for the guy that Ferry's had.

One of the boards had a red pentagram on it, similar in design to the Satan Bugg logo. The name on the board was Deep Sea Ryder. "Is that one of his creations?"

"Oh, yeah. They're all originals—instant classics. Ride a Legend is his brand." She went over to the worktable and picked up a clipboard. As she clamped my card to it, she riffled through pages of paper for a moment, stopping to examine one. "What was that name you asked me before if I knew him?"

"Ben Nickerson."

" 'B. Nickerson,' " she read. "Hmm, same person?"

I looked.

"If so," she said, "that Deep Sea Ryder is his. He ordered it."

"Does it say when?"

"Three sixteen. When's that . . . March? There's a phone number." She turned the clipboard for me to see. "I don't know this exchange."

I did, but I checked to be sure. I had the same number in my notebook. Paula Jensen had given it to me. "It's near San Diego. What does the rest of that mean?"

She scanned the sheet again. "Dimensions. Is he small? I can tell by this it's for someone like my height and weight. It's being held for pickup on . . . hmm. Supposed to be two days ago."

Outside, I already had the key in the ignition when I saw the writing on my windshield: "em llac" and some numbers. The words and numbers were backward but I could read them. Even so, I got out and looked around to see who might have put them there, but I saw no one. They were written in lipstick. Something about the message was familiar.

I fetched my cell phone and dialed the number. After several rings a peppy-sounding female voice I didn't know said, "Hi, can't talk right now, but the machine can put us in touch. Do your thing after the beep." Which took forever to come. I gave my name and location. "You left a note on my car. I'll try again later."

I jotted the number into my pocket notebook, then used my handkerchief and wiped the lipstick away.

At the beach house I called my service and picked up messages. Bob Whitaker at the *Sun* had called me back. I tried him but was told he was out on a shoot. I got *The Torch,* the yearbook that Paula had brought. In the pages of photographs, where classmates had scrawled communiqués of naive hope and false sincerity on their likenesses, relatively few had written anything for Ben Nickerson—mostly fellow members of the Key and biology clubs and the band. On a thought I flipped ahead to the *R*'s, and there was Theodore "TJ" Rand.

Rand was a handsome kid, with an expression that seemed at once serious and sincere, innocent and full of knowledge. It was a look that promised success in school—and maybe in life, too. He had his father's curly hair. The list of activities by his name was long: football, baseball, basketball all three years, class president, high honor roll, to name but a few. His future included Dartmouth College, and, opined the editors, "big things!" Next to his own picture, he had inscribed: *"To Ben—I hope you find a beach without footprints, so you can leave your own. Good luck in the future. TJ."*

Contrasted with the pap most of their classmates had turned out, it was a surprisingly fresh expression. Taking another shot, I flipped forward to the *V*'s, and there was Chet Van Owen. "Red Dog." In the black-and-white portrait, he had thick, sun-bleached hair and a faintly menacing look. Like Rand, he had been an athlete—football and track—but there were no academic honors, nor other signs of school involvement, and no predictions of future success. In the line where grads projected a career for themselves, he had written "chase waves." He hadn't signed Ben Nickerson's yearbook.

I pondered a moment the fact of these three names, two of which I hadn't even known until a few hours ago, orbiting in the same little solar system. And yet, why should that be a surprise? In Lowell, where graduating classes ran to the thousands, it might have been more coincidence than possibility could bear; here, in a small town, it added up. I called Nickerson's California number again. When the voice mail message came on, I left my name and number once more. On a hunch, I retrieved the roach I'd recovered from a wastebasket that morning. I laid it on my handkerchief, next to the smudged lipstick stain from my windshield. Either that shade of purple was a summer hit, or the same person had left both. I dialed that phone number again and got the same brisk message. I repeated myself. It seemed to be all I was doing.

Sunshine and sea air had made me sleepy, so I lay on the living room couch for just a moment. The phone woke me. Outside, dusk was inking the sky. "Mr. Rasmussen?" a young woman asked. "Can we talk?"

I swallowed the dust in my throat. "Let's. Who's this?"

"I overheard you asking about someone at the sports store today."

"Chet Van Owen," I said.

"Ben Nickerson. I wrote the note on your windshield." She had to have been the young woman looking at sunglasses, but I had only an impression of hair. "I'd like to talk with you."

"Go ahead, Ms.—?"

"No, I mean like in person. Maybe tonight?" Her voice lacked the perky note it had on the answering machine. In fact, it had lowered to a near whisper. "Do you know where the Cliff House is?"

She gave me directions, and we agreed to meet there in half an hour. She said she drove a red Daytona. My detecting powers told me she wore purple lipstick. But I still didn't know her name.

9

The coast road wound north. I drove with my windows down, breathing the sea air, my senses alert. I believed that to do the job I was being paid to do, there was still a lot I needed to know about Standish, and the time I had to learn it in felt as if it was growing short. Except for one shaky moment, Paula Jensen had been maintaining her composure that afternoon, assuring herself that there was a logical explanation to her daughter's and her ex-husband's disappearance, but underneath her surface I sensed she was starting to unravel. Before leaving, I had considered calling her to tell her about the surfboard Ben had ordered; but it didn't answer any questions yet, and I didn't want to get her hopes up needlessly. I'd wait at least until after I'd talked with the mystery woman. I wanted to get some solid information to her and her husband before the case became fodder for the TV news.

The Cliff House sat on a rise on the inland side of the winding coastal road. On the opposite side, the land sloped a short distance to low cliffs above the sea. The nightclub was a large old colonial-style place, white with black shutters and a veranda. Tiny white lights twinkled in the ornamental trees, and lamps glowed beyond the screened windows. I drove up the sloping driveway and looped around the busy parking lot looking for a red Daytona but didn't see it. I parked and got out.

Light jazz floated on the lilac summer evening. People were sitting in wicker chairs on the porch. Nearby, at a big picnic table on the lawn were members of a softball team. They had several rounds of beers sitting before them and were laughing in the jolly way of winners. I recognized the pine-tree logo on the uniform shirts. Evidently, Ted Rand's local spirit included sponsoring a team.

At the sudden squeal of tires, I looked to see a car turn sharply off the ocean road and come blasting up the drive, music punching from its open windows with the percussive thud of mortar rounds. It was a red Daytona. As it pinged around the parking lot, I walked back and waited for it to come to rest.

A young woman got out, looked around and spotted me. We recognized each other from the brief encounter at the Wide World of Sporting Goods. She was about twenty-five, slender and on the short side, with a lot of brassy-blonde hair teased up and lacquered in a party-girl style, which went with the tight jeans and sleeveless blouse, never mind the dance beat still pummeling from the car. Her breasts made pert shapes in the satiny material. I couldn't see the shade of her lipstick.

"This isn't a good idea" were her opening words.

"What isn't?"

"Us meeting."

"You suggested it. What did you have in mind?"

"It really isn't." She was glancing toward the Cliff House. "At least not out here."

I wanted to point out that that was her idea, too, and that I hadn't entered the scene to an orchestral accompaniment, but I said, "Maybe we should get properly introduced. I'm Alex Rasmussen."

"Jillian," she said hurriedly.

"Do you want to go inside and get a drink, Jillian? Or talk in the car?"

"No, no."

"Should we get right to it then?" I was growing impatient with her seeming unwillingness to come clean about anything.

"Okay, the reason I left that—" She broke off. "Oh, shit."

She was looking past me again, and I followed her gaze. One of the softball players was headed our way. She ducked back into her car and shut off the music. The man was broad-chested, slightly older-looking than some of his teammates, his teeth white in his tanned face, dark shaggy hair hugging his head. "I can't see this guy right now," she whispered.

"Trouble?"

"Look, did you pass the lighthouse coming here?"

"I saw it."

"Let me get rid of him, okay?" She made smoothing motions at her hips, preparing herself. "I'll meet you there."

"When?"

"Soon as I can."

I started toward my car, not looking back, but walking slowly, listening: one of my professional reflexes. "Hey, Caro-line," the soft-ball player called, drawing out the name, in a way that might have been flirtatious or mocking. Now I did glance back. Caroline? The pair faced each other in an aisle of parked cars with him towering over her. "Long time no see, baby," he said to her, still grinning.

The lighthouse rose from a grassy bluff at the edge of the continent, squat and white against the coming night. There was a gravel turnout near its base and parking enough for maybe ten cars, most of the spaces filled, the cars silent and dark: couples catching the ever popular submarine races, no doubt. I didn't blame them. Hell, I was envious; it was that kind of summer evening. I gave them as much space as the small lot would allow and drew in and shut off the motor. The lighthouse had gone the way of most lighthouses along U.S. coasts, turning away the loners and would-be poets who used to people them in favor of mechanical operations. Boston Light was the only one that was still manned, as it has been for almost three hundred years. After ten minutes I began to feel peculiar sitting there alone.

I *felt* the car before I saw it. When it appeared, it drew in next to me and its lights went out, but not the noise. I fairly expected to see the doors pulsing outward, cartoon fashion, with the beauty-parlor beat. The woman looked over, studying me a moment, as if trying to decide something; then motioned for me to get in the Daytona. I went around and slid into the passenger side bucket. She lowered the volume slightly. The car smelled of cigarette smoke and cosmetics. I still couldn't figure out whether the driver was pretty or not; she definitely caught the eye. The hair wasn't the end of it. There was her round face, the full lips glossy with the purple shade I was starting to know so well. It was the same color as that on her long nails, which tapped restlessly on the steering wheel. The nipples of her breasts poked tantalizingly at her blouse.

"Was there any trouble back there?" I asked.

"No, I took care of it. I hope I'm doing the right thing."

"We're probably not doing much for the mating rituals of our neighbors. Can we cultivate the art of silence a bit?"

Reluctantly, as if she were forsaking a friend, she shut off the music. "That wasn't Satan Bugg, by any chance, was it?" I asked.

"What? You think I listen to that garbage?" She frowned and looked outside. "I don't know if this is such a good idea."

"Why don't you tell me what you have in mind," I said, "and then we can decide."

She sighed. "I might not be here at all if I hadn't overheard what you asked that salesgirl today about Ben Nickerson."

"So you know Nickerson?"

"Hardly at all, really. We met over at Nantasket Beach the other night, both just happened to be there, sitting at the bar. We started talking. I don't know, maybe he was picking me up." She flicked her hair, perhaps replaying it in her mind. "It got pretty noisy in there, so he said he had a beach house in Standish where he was staying and did I want to go see it. I live in Standish, too, so I said okay, and we went."

"Just the two of you?"

"Who else?"

"Go on."

"I don't party with groups of guys, hey."

"I just meant, was anyone else there at his house?"

"I didn't see anyone else. Anyway, we took a walk on the beach by the house, then went inside."

"What did you talk about?"

"Everyday stuff. Work, life. He's got a successful business."

"He said that? Successful?"

"Out in California."

"He didn't mention his daughter?"

"He said he'd been married once a long time ago and had a girl, yeah."

"And she wasn't there at the house?"

"I think I'd remember that. Why? What's this about? He still married or something?"

"No. What about his business, Jillian? Did he say what he did?"

"He told me he was like some kind of crab."

"That *he* was a crab?"

"That's outgrown its shell and he was gonna move into a fancier one."

"A hermit crab."

"I guess. Crabs I don't care about. That wasn't the focus of us getting together."

"What was? Do you know?"

"Duh."

I grinned.

"We met at the Sand Bar, like I said. It's right on the strip at Nantasket Beach. He bought me a drink. We liked each other's company."

I couldn't readily picture Ben Nickerson picking her up; it didn't seem to be a knack the man possessed. Though, what did I know? His line had worked with a woman as lovely as Paula Jensen. My information was all secondhand. "Now, how about you?" she asked. "Do you know him?"

"Never met him. I'm trying to locate him—or his daughter, actually. I'm a private investigator."

Her smooth brow got a nick of concern. "He done anything wrong?"

"Not that I know of. His ex-wife just hasn't heard from her daughter or him in a few days."

Jillian looked downcast. "I haven't either. I was hoping I would."

"Did the two of you toke up together?"

Her eyes narrowed. "You think I smoke dope?"

"And I think you're being careless about it, leaving roaches in people's ashtrays."

"That could be anyone's."

"With purple lipstick on it?"

She drew her lips in as if she wanted to nibble away incriminating evidence. "You hit low. I suppose you never smoked a joint."

"No, never. Nor have I ever had a hangover, lied about my age, or read *Playboy* for anything but the articles. Look, personally, Jillian, I don't care. What people do at home is their business. Pot isn't a killer drug, but I have a hunch the cops here will take you down just as hard. Was the weed his or yours?"

She was silent a moment. "Mine. We smoked half a joint. Big deal. Next time I'll be sure to eat the roach, like some sad old hippie."

I smiled. "You'll never be that."

"Okay, you said his daughter, but why you interested in him?"

"His daughter was supposedly staying with him, and as I said, her mom's worried. Her name's Michelle."

"I'm sorry, I don't know a thing."

"Why the first note on my car?"

"Guess."

"You want to see him again, so you came by the house."

"I knocked on the door, but no one seemed to be there." Probably when I was over yakking with old Mrs. Rand about kidney stones. Jillian sighed and checked the mirror for her image. "This shade is called Paradise Plum, by the way. You like it?"

"Yeah."

"I haven't decided yet." She adjusted the mirror.

"Did you see what kind of car Nickerson was driving?"

"A blue Jeep, California plates. That's why when I saw your car there, I wasn't sure, so I just left that little smiley face. But that's all I would've done. I'm not like that woman in that movie who stalks the guy with a knife. He has my phone number, so if he wants, he can call. When I overheard you asking about him at the sports store, I thought maybe you knew him." She nibbled her lip again. "I guess

I was hoping it wasn't gonna be just a one-night stand."

I felt no pang of prejudice at seeing Jillian—or Caroline—as one of those young women for whom a broken nail was a whole other order of tragedy from twenty thousand souls lost in a China typhoon. I could picture her at a stoplight: brush of hair, dab of lip gloss, then zooming off to her own hyper soundtrack, eager to be someplace, but it was never here, never now. And yet there was a quality about her I liked. How many men had promised to call? She'd met someone she liked, and she was willing to risk a little vulnerability to let him know. And she'd thought enough to contact me. But why? Only to ask about Nickerson? Or was there something she wanted to tell me? Before I could frame words to find out, she pushed open the door and got out. I followed.

In front of the cars was a low white guardrail fence that separated the parking area from the cliff. She walked along beside the rail to where it ended near thick bushes. On the other side there was a path worn in the short grass that traced the top of the cliff behind the lighthouse. Below, the water whispered against rocks. She set off along it. I caught up, not hard to do trailing a woman in heels. She stopped and turned abruptly, as if she hadn't intended for me to be still there. "Damn it, what do you want from me? You want to know if we got it on? Whether I left lipstick on his body, too?"

The outburst surprised both of us. She looked pained, embarrassed. "No, that stuff is your business," I said, "not mine. I gather that you liked him."

"I didn't get to know him too well, but he seemed like a nice guy. Decent . . . and smart. I saw that right away when we first talked. It's why I was willing to go with him."

Her words had to compete with the swishing of waves on the rocks below, and the wind was blowing her hair awry. She asked if we could go back. In the Daytona, she reached for the CD player, thought better of it, and sat back. "When we were at the beach house, I was in the bathroom at one point, and the phone rang. He took it and went out on the deck. He shut the slider door, but the bathroom window was open. I overheard some of what he was saying. He was pretty upset. It was after that I said I should maybe leave. But he said no, he just needed to relax. I said did he want a back rub—you know, to relax him. We went to bed."

I didn't need the details. It made the world go round, sure; but we had to walk upright in that world, too. "Did he say what had upset him?"

"No, and I didn't hear the other side of the talk, obviously, but it sounded like it was maybe a business deal. He kept saying, 'That wasn't the arrangement.' Something like that."

" 'Arrangement' could mean other things, too, no?" I found myself thinking about a domestic arrangement. "Could you tell if the speaker was a man or a woman?"

"No. All I know is he seemed angry and a little . . . spooked."

"Scared?"

"Just a feeling I got. Anyway, he made plans to meet."

"Meet the person he was talking to?"

"I think so."

"Did he say when?"

"No. He mentioned the beach."

"To meet?"

"Seemed like it. He said 'surf'?"

"Was anyone else mentioned?"

She hesitated. "I . . . don't know."

I had the idea that she might. "Any names at all?"

"No, not that I heard. Anyway, after that's when he said he was uptight. I brought out my stash."

"And you both lit up?"

"Yeah. Wait. I didn't have any matches—well, I did, I mean, but I collect matchbooks, kind of a hobby, but they have to be like virgin, no matches gone. So I looked in a drawer, and I see a gun in there. That shook me."

"A handgun?"

"Yeah. In the kitchen counter, by the stove."

"Did he take the gun out?"

"He didn't have to. A person you've only just met and he's got a gun there . . . that's a little random."

"Did he seem scary to you?"

"No, that's just it—he was nice. Personal. Person*able*."

"And you didn't stay all night?"

"Uh-uh. He said he had to go out later."

"For his meeting?"

"Sounded that way. I left just before midnight."

"Did he mention his daughter at all? Or his ex-wife?"

"You keep asking me that. No. Now—I'm going to cultivate the art of silence."

I thanked her and opened the door and stepped out. She leaned toward me. "Look, this won't get . . . back to Ben, will it? Or anyone else?"

"Like who?'

"I just mean . . . can you keep my name out of it?"

"I promise. Speaking of which, is it Jillian or Caroline?"

"It's both."

Farther down the row of parked cars, a motor started. A van, I saw. She noticed it, too, and watched the van a moment, but it was soon gone. She checked herself in the mirror, patting her hair, then tossed me a jaunty little wave. The music came like offshore blasting. Seconds later she was slinging gravel as she swerved out onto the paved coast road. Even after her taillights had gone from sight, I still rocked in her wake.

10

I found a quick mart and bought a few provisions for the morning. Back at the house I put the groceries away, except for a bottle of tonic water, a lime, and a pint of Beefeater. I needed to do some thinking. I got a good-sized glass from a cupboard and fisted in some ice cubes. As I was cutting the lime, there was a rap on the screen door. Out past where moths were swarming the deck light, Ted Rand raised a hand in greeting. "I saw your light. I hope I'm not interrupting you?"

"Only if you're from the temperance union. I was just about to fix a drink. Join me?"

He waved at the moths, slid open the screen and stepped in. I'd lost track of the time. The kitchen wall clock showed it was almost ten. Rand was wearing a Dartmouth sweatshirt and a pair of orange swim trunks, a white towel slung around his neck. With his deep tan and white hair, he looked like an old lifeguard.

"I was just over checking on my mother."

"How is she?"

"She's got a bunch of things wrong, none serious enough to kill her. She'll outlive me for spite. I heard you were looking for me earlier." Rand must've read my surprise, because he laughed. "No, my mother didn't remember, but it's a small town."

"Actually, that's the reason I was looking for you, hoping you might be able to shed some light on Ben Nickerson's visit to Standish. I didn't mention it yesterday, but I'm a private investigator."

"I heard that, too. And the answer is, certainly. If I can help, I'm glad to. What's up?"

"Gin and tonic okay?"

"I'll pass. I've got something else in mind." His blue eyes twinkled. Was he a closet doper? "It's Mr. Rasmussen—have I got that right?"

"Alex is fine."

He crooked a finger. "Come with me, Alex."

I followed him out and down the steps to the sand, away from the house. Over the ocean, the moon was a half-shut eye. Picking up its glow, tiny waves lapped the beach. "Isn't that pretty?" he said. "It's like a golden road to somewhere."

"It is pretty," I agreed.

"Let's swim."

"Now?"

"There's nothing more refreshing. The tide's about to turn, and there'll be fog later."

"I'm not much of a swimmer."

"The sea will take care of you. It's the mother of us all."

"Then my excuse is I haven't got a swimsuit."

Rand's shoulders bobbed with a silent laugh. He stretched out a hand. " 'The Sea of Faith was once, too, at the full, and round earth's shore lay like the folds of a bright girdle furled.' " He looked at me. "Know it?"

"Shakespeare?"

"Listen. 'But now I only hear its melancholy, long, withdrawing roar, retreating, to the breath of the night-wind, down the vast edges drear and naked shingles of the world.' " He paused, giving me another chance. "Matthew Arnold. 'Dover Beach.' "

"Off by only a few centuries," I said.

"You're an educated man, Mr. Rasmussen. Alex. I had a feeling an investigator would have to be. Most folks wouldn't have a clue. Do you remember how the poem ends?"

"Let's go back to the part about me being an educated man and leave it there."

He laughed. "What did you want my help with?"

"I've got some information that Ben Nickerson may have been working on a business deal in town. You seem to be the local burgomaster. Any idea what he might have been up to? Or with whom?"

"Well, I'm flattered you consider me a credible source. Burgomaster, huh? And here I've been thinking I was just a bumpkin." His smile lingered a moment, then his expression grew serious. "A business deal. Hmm. Here in town?"

"I'm not sure."

Rand tipped his head in a gesture that said he wished he could be more helpful. "I saw him only once, and he didn't say much. Though that doesn't mean you're not right. There's opportunity in Standish. Have you spoken with Vin Delcastro?"

"Briefly, yes."

"Well, I'll certainly keep my ears open."

"Nickerson evidently had a surfboard made here for his daughter."

"And you're coming to *me* to get information?" Rand chuckled. "You seem to know more about our little town's goings-on than I do. Sorry I don't have much to offer. I keep myself pretty buried in my project." He gestured toward the dark sweep of Shawmut Point off to the left. "That's all mine," he said, with a note of half-surprise. "Not literally. Some of it is. But I possess it in my imagination. I've envisioned what it can become and have taken steps to make it happen."

"I heard something about it. Point Pines, right?" He glanced my way. I lifted a shoulder. "As you say, it's a small town."

"Understand that not everyone is happy with the idea. I'd like them to be, of course. I try to spread things about and make it good for all. I can't worry too much about folks who choose not to see it that way. There'll be some attempts to block me. Obscure zoning laws or EPA rules no one ever noticed before will come up, but I'm prepared for that. You see, I've got a vision for Standish." He gave a low laugh. "I didn't come by to bend your ear."

"Then we're even," I said.

"Well, it's getting a bit late for a swim. The fog is on the move." Sure enough, the bank that had shimmered on the horizon earlier had drifted closer to land. "And you don't want to be out there in the fog," he said. "It invites monsters." He laughed.

"The bar's still open."

He said he had to get back home; he lived on the other end of town and was an early-to-bed-early-to-rise type. "Next time," he promised. "We'll swim and then have a drink. My treat." He started away, then stopped and came back. "In fact, I'm having a little soiree at my house tomorrow night. Kind of a meet-and-greet for some of the wash-ashores who've bought homes in the phase one of Point Pines, plus a few town folk. Why don't you come? It'll give you a chance to meet some people."

"No poetry quiz?"

His shoulders bounced with silent laughter again. "I can't promise that, but it will be fun."

I said I'd be glad to come, and he gave me directions. "Anytime after nine. Bring swim trunks."

Inside, I completed my bartending chores and then sat in the semidarkness, sipping the drink and allowing my mind a slow access to the events of the day. So far, I knew that Ben Nickerson had ordered a surfboard prior to coming east, probably as a gift for his daughter, but he hadn't picked it up yet. What he had picked up was Jillian, or Caroline, depending on who was talking; and she had left by midnight. I also knew that Michelle Nickerson hadn't been in evidence at the beach house that night. Ben had argued on the phone with someone. Who? Remembering something, I checked the top drawer in the counter by the stove and then the other drawers. No gun. So that's what I had: details that, thus far, netted out to zero.

In sports, people talk about impact players, athletes who can enter a game when the chips are down and make things happen. That's what I was supposed to be. Impact Investigator. I added that to a mental list of possible ad copy to run by Fred Meecham if I ever decided to take his counsel and shill my wares. I checked my answering service, hoping that Sergeant Ed St. Onge had called. He hadn't.

I looked at my watch. Ten-twenty. I rinsed my glass, got my keys and headed for the car. By Ted Rand's measure it might be late, but I had to figure that young folks on summer vacation used a different clock.

11

The Beachcomber was a mile south of the town center. When the kids playing Haki Sack on the common had told me that it was a twenty-one-and-under place, with soft drinks and sandwiches and live bands, I was having a hard time imagining it, but I thought it was worth a look. The parking lot was full of cars, including a Standish prowl car. Sitting at the wheel was the same shaggy-haired officer I'd seen in town with Chief Delcastro that afternoon, with the mirror sunglasses. He still wore them at 10:45 P.M. It's possible he was snoozing behind them, but in case he wasn't, I parked where he wouldn't notice me and got out. Muted music and the crickets mingled in the salt-fragrant air.

I moseyed up to the door. I might have been a parent looking for a tardy teen. In fact, I'd more or less decided on some sort of cover—friend of the family, who were away for a few days and asked me to check in with their daughter—but I'd wing it. Feeling only slightly self-conscious, I went inside. I needn't have worried. The doorman stamped my hand without a second look.

But any idea of wandering around bracing people about whether or not they had seen Michelle Nickerson was out. The place was so crowded and humid with bodies and smoke, I could barely see or move. On a low stage three guitar players had their amps cranked up full. The audience seemed happy enough, though. In front, lots of kids were thrashing around in jerky movements, which were to dancing what the noise coming from the stage was to music. I made my way to the bar, where several college-age youth were fetching sodas and working an exotic espresso machine. After several attempts, I made one of the youths understand that I wanted information, not caffeine. He looked at the photograph of Michelle Nickerson and then at me, and I think he had the idea I was looking to pick her up. He shook his head. I tried several other people, but got the same response. Finally, with no new information to go with my ringing ears, I went outside.

In the parking lot, a broad fellow with longish hair and wearing a Hawaiian shirt and jeans was leaning against an old pickup truck moored alongside my car. He was older than any of the people inside, though not yet my age. He listened to my canned intro and took the photograph. Clamping a cigarette in his lips, he held the photograph at a distance, squinting against the smoke, as if attempting to draw a bead. "I think I saw her once."

"When?"

"I'm trying to recall."

He seemed a little spaced. "Recently?"

"Yeah. Not here, though. This isn't my scene." He made a brief effort to remember, then shook his head and handed the photograph back. "Who is she, anyway?"

"Her name is Michelle Nickerson."

He straightened up and waved his fingers in a "gimme" gesture. He gave the photo another look. "Is this Ben Nickerson's girl?"

"His daughter, yeah."

"How old is this?"

"A few years." I was watching him closely. "Do you know Nickerson?"

"I'd like to find him," he said.

"So would I."

The man sucked the last smoke from his cigarette, pitched it down and stepped on it. "What's your interest?"

"I'm trying to locate him or his daughter. What about you?"

He ran a hand across his mouth, watching me, like a man deciding whether or not to come clean. "You're not really interested in a board, are you, bro," he said.

"A board?"

"Actually, I followed you. I went over to the place on the beach you're staying, but you were just splitting. I tagged along. I got your message."

I wasn't expecting a tail, so I'd missed it. I hadn't been expecting company, either, but I made the connection now. "Are you Van Owen?"

"You're a private investigator, huh?"

Somehow I'd expected a lean, blond-haired guy, younger. "I've been hired by Nickerson's former wife."

"What did Ben do?"

"He and his teenage daughter seem to be missing."

"Hmm. Maybe why he hasn't picked up his stick. The blue one," he added for my sake. "In the shop."

"Deep Sea Ryder." I was making all kinds of connections now.

"I saw him in town the other day, coming out of the bank. We only got to talk for a minute. He seemed hurried—so much for California laid-back. I told him his board was ready. He said he'd be by to get it."

"What day was that?"

"Day before . . . three days ago, actually."

"Is the board paid for?"

"On a custom job I'd generally take a deposit, but I know him." Van Owen shrugged his thick shoulders. "He said he'd square with me when he got here."

The cruiser I'd spotted earlier was back, doing a slow prowl among the rows of parked vehicles, coming our way. Van Owen reacted first. "I've got to rock," he said. He was already climbing into the beat-up truck.

It was full dark now, the moon down, but in the light from the teen club I could make out the shine of the cop's reflective lenses. I went around to the other side of Van Owen's truck and climbed in, too. He looked at me but said nothing. When the cruiser had crawled past, I said, "That looked like an instinctive shying away from the law."

Van Owen grinned. "The chief sends a car out here on a regular run. Community-policing effort, keep the youth of Standish on the straight and narrow. Parents around here love him."

"But you don't?"

"The chief and I are both townies. Let's say I'm warily respectful of him, but I believe policing works better if it's a cooperative arrangement. I don't think keeping people under constant surveillance and making them afraid is good policy. That spook in the car— Shanley—he can be a hassler." He didn't elaborate. "That do it for you? Or do you want to ride awhile?"

We headed north. The truck's interior was pasted with decals for surfboard makers, the dashboard covered with tattered maps and papers, the floor littered with fast food wrappers and coffee cups, the remnants of gulped meals en route to secret surfing spots, I imagined. Van Owen checked his mirrors several times, but the road behind us was dark. He pulled a deck of Old Golds from the pocket of his island shirt and offered them. It seemed an oddly old-fashioned gesture, though I guess it could be considered hostile these days. I declined, and he tapped out a cigarette on the steering wheel and used the dashboard lighter. His arm was thick and muscular. I reeled the conversation back to Ben Nickerson and his surfboard.

"He ordered it by phone back in late winter. Wanted something a kid could learn on. I shaped it to the specs he gave me."

"That design on it—the red logo—"

"He drew it in his letter and—" He snapped his fingers. "That's where I saw the girl. My boards are all about performance. I build them to the person, to their body style. Usually I like them to come in and I take measurements, but because he was in California, I asked him to send a photo. I've probably still got it in the shop. It's newer than what you have there."

"May I see it?"

"Next time I'm there I'll look for it."

"I'd like to see it now if possible."

He glanced over. "Hell, man, it's late."

"That's what I'm thinking, too. If the Nickersons have disappeared, it's getting later all the time."

He was silent a moment, then he slowed and swung a U-turn. I thought he was bringing me back to the Beachcomber and my car, but he took a side road and turned inland. We rode awhile on roads winding through farm- and woodland. In the mild air I could smell mown hay and see fireflies winking in the meadows. Considering the crowding on the South Shore, I was surprised any open land still existed. Taking my cue from Van Owen, I kept silent. The old truck rattled along. Soon, we crossed the highway, and I recognized the Hanover Mall, night-lit and deserted. Actually, somebody was still inside the Wide World of Sporting Goods, doing inventory. The man recognized Van Owen and let us in with minimal explanation. At this hour, nearing midnight, the place had a strange feel: all this equipment for the active life seemed ghostly. Van Owen led me back to his fabrication area, and after a brief hunt among papers, he found what he was after.

It was a Polaroid snapshot taken only a few months ago, according to the date stamp. It showed Michelle Nickerson standing under a tree. She was a pale, pretty girl, with short, jet-black hair. She was wearing a long black skirt, black T-shirt and a studded vest. A small ring glinted above her right eyebrow. Van Owen moved beside me to see it. "Under the goth garb," he said, "she looks athletic enough, like she could handle a board. That's the kind of thing I'd look for in custom-fitting a board."

"Can I hang on to this?"

"Take it. Do you think something happened to her?"

"I don't know. I hope not. Do you?"

"No reason to. Still . . ." He went over to the surfboard, Deep Sea Ryder. An instant classic, the salesgirl had called it. "I was hoping Nickerson would be eager to get it."

"Did you know beforehand that he was going to be staying out there at the beach?"

"No. Not till you told me."

"Do you know a young woman who drives a red Daytona? Jillian something?"

"Big hair and a brain no bigger than you'd expect?"

"Who is she?"

"A club rat. I don't know her last name. Does she figure in this?"

"I don't know. Nickerson seems to have picked her up in a place called the Sand Bar three nights ago. They spent some time together. What's her scene?"

"What else? Girls just want to have fun."

I slipped the Polaroid into my shirt pocket.

"Are the cops in on any of this?" Van Owen asked.

"I've met with Delcastro, but they're not officially involved yet. Nickerson's former wife and her husband believe Ben and the girl will turn up, that maybe they've been away for a few days."

"Off beachcombing?"

"Is that possible?"

He lifted his shoulders. "Nickerson was always poking around tide pools and marshes. He did tenth-grade science projects even the teachers couldn't understand."

"So did I."

"I hope that's what it is—his being off on a brainstorm."

Something in the way he said it made me curious. He said, "There was a case five or six years back of a girl about that age, a runaway. Apparently she was hitching through town, supposed to meet some friends in Boston. Several people saw her because she'd camped out in a field along the Old Cape Road—but she disappeared. You got me thinking, that's all. But this doesn't sound like that."

"No," I agreed.

The outside air had cooled. He brought me back to my car and let me out. "I hope they turn up," he said.

"Me, too. What are you out on the surfboard?"

"No big deal. I can find a buyer if need be."

"There's a cute little salesclerk at the sports store who sounds as if she'd like some surfing lessons."

He grinned. "Save it. She and I have been there. What she really wants is a ring on her finger—or through my nose."

I handed him another of my cards, which he glanced at. "Is that how you spell it?"

"It's a misprint. Hang on to that; it's an instant classic."

He laid the card on the cluttered dashboard, then gave me a hand sign, thumb and pinky finger extended. "Paddle easy, Dog. Old hodaddy's advice—keep one eye on the horizon and one on the shore. This is where the hungriest sharks are."

When he had gone, I stood in the cool night. The Beachcomber parking lot was still packed, the club still going strong, rampant with teen hormones and metal music. I had a yearning for something to drink, but espresso wasn't going to do it for me. Out on the starlit sea, the mantle of fog had crept closer to shore. I could see the rhythmic sweep of the lighthouse farther up the coast, like a blurred and restless eye. The tide evidently had turned, bringing the tangy brine of ocean. In Lowell, once a year if the wind was right and you were lucky, the scent might carry upriver from Plum Island, make its way past the brackish currents at Newburyport and Amesbury, through the industrial stinks of Haverhill and Lawrence, sneak by the dank churn of the Duck Island wastewater treatment plant, and on a downtown street, thirty miles from the sea, you'd flare your nostrils bracingly and say "Smell that!" Then the wind would shift, and in fifteen minutes it was all a dream. Here in Standish, I was becoming aware that the sea was a constant, bearing change, moment-to-moment, oblivious to the tides of human affairs around whose puny shorelines it washed.

No wonder Matthew Arnold and Rod McKuen were poets.

12

Standish Center was night-wrapped when I drove through it: locked up, buttoned down, rolled tight. In my city, things would just be starting to cook. I wasn't sure which to prefer. Just beyond the center, I stopped at a late-night gas station to fill up. I paid for a bag of ice, and the clerk gave me a key for a refrigerated locker outside. As I unlocked the insulated chest, I happened to glance across the street. On the opposite corner, fifty yards from me, two men were standing in a small alley between the Wash Tub laundry and a martial arts studio, both enterprises closed at this hour, talking. The men were just out of the glow of an overhead lamp, but my eye was struck by a gleam of white hair. I realized one of them was Ted Rand. I glanced at my watch. Midnight. Rand looked as if he had thrown on clothes over pajamas. The other man wore jeans and a windbreaker, so it took me a moment to recognize him, too. It was Police Chief Delcastro.

I watched from my shadows. At this distance, I couldn't hear a word of their conversation, but the way they were facing each other gave me to believe it was tense. Ted Rand's hand gestures looked insistent. Delcastro stood with a kind of glowering posture, making only occasional replies. Above them, moths spiraled in the cone of lamplight. I had an idea to try to move closer, but it would mean getting across the bright-lit gas station lot, so I let it go. I'd learned that almost any detail, no matter how small or insignificant seeming, was worth noting. I'd also learned that it was important to be curious without being paranoid. I returned the key, and when I came out, the two men were gone.

13

On the stage, a group of musicians stood in a smoky glow of spot-lights. A corpse-white man was singing, his voice a guttural snarl. The lead guitarist worked his instrument with such furious intensity, there was a physical discomfort in listening to the sound. I wanted to get away from it, had even turned to go . . . when I saw the child. She stood to one side of the stage, as if frozen. Around her, oblivious to her presence, couples were moving in a jerky dance rhythm. The air was almost opaque with smoke, giving the figures on stage a dreamlike presence. At the rim of the sound another vocal had begun, a frail voice crying in the wilderness of noise. It was the child, I realized. Her words were indistinct, but I *felt* them, felt their pain and fear, and all at once I was slick with sweat. My muscles were tight, and breathing was difficult. The drumming kept on, like the thunderous footsteps of something terrible approaching. The sound banged off the walls, trying to escape. I needed to escape, too.

But not without the child.

I started forward. I edged around dancers, avoiding contact (something told me it wouldn't be a good idea to touch them) until at last I was close. I was reaching for the child, about to gather her to myself, when a laser beam blistered my face and sent me recoiling.

Bars of moving light drew my eyes open, and I was suddenly awake. I'd been dreaming. I was in a bed in a dark room, both unfamiliar. I stank of tobacco smoke. There were bright shapes sliding over the ceiling. Headlights? I knew then where I was. Except the lights weren't coming from the narrow road in front of the house, but rather from in back, from the beach. With a pounding heart I lay frozen between wanting to know what was going on and simply willing it to go away. I eased back the sheet and rolled quietly from the bed. The rattan roughness on my bare feet wakened me more fully. I drew on pants and moved with hushed steps to a window on the seaward-facing side of the room. Keeping to one side, I peered out.

Two high, close-set lights were piercing yellow eyes. Fog had engulfed the house, and it was as though some beast from the sea had come with it. Through the glare I could make out its vague, elongated shape. I thought I could hear a sound now, too—a low rumble, as of an engine, though I wasn't sure.

I made my way downstairs, cat-footed through the dark house to the kitchen, but when I reached the door to the deck, the lights were gone. The sound seemed to taper to the thin edge of dream, and then it disappeared. The beach was fog-bound again, silent. I drew open the sliding door and smelled the sea. I stepped out onto the deck, the planks cold underfoot, and blinked into the seamless shroud. Was there a large, humped form going down the beach toward the water? Perhaps I imagined it. I stood in the cold night, feeling the wild thud of my heart. I didn't begin to shiver until I got back inside.

I left the lights off. The digital clock on the kitchen counter said 3:33. It was about as wee as the hour got. A slot player might have listened for a jingle of coins, or a prophet warned of a cut-rate beast of the Apocalypse. I tried to remember my dream, but it was hash. I told myself to make a list of things to bring back from Lowell and at the top to put my .38. I sat in the dark and watched the clock go through a lot of numbers before I finally dozed upright in the chair. I woke once around dawn, stiff-necked, and went to the slider and looked out.

The mist had thinned and paled. The beach had been swept

clean by the tide. Waves were gliding shoreward in calm, unruffled rows. I started to go back upstairs to finish my sleep when I noticed something in the sea off the point. A lone figure in a wet suit sat on a surfboard, gently rising and falling with the waves. More from lethargy than real interest, I watched him for a few moments, wondering if he'd catch a ride, but he let the water roll emptily under him and just sat out there, like a sentry on watch. I roused myself and went up to bed.

The next time I woke, it was to sunlight and the high music of children's voices outside. It was after nine. I went downstairs and stepped out onto the deck, squinting. People with beach chairs and blankets had materialized. I thought that some of them were looking up at me, but I rubbed my eyes and realized it was just the leftover heebie-jeebies of my busted sleep. The beach folk had other agendas, chief among them working on tans. I could smell the sunscreen. A jagged line of seaweed, broken shells, and bits of trash delineated the high-tide mark: flotsam and jetsam, I imagined, though don't ask me which is which. Seagulls chuckled overhead. Thirty minutes later, showered and shaved and dressed in a gray rough-silk sport coat, pale blue shirt, and chinos, I was at the police station. The young female officer at the desk frowned in consternation when I told her what I'd seen on the beach during the night.

"It wasn't a squad car," she assured me. "Not down on the sand. Around three A.M., you say?" She checked the log. "No one called in to report anything unusual. But that doesn't necessarily prove much. This time of year, we sometimes get off-roaders, or kids on a toot. Though that's a pretty private stretch of beach. I'm noting it now, sir. How do you spell your name?"

As she wrote it in, I was scanning the notebook that served as the Standish police log—an old cop habit, I suppose. An entry from several nights before caught my eye. "What's that?" I asked, pointing at it when she'd finished writing.

The officer looked. "A call came in just before midnight that a young female was walking along Sea Street. It was just a safety issue—there's no sidewalk along there. An officer was sent over, but the person wasn't there when he arrived."

Before I could ask if there were any further details, a cop rushed in to say there'd been a bad accident. A car had gone off the road south of town sometime overnight. They were pulling it from the ocean now: a red Daytona.

I fought a desire to speed. At last I came around a curve and onto the scene. The already narrow coast road was further narrowed to a single lane by a line of emergency flares. In the midmorning sun they were no brighter than Fourth of July sparklers. It appeared that most of the town's police force was already on site. I made out Chief Delcastro talking with several people. The Daytona, its windshield gone and its roof crunched at an angle, oozing water from every seam, was being winched onto the back of a wrecker. I told the officer directing traffic that I had information to share with Chief Delcastro. Trustingly, he waved me through.

When Delcastro saw me, he did a double take. "Get out of here," he snapped.

"What about the driver?" I demanded. "Was it a young woman named Jillian?"

He fixed me with his gaze. "What do you know about this?"

"Was she inside?"

His silence was all the answer I needed. I felt as if I'd been punched. I let out a breath and looked away and for the first time saw that a length of wooden guardrail had been broken off.

"She didn't make it," Delcastro said in a quieter voice. "We took her out already."

It was my duty as a citizen to report what I knew. It wasn't much—I didn't even know the young woman's name for sure—but I gave him what I had. I realized that I was probably one of the last people to have seen and spoken with her, possibly the very last; and oddly Delcastro kept a firm look on me, then motioned me over to his cruiser, out of earshot of others. "Around nine-fifteen P.M., you said. At the lighthouse."

I nodded. "We spoke for ten minutes, maybe less, and then she left."

"And what did you do?"

"I made a quick stop to get some food supplies, then went back to where I'm staying." I was about to add that Ted Rand could vouch for me but realized that I didn't have to; no one suspected me of anything. I did tell him that I drove out to the Beachcomber, and I said I'd just been at the police station, since he'd find out anyway. He didn't seem much interested in lights on the beach at night; he had a fatality on his hands. "Okay, the driver's last name was Kearns. How was she involved with this allegedly missing Nickerson girl?"

"I'm not sure she was. She overheard me asking questions out at the sports market and left the note on my car. I called and set up a meeting. She and Ben Nickerson evidently picked each other up in a bar Tuesday night. She said she went back to his rented house with him and they partied a little, but she left just before midnight."

"And Nickerson's daughter?"

"She claimed she never saw her."

He posed a few more questions, and I replayed what I could. "You still have the note?" he asked me.

"It was on my windshield in lipstick," I said. "Paradise Plum, if it matters."

He didn't seem stirred by anything I'd told him, or convinced of its importance. "Well, I appreciate your coming forward, but I don't think there's any mystery to solve." He glanced toward the Daytona sitting atop the wrecker, one headlight goggling out like a displaced eye, a brown frond of seaweed dangling from a broken door mirror. "This is a bad road, and people sometimes go at it wrong for the conditions. It got foggy last night. Add in the fact that the victim may have been drinking . . ."

"I don't think she had been when I spoke with her."

"I've got witnesses who put her at the Cliff House near closing."

"Which is how you came up with the estimated time of her crash?"

He shot me a glance. "Dashboard clocks aren't what they used to be. They don't freeze the moment of impact."

"Was she with anyone at the Cliff House?"

He pointedly ignored the query.

"Who claims they saw her?"

Ditto.

"Do you happen to know her real first name? It seemed a multiple choice last night."

"To answer the *next* question I know you're going to ask—and so you won't think I'm being rude—we will investigate the accident." He turned and headed back to the scene.

"I never doubted it, Chief," I called after him.

As I reached my car, the wrecker drew past, and it occurred to me to do what I hadn't thought of last night: I jotted down the Daytona's plate number. For an instant, as I put my notebook away, something stirred at the edge of my memory, but a police siren whooped and the something was gone before I could grab it. I slid the Ford back into the halting flow of the curious.

I'd told Delcastro that I didn't doubt he would investigate the car crash, and I assumed there would be an autopsy; what I did have doubts about—and mulled as I drove back to Standish Center, slowly—was whether my meeting with the woman in the Daytona had somehow contributed to her death, directly or otherwise. As I'd said to Delcastro, she had seemed nervous last night, but when he'd pressed me on it, I didn't have a reason. I played with possibilities now. Was it about the softball player she'd wanted to duck at the Cliff House? Someone in the van that had cruised the lighthouse? Being seen talking to me? Did it concern Ben Nickerson? If she'd been inebriated and driving dangerously on account of it, as the police seemed to be promoting, I could let myself off the hook because that had come later. She wouldn't have been my bet to win any safe-driver awards, and yet I had to ask myself what, if anything, I might have done to prevent it. Until I knew more, I was going to wonder.

Of course, it was entirely possible that the accident went down just as Delcastro had read it. The road was curvy, and certainly by the time she went off, the fog had rolled in so thickly that visibility would've been dicey. I used my cell phone and called the RMV in Lowell and asked for a woman I knew. The wait took only half as long as if I'd been there, standing on line to get a license. She sounded happy to hear from me.

"I need an ID to go with a tag number," I said.

She played coy awhile, reminding me how she couldn't *possibly* give out that information to anyone except a *real* cop; it wouldn't be professional.

"You're tough," I said.

"Go on, you think so?"

"Armor-clad. You could be a CIA spook."

"Seriously?"

"You'd get an ultra top-secret clearance easy."

"Oh, you're sweet." I heard a tap-tapping of keys. "Okay, here's the name."

Lucky thing it wasn't her virtue I was assailing. From my car, I called directory assistance and got a phone number and an address. I felt like Nero Wolfe on wheels.

14

The full name, according to the Commonwealth of Big Brother, was Caroline J. (for Jillian, I surmised) Kearns, with a Standish address. I located the apartment house on the inland side of town, an old wood-frame with sand-colored vinyl siding and a large front door that led into a vestibule. There were mailboxes and bell pushes for the six units. The inner door was locked. A label by number 5 said "C. J. Kearns." No one answered my ring. I stood there for a moment, like a bit of flotsam—or jetsam—left by a wayward tide. I felt a sadness that the young woman would never answer a doorbell again. We never would've been dear friends, but her liveliness beat like a muted echo of her music.

My habit is curiosity. The day's mail had already come, and there were a few envelopes visible inside her locked box. Too big for the slots, an assortment of flyers and magazines was spread across the table. I found two for C. J. Kearns: a lingerie catalog featuring the Love Potion collection and a copy of *Cat Fancy* magazine. Did she have a pet in the apartment? Something about her gallivanting lifestyle suggested that anything more than a guppy was unlikely.

When I got back to the town center I was hungry. I hadn't eaten a thing all day. I went to the Storm Warning restaurant. A pointing-hand sign, smaller than the one at the town hall, directed me through the main dining room (empty at this hour and set up for dinner) out to a screened area in back overlooking the inlet of the bay. There were a few small parties at the picnic-style tables. The same waitress as yesterday, Fran, wearing her yellow rain hat, came to take my order. "We meet again," she said amiably.

"Isn't it fun?"

She grinned. "Are you on vacation?"

I told her what I was doing. I didn't see any reason not to, though I left out mention of Jillian Kearns's fatality; I'd let Delcastro and his department handle it their way. Her expression got very serious when I told her about Ben and Michelle Nickerson.

"Ben, yes," she said. "I remember him from long ago. He grew up here. If it's the same Ben Nickerson."

"It is. Evidently he was here earlier this week."

"Visiting? I didn't think he still had family here."

"He wanted to show his daughter where he grew up. The girl's mother hasn't heard from them, so she's worried."

"Of course. Do you have any idea what happened?"

"I'm trying to find out." I showed her the Polaroid of Michelle Nickerson that Red Dog Van Owen had given me last night.

"She's lovely. I'd know if I'd seen her. I'll certainly keep my eyes peeled."

She went to place my order. I watched lobster boats move out of the inlet, trailed by opportunistic seagulls. When the food came, since Fran was of Ben Nickerson's generation, or close to it, I asked her what she remembered of him.

"My impressions are pretty vague, I'm afraid. He was one year ahead of my older sister Ginny in school. Along with Teddy Rand. My dad might recall more—he used to be a schoolteacher."

"What about Chet Van Owen?"

"He was in that group, too." The other patrons cleared out, and we were alone in the restaurant. She kept busy as we talked, filling salt and sugar dispensers. "Red Dog's still around."

"I met him. I'm not quite sure how to take him."

She smiled knowingly. "He's hard to read sometimes. Sometimes he seems like a big teddy bear, or a guru or something. Other times he's someone to steer clear of."

"Yeah? Why's that?"

"He just is. He used to run a little surf shop out there on the jetty." She pointed past the open window to the line of big rocks jutting into the harbor mouth. "He didn't make much money. I think it was something to do, because he loves surfing and the life that goes with it. Eventually, the town got on him to fix up the shop—it was little more than an old fishing shack, really—or get rid of it. It didn't meet the town codes, or something. Anyway, no one here would give him a loan. That's the story anyhow. I was living out west in those days." There was that wistful note again, as if it was something she would've liked to be still doing. "I should let you eat in peace."

"No, I like talking." She smiled, as though not quite convinced. "What happened?" I asked.

"My husband decided he didn't want to be married anymore." I'd meant with Van Owen, but she seemed to want to talk about her situation, so I listened. "He said he'd missed his youth being responsible and now he wanted it back. He was going to live in Vail and be a ski bum." She lifted a shoulder. "You can't reason someone into loving you. My dad needed help with his business back here, so I came home." She stopped wiping and laughed. "I'm sorry, you didn't mean me. You were asking about Red Dog."

I smiled. "I was interested in both," I said truthfully.

"Well, you're nice. End of *my* story. I'm living with Dad. Red Dog, though—he couldn't get a loan, and then his shop burned down one night. It blazed out there on the jetty like a Roman candle."

"Poor man's lightning?"

"I'm sorry?"

"Was it burned to collect insurance?"

"Oh, I doubt he had any at all. I don't really know. Afterward Mr. Rand stepped in and set him up as manager at the sports store. That's what Red Dog does now."

"Rand has pull, huh?"

"Oh, yeah. He owns the store."

"That sports supermarket?"

"He's a silent partner I guess you'd call him." A party of four had come in. She gave them time to get settled, then rose. "Duty calls. Nice talking with you, Mr. Rasmussen. I sure hope you find Ben and his daughter and they're okay."

This was the day I'd promised Ross Jensen we would talk about the progress of the investigation. As far as I could tell, there wasn't much. I was circling around, learning bits of Standish's history, but they weren't adding up yet to anything that helped me. Still, there was some kind of method to it, and at the moment, it was all I had.

Recalling the item in the police log from three nights ago—the same night that Jillian Kearns had visited Nickerson at the beach house, and left before midnight—I drove out Sea Street in that direction. There was a sidewalk along it. I passed the Strand Theater and beyond that I noted that the sidewalk ended as the road grew narrow. Had the young woman who'd been seen walking along here been Michelle Nickerson? Was she going back to the beach house? If so, from where? I U-turned and went back. I stopped at the Strand Theater, which was closed, not scheduled to open until 5 P.M. I rapped on the glass a few times and waited. Finally, I saw a man approaching from inside. He was a rotund, dark-haired young man, with long greased-back hair. He pushed open the door. "First show's not till five-forty," he said.

I told him what I was there for and handed him Michelle Nickerson's photo. He looked at it thoughtfully. "Geez, I don't know—this flick we're screening now brings in a lot of youths." Mr. Old-Timer: he looked all of twenty-two. "But, hmmm . . . I might've seen her. The night you're talking, I saw a kid about her age standing outside after the last showing."

"What time would that have been?"

"Show gets out at eleven-forty. I saw a kid standing out here like she was waiting around for a ride. When I came out later—maybe twelve-twenty—she was gone. I didn't even remember it till now, on account of you asking."

"You didn't see anything else? Other people, or a car hanging around? Anything?"

"No. Is there a problem?" He seemed genuinely concerned. I thanked him for his help.

So what did it mean? The last show let out shortly before midnight, and a teenage girl who might possibly have been Michelle Nickerson had waited for a ride. So what if Nickerson, wanting an evening alone with a woman, had dropped his daughter at the theater, say, around eight-thirty or nine. No, he hadn't known yet that he'd meet a woman. But what had Jillian Kearns said? That they met at the Sand Bar and talked only briefly before they left together and went to the beach house. She'd said that Nickerson had a phone call that seemed to be about meeting someone. And if he'd gone to meet someone, perhaps he'd missed the pickup time for his daughter at the Strand. It was a stretch, without a lot to hang it on, and yet I felt an eerie sense of possibility.

I phoned the confidential number on the card that Ross Jensen had given me. Someone else answered it and said attorney Jensen was in court and she thought he'd be back late, did I want to leave a message? Jensen had made it sound as if the number was a hot line that would put us in instant touch. Serves me right for believing a lawyer who wasn't under oath. I left no message. I tried Paula Jensen at home and got her.

"Alex—hi. Anything?"

I gave her what I'd learned, including Nickerson's apparent date with the Kearns woman. There was a brief silence. "I wonder where Shel was if she wasn't with Ben?"

"That's what I'm curious about, too. Would she have gone to a movie here in town alone? If Ben dropped her off?" I gave the name of the film that was being screened at the Strand.

"That is one she'd mentioned wanting to see. Still, I'd think Ben would've gone with her. Though they've been together since Shel flew out to California, so maybe they wanted a little space. But where would they go afterward?"

Of course, I had no answer. I told her what I'd seen on the police blotter, and I said I was going to check that teen club again. "Did Ben ever mention the name Van Owen?"

"He may have, I'm not sure."

"How about Teddy Rand?"

"Why is that familiar?"

"He's in that high school yearbook—they both are, actually. They were Ben's classmates. And I met the sister of another contemporary today. Ginny Carvalho was one year behind them in high school."

It didn't ring any bell. "Teddy Rand, though," Paula repeated. "Was he TJ?"

"TJ, right."

"He and Ben were friends, I remember that now. He wrote in Ben's book. I don't think they kept in touch. Not while we were together, at least. Why?"

But I had no answer. I ran through a few more details, mostly trying to find something to probe and wanting to encourage Paula to be optimistic. Though she didn't say so, I had the idea that Ross Jensen was too consumed by his court case to be much support. "I'm starting to wonder if Nickerson's business was doing as well as we've imagined," I said. "When I call there, I get only a voice message that it's closed for vacation. Is that likely if he sells live specimens?"

"It could be, if he sold out his inventory. Tanks need periodic cleaning and repair, and he'd been planning the trip with Michelle for a while."

"Is there any way you could find out?" I thought maybe a little task might keep her mind away from worrying.

She considered it for a moment. "Well, this goes back, but he did file an amended child support form when Shel turned thirteen. I probably still have his accountant's name. I could try it."

I told her that anything she could learn might help. I would keep my focus on finding Michelle. I said that she and Ross could expect to hear from me that evening with an update. As we were about to sign off, she said, "Alex?"

"Yes?"

"Thank you."

"For?"

"What you're doing." Her voice held the same shy gratitude

that I'd seen in her eyes that first day we'd met. "You're turning over a lot of stones."

"Stay hopeful," I said.

Despite my pep talk to Paula Jensen, I had begun to think that I was looking for phantoms in a fog. Or, as Ed St. Onge liked to say, hunting elephants with a BB gun. Though now that I thought about it, I realized I didn't have *any* firepower. My rod was back in Lowell, locked in a drawer, where I couldn't hurt myself with it. That was okay for now, as long as I didn't come up against a situation where I needed it, like a real live monster emerging from the sea—or one trying to put me into the sea. Remembering to start a list of things to get when I returned to Lowell, I opened my pocket notebook and wrote "gun." I also made a note to. send flowers for Jillian Kearns, if I could find out to whom.

On a separate page I started inscribing names, several of which had turned up more than once so far. Red Dog Van Owen's name went on there. And Ted Rand's. Clustered around that one I wrote "Teddy/TJ" and "old Mrs. Rand," that wheelchair-bound apparition from yesterday. I also wrote "Jillian" and "Mirror Shades." If I had a Dr. Watson chronicling my cases, the notebook would be a treasure trove of character ideas. As an afterthought, I wrote "Mrs. Ted Rand," followed by a question mark. They were all question marks as far as that went. As I put my notebook away, the fleeting thought that had eluded me at the crash site earlier abruptly materialized. Jillian had left Ben Nickerson before midnight, which might have put another car on the road, another pair of eyes, around the time that Michelle Nickerson might have been walking along the road. It was a lot of "mights."

I trundled over to the real estate office in the center. The man with the commercial solutions, Andy Royce, was on the phone again. He got in his patented "No kidding" a few times and finally hung up. I wondered what he used for a closer. He glanced my way and drew on a blazer the color of ballpark mustard. "Did you find someplace to rent?" he asked me.

"I'm all set, thanks." I had a question and wasn't sure how it would play, but a realtor's stock-in-trade was knowing what was going on, same as mine; the difference was that in my game, tight lips were a virtue. "My neighbor is Ted Rand," I said. "Out of curiosity: Does he own that house at the beach?"

"He owns several houses around town. The one you're talking, he and his wife used to live there. His mother's in there now, I think. Ted lives on Maple Street."

"His wife, too?"

"Iva? Iva bought a condo over in Hull. I want to say the Sea View . . . Sea Crest . . . Sea something. Are you interested in a condo?"

"Not at the moment. Is Iva's last name still Rand?"

"As far as I know. How about a business? I was just on the phone to somebody who's selling a Laundromat."

"I'm not sure that's a solution for me," I said. "I like to feel I'm free to move."

"Hmm . . . well, when you're ready, you come see us first."

I promised I would. At the village drugstore, I used a local directory and looked up Rand. Iva was listed, with a Hull exchange. I called and got her. After taking a moment to make plain who I was, I said I'd like to speak with her. Without bothering to ask what about, she gave me directions and said to come on over. I think her voice was a little slurred.

15

The condominium complex where Mrs. Iva Rand lived was on Nantasket Avenue, near where the old Paragon Park had been, she had said. I cruised along the strip in afternoon traffic, looking for the address. The amusement park was long gone, the land, with its ocean proximity, having become too valuable for childish fun, though Paragon had left some of its funk behind, the way spicy food will. A stretch of pinball arcades, cheap souvenir stands, and biker bars occupied one side, and across from them was the long graceful swoop of Nantasket Beach. I braked to let a pair of round young women with a posse of small kids play through. A little farther along there was still an old merry-go-round, which gave one of the housing complexes its name. CAROUSEL CONDOMINIUMS a sign trumpeted. "Coming Soon! Luxury Units Going Fast!" But the project didn't seem to know if it was coming or going. Judging by the unfinished construction, it looked as if it had been begun with more optimism than ready capital. There were probably prospective buyers who'd need a cemetery plot before they got their dream home.

The complex I sought wasn't half so fancy, but at least it existed in more than a four-color brochure. The Sea Chimes was a cluster of gray buildings fashioned at angles so as to give each small unit a view across Ocean Avenue to the seawall and the beach while restricting any glimpse into the neighbors' lives. It couldn't have been more than a decade old, but already it was showing signs of weather and wear. I parked in the area designated for visitors. A panel truck that said LIQUOR LOCKER on the side was idling in the shade at the front entrance. I went into the hallway and found the stairs to the upper levels. Mrs. Rand had told me 3-B.

"Hey, ma'am?" a man's voice was saying in the dimness at the top of the stairs. "I wouldn't know, okay? He says no checks. I don't make the rules. He just says have it paid next time or no merchandise." A flushed and balding young man came out. Seeing me, he gave an exasperated look and tossed his head. "For her there should be a whiskey wagon, tinkle a little bell when it drives through the neighborhood, playing 'One for the Road.' Good Humor for adults, unlimited credit." He went on down the stairs.

I realized he belonged with the panel truck in front. I climbed to the next gray-carpeted landing. The door to 3-B stood open. "Knock, knock," I said into the doorway.

A woman in a gold velour sweat suit and red espadrilles with stack heels stood in the center of a white room, holding an empty glass in her hand. She was slender and middle-aged. Without looking at me she said, "You made your point. Go."

"I just got here," I said.

Now she glanced my way. Evidently seeing that I wasn't with the Liquor Locker, she frowned. "If you're looking for Randy, you missed him. He keeps it short these days. Ignore the pun."

I ignored. "If you're Mrs. Rand, I'm looking for you. I'm Rasmussen."

"Oh, you." Her enthusiasm lacked a lot. She waved me in. Her long reddish-gold hair was held back with a green silk scarf. She was attractive, and once had been very attractive. Her eyebrows were plucked as thin as razor cuts. She had small whiskey welts under her eyes; her voice was Lauren Bacall without the purr. "I thought you wanted Mr. Big Shot."

"Rand? I understood he lives in Standish."

"He deigns to visit me here from time to time. Usually when

he wants something, or when it's convenient, like today. He was going to check out the Surf."

Rand was a surfer, too? It seemed to be a cult down here.

"Do you want a drink?" she asked.

"No, thanks. I just wanted—"

"Well, I sure wouldn't mind a splash."

I glanced around, half-anticipating a cash bar where I was expected to buy her a highball, but she managed it by herself. I had imagined the man I'd seen departing had shut off the tap somehow, but on an ornate sideboard there was a set of crystal decanters: drinks for all occasions. Iva Rand didn't bother with any of them; she poured straight from a fifth of J & B. I hadn't imagined the slight slurring in her voice on the telephone.

"You have a nice place here," I said. Despite its limited space, the condo was tastefully and expensively furnished, with cream-colored rugs, bright acrylic abstract paintings, and antique furniture. There was a balcony where two people could dine if they ate standing up. The wall facing the balcony, with the beach beyond, was a mirror, giving the room a moving seascape and an illusory expansiveness.

"Built on the bones of Paragon Park," she said. "You're old enough to remember the park."

"I made the trip from Lowell on several occasions to ride the roller coaster."

"Lowell? Is that where you live now? No wonder you look pasty. You need to get some sun. What's your name again?"

I told her.

"And you're here why?"

I told her that again, too, but she seemed no more curious than she had been on the phone. "When they demolished the park," she went on, "right near the exit from the Tunnel of Love, workers uncovered an old dry well. Guess what it was full of?"

"I don't know—broken hearts?"

"Wallets. I love it. Wallets from the nineteen forties and fifties, not a lousy dime in any of them. What the police think, they think it was from pickpockets working the crowds." She gave a bray of laughter. "Randy and I used to come here from Boston when we first met. We'd make out on the beach at night. Burt Lancaster and Deborah Kerr had nothing on us. God, that was ages ago. We haven't seen moonlight and love songs around here in a long time."

"Are you and your husband divorced?"

"Nosy, aren't you."

"I guess so," I said. "Though I like to think of myself as a skilled conversationalist with a robust curiosity."

She frowned and took a drink. We were still standing in the living room. "I don't live there in Standish because the house gets a little too tight, thank you. Not to mention the town. Since you're some kind of private snoop, you've probably noticed that my husband owns Standish."

"Owns?"

"*Owns*. Understand English? He owns people and places and things. He paying you?"

"No."

She didn't look as if she quite believed me, or cared especially, either, but she did wave me to a chair and I took it. She went on standing.

"What people and places does he own?" I asked.

"Let's just say that Standish is being shaped in Ted Rand's image and leave it at that."

I was suddenly thinking about what Rand had told me on the beach last night, about having a vision and making things happen. Carrying her drink, Iva Rand stepped before the mirrored wall, put one hand on her waist and flounced a hip to one side. "I was a real piece," she said to her full-length image. The sweat suit hid her figure, so I couldn't make any judgment there, but facially she had been a beauty. I wasn't thinking of Deborah Kerr so much, though, as Geraldine Page's character in *Sweet Bird of Youth*. "Randy robbed the cradle with me. You should've seen me in Capri pants."

"I believe it." I could still see her beauty there underneath the adipose tissue, like an artifact poking through the desolations of time.

"Then I got too *old* for him." She gave the word a sour emphasis, still studying some image cast there in the reflecting glass. "I'm ten years younger than he is, and I'm too old. That hypocrite.

But he'll come around." She made a pursed-lips expression in the mirror. "I'm getting it all back." She made a vague gesture toward some stainless-steel dumbbells piled on the edge of the carpet in a corner. "He'll see what he's got here. *If* I take him back." She shot me a firm expression to leave no doubt as to who was in charge, then turned away from the inspection and went and refreshed her drink. I didn't ask her if she was going to Rand's soiree that evening. Intuition told me she didn't even know about it. Carrying her drink, she came back over. "What do you want?"

"A glass of water would be fine."

"With me," she said querulously. "Why are you here?"

"As I mentioned on the phone, I'm trying to find some people."

"They live *here*?"

"One of them used to live in Standish. Do you know Ben Nickerson?"

"What about him?"

"I'm trying to locate him. He came back to Standish with his daughter several days ago for a vacation. I'm looking for anyone who may have seen them."

"You think I did?"

"Someone told me he was a friend of your son's."

Her face looked as if someone had given it a sudden twist from behind. It tightened and clenched in an unattractive way for a moment, then let go. "Yeah?" She came nearer. "For your information, Ben Nickerson was a very socially misfit young man. You can ask anyone. Inept. He has children?"

"A teenage daughter."

"Well . . . Anyhow." She got me a glass of water. "Teddy didn't care about things like the high school caste system—and he would've been at the top of it. My Teddy was a remarkable boy. Generous and trusting. Gifted. He had a talent for making friends. Unfortunately, his choices of people weren't always wise."

"Meaning Nickerson?"

She waved an impatient hand. "He wasn't important. I mean that devious bastard who *pretended* to be his friend all those years and in the end just destroyed him." Her words dripped acid. As if to wash away the taste, she drained her glass. I waited for her to resume, but she didn't. She poured more whiskey and went into the adjoining kitchenette. I followed. She broke several cubes loose from an ice tray and dropped them into the glass. A section of counter was cluttered with bottles of vitamins and herbal concoctions, potions and emollients and other things promising long life and beauty. She saw me looking. "I'm a health nut," she said a little giddily. She raised her glass. "To yours." She took a drink.

"Who were you referring to before?" I asked.

"What?"

"Someone pretending to be your son's friend."

"I won't have his name uttered in this house."

"Was it Chet Van Owen?"

"That's enough!"

In the abrupt silence, the ice cubes crackled. Her eyes were getting glassy. I trailed her back into the living room, wanting to ask my questions while I could still understand the responses. "Have you heard of a young woman named Michelle Nickerson? She's sometimes called Shel or Shelly?"

"Am I s'posed to have? Look, why don't you go ask Randy about all this? You can probably still catch him at the Surf."

"Is he a surfer?"

"Huh?" She stepped back, her gaze narrowed in foggy comprehension. "The Surf ballroom. It's for sale. He buys things. People and things." She gave an exaggerated sigh. "You don't really know what you're talking about. You can't possibly. Do y'self a favor. Forget the beach. They got crème tanners you can use. Go back to . . . wh'rever you're from." She shook her head in dismissal, and I saw her take a quick sidewise step to keep from stumbling. Even so, a couple of ice cubes tipped from her glass and wobbled across the carpet like a pair of misshapen dice. I moved toward her, but she held up a hand in a "stop" sign. "Oh, my husband has done good things, and bad things. But there's one thing that was unforgivable."

"Why don't you sit down, Mrs. Rand—"

"Like hell." She gave me a blurred look. "Next you'll want me to *lie* down. What kind of wife you think I am? Huh? Pumping me. And where d'you get off comin' around ingratiating yourself, pretendin' you're better'n me, not drinkin' my whiskey." Her husky voice rose. "I was one hot babe! You hear me?" She stumbled and a slosh of booze slurped over the rim of her glass. "You think I'd tell you a goddamn thing, you goddamn snoop! *Get out!*"

I got.

16

Pressured by my sense that I needed to be doing *some*thing to locate the Nickersons, I drove through the heat shimmer of the busy strip along Nantasket Beach. In midafternoon traffic I passed Skee Ball arcades, T-shirt emporiums, shop fronts selling fried seafood, frozen custard, caramel popcorn, and postcards of young women in bathing suits that you never saw here—neither the bathing suits nor the women. Music came from a dozen sources in an aural collage that canceled out any particular song and formed a generalized sound track of noise for the roving masses of sun worshipers and beachniks. I suppose there was a honky-tonk charm to it all, but I was preoccupied. And then I saw what I was looking for and parked.

The Sand Bar had a dim, underwater feel, like any barroom on a sunny day, but here the effect was heightened by the room's narrowness and low ceiling, and a funky decor of fishnets with rubber lobsters and starfish woven into the strands, and big worn tables that might once have been the dragger doors of a trawler, glossy now under coats of polyurethane. I didn't check, but even money said the bathroom doors were labeled "Gulls" and "Buoys." The barman, at least, looked like a landlubber: a longhair clad in painter's pants and a tank top with a faded yin/yang symbol that rounded over his potbelly. Behind him, intermixed with the bottled paraphernalia of his trade, was an array of sports trophies and team photos. I wasn't the sole patron of the establishment, but near enough. I sat and ordered a draft.

Since this was the place where Jillian Kearns said she'd met Ben Nickerson, I improvised, and when the brew came, I said, "I met a young woman in here a while back. Jillian something. Cute, with a lot of hair? I heard she was in a car crash."

He drew hair away from his round face. "It's a drag, man. Jilly used to come in and brighten up this sad scene. She went off the Coast Road in fog. I overheard somebody saying the cops think she'd been drinking, but that's a crock. The only thing I ever knew her to drink was maybe one Pink Slipper."

"You know how to make one?"

"Me and Olde Mr. Boston." We exchanged a smile, and then he grew glum again. "I've got a theory," he said.

I was careful not to appear anything more than polite.

"She seemed like a lonely kid," he expanded. "Looking for love. Sure, she often seemed to be with some new guy, full of eager hope, but what it was, deep down, she was . . . bereft. My take is she never had a relationship with her father, so she was seeking it in the men she met."

Pay the barstool philosopher a little court, and he's yours. "That's kind of deep."

"She wanted the missing piece. Completion. The yin."

"Definitely deep," I said. "What about the man she was with the last time you saw her—who was he?"

He gave me a closer inspection. "What, you carrying a torch for her, brother?"

I shrugged. "I thought maybe I'd see her again."

"Goes to show. We never know. That guy? I don't care who he was. He was wrong for her, I'll tell you that."

"Wrong how?"

"Something about him just looked kind of . . . mean."

It was a new word for Nickerson. I wished I had the high school yearbook to show him Nickerson's mug, but I tried describing him. Dark hair, yeah, that sounded right, but the bartender didn't seem quite sure about the rest. The joint had been hopping that night, so he couldn't be certain. "Why?"

I lifted a shoulder and drank ale. He leaned close to me. "Want some free advice? Pay your respects and move on. Ashes to ashes. Our days keep sailing over the horizon, friend."

"I'm not a flat-earther."

"Well, that's when it's tough."

I put down money for the beer and a tip. "Thanks for the existentialism."

"We're all just God's laundry, blowing in the breeze."

A half mile down, the commercial area thinned, giving way to apartments and vacant lots. Then, there it was. I'd heard Iva Rand *say* it, but I hadn't really imagined she meant the same place. I drew off the road onto the cracked pavement of a parking lot, shut off the car and got out. There was another AT&T truck parked nearby, and a young man getting ready to climb. My secret eyes and ears. I wondered if Ma was quietly trying to hook things up and put it all back the way it was before de-reg. Part of me wished she would.

"Pardon me," I called, "did that used to be the old Surf ballroom?"

He looked where I was pointing. "Yes, sir, that was it. Long ago. My grandfather used to go there."

"Yeah, so did mine," I said, trying to stanch the bleeding.

The 1970s *were* long ago, as nightclubs went; most of them seemed to change style and theme before you'd fairly learned the dances of the current scene or the names of the mind candy of choice. The original deco sign was history, as no doubt the signs of half a dozen other enterprises gone from the site were, replaced now with a realtor's placard, but I knew this was the spot. The Surf ballroom had rung to its last line dance around the time Travolta's white suit began to show marinara stains. The pale stucco, which had once been pink, had faded and was cracked, and the big windows were covered with plywood. It was a far sad cry from the club I'd come to two or three times with Lauren when we were courting.

Who knew, though? Where I saw desolation, maybe a shrewder eye saw opportunity. Wasn't that Ted Rand's specialty?

I walked down the beach to the seaward front of the building, hoping to get a look inside, but only got my shoes full of sand for my trouble. I stayed clear of an area of old paving where seagulls were smart-bombing with surf clams, eager to crack the thick shells and get at the tasty morsels inside. The gulls in Lowell wouldn't know a clam if it waved at them; their lunch du jour came off the city landfill. I watched a rat the size of a bread box scurry to cover beneath the eroded concrete steps. I looked for the ghosts of a young couple stepping out onto the runway for a cigarette and a kiss as the sea foamed in hissing white lines in a summer dusk. I looked and listened in vain. The sun shone bright, and the ocean was as flat as last week's beer. Heading back to my car, I glanced at the realtor's sign. Small world. It was the Standish agency, along with the name and phone number of the contact agent. Andy Royce. No kidding.

On the way back to Standish, I dialed Red Dog Van Owen's number. He picked up, sounding as if he'd been asleep. "Not out hanging ten?" I said.

"At dawn I was. Who's this?"

I told him.

"I should've known. Where'd you pick up the lingo? Off a Jan and Dean album from thirty years ago?"

"Probably, yeah. Look, I find myself going around asking the wrong questions to the wrong people. Now I'm thinking maybe it's you I should be talking to."

"What's your curiosity? Nickerson still?"

"Right, but hang on to your huaraches, there's more. Are you awake enough for a late lunch? My treat?"

"I've got some things to do."

"I'm easy, you say when."

I heard him drag on a cigarette, or sigh. "Why don't you fall by my place around six? Keep your appetite; you can share *my* humble meal." He gave me directions.

"Harwell's Cove," I repeated. "Is that a street?"

"What street? It's water, man."

I hadn't let go of the idea of checking Jillian Kearns's background. Maybe one of her neighbors had something. I made a stop at a 7-Eleven and then drove over to her apartment building. A town cruiser was parked in the side lot. The small number "1" on the side panel told me whose it was. In the foyer I pressed the bell for Jillian's unit. I expected to be challenged over the intercom, but a buzzer sounded and the outer latch clicked and I was in. The carpeted stairs creaked as I climbed to the second floor. The door to apartment 5 was open. I approached it carefully, looked in and saw Delcastro. He stood in the front room, waiting. "What the hell are you doing here?" he demanded.

"Great minds," I said, "and all that. Boy, that was a nice little move, letting the mystery caller in without a challenge—looking to see who might turn up."

"Relax, this isn't a crime scene."

"That's what I figured. May I come in?"

"What for?"

"A look." I held up the bag of Little Whiskers I'd just bought and gave it a jiggle. He paid no attention to it. I said, "She may have been the last person around here who actually saw and talked to Ben Nickerson."

"That again."

"You know how it is. Sometimes you have to make a stretch when you're looking for connections." He didn't bite. I shrugged. "Was my guess that she had a cat faulty?"

He relented. "In there." He nodded toward a door. If he was curious as to how I'd known, he didn't ask; maybe he'd scanned the magazines in the foyer, too. He said, "We don't have experienced investigators on the force—we don't have the need—but I like to check things out, just to be thorough."

"Anything?"

He gauged me. "Nothing to say her dying wasn't an accident."

I opened the door and looked into a bedroom. A cat peered out from under a pink dust ruffle and stared at me with green-eyed alarm. I rattled the goodies again, but got even less reaction than Delcastro had shown. I found the cat's double bowl in the kitchenette, put in fresh water and some of the food, and set it on the floor. Delcastro said, "I know a retired couple who live in the building. I'll ask them to look after the cat for the time being, or call the MSPCA."

We wandered around the small apartment together. It was what I had envisioned, from the hand-me-down furniture to the dime-store painting over the couch. The most costly possessions were the TV set and DVD player in the bedroom. Her film tastes ran to tearjerkers with Julia Roberts in them. On her dresser sat a fishbowl-sized snifter half-full of matchbooks. I scooped out a handful. They were from clubs and bars around greater Boston. She got around, looking for love in all kinds of places. I upped my rating of the yin/yang barman. "Did you find out her blood alcohol level?"

Delcastro scoped me. "Why?"

I dropped the matchbooks back. "Come on, I can read it in the newspaper."

He frowned. "She was well below the limit. But accidents happen anyway."

"True. So does crime."

He turned to face me squarely. "What are you driving at, Rasmussen? Are you sniffing around here after something I should know about?"

"No, just what I've already told you."

"That she partied with Ben Nickerson, and about the van at the lighthouse. Well, we've checked, believe it or not, and you seem to be the only one who saw anything."

That quieted me. At least he'd checked. He struck me as an efficient cop, if not an overly friendly one, and I was mostly satisfied. But he seemed to have drawn a bead on me. "Don't hold your breath that the presses are grinding out a late edition with all the gory details," he said. "This isn't one of those creepy little Edens they love on nighttime TV, with evil lurking behind the picket fences and monsters by the school yard."

"Never said it was, Chief."

"But I'll tell you," he went on, pointing a finger my way, "if a crime has been committed, I'll nail the dumb bastard who did it. Thanks for your big-city efforts to help us poor country cops, it's right nice of you. But we'll struggle along without it. Let's go." He jerked his chin at the door. "The ghoul tour is over."

17

If I'd been right in envisioning Jillian Kearns's apartment, I missed Harwell's Cove Marina by a nautical mile. What I'd pictured as a posh yacht club proved to be a meager assortment of small sailboats and stubby cabin cruisers tied to a sagging wooden dock in an inlet that appeared as though it would maintain just enough water at low tide to float them off the mud. Seagulls and terns wheeled above the marsh grasses, and a white egret fished the banks. None of the boats looked fancy enough to require a security gate to keep the curious away, which probably explained why the marina didn't have one. I tromped right onto the dock.

Van Owen's home was a Chris Craft, old but reasonably well-kept, though time and the elements were exacting a toll. Lettered in white script across the mahogany transom was the name *Goofy Foot*. Van Owen met me, looking sun-browned and salted, his hair still damp. I handed him a bottle of Chianti, and he waved me aboard. He had on cutoffs and a faded red, yellow and green island shirt. "Hope you like flounder, caught today."

"Which makes it about a week fresher than what I'm used to. Love it."

A hibachi was heating on the cabin roof. On one side of the

deck—starboard, if it matters—three surfboards lay stacked together. Forward was a small vinyl table and two canvas chairs. At the stern, on a square of all-weather carpet, stood a weight bench and a set of rusty barbells. I followed Van Owen below.

The cabin was tight but cozy. There were two chairs and a reading lamp. On built-in shelves was a Bang & Olufsen stereo setup—like the boat, old but top quality. The paneled walls held a collage of framed pictures. Van Owen reached into a small drawer and held up a baggie of weed. "Want to burn one for appetite?"

"Everyone else seems to think I should burn my skin. I'm starting to feel like Moby Dick."

"Doesn't the sun shine up there in Lowell?"

"Not at night."

"Is that a 'no' to the weed?"

"If it cleanses your doors of perception, go for it. It never did for mine."

"And booze does?"

"Hey, that's a nine-dollar bottle of grape—it bruises easily."

He put away the weed and stepped into the little galley. "I'll save the wine for the chow. Gin okay?" I said it was. Ice cubes plinked into glasses. When he'd handed me a drink, he put on a CD. Following a bluesy piano intro, a wonderful voice came from the speakers. I listened a moment. "Dinah Washington?"

"You were figuring Dick Dale and the Del-Tones."

"It was one of my suspicions." I clinked his glass with mine. "To stereotypes."

He got the fish started on the hibachi, then brought out a basket of bread sticks and we took our drinks onto the deck, where the music reached softly. The tidal river was rising, and grasses shimmered green in the golden light of late afternoon. "This is nice," I said.

"It's the low-rent district, but it suits me. There's a whole series of little brooks that snake up through salt marshes and feed into the North River. In the seventeen hundreds there was more tonnage launched on the river than anyplace else in America." Between sips of our drinks he told it, how the boatyards were well protected, had a ready supply of trees for hulls and masts. Eventually, the trade went to bigger ships, with deeper drafts, then steel hulls, and the local trade was done. "Now Standish has got plans to reinvent itself."

"You sound like *Boston* magazine."

He pointed in the other direction, toward a jut of land, the wooded top of it just visible above the low trees flanking the river. "That's going to be the fat-cat district, with an eighteen-hole private golf course and private moorings."

Ted Rand's project—Point Pines—I realized but I wasn't here for the heritage tour. "I looked you up in Ben Nickerson's yearbook," I said.

"Really? That must've been good for a laugh."

"Career ambition—'chase waves'?"

He shrugged. "You had to say something. I could've said stockbroker or brain surgeon, but frankly no one would've believed it."

"It seems like you've done what you set out to do. I wonder how many of your classmates can say the same?"

"Nickerson, for instance? To tell you the truth, I don't know what he does. He never said."

"He catches things." I told him what I knew of Ben Nickerson's marine biological supply business. He said it made sense.

"I thought more about what we talked about," Van Owen offered. "About how he seemed the other day when I ran into him. Sometimes, sitting on a board, you can see right through the surfaces, through ten feet of water, and you see rockweed on the bottom, or the way a sandbar shoals, a crab scuttling along. You can see like that into people sometimes, past the social smoke screen, straight to the core. It's . . ." He waved a hand, looking for words—"Goofy foot."

"The name of your boat?"

He frowned a moment, then seemed to find inspiration. He rose and pointed to the deck. "That's a surfboard. How would you stand on it?"

Feeling I was humoring him, I stood. I set one foot ahead of the other on the floor. He nodded. "Right foot forward. It's the surf equivalent of being left-handed. Goofy foot. The term also means how you sometimes get the intuitive stuff . . . inklings."

I was thinking of Paula Jensen just then, of her dream.

"With Nickerson it was often like that."

"Someone who could see beyond the superficial?"

"No, no, I mean somebody who could be seen *into*. Transparent."

"And what did you see in his core?"

He grabbed at the hair on the back of his head, as if trying to pull loose a reluctant thought. "I saw it again the other day when I ran into him. He was very nervous."

I was alert, as if the alcohol had sharpened my brain.

"I mean, he always was, but more now. He seemed . . . I don't know. Just funny. Like maybe he'd stepped in some quicksand and knew it, only he didn't realize how deep yet."

Van Owen went into the cabin. I sat there wondering: Did I really credit his perception? Was he a person of genuine insight or merely one who believed he was? He brought out plates, utensils and a salad as I uncorked the wine. No more was said about Ben Nickerson. I discovered that the aromas and the fresh air had given me a serious appetite. I had more questions, but they could wait. We ate and then ate some more. Everyone has his own tempo for eating: Red Dog put his food away fast; I took it more slowly. We matched each other on the Chianti. For dessert there was store-bought blueberry pie that tasted great, the way store-bought hot dogs do at the ballpark. Someone had rung a dinner bell for the mosquitoes, too. Knowing that I'd better move or I was going to be in the same spot come morning, I stood and began carrying things back inside. As Van Owen washed dishes in his small galley, I put on a lamp and perused the photos on the walls of the cabin. Most of them were pretty old, the people in them young. One in particular caught my eye. "Is this Teddy Rand?" I called to him.

He turned, wiping his hands on a towel. "It's TJ, yeah."

Another shot included a girl with dark hair and a nice smile and wearing a cheerleader's sweater. She had sturdy legs, tanned against the short white pleated skirt and the bobby socks and tennis sneakers. She was standing between Van Owen and TJ Rand, who were in their football uniforms, grass-stained and disheveled in that flush of glad exertion that is the sole property of the young. Did kids still feel that exuberance? I thought of the dour posse on the town common. Did Michelle Nickerson feel it? "Who's she?" I asked.

"Ginny Carvalho."

"You gotta be a football hero to fall in love with the beautiful girl."

"She was that. So who got her, do you think?"

She was with them both, proud of the fact, and of them, but her head was canted ever so slightly toward Teddy Rand's shoulder.

"Not you."

"They went together our last two years of school."

I looked at the trio again, drawn to them. There was a quality in them—the men broad-shouldered, the woman slim-waisted, perky—a total physical confidence that comes with doing something well and for the pure joy of it. Ginny Carvalho's stare was direct and challenging—possessed, I thought, of a hint of defiance. "Why does she look familiar?"

He glanced at me.

"I feel like I've seen her somewhere."

"Have you been in the Storm Warning?"

"The waitress—Fran something."

"Fran Albright. That's her sister."

"Fran doesn't look this confident, though."

"Fran always seems eager to please others and is never quite sure if it's working. She went out to Colorado and had a marriage for a while, but it didn't take any better than mine. She moved back a few years ago; now she and her old man struggle to make a motel break even."

"I thought her father was a teacher?"

"Used to be. He got out. He owns a motel out on the Old Cape Road. The place that time forgot."

"The motel or the road?"

"Both."

"Is Ginny still around? I'd like to talk to her."

Van Owen was still for a moment. "You'd look a long time. She died—three or four years after that was taken."

I studied the photograph again, as if trying to fix her in life. Her vitality in the image seemed to be the very denial of death. Outside, a fender creaked as the boat shifted slightly with the running tide. "What happened?"

"She'd been drinking and skinny-dipping one night. She washed in on Shawmut Point next morning. It was briefly investigated, ruled accidental. Her folks never really recovered from it. Her mom died a year or so later."

"Was she swimming with other people?"

"Alone—according to one story, after gangbanging a carload of high school kids. I don't know, though. No one ever came forward, naturally. Ginny's drowning became one of those tales a town tells itself."

"The evils of wanton behavior?"

"I guess so."

"But?"

"But what?"

"I thought your tone left it open a crack."

"Wrong. You've got to quit being a detective sometimes. She was a beautiful girl. We all had some fun times together. I'm sorry she went. End of story."

There were other photos, other stories: old chestnuts of high school heroics, some shots of people riding waves. In one of these, the rider was in a crouch, just emerging from the large curling wave, his arms spread in a balancing act. "You?" I asked.

"Yours truly, in Fiji." He said it longingly, as if it was a place he would prefer to be now.

"You've surfed a lot."

"Every chance I get. I've broken some ribs, my right hand, lost teeth. Bruised my ego once or twice. Almost drowned a few times."

"You make it sound awfully tempting."

"It is."

"I'll stick to channel surfing. Tell me about Ben Nickerson back when. Is he in any of these?"

"No. And I don't remember much."

"You weren't that close?"

"Get real. He was the class brain." Van Owen was silent a moment, thinking, then laughed. "I caught him cheating off me on a test one time. A straight-A student, copying off my paper."

"Maybe he hadn't studied."

"I'm no Rhodes scholar, Rasmussen."

"You think he just wanted to fit in?"

"He didn't know yet that he didn't have to. A smart person . . . time takes care of them."

Sometimes, I thought. Nickerson had married a pretty wife, though he'd lost her, too. And now she was wondering where he was. And where was Michelle? The food and wine had lulled me into a lethargy I didn't want. I scrubbed a hand across my face. "Teddy Rand's write-up in *The Torch* had him destined to be a mover and a shaker. Tell me about Teddy Rand."

"What the hell's that got to do with Nickerson?"

"Maybe nothing, but he seems a presence here." I nodded at the wall of photographs.

He looked at them a moment, too. "Funny," he said, "digging all this up. I've had these so long, they're wallpaper. I don't even see them anymore."

"Maybe they want to speak." Or maybe he did.

He didn't hurry to tell it. We took seats, and he lit a cigarette. There was still daylight outside, but it was reddening. "We were born on the same date, one year apart. I was older, but I got kept back in sixth grade, so we were both going into tenth when his family moved down from the city. He transferred out of Boston Latin. That first summer, we became friends. You know the way it happens sometimes? You meet, and inside of five minutes you both know you can do or say or be anything you want, and it's cool."

I nodded. It was how I'd once felt with Ed St. Onge.

"We lifted and ran all summer—he had the best natural build on a kid I ever saw. He went out for football the first time ever that fall. I'd played through junior high. We both made varsity. First game of the year, his first play from scrimmage, he broke wide and went seventy yards. I'll never forget it. He had this lazy, loping stride, deceptive as a bastard. He looked *slow* till you tried to close on him and then realized he was moving that fast. He scored a hundred points his first year, made All-Scholastic."

"You made it, too. Led the league in sacks."

"A year later. You already know all this?"

"I know it because there's a young cop here who seems to think you were Sam Huff."

He frowned. "His perception's skewed. The town hasn't fielded a decent team in years."

"Is that where your nickname came from?" I hadn't thought of the term since I'd played high school ball. I didn't even know if it was still used.

"Coaches thought I was quick reading the opposing offense. Ha! I had all I could do to keep a half dozen of *our* plays in my head. No, it was this right-brain perception thing I have. Anyway, TJ knew Latin—from having gone to Latin school—so he made a link with Ben Nickerson, too. TJ was friendly with everyone. It was a knack he had."

For making friends, Iva Rand had said.

"Teddy was smart *and* well-rounded. Three-sport letterman, student council."

"Pretty girlfriend," I added. "Good family."

He blew smoke toward an open porthole. "He had it aced. And he was a nice guy, too. We stuck together. We double-dated, drank our first brews together. He graduated at the top of our class. He was headed for Dartmouth that fall, to get a degree and come back to run his old man's business. That's where that bit in *The Torch* came from."

"Did you keep in touch?"

"Hold on. He was going Ivy League; I was *may*be going to get into junior college. Instead I caught a dose of the teenage dumbs." He waved a hand, dispersing smoke, and maybe his trouble along with it. "I borrowed a skiff without the owner's permission and got it kind of sunk. The judge gave me an option of jail or the service. We had a president who was trying to make military duty glamorous again—the way these jokers who never got anywhere near a war like to do. We were dancing into that Panama bullshit, so what the hell? TJ tried to talk me out of it, said his father could get me a lawyer to fight it. I didn't want lawyers. But he was really getting into it. He came up with all these ideas. The one he picked . . . I remember it so well."

"You remember a lot of things well when you get going."

He sent a look my way. "Some dipstick keeps reminding me."

"Keep rolling."

"We drove around half the night, TJ giving all these reasons why the U.S. shouldn't be doing what it was doing, and how maybe we should all be pacifists, win hearts and minds. I think he was working it out for himself. We wound up on Shawmut Point. His folks had this old summer house out there. And we're drinking—Scotch, I remember. Maybe because it's an adult drink and we're trying to make adult decisions. So we get out there and we finish the bottle, and TJ goes in his old man's locker for more, and he comes out instead with this big-ass gun—his old man's forty-five, which he kept for blasting rats. And TJ racks one into the chamber. It's remote out there—pretty dead before Memorial Day. Anyway, he gets this plan. We go out in this old aluminum boat they kept out there, and we go out to the channel and cut the motor and drift. The idea is, he'll shoot me in the leg—the fleshy part—so I can't go in the army and probably won't have to go to jail, either. But I say, very calm, like he's not some maniac, 'What about you? You think Dartmouth's gonna want a guy who shot his best friend'?"

"These days there'd be a scholarship in it," I said. "Adds diversity."

"No shit. So he hands me the gun. He decides *I'll* shoot *him*. It got crazy."

"Never mind that a forty-five would blow your leg off and sink the boat. What happened?"

"I had a wicked hangover next day, and a few days after that I joined the Marines."

"I thought you'd sobered up?"

"Yeah, well . . ."

"And TJ went to Dartmouth."

He cast a glance out where a lobster boat was chugging westward on the sunset tide. For a long moment, he didn't speak, watching the red flicker of wind on the water. "Man, how many times I've wished he had."

I waited. He opened his mouth, shut it again. Finally he crushed out his cigarette. His chair creaked as he rose. "Let's take a ride. I want to show you something."

"Can't you just tell me?"

"For Christ's sake, Rasmussen, you started this."

18

Actually, I had plans later to take up Ted Rand on his invitation, but I *had* started this, and now I was curious. Besides, a ride might do me good, knock the edge off the food and the alcohol. "Ever been to Brockton?" Van Owen asked when we were rolling west in his rattle-bang truck.

I had, once or twice, though it had been years since the last time. What textiles had been to Lowell, shoes had been to Brockton. All the major American manufacturers had operations there, but after World War II, shoe city had died hard, too—harder—with one outfit after another closing, broken down like some old brogan. Lowell had risen from the dead, but this was still a corpse from what I could see. I didn't need a guided tour. Long ago the area had been called Hokomock and had seen the likes of great Indian warriors like Squanto and Massasoit. As Brockton, it had been home to men with cannonball muscles and tough spirits—Rocky Marciano and later Marvin Hagler both hailed from there—but the city was a husk of what it had been, and when it made news at all it was unpleasant: one more senseless shooting or an administrator at the local community college hiring hookers to teach night classes. Out the truck window I could see soot-stained brick and curb-stoop gangs waiting for night. Without the surrounding presence of TJ Rand, I needed to prompt Van Owen to finish his tale.

"Does this still connect to Nickerson somehow?" he asked.

I hoped so, but I was no longer sure. According to Van Owen, when his friend could not come up with an absolute reason why *he,* TJ, shouldn't be in uniform instead of Van Owen, he decided that the only honest thing to do was to enlist with him.

"He joined the Marines?"

"I told you he was nuts. He should've been running touchdowns on October afternoons for the simple reason that he was that good. And yet, I don't know, it seemed . . . natural that he'd stuck with me." He glanced my way, maybe looking for verification that TJ's actions made any sense at all. "Whatever the case, he got into it. After a while, when a chance came to apply for officer training, he took it. Now I was the one telling him *he* was crazy. Let's do the original tour, I said, and get the hell out. But he had his mind made up, stubborn bastard. After boot camp he went OCS, and I was a grunt. Then the president found this silly little hornet's nest in Panama and decided it was time to make men out of boys."

"You went?" I asked.

"I went to Pendleton. The San Onofre surf tour. My ass was safe the whole time. TJ went, though. When we both got out, we came back here. I didn't go see him right away, though I knew he was already home. He was staying out at the Shawmut house. The second week I was back I took a ride out. His mother welcomed me. I remember him lying upstairs in this big old brass bed reading, and tossing the magazine aside—it was *Rolling Stone,* with Bob Seeger on the cover—and him saying, 'What kept you, bro?' And it was like nothing had changed. He didn't look different—still had a hell of a build, only leaner—but stuff *had* changed. For both of us." Van Owen's voice had gone lower. "Remember that idea I told you? What he wanted me to do?"

"Shoot him in the leg?"

Van Owen glanced over at me. The shimmer of late-dying sunlight between trees and city buildings flickered across his face, like the speedup of all of his days. He looked weathered and worn.

When he said nothing, a bad feeling crept over me. "What happened?"

He slowed and turned past a sign that said BROCKTON VETERANS' ADMINISTRATION HOSPITAL. He pulled into the parking lot, into a space underneath a maple tree. Ahead of us stood a four-story brick hospital wing. "Story's almost done." He lit a cigarette, doing it slow. "That day I visited him at home, we made a plan for a little surf trip—like old times. He'd got to be a pretty decent surfer for a guy who'd come from the city. Not smooth, but he was big and strong— he could push his way around in the water. A week later, we ended up out at Nauset on the Cape. This was September, and there was a tropical storm kicking up a surge. Biggest I'd ever seen. I hadn't been to Fiji yet. Big rugged barrels this deep stone-green, danger written all over them. Eight to ten feet, I'm not kidding. Black-flag city. No one was supposed to go out, and no one was."

Van Owen drew smoke and let it out in a slow breath. "There's a simple way to figure out who a friend is. Say a guy gets the notion to do some crazy-ass, half-suicidal thing. You tell him, no way. You stop him if you can. But if he's determined? You walk, right?"

"Unless he's a friend," I said.

"Friendship trumps all the rest—caution, responsibility, common sense. If those don't work, you go along." He set the cigarette in the dashboard tray and tugged back his hair, holding it there behind his head like a bundle of copper wire. It tightened the flesh of his face, which looked younger but still ravaged, and afraid, too. "Getting out was near to impossible. My arms were dead from paddling. I was just cresting a wall, and I saw him paddling way, way out. I went down in the pit, and when I rode up the next crest, I saw him take a wave. But something was off. There may have been a sandbar, or a rip current . . . the wave didn't form right. It got all this big mass, but it looked bogus, I could see that from where I was. He couldn't. And he didn't have the water knowledge to read it right. I tried to flag him off. He came skidding down the wall, and I knew he was in for the ride. Then, just like that, it collapsed on him. Gone. I kept looking, frantic, man—but where do you look? You've got this whole ocean, and it keeps churning, wave after wave. You want to talk panic? Then his board shoots up into the air like a rocket, the broken leash dangling. No TJ.

"I dug hard to get to where the board had come up. Waves kept falling. I was freaking, never been so scared in my life. He'd been under a long time. I reached the spot and I prayed and I dove. I found him. Sheer chance. His leash had gotten tangled. I got him up. I have no recall of either of us getting back to shore."

In the silence he took up his cigarette, sucked it back to life. "Someone called an ambulance. I broke ribs, busted up this hand." He held it out, and I saw that the hand was misshapen. "TJ, on the other hand, he *looked* okay. It was a while before they figured his back was broken. It probably hadn't done him any good me dragging him in, but that wasn't the worst thing. He'd been under water too long. Without air, man . . ." He stared at the hospital building for a moment; then shifted his gaze, letting his eyes go wide and unfocused. "He's up there. Fourth floor, C Wing, room four-oh-six."

I waited for him to get out, but he didn't move. "Aren't you going in?"

"What for?"

I looked at him, trying to understand. He started the truck. "I've never been. Never will. There are times," he said, "I wish he'd just die."

We had little to say on the ride back to the boat. He let me off, and as I unlocked my car, I thought of something. I went back over. "When you visited TJ at home that first time, after you were both back from the service—you said he was different. How?"

"I don't know, just was."

"Was it bravado, going out in the waves like that? Some reckless thrill?"

"What're you asking? Was he a gung-ho marine with a death wish? Bull. If anything, he was quieter than he'd used to be, more subdued."

I considered this a moment. "Was this before or after Ginny Carvalho drowned?"

He frowned. "After. She'd died the previous June. Who the hell are you supposed to be now, a shrink?"

"No. Thanks for dinner."

Back at the beach house I experienced a letdown in my energy. The drinks had leached some of it away, but I also felt I'd been spinning down avenues that might lie beyond where I needed to be. It was as if Standish were pulling me into its own elliptical orbit. There had been an intensity to the day that had sneaked up on me, and now I was sinking. Van Owen's tale and the trip to the VA hospital had been the hammer blow. I craved sleep, though I knew if I succumbed, it would be impossible to get moving again. My perception of time running away from me had returned. It was eight-fifteen. I checked my answering service, and there was a message from an hour ago from Paula Jensen. It was marked urgent.

She sounded glad to hear from me. "I talked to the accountant that I mentioned. It turns out he hasn't worked for Ben for over a year now—Ben fired him. Evidently they had a disagreement over Ben's tax filings, but he wouldn't get specific. Does that mean anything?"

"It's interesting," I said. "It may mean that Nickerson's business is in trouble."

"But Ben's got clients all over the country."

"So did Polaroid. It's just a theory, but what if he came east with an idea of saving his business, with raising some cash?"

"Holding Shel for ransom?"

"I haven't gone that far with it yet."

"He could've just asked me for money."

"I think he did. He presented your husband with an investment opportunity, but he never gave Ross any details, and Ross declined. Ben told Van Owen he'd pay for the surfboard when he got here, that money wouldn't be a problem. Didn't he give you the same idea about reimbursing you for the rental on this place?"

"Well . . . he wasn't the greatest businessman." She sounded shaken by the idea that I was laying out. "He was wonderful with the science end, but in the early days, when we were building the business, I was the people person. Frankly, I thought he should have stuck with teaching; that was his gift. But that's all hindsight, isn't it? Alex . . . where's Shelly?"

I told her I was trying to find out. When we'd signed off, I got a number for the Cape Way Motor Lodge and called there. It rang several times before a scratchy answering machine tape kicked on. A woman's voice said that I had reached the Cape Way Motor Lodge in historic Standish, Massachusetts, that rooms were available, et cetera. The only thing historic was the recording, but despite the poor quality, I recognized the voice. I hung up and got the local number for the Storm Warning, which I called and caught Fran Albright in person. I reminded her who I was and what I was doing.

"Oh, yes," she said tentatively.

"I'd like to speak with you about your sister."

"About Ginny?"

"Yes, with you and maybe with your father."

"I don't know how much help I can be, but Dad and I will be at home later."

"Can I call then?"

"My father's not comfortable with the telephone. Why don't you come out? We're on Route Fifty-three, in the little house right behind the Motor Lodge. Could you be there at nine-fifteen?"

I took a fast shower and changed into a tan summer-weight suit, pale blue shirt. I hesitated over the assortment of ties I'd brought. Ted Rand had said to bring a bathing suit to his soiree, so I wasn't sure of protocols. One of the things—one of the many—I had loved about being married to Lauren was her unfailing sense of protocol. Okay, it isn't think-tank research, and I manage it myself now, but I'm never quite sure. When she told me, I always listened. I'd listened, too, when she advised me to forget about whether people believed I'd taken a bribe when I was a cop; what mattered was that *I* knew I hadn't. I should get on with my life—*our* lives—she said. I'd listened, but had I taken her advice? Too late now. I settled on a blue-and-gold-striped rep.

19

With daylight dwindling, I drove down the meandering Route 53. Before the highway was built, this had been the primary road to Cape Cod. Now it was a string of old and bypassed small businesses: a sail-maker's, a dry cleaner's, auto repair shops, a flower nursery with several old broken-paned greenhouses doing a brisk business in weeds. None of the enterprises looked very prosperous, a theme that was picked up by the Cape Way Motor Lodge. The sign had a catchy little red-and-yellow pulsing-light pattern, but there weren't many eyes to catch. As I turned off the engine and opened my door, I felt the silence.

The motel was a long one-story unit with about twenty rooms. The stucco exterior looked mossy. I counted three cars in the lot. A short distance beyond the motel building, set back from the road, was a small house. Parked in front were a new Toyota Celica and a Dodge station wagon that could have worn an antique plate. Much farther back on the property were eight or ten tiny housekeeping cabins, no lights on in any of them. Fran Albright had made a point of my being here at nine-fifteen, and I was.

As I reached the door, I heard a jingle in the tree shadows off to my right and saw the shape as it lunged. Luckily it was on a short chain. It looked like a pit bull that was on steroids, or had eaten someone who was.

"Gruff! Get down!" a woman called from the door. It was Fran Albright, who recognized me from earlier. "Best come in quick," she said.

"Is he hungry?"

"No, it's the bats." She glanced nervously over my head. "They see the light and they sometimes fly in."

I checked my vicinity for aerial bombardment and went inside. She shut the door quickly behind me. She was still in her waitress uniform and apron, minus the oilskin hat.

"Gruff?" I asked.

"Isn't that dumb? He came with it when my father took him in as a stray. I wanted to call him Lambert. Remember him? The sheepish lion?"

"Gruff doesn't seem sheepish or leonine."

Her pretty smile was tired. "Come through here."

The room was dim, crowded almost to the ceiling with stacks of old newspapers, as if they had been saved for a Boy Scout paper drive that had never occurred. They gave the house a musty scent and me a sense of claustrophobia. I followed her through and into a small adjoining den. The wallpaper looked as old as the newspapers, and gauze curtains hung before a picture window that hadn't seen a squeegee since Nixon, but the rich finale of sundown forgave a lot of sins.

"Please have a seat."

I sat gingerly on an old foam-cushion davenport covered in coarse flowered-print fabric. From somewhere else in the small house I could hear radio voices. Fran untied her apron and set it aside. In the yellow light, she could have been an older version of the girl in the photos on Van Owen's walls. She was actually the younger sister by several years, but her clock hadn't been stopped as Ginny Carvalho's had. Now there were time and miles and a broken marriage on her, but they gave her face character, and her kindness some meaning. She moved quietly to a doorway and drew aside a drape.

"Dad, Mr. Rasmussen is here." She glanced back at me. "Am I saying that right?"

"Perfectly."

"One moment." She went through the doorway. On a bookshelf below the window was a row of thick binders bearing dates on the spines, going back I saw, to the early nineties. On a lower shelf were more newspapers and some literature from right-wing groups. Fran Albright reappeared. "Come on through here."

The inner room looked to have once been a small alcove or a breakfast nook. It was a home office now, with a desk full of drawers, a large old computer, and a world map. A thickset man sat writing on a yellow pad, his big hand crabbing along slowly. The radio I'd heard was an old Admiral on the shelf above him, and alongside it was a Bearcat police scanner.

"Dad, this is Mr. Rasmussen. My father, John Carvalho."

"Make it Alex," I told the man's back.

"Dad."

After another moment of scribbling, he turned. His face was round, with a bulb of nose and small suspicious eyes. He was in faded green twill work clothes, his thinning brown hair combed across his large head. He had a humped shoulder, and his hands were stubby and powerful and looked to be studded with warts or carbuncles. I wasn't sorry not to shake one. He studied my investigator's license with silent intensity. There are worse sights than the pasty flesh of a man's leg showing at the bottom of his pant cuff, but none came immediately to mind.

"You're not with the gub'ment?" he said.

"Strictly independent."

"Who's Eugene Horsman?"

"Who?"

He was staring at the ID. I looked above his thick thumbnail at a scribble of official signature. "You can read that?" I said.

He tried the name aloud in several variations, then turned to his keyboard and poked at it awhile. Names came on the screen, a long alphabetical list, and scrolled down. There had to be several score of names.

"There was a V. Ramsey *Horzmann* in the State Department," he said. "Different spelling, but we know how they change them. Don't forget Rosenfelt and Cantor."

"Who?"

"Franklin D. and John F. Puppets."

"Look, this is just a PI license. I pay the Commonwealth five hundred bucks a year for it, and they let me sit in my office and play gumshoe. I don't think there's any connection to—"

"That's what they *want* you to think."

His daughter turned down the radio. "Dad," she said patiently, "I don't think the gentleman wants to get into that. He's here to ask about Ginny."

"The Commission," Carvalho went on. "They control every message on every television broadcast, Hollywood picture, and highway billboard. Let's not even talk about the World Wide Web."

The woman gave me a look of plea. "He listens to those radio call-in shows all the time—Lush Rimjaub and that late-night kook. All that jittery, fear-mongering . . . Dad's convinced there's a world conspiracy."

"The Tri-Lateral Commission is a proven fact," he said evenly. "The illuminati."

"Well, let's see if we can be helpful to Mr. Rasmussen, Dad."

I was having my doubts they could be, but I explained that I was trying to get information about a young man Ginny Carvalho had gone to high school with.

"Ben Nickerson, Dad," Fran added quickly. "I told you."

Carvalho was silent awhile, then murmured, "Show him."

She directed my attention to a photograph on a bookcase. It was a color-tinted portrait of the beautiful young woman I'd seen in a photograph on Red Dog Van Owen's boat. Ginny was short and dark, in a long dress, holding a corsage. There was a rosary looped around the picture frame.

"That was her prom picture," Fran Albright said. "She went with Teddy Rand." Fran smiled. "They were king and queen that year. TJ was so handsome in his tuxedo. And Ginny—"

"She was our firstborn, but our baby just the same," Carvalho said, his eyes not meeting mine. His voice sounded hoarse with old pain. "This place I bought off Mr. Rand. Before the highway went by." And all the travelers with it, apparently. I thought he might go on, but he leaned over, peeled up a corner of the drawn shade and peered out at the twilight. "We've got a little window now. I want to show you something."

I looked at Fran Albright, who shrugged. "He wants to take you on a field trip."

"Wait here a minute." With a grunt, Carvalho heaved himself out of his chair and went through the drape-hung door.

Fran stepped closer and whispered, "That's about all he'll ever say of Ginny. I honestly don't know what to tell you about Ben Nickerson or his daughter. I certainly hope they're okay." She hesitated, then said, "Ginny was . . . adventurous. She had an idea about being a fashion model. She probably could've—she didn't have the long thin body, but she was adorable, and she had plenty of spunk. It tore us up when she died. My mom's heart was broken in two."

I nodded sympathetically. I wanted to ask about the story of Ginny's being with a group of boys the night she died, but it wasn't the moment. Carvalho reappeared holding a large handgun that gleamed with oil.

"Dad, is that necessary?"

He raised it, and she glanced at me. "He has a permit," she said.

It was a .44 Colt Python, enough weapon to stop a water buffalo, though not my first choice against bats. He swung open the chamber and inspected the load, then snapped the weapon shut and put it into a leather holster belted on his thick waist. I looked at his daughter, who was watching him with concern, but she kept silent. He led the way back out through the roomful of stacked newspapers and outside. He unchained Gruff, who took only a passing sniff at me before lunging into the backseat of the geriatric Dodge wagon. I climbed in beside Carvalho. Out of habit I reached for a seat belt, but there was none. We drove east, toward the descending edge of night.

I noted that he had a police scanner here, too. With its volume down I could hear only the faint garble of voices. His preference for sound was the dashboard radio tuned to some syndicated AM talk guy, with open lines to the heartland crazies. Host and callers shared that odd combination of ultra right-wing, libertarian and white male paranoia, and spun out history about as accurate as a drive-by shooting. Listening to them was the aural equivalent of boils being lanced. "Can we lose that?" I said. Carvalho winced, as if I'd asked him to sever an artery, but he turned the volume lower, at least, to where it blended with the scanner in an unintelligible mutter. "Where are we going?" I asked.

"Shh."

I brought up TJ Rand and Ben Nickerson, but I got even less response, so I clammed up. In the years since the Dodge had rolled off the assembly line, Detroit had gone to building them small enough to fit three in this baby's spare-tire well, and then to building them a ton heavier than this and three feet taller. This represented some kind of a mean between extremes. It had its shifter on the column and a dimmer switch on the floor, where Carvalho would click it with his toe, the high beams tunneling the dusk on the narrow winding road until he would kill them at the approach of an occasional oncoming car. He didn't have to do it often. We drove for about three miles, the land opening up in a coastal plain, with salt marsh astir in the soft wind and tidal streams gleaming like copper snakes in the fast-fading light, and then Carvalho slowed and turned onto an unpaved road. He babied the car over the rutted dirt, but even so the shocks clunked and my teeth rattled. When we came upon a weathered barn, he drew into the yard and shut off the motor.

"Bring these." He handed me a pair of binoculars. He opened his door and got out. I did, too. I slung the binoculars around my neck. I wasn't sure what to make of Carvalho's carrying a weapon, but I wanted to keep my hands free, at least. He left Gruff in the car with the windows partway down. The dog seemed to know the drill. It leaped into the front seat and sat alertly by the steering wheel and didn't so much as twitch as Carvalho started off on foot.

The barn was straight from Charles Addams, with a tilted cupola and a weather vane. Swallows swooped in the dusk. Beyond, at some distance, in deep grass, a large boat sat on a wooden cradle. The boat hadn't seen paint or varnish—or the ocean, for that matter—in a long time. There was a suggestion of a pathway through the grass. I remembered the Lyme disease alert I'd seen in the town hall, but Carvalho didn't seem concerned, so I pushed my worry aside and kept my attention on his broad, slightly humped form. After a few minutes, the path joined an unpaved road. It was soft sand, deeply rutted on both sides by the passage of four-wheel-drive vehicles. Just ahead of us, a cable, slung between two posts, blocked the road. Carvalho stopped. From the cable hung a sign, whose dark words I could just make out against the pale background: KEEP OUT per order SELECTMEN TOWN OF STANDISH.

Carvalho drew his watch close to his face. "I wait till now," he said, his breathing labored from walking. "It fouls their cameras."

"The selectmen?"

"But it's not dark enough yet for them to use the night scopes. Satellites, there's nothing for that but timing."

I looked around, wondering who *they* were. He stepped over the cable and started along a faint path through the high grass. I trailed him up a dune. From the top, where it sloped down to a stretch of beach, he pointed. Across the water lay a dusky strip of land and the silhouettes of several buildings, including a mound-shaped one with lights winking along the top.

"They almost got us on that one. Use the binoculars."

I did. I realized I was looking at the Pilgrim nuclear plant.

"Notice the lights?" he said.

"To warn off planes."

"Look again. See the pattern? Imagine an eye on top."

"An eye."

"The pyramid on a dollar bill? The illuminati?" The Commission again. I let the binoculars dangle. "They're messing with my mind," he said. "Because I know."

"What is it that you know?"

He peered again at his watch. His fear seemed to be intensifying. He kept looking around, like a skittish hound. I wasn't crazy about the thought of him packing the loaded Python. I pointed to a jut of land off to the right. "What's that?"

Carvalho shuddered, as if with cold, or revulsion. "We'd better get back."

"Is that Shawmut Point?" I pressed.

He glanced skyward, his brow clenched. He looked like one of the hunching figures in Picasso's *Guernica*. "Satellite will go over in three minutes."

I glanced at the sky, too; I was getting a contact scare being with him. I did see a small bat fluttering past, but I didn't fear it. Taking a chance, I said, "Isn't that where your daughter was found?"

His small eyes seemed bright with emotion. For a moment, the paranoia, the gun, the big dog faded away. He was just an old man, still in pain over a lost child. "We need to be moving," he murmured.

I took a few steps closer to him. "Do you know where your daughter was swimming when she drowned?"

"Drowned. Yeah, that's the way they put it."

"Wait—who? The high school kids?"

He slanted a look at me: disappointment or anger—or both. "That was disinformation. The ones who killed her planted that. Come on."

My heartbeat quickened. "What people?"

He was growing frightened, a sensation that was spreading to me. "Mr. Carvalho, are you saying someone murdered your daughter?"

"We're almost out of time. We've got to go." He looked skyward again. His broad dome of forehead was slick with sweat. Wind stirred the brittle dune grasses. "They'll be switching to infrared." I heard a chord of true panic in his voice.

"Please, what did you mean?"

But he was moved by other terrors now. He pushed bluntly past me, his thick legs churning through the sand, back toward the high grass. "Come *on!*" he cried.

He drove in taut silence, his eyes scanning his mirrors. Warm from exertion, I loosened my tie. I had sand in my shoes. I turned the little handle of the vent window and pushed it out and let the night air stream in at me. Once a car approached and Carvalho clicked off his high beams; when it passed, he stomped the floor button again as if he were firing a salvo of heat-seeking missiles at an unseen enemy, and the beams stabbed the night again.

The Cape Way's VACANCY sign looked hopeful, but it was a

fading hope. The only living things drawn to it were moths, and maybe the occasional bat; the rest seemed all about ghosts. The parking lot was mostly empty. The forlorn cottages loomed palely at the edge of the woods in the back a moment before Carvalho turned off the car's lights. He put his dog into its pen. "Good-bye," he said emphatically, letting me know my questions would go unanswered. "Word of advice," he added from his doorstep. "You ought to get another car."

"One of these days. Where I'm from, though, I'm still ahead of the curve."

In the pulsing red-and-yellow light, he looked shocked. "I mean *older*. You don't know about that? Everything built from '87 on, the government installed a chip. In case they want to mobilize. Never mind the fact that Arabs will soon control every gas pump in the country, that's irrelevant. One central switch someplace in a cave in Utah—they hit it, and *bango*. The highways are full of dead machines and helpless citizens, and the black helicopters come. Sitting ducks."

"Been on the X-way lately?" I said.

"Eternal vigilance, Mr. Rasmussen."

20

It was going on ten o'clock when I found Maple Street, a tree-lined road west of the town center. Part of me wanted only to go to the beach house and sleep; another part wanted to get back to Apple Valley and speak with the Jensens; but I was curious, too. Ted Rand had said there'd be an assortment of outsiders and locals at his soiree; maybe I could find some answers to my growing list of questions. I knew which house was Rand's by the way a kid in chinos and a teal Izod shirt came jogging out and practically wrestled the wheel from the driver of the BMW ahead of me. A second kid, same uniform, was slower getting to me. I climbed out and let him take it. "Nice ride," he said under his breath, but he seemed ready to forgive me when he caught sight of the 8-ball shift knob. He whacked it into gear and wheeled the Ford away in the Beemer's dust.

The house was an old colonial, agleam with floodlights that lit its white brick facade. There was a modern addition blended to the main house with such inspiration and skill, it was hard to tell it hadn't been part of the original structure. A pretty woman in a soft green summer dress greeted me at the door. I gave her my name. "Ah, y'all are the detective!"

"Look who's talking."

Her grin grew wide as a country sky. "C'mon in. I'm Clarissa."

"Hi, Clarissa." She was a few years younger that Paula Jensen, with coppery hair that fanned away from becomingly freckled cheeks.

"Ted's told me about y'all. You're looking for someone from town."

"And his daughter." I showed her the Polaroid.

She shook her head. "Sorry. Of course, I'm not a native—I'm a wash-ashore, Ted calls me. I'm from Texas."

"No fooling?" Her drawl should've been served with pinto beans.

She seemed to be performing the role of hostess. I followed her through the house, not hard to do: she moved with a shapely grace. Was she Iva Rand's replacement? A set of French doors stood open to a large enclosed courtyard. "Ted went to Italy one time," Clarissa told me, "and he wanted to re-create a Tuscan courtyard." Decorative trees were strung with strands of tiny white lights, giving the space a festive air. The walls were made of stone, flanked with gardens; there were little niches and mossy benches and garden statuary. A crushed-stone walk went around the swimming pool, which was the courtyard's centerpiece. The pool was lit from below and the beautiful people surrounding it glowed. In the water several bikini-clad women were splashing about.

Clarissa made sure I got a drink and then introduced me around. Among the guests were a number of prominent locals, including bankers and selectmen, making me think of the sign out at Shawmut. Mitzi Dineen, the realtor, was there and happily took over duties of showing me around as if I were a new listing. She presented me to her colleague, Andy Royce, who pumped my hand, maybe thinking the third time was the charm. Among the "wash-ashores" that Ted Rand's luxury project was bringing to town were a young comer from the state senate, whose face was familiar to any *Globe* reader, and a prominent elderly cosmetic surgeon—at least I was told he was prominent; he was definitely elderly, though his wife appeared to be still decades away from needing his skills. There was also an old white-mustached fellow in the Jacuzzi talking to several bathing beauties; he looked familiar though I couldn't place him.

I chatted with guests, probing for the occasional scrap of information that might relate to the case I was working on. I wasn't sure what I was likely to learn; I had the sense that I was examining an interesting tide pool, looking at scattered forms, trying to discover some element that linked them. Fortunately most of the people were too full of themselves to wonder why I wanted to know.

Ted Rand spotted me and came over. He was in an elegant blue sport coat and tan slacks over a white polo shirt. In the glow from the tiny white lights he had the burnish of prosperity and good health. "I see you're mixing and mingling just fine," he greeted. "Did you bring your bathing suit?"

"I'm not much of a swimmer. The pool looks good, though."

"I never use it. I prefer the Atlantic. But," he added, smiling toward the pretty pool users, "the guests are friendly, so make yourself at home."

"Who's the gentleman in the spa?" I asked.

Rand told me his name, and I recognized him as a former superior court judge. He'd heard cases in Lowell for years. Generally the bench was a seat for life, and most judges dug in like Mississippi wood ticks, so either he'd voluntarily given it up for something else or had been made to. Ted Rand went off to spread charm, and I wandered about the courtyard, sampling canapés and capping the occasional yawn. Drinks and the festive mood soon had people dancing to seventies club music. I wandered over to the deejay set up in a cabana beyond the pool. "You don't look like that's the music you grew up with," I said. He was far from old enough to use the bar.

He grinned vacantly. "No, it's all programmed. I just spin the play list the boss gives me. Any requests?"

"Got Satan Bugg's latest?"

He laughed and gave me a bit more attention. "That'd rock this scene."

"What's their appeal?" I asked.

"These people?"

"Satan Bugg. They're popular, no?"

Now he was into me. "Their last album went double platinum. Their appeal? They're angry, man."

"Angry."

"You know. British working-class angst. Pissed off."

"At what?"

"At all of this . . . this . . ." At a loss for words, he waved a hand. "Opulence. Excess. It's random. You see the cars parked out there?"

Yeah. That made sense. The band members undoubtedly drove old wrecks, like John Carvalho, and lived in packing crates. "Does the band have any strange trips?" I asked. "Any hidden meanings to their lyrics?"

"You mean like back masking? Satanic messages?"

"Whatever."

He laughed. "Yeah, right. It's music. It helps if you're sixteen—something to outgrow. Unfortunately, no one told this crowd to outgrow Cher and the Captain and Tennille. No offense, hey."

I grinned. "One more question." I took out the snapshot of Michelle Nickerson. "Ever see her around?"

He gave it his attention but shook his head. "I'd like to. She's cute."

"Thanks for the music lesson."

I wandered into the house. In the living room a handful of guests were standing around the young Beacon Hill pol, who was holding forth as if it were the senate floor. I went and stood on the fringe.

"And when they started the excavations they found some old bones," he was saying. "Some federal agency came in and tested them, and they were five thousand years old. Well, that was that. They threw the red tape like frat boys throw toilet paper. Ted had to hold up the project a month while archaeologists checked it out. Evidently the bones were from Indians. Excuse me—'native peoples.' That put a few folks on the warpath. Could've held up things indefinitely, but Ted got everyone's feathers unruffled—no pun intended."

"Like hell, Steve," someone quipped. Chuckle, chuckle.

"Ted had a powwow with some tribal leaders and soon everyone was all smiles and the project was back in business. He's a master at compromise. I keep telling him he's got a future in the state house if he ever gets tired of development."

"He's got a future here," Andy Royce said. "And we need him."

"We certainly do," piped a lean young woman, her blonde hair still wet from the pool "He gives great party. And in the winter he's got a theater downstairs and has these movie nights? He shows all those old classics, like *Sleepless in Seattle* and *Basic Instinct.*" She beamed.

"I heard he promised the Indians backup if they try for a casino license."

"And maybe a location for said casino right here on Shawmut Point," said Royce.

One member of the circle seemed to be paying little attention to the talk and instead was watching me with baggy-eyed appraisal. It was the former judge, wrapped in a thick white terry pool robe now, as if he'd wandered in from the set of *Playboy After Hours.* I met his gaze and nodded, but he twitched his mustache and turned away. Mr. Beacon Hill was settling in for a filibuster, so I broke free of his charisma and wandered into the next room.

If the courtyard was Tuscan, this appeared to be a Bavarian hunting lodge, the dark-paneled walls hung with trophy heads of deer, a cuckoo clock, plaques of appreciation for civic and charitable work. Something—was it a potpourri?—gave the room the piney scent of the Schwarzwald. I went for the framed photographs. Ted Rand sitting in a golf cart with the governor. Standing with Frank Sinatra. Posing with members of his softball team, each player holding a "Number One!" finger in the air. Several photos were of Ted and his son when the kid was young. In one, TJ, in a football uniform and smiling almost shyly, held a trophy the size of a beer keg. In another he wore the dress uniform of a marine lieutenant. There was no appearance of his loyal sidekick, Red Dog, or his prom queen. The photograph that caught me, however, was of a young Iva Rand. She glowed with beauty. She was smiling and tightly holding her toddler son, as if he might slip from her grasp and disappear.

I grew aware that someone had come into the room and was standing beside me. It was the former judge. He was dressed now, in sport clothes in the sober hues and costly cuts that befit a man of his position.

"They're quite a family," I said conversationally. "I'm Alex Rasmussen, by the way."

Either he was hard of hearing or short on social grace. He ignored my hand and went on looking at the Marine Corps photograph.

"Rough what happened to Teddy," I said. "Do you know the story?"

He looked at me as if I were being distasteful. I hesitated, and groped for a fresh start. "Do the Rands have other children?" I tried.

"Only the one."

I turned to see Ted Rand, who'd spoken. The former judge looked at him, too, sent a cursory scan at the photos, then moved off without a word.

Rand wore a tight smile. His cheeks looked sunburned. "I invited you to give you a respite," he said. "Bracing me is one thing, but I hope you're not going to subject my guests to an interrogation. Clarissa told me you showed her the Nickerson girl's photograph."

I raised a hand, palm out. "Sorry. I've got this bad habit of forgetting to punch out when I leave the job. In fact, one thing I meant to ask you—if I may?"

Rand shrugged. I said, "When you saw Nickerson the other day, did he talk with you about money? Or about business opportunities?"

"We've been there already, haven't we? Is that the route you're following? That Ben Nickerson has some business connection to Standish? Because, if so, I'm sorry I can't be more helpful—I simply don't know anything." He smiled. "It was your notion that I'm the burgomaster, not mine."

"Don't be modest. Look at your guests tonight. And golf with the governor? You've got to admit you're a high-profile citizen. But what I'm thinking is that Nickerson's business may not be as sound as he's let on, that possibly he came back to Standish looking for an opportunity, or a loan. He has the local newspaper mailed to him in California. It's likely he's kept aware of your Point Pines project."

Rand gave a little snort of laughter. "Ben? I can more likely imagine him trying to convince me not to build anywhere near the coast, for fear I'd be endangering some species of jellyfish." His smile faded. "Are you thinking that he might want to extort money somehow?"

I hadn't thought it, but I couldn't rule out any reasonable possibility. "Well?"

"The fact is, I've been even more stringent than the EPA requires. After all, what would be the point in spoiling the natural beauty of the area? People paying what Point Pines costs damn sure don't want a wasteland. Anyway, curiosity is a habit I tend to share—but in the right time and place. Let's suspend it for tonight. What do you say? I want to enjoy myself."

I'd been hoping to find a way to bring up his son's accident without revealing where I'd heard it, but I couldn't now. "Can I ask you one more question?"

"All right, a quick one, but I've got my lawyer right over there." His tone was jocular, but he nodded, and I looked and saw the former judge. In an instant I had an answer to my question of earlier—of why a judge would leave his bench—and the answer was simple: better pay.

"Very quick," I said, changing tack and gesturing to the photograph of Rand with Old Blue Eyes. "Did he sing 'My Way'?"

He gave me a complex smile. "Sometimes it's smarter to let the other person think he's had *his* way."

One of the catering staff came in and told Rand he had a telephone call. He excused himself and went out. I saw my opportunity to leave. I wanted to get back to Lowell tonight to check out some things in the morning. I found hostess Clarissa and told her I was going. "Aw, aren't y'all stayin' for the fun? I'm just puttin' up some coffee."

"I always end up with a lamp shade on my head and hunting for my clothes."

"Oh, you." She made a gracious little pout. "How'm I gonna hold my own with all these Yankees?"

"You'll do fine, girl," I assured her, "just remember that around here, 'yawl' is a sailboat."

The valets were huddled in the bushes as I went out. There was no disguising their teal shirts or the pot smoke. When my kid brought the Ford around, I showed him Michelle's photograph. His partner joined us. They gave it glassy-eyed regard, and then my kid nodded. "Yeah, dude, I've seen her."

"Where?"

"I know exactly where." He glanced at his partner. "How about on a mattress in the back of my van." He slapped his partner's upraised palm.

He snickered and turned away. I caught him from behind and yanked the hem of the shirt up around his shoulders and ears. As he struggled against the tight fabric, I spun him in three quick circles and pushed him into a clump of forsythia. His partner just cowered and gaped at the whole show. Driving out, I spotted the old judge. He was looking past an earnest young woman who was trying to tell him something, staring at me as though he were weighing evidence. I flashed him Red Dog's thumb and pinky finger surfer sign.

21

Before I hit the highway, I stopped and bought a coffee—the old-fashioned kind, with just coffee in it—and actually got halfway back to Lowell before opening my eyes between blinks came less and less often. I drew off at a rest area and climbed out. Inland there was not a whisper of a cool breeze. I stood in the hot, buggy dark, sharing the night with a steel hauler tightening his load. I pin-wheeled my arms and then leaned against the car and stretched the way, at my age, I should before and after a run but never do. When I felt as awake as I was going to get without amphetamines, I got back on 128 and put the Probe at seventy-five.

It was the hushed time long past midnight when the highway was a quiet canyon and the mostly empty parking lots of the high-tech companies gleamed with sodium-vapor light. The janitors had gone home, and the night watchmen were sacked out surveilling the inside of their eyelids, and only the workaholics intent on making associate VP were still at it. That was the brief hour of inward gazing when you realized how America got so strong and wondered if it really was our destiny or just a sorry wrong turn we'd made. I didn't invest my time pondering it. I got back to my apartment exhausted but wide-awake and thinking about Michelle Nickerson. I wanted to speak with her mother and ask some of the questions that had begun to take root in my mind, but it would have to wait for a more civil hour. Paula Jensen didn't stay as pretty as she was by receiving phone calls at 2 A.M.

I poured a nightcap and tipped back in my lounger, but still my brain whined along at a highway hum. Had the evening netted me anything other than more questions? Add that one. Maybe an old movie would help me focus, something of earlier vintage than *Pretty Woman*, but all I got were people in K-Mart suits talking about how to get rich and stay rich, and ads for the Harmonicats' biggest hits, on CD or cassette, which I probably already had around there on vinyl somewhere—for all I knew I had them wedged into the cassette player in my car. TV programmers ran the purest crap at this hour because no one was watching it, and if anyone was, they deserved it. I killed the dreck, poured a nightcap and went out on my tiny porch. It was a far cry from Ted Rand's Tuscan courtyard, and the air was humid as a viewing booth at an adult bookstore, but it was home.

If I were Nero Wolfe, this would be the time when I'd start laying things out for Archie Goodwin, making clear all the connections I'd put together in my head. Alas, I had only me. I got in bed. One thing I could do was quit wondering about Satan Bugg. Beyond Michelle's interest in their music, I realized they had no link to this. But I didn't seem to be so clear about much else. It was as if Standish, for all of my status as an outsider, was determined to draw me into its warp and woof, and given what I had seen tonight, I sensed that the town had threads running right up to Beacon Hill. Though trying to find a link there to the Nickersons' being missing was a stretch I couldn't make. No, I was still thinking about the idea that Ben had come to town looking for something, probably money, to keep his business afloat. He'd been there five days. He'd have made his play by now. And yet, no one had heard a word. I had a bad feeling. I didn't want to have it, but I had it nevertheless. It churned around on the surface of my brain for a while, then it sank, and I did, too.

22

At 9 A.M. I phoned the Major Crimes Bureau and asked for Ed St. Onge. His greeting sounded testy. "Hot," I said, to soften him up.

"It's not the heat; it's the stupidity. Where the hell have you been?"

"Me? Tokyo, Nairobi, London. I came back when I got homesick."

"Get down to your office if you're not there already."

Before I could wish him a pleasant morning, a hang-up clattered in my ear. I got downtown in twenty minutes. As I stepped into the lobby, I was almost knocked over by St. Onge, or by what he shoved at me. It was a manila folder. "From department files," he said.

"Personal delivery?"

"I don't like to advertise." He nodded toward the elevator door. "That out of service again?"

"No, it just doesn't work. Do we need to talk?"

"In private. Upstairs."

I gathered the mail from a box marked "third floor" and we climbed the zigzagging flights together, our combined eighty-plus years weighing on us like destiny and making us breathe hard. He was a native, like I was; he'd grown up in Little Canada. He got through school a few years ahead of me, and through the service, too, but neither of us had hit escape velocity. As cops we'd worked in the Major Crimes unit together, had been friends, danced with each other's wives at the policeman's ball. I was his daughter's god-father. Ed was still a cop, and he and Leona were still together, with their daughter doing a medical residency out west. He was the best police detective in the city, if you didn't count his suits. He bought clothes the way most people bought milk, grabbing the first unit on the shelf; they didn't come with an expiration date, though. His current drape was a polyester-sport-coat-and-wool-slacks combo in shades of mustard and maroon. He was the one person in Lowell who didn't mention the city golf tournament, because, like me, he didn't care crap about it. I wasn't sure what we were to each other anymore—"friends" didn't seem to cover it—but I didn't waste time trying to figure it out, and I doubted he did, either. He held his tongue until I unlocked the waiting room door and we stepped into the nerve center. "I'm sweating already. No AC either?"

I hauled open a window and emancipated several days' worth of trapped heat and an exasperated bluebottle, which bumbled out into the city day. St. Onge peeled off his sport coat and tossed it on the chair. "You ought to take a vacation from this," he said.

"Are you paying? Didn't think so. Anyway, on *Hollywood Squares,* they asked, 'What goes down after a two-week vacation?' Know the answer?"

"Goes down?"

"Gets lower, yeah. Guess."

"Bank account? I don't know. Blood pressure?"

"IQ. People come back dumber than they went."

He frowned. "But it comes back, right? Once the challenges of the job return?"

"This was *Hollywood Squares,* not *Nova.* The point is I'm a one-man think tank. I can't afford the brain drain. Take a seat," I said. "Something cold to drink?"

He took neither. He gestured at the manila folder he'd given me in the lobby. "The kid you asked about is Ross Jensen's stepdaugh-ter."

"I know."

"Then why the hell—?"

I was surprised, too. "You know Jensen?"

"You could say that. He cost you and me tax dollars, and Grady Stinson his badge."

I sat down. Stinson was a patrolman who'd been suspended after a complaint from someone who said the cop broke his arm during a traffic stop. "Jensen brought that case?"

"His firm."

"Randolph, Blinkman and Bearse."

St. Onge sat, too, and gauged me a moment, probably trying to see what else I was holding from him. The truth is, I hadn't known who had represented the plaintiff, but it came to me now. It wasn't the first complaint in Grady Stinson's file. "The city settled out of court," Ed said. "I heard one-point-something. Stinson's still on suspension pending a job hearing." St. Onge shook his head. "Between us, it isn't going to happen for him. He was walking toward a deep hole for a long time. I've got no tears. But I hate to see the dirt thrown onto good cops, and I don't like seeing the city bleed bucks it needs for important things because some gang of pinstripes gets greedy."

"I'm just looking into a missing kid, Ed."

St. Onge grunted. "Jensen's?"

"Off the record. His stepdaughter."

Ed ran a hand over his graying mustache. "I didn't hear about it."

"That's how the family has wanted it."

"Domestic?"

"It may be. She was on vacation with her father. I've been down on the South Shore, trying to backtrack them."

He nodded. "Cops down there in—where the hell is it?"

"Standish."

"—they doing anything?"

I told him how it stood with Chief Delcastro and his crew. He listened and made sounds of empathy and wished me luck. As he started out, he paused and frowned at the water-stained ceiling above the door. "Won't the landlord fix the roof?"

"Right after the elevator and the AC. I give Rorschach tests in my spare time."

"Keep wisecracking, one of these days the tiles will start dropping on your head."

"The whole universe is in entropy, Ed. Why should I expect special treatment?" I picked up the manila folder. "Thanks for this."

"What the hell, if it'll help you find the kid. Plus taking some of Ross Jensen's money can never be a bad thing."

I gave my morning's mail the five seconds it deserved, put my attorney neighbor's batch in a separate pile and made coffee. I went through the file Ed St. Onge had left. It was the police report for the night that Michelle Nickerson and three other juveniles and one eighteen-year-old were picked up after a concert at the Auditorium. There was also the case's disposition. Beyond a loitering charge for the adult, later dismissed, no charges were filed.

In this business, when leads are scarce, you give up or you keep scraping the pan. I called Bob Whitaker across the street at the *Sun* and laid out what I was after. He said he might have something, why didn't I drop by in an hour when he took his break. I told him I'd bring lunch.

I tracked an address and phone number for Grady Stinson. As with too many cops, his domestic situation and his home address were subject to change. He was currently rooming in a place over in the Lower Highlands. I dialed it and got a man with a voice like a rusty damper grating in a chimney.

"Stinson?"

"Who's this?"

I told him and mentioned that we'd overlapped on the LPD for a few years. "Oh," he said. "Yeah."

I told him what I was after.

"Can't yap right now, bud. I'm on my way to the golf tourney."

Suspension with pay was good work if you could get it. "How about later? Have you got any openings?"

"Come three o'clock I always get thirsty. Know where the Mill Stone is? On Decatur, off Moody?"

I said I thought I could find it.

Remembering a mental note, I opened my closet and retrieved the old sawed-off twelve-gauge I'd inherited. It didn't seem quite so ugly as it had the day before yesterday, maybe because it wasn't pointed at me. Mostly, it just looked grimly efficient. I took a pair of running shoes and sweats out of a gym bag and put the shotgun inside and zipped the bag up. It could pass for a fungo bat. I took it down to the parking lot behind the building and locked it in the trunk of my car, then went around the corner to the pizzeria.

"Ehh, my friend!" Vito called out when he saw me. We shook hands and I told him my visit was strictly food-related. I ordered a pair of sandwiches for take-out. In the *Sun* I checked the box scores for the Spinners, the Red Sox farm club that the city was crazy about. When Vito brought over the sandwiches, wrapped to go, along with a large antipasto salad I hadn't ordered, he waved away payment. "Just to tell you, I'm going to have a dealer look at—" I mimed pulling a trigger. "If it's worth anything, I'll let you know."

"Whatever you say, Mr. Rasmussen, it's good with me."

I walked over to the *Sun,* whose headquarters building faced mine in a flatiron across Kearney Square. I had told Bob Whitaker about Michelle Nickerson's having been picked up with some other kids in February for loitering. At his desk in the newsroom he opened an envelope and took out an eight-by-ten photo. It was of Michelle Nickerson, playing field hockey.

"The name rang a bell when you told me, so I checked my shoot notes and realized I'd taken some team stuff at a game in Apple Valley last year."

She had her mother's looks: delicate features and shining hair, a little defiance in the mouth, a lot of uncertainty in the eyes, which, though the black-and-white didn't show me, I knew would be pale blue. Maybe Red Dog Van Owen could tell if she was a natural athlete from a photo, but I couldn't. "Would you have anything from the police roust?"

"Only a mental image. I recognized her as the same kid. I didn't shoot anything that night—hell, they were children. If they keep coming back for more, my heart quits bleeding, but what kid doesn't make a mistake? Her father's Ross Jensen, no?"

"Stepfather."

"I happened to be at the cop shop that night when he came in to get her. He was doing a controlled burn, one of those things when the mouth goes a little wobbly and the ears get red from the pressure inside, but the words and the mannerisms are all checked and civil. When do guys like that blow off steam? Clapping at a polo match?"

"Do you recall what *she* looked like that night?"

He nodded at the field-hockey shot. "Different from that. Hair as flat black as auto primer, whitish skin, ring in her eyebrow—you know the look. Goth. Black T-shirt and skirt, black tights, a pair of Docs."

"Docksiders with black tights?"

"Martens."

"Right."

"I could hear the 'That does it, young lady' talk coming, but she seemed as if she knew it, too. I liked her spunk. Hang on to that if you want."

I slipped the print back into the envelope. It filled a gap between what the Jensens had given me and the Polaroid Red Dog Van Owen had supplied. I was assembling a gallery of photographs, but I wanted to find the girl.

Back across the square, I paused before the window of World Wide pawnshop. I wondered if the shotgun would yield a few dollars, but I didn't go in to find out. I peered in at the cheap wristwatches and fourteen-karat jewelry, beat guitars that hadn't seen action since Gerry and the Pacemakers, jackknives, hot plates and bowling trophies. It was the detritus of troubled lives. In Ross Jensen's world, stuff merely collected in garages and basements; here it was turned to meager cash to pay the rent, to buy a drink, or a bus ticket out of town. And yet trouble had invaded the Jensens' world, too. No one was immune. I still had a couple hours before I saw Grady Stinson. I got my car and drove over to south Lowell.

This was the plug-ugly side of the city, with its rusty rail yards, soot-stained warehouses, boiler works, steam plants, stagnant canals, and, a little farther out, more graveyards than in Transylvania. The brick buildings all had a glum air of entrenchment, and the horizon was pricked by tall stacks that had last blown smoke when Reagan had, in his cowboy getup, shilling for cancer sticks in *Collier's*. Students from the U. sometimes trekked over with notebooks and mini tape recorders to sample real life and write papers for Sociology 101. If Bukowski were still kicking, he'd make a poem of it, but he wasn't and it wasn't—a poem, that is. It was blackened structures, and vacant lots with last-month's news yellowing crisp in the high weeds, and crapped-out lottery tickets, like the windblown hopes of life's original survivors, the losers. It was a district of gang graffiti and vicious dogs caged behind chain-link, some with four legs. My car stood out by having tires. Somewhere, a pile driver was hammering, shaking my fillings as I got out, and the wind blew cold, even in July.

Some things in life don't change. Charley Moscowitz, for one. He was the son of a Lowell Greek who'd married a Lowell Jew. In the backyard, beyond a corrugated sheet-metal fence, rose a ziggurat of cubed rust. Moscowitz's living was scrap metal; his passion was guns. He operated out of a Quonset hut with tin signs for makes of car that hadn't rolled off assembly lines since Iacocca was in knickerbockers. Charley was out back, lying in a nylon-mesh chaise, holding one of those winged aluminum reflectors under his chin, so that his face glowed with otherworldly light. "You take that thing in trade?" I greeted.

He lowered the contraption and sat up, squinting as his eyes focused. "Somebody pinch me. Can it be? Lowell's finest."

"I don't carry a badge anymore."

"That's what I'm saying." He sprang out of the chair more spryly than his sixty-odd years ought to allow and took my hand in a vise grip. "Sunlight's good for you," he said.

"On Neptune, maybe. Here it causes cancer—they just found that out about twenty years ago."

His dark hair was combed in a pompadour you could have surfed on and was only faintly threaded with gray—and he did have a hell of a tan, I had to give him that. "Come on inside."

The building was equipped with rebar over the windows and an alarm system. FORGET THE DOG: BEWARE OF OWNER, read one sign and, to show he was full of good humor, PREMISES GUARDED BY— and a taped-on picture of Woody Allen from *Take the Money and Run,* holding a gun carved from soap.

"Lowell's finest PI," he said when we were in, as if he were trying to immortalize it. "I tell you, I sleep better knowing you're out there, Rasmussen."

"Me and Woody."

"I'm not just talking this neighborhood. Crime keeps getting uglier all over."

"I hear retirement in Florida is still a good value."

He scowled. "What do I need Florida? I dig it here. I was brought up in this neighborhood all my life."

"I like it that I don't have to keep pulling your card off my Rolodex and throwing it away."

"Sunshine. You could use some, brother. You're light. Okay, we kibitzed enough. What brings you? I know you ain't got old jock-straps in that canvas sack."

I set the gym bag on a long worktable, unzipped it and drew out the sawed-off shotgun. "I came into possession of this recently."

He licked his lips and ran a hand across them a few times, but he didn't reach.

"Is it any good?" I asked.

"Not to win beauty contests, it ain't. Set it down there a minute." He stepped over to an oak rolltop desk and pulled up the top with a clatter. Inside he found a visor with a magnifying lens built in, the kind that aging dentists wear, and he put it on. He drew on white cotton gloves. Now he did pick up the shotgun, handling it with care, turning it over, microscoping it with his eyes, which had become the size of beer coasters. He didn't say anything for a few minutes, and I let him look. *I* looked.

The office was vintage, from the rolltop and the black rotary-dial telephone to the big water carboy in the corner with the pointed paper cones. Even the pinup calendar on the wall looked quaint, July's buxom nudie discreetly wrapped in a ribbon of Old Glory. The hat rack was home to a solitary pearl-gray fedora with dust in its crease. Add a brass spitoon and the place could be closed off with a velvet rope: "American Office, circa 1935." The desk had a warren of little cubbyholes that I'd have bet were stuffed full of old shipping tags and yellowing bills of lading for cargoes that had reached their destinations lifetimes ago. In some drawer, perhaps, secured with a crisp rubber band, was a stack of faded index cards that, if you could shuffle them in just the right order, might solve all our enigmas. Behind the wainscoting, mice nibbled the cheese of time. I felt as if I was slumming in an earlier decade. It was nice, but the present was calling me back.

"How'd you say you got this?" Charley Moscowitz asked.

I hadn't, but I told him now. I knew that neither the story nor the gun would end up anywhere it wasn't supposed to. "A cop friend said it hasn't been flagged in any crimes. Nothing recent, anyway."

"Entirely likely. Some of those downtown shops look the way they did during Prohibition. Proprietors used to keep their own peacemakers against the strong-arm that went down—and I'm not just talking crooks. There were bulls on the force you wouldn't bring home to Mother, unless she was Ma Barker." He looked at the shotgun again. "Decent workmanship went into this. Some sawed-offs there are steel filings all over 'em, and you just know the missing barrel's still clamped in the owner's basement vise, waiting for the cops. Even Mark Fuhrman could make that case."

Charley ran a white-gloved hand over the shortened double barrels, and, aside from some rust, it came away clean. Likewise with the breech. "I'd venture to say it's never been fired." He took off the gloves and scratched some of the corrosion off with his thumbnail. "Did you see this?"

I squinted and made out a year etched into the metal: 1928.

"Parker Brothers was out of Connecticut," he said. "They produced a line of sporting arms, then, the early thirties or thereabouts, they quit. I think Remington took them over. A good firearm is like a good violin."

"And plenty have been carried in a violin case."

"If it's cared for, it keeps making music."

"Is that a good one?"

"It's no Stradivarius, and it's chopped, but, yeah, it *was* good. Cleaned up, it'll work fine." He took off the visor and turned his normal-sized eyes on me. "You want it should work?"

"I'd like to have it cleaned."

"Who you planning to shoot?"

"The wolf at my door. Would a gun collector be interested?"

"There are some. People are into quirky things. Restored, you're looking at maybe a grand."

I whistled. "For a sawed-off?"

"If it's had a colorful life, maybe more. Bad guns, like bad girls, have a following."

"How much to restore it?"

"Let me do the work first. Later we'll talk."

It sounded okay to me. If it sold, I told him I'd go threes with him and with Vito at the pizza shop. "You want a down payment?" I asked.

"What down payment? I've got the gun, don't I?"

He walked me out, taking his sun reflector with him to go back to work on his George Hamilton tan, but the sky had grayed. He glowered up at it. "Figures."

From my car I pointed at the sign with Woody Allen on it. "You should get Chuck Heston."

"Nah. That name makes a dirty pun in Greek, you know."

"Heston?"

"Very dirty."

I didn't know, and I didn't ask to be let in.

23

You can live in Lowell a long time and never know all the barrooms, and if you tried, you wouldn't live a long time. There's logic there; I just can't express it right. The Mill Stone was a rat hole on Decatur, between a twenty-four-hour Asian market and a rooming house with an improbable striped canvas awning over the door. More improbable was the name—the Ritz Manor—but the ersatz dignity didn't hide the laundry blowing from clotheslines on the side porches of the triple-decker. A neon sign in the bar window gleamed on the shadowed sidewalk and said FINE FOOD & CHOICE LIQUORS. A little past three o'clock I stepped inside and waited as my sudden blindness faded.

Half a dozen souls were arrayed along the bar. Off to one side were a Keno screen and an Instant Action lottery machine, both unoccupied for the moment. Grady Stinson sat alone in a booth, wreathed in cigarette smoke. My notion was that perhaps Stinson might have a motive to come back at the lawyer who'd kept him out of uniform. I started having doubts as soon as I started over. Though only five or so years older than I, he had the potty physique of a man who takes his exercise on a barstool. There were patches of stubble on his sunburned cheeks and scabs on his nose and chin, as if someone had taken out divots at Pleasant Valley that afternoon. I x'd him off my possible suspects list. He'd have been no match for a feisty sixteen-year-old. He took a deep drag on the butt and squashed it in a foil ashtray.

"Good to see you," he greeted me, in a wood-rasp voice. We shook hands. As I was about to sit, he flapped open my sport jacket. "Not up to anything sneaky, are you?"

"Like getting you on tape? What'd be the point?"

"My case is on appeal," he said, waving me into the booth. "I'm gonna get my shield back."

Not according to Ed St. Onge, I knew, but I just nodded.

"Name your poison," he said.

It wasn't necessarily a euphemism. I asked the bartender for coffee. He brought it and poured another shot for Stinson. Bushmills chased by Guinness. He was going all-Irish. "You want any food with that?" I offered. "That stuff drinks hard."

He belched softly. "Nah, I already had a coupla tube steaks," he said, as if I wouldn't have guessed.

"Tell me about you and Ross Jensen."

"That lousy bloodsucking SOB. Am I making my point?"

"Go on."

"Some gold dust'd be a nice thing."

"You're on paid leave."

"I got expenses. Drinking top shelf ain't cheap."

"Bad info is. Show me your line, then we'll talk what it's worth."

He frowned. "An honest cop doing his job is a target for lawyers. Their job is to bend the law. Difference between them and crooks is lawyers get to *make* the rules, too. And it's all a lousy game. They win, and they do that phony dance about how the system works and how it's flawed but it's the best there is. Justice be damned, it's who wins and who loses. It's all mental macho."

"What about Jensen?" I asked.

"That's what I'm saying. I hate him, okay? If there was an open season, I'd choke the bastard myself. But if you're asking did I hassle with his kid—the answer is n-o."

"Okay."

He lit another weed and forked smoke from his nostrils. "So, you're working for his old lady? What's she like?"

"She likes her children. Have you spoken to Ross Jensen since your case?"

"Threatened him, you mean?" It was an interesting word choice. I let it hang.

"Not a chance." Stinson huffed more smoke. "You don't talk to lawyers. You pay, they talk. They're too in love with the sound of their own bullshit to listen."

As a legal commentator he was a half bottle ahead of me, and I had no interest in catching up. I took a twenty from my wallet and palmed it on the table.

"Gee, I'm going all giddy," he said.

I laid a ten on top of it. "I'm trying to get a line on his stepdaughter."

He scrubbed his whiskered chin a moment. "Well, now, here's a tale." He leaned forward, a gleam in his eye, glad to tell it. "I went to his office a couple weeks ago."

"I thought you said you hadn't seen him."

"Keep listening. I went at night, after closing." He gauged me, weighing my reaction. When I showed nothing, he said, "Fancy lobby, skylights, palm trees. The building's constipated with lawyers. You'd need a suppository the size of a hand grenade to clean out the joint. Randolph, Blinkman and Bearse were on the second floor. But security was nothing; a Girl Scout could break in. People like that are so arrogant they think no one's going to come at them." He spilled more Guinness into his mouth and wiped his lips. "I went in and sat in his big soft chair—like sitting in God's hand. You got the picture? We're probably looking at a couple grand for the desk alone. At first I thought I'd trash the place, toss files all over, maybe take a leak on his rug." Stinson gave me an expression that was more grimace than grin. "I'm kidding. In the end, it was enough to be there. To be there and to know it. You getting this?"

"It's got 'movie' written all over it."

"Wait. He had the photo there. 'The family.' The photo that big shots always have that says, 'I'm jus' plain folks. My family comes first.' Meanwhile, they're sticking it to the rest of us working stiffs and hauling off the seven-figure bonuses and a home on Nantucket. You notice that?"

"The photo," I said.

"It was Jensen and his old lady—nice-looking broady, from the picture. You're working for her. She hot?"

"Keep going."

"Okay, and a little kid in pigtails. Seven, eight. The one you're talking about was out of the picture."

"She wasn't in the photo?"

He was shaking his head, his face damp in the neon gleam. "She was out of the picture. It was one of those clear plastic frames. I turned it over and saw she was folded over on the back, so the rest of the family could fit. I mean, c'mon, would it kill the guy to get a bigger frame?"

"You recall what she looked like?"

"The fold-over?" He rolled his shoulders. "The way they do these days—short black hair and ratty clothes, kind of an 'I'm-pissed-at-the-world' look. But she wasn't any dog. Had her old lady's looks."

I uncovered the bills. He scooped them up. "Have a drink," he said.

"Another time." I was on my feet.

"You say when. Hell, if things don't work out with the job, I'll get into *your* dodge." He laughed. "That's gotta be nice—no heavy lifting, except your client's wallet. 'Cause I got it coming," he called after me with bitter relish. "You know what it's like, Rasmussen. To've been a cop and been shafted. We're two of a kind!"

As I drove back downtown, I cooled. I was even able to summon a small ration of pity for Stinson, but no sympathy. He could rant about the stacked deck and about Ross Jensen, and maybe he was right—I wasn't Jensen's biggest fan, either—but Stinson's real enemy was the man in the mirror. As Ed St. Onge had said, a bent cop has to go. Some people had felt that way about me.

24

I got back to my building to find Jensen himself in the lobby staring at the pedestal ashtray with its collection of stale cigar butts. "Oh, here you are," he said quickly.

"Is she back?" I said at once.

"What? No, but we need to talk."

I led him upstairs. I felt restless, but I sat, and he did, too. He cleared his throat. "The fact is we won't need your services any longer. Things are moving to the next level."

"What level is that?"

"The Standish police have agreed to take a close look."

"As close as they did the first time?"

Jensen scratched his lean jaw. He glanced past the gold lettering on my windows to the stone sill where a troop of pigeons sat atop the spikes meant to keep them off. They looked like plump yogi mystics. He sighed. "Look, I know you were a cop here, and I heard about State Senator Cavanaugh. My guess is the reason you lost your job is you stood up to him—because I also know you speak your mind." It was a more balanced view than many people had been willing to give it. "The fact is—and this hasn't changed since when we first talked—now more than ever, since the litigation I'm working on is just about wrapped up, I can't risk any sort of scandal over Michelle's being gone."

"What scandal?" I sat forward. "Do you know things I don't?"

"Cavanaugh's one kind of lawyer. He sees a license to practice as permission to steal. As you may or may not know, he's chairing a committee looking at casino gambling."

A faint alarm bell had begun to sound in a back corridor of my brain. "You want to talk specifics?"

"Do you think it matters?"

"Let's try."

"Something about an initiative from a Native American group who want to build a casino down on the South Shore."

"In Standish?"

"I don't know exactly where. I don't know when or what tribe. What I do know is that Massachusetts is one of the few states that hasn't rolled over and wiggled its tush at big gambling. This could change that, and I believe it would open the door to woes we haven't seen yet."

"What's Cavanaugh's role in it?"

"Beyond the fact that he's progaming—this month, at least—I have no idea."

"You don't know a hell of a lot, do you? Why bring it up? What's it got to do with you?" I was more frustrated than angry. Jensen's jaw tightened. "Or is it about me?" I said.

"My point is he's one kind of lawyer and he's a loose cannon, likely to hit anything that happens to be around. You working, in that town . . . it's a stretch, but I can't risk it. My name turning up in the newspapers, in any context, could torpedo what my firm's been working on for months."

"What are the other kinds?"

Jensen frowned. "What?"

"If Cavanaugh is one kind of lawyer, what are the others? What kind are you?"

"One who sees his job being to serve his client's and his firm's best interests."

The sonic boom of Latin rap from a car passing in the street below rattled the panes. I was trying to stay in the conversation and to make sense of something, but it lay just beyond me. "Fair enough—you letting me go. It's your prerogative. And, yeah, the cops can do things I can't. My strong suit is information—I'm not in the business of solving crimes. But if the cops don't *see* a crime, they fade. You're the one who's been saying all along that no crime's been committed. I hope that's true. But it's a fact that your stepdaughter and Nickerson seem to have vanished, that a woman Nickerson met in a bar turned up dead a few days later, and there are questions that no one seems to be able to answer, or to be trying very hard to find answers to."

"What are you so angry about?"

"That you're *not* angry, dammit. Look . . . I'm nervous. Forget the firm for a moment—Michelle's your family. I would think it'd make sense to find out everything you can, damn the torpedoes."

Jensen's color stayed high, but his words were steady: his courtroom training, no doubt. "I'm confident that the Standish police will help with that."

"I wish I were."

"What do you mean?"

If I told him the truth, he was going to think I just wanted to keep the job, but I couldn't worry about what he thought. I said, "I believe something has happened to Nickerson. I think he was trying to get money and it may have gone wrong."

He swallowed. "Jesus, do you think he's . . . dead? Do you think Michelle's . . . ?"

"I don't know. I do know Delcastro's overextended and, frankly, some of his help don't have much experience. Waving white gloves at beach traffic isn't crime investigation."

He pulled himself back together. "I've addressed that, and I'm satisfied that there'll be extra resources committed to finding Michelle."

"That's good to hear. Did the chief inform you, too, that by his working the case, it's going to be on the blotter and it'll become news? You know that, because we've already talked about it. In my opinion, news could be a plus because there may be people who've seen Michelle and Nickerson, but you should be prepared for it."

"I've addressed that, too. I've got assurances that their investigation won't become headline fodder."

Who could guarantee that? Cops were public servants. But I nodded. He'd made his closing argument and rested his case, and when he drew a check from his inside pocket and slipped it across the desk, already made out, I knew any more words from me would just be blowback. "I've included a little extra there," he said.

The check was for nearly twice what I'd earned. "Call it a severance package," he said. "I'm sure you've had expenses, and I value what you've done." He rose. "If you've still got things at the beach house, I'll have Paula box them and get them to you."

What could I do? He was paying me, even handing me a little parachute so the landing wouldn't hit so hard; he had say over axing me, too. I considered mentioning the family photo Grady Stinson claimed to have seen in Jensen's office, but there was no way to do so without an explanation. The very fact of my consorting with Stinson would likely put someone in jeopardy, probably me. I recalled what Bob Whitaker had said about Jensen at the police station the night his stepdaughter had been pulled in for loitering, and even on that I had to award him some points. He'd shown up. The kids you really worried about were the ones whose parents had given up on them. I thanked him, and we shook hands. I said I'd prepare my final report for him, and he left and that was that.

Since the demise of the building's elevator, the postal carrier had taken to putting mail for the upper-floor offices into a bin in the lobby. Either Fred Meecham or his paralegal assistant, Courtney, or I, whoever happened by first, would bring the other's mail up with his own. I'd done so this time, and Meecham stopped by now to get his. "Where have you been?" he asked.

"Working. But I'm through now."

"Bad timing. The city golf tournament just ended."

"Yeah, tough break."

"Did you see this?" He held up the late edition of the *Sun* to show me a page-one photo of a grinning state senator Cavanaugh,

Lowell's own. He was at Nabnasset Lake Country Club, according to the cutline, giving tips to the club pro. Fred Meecham shook his head. "The pompous son of a bitch. He'd tell Ben and Jerry how to make ice cream."

But I wasn't looking at Cavanaugh. I was gazing at a face in the crowd, one of the ever-present gallery at the fringe of the action, generally as anonymous as the faces on the post office wall—until you recognized one. Like the portly old gent with a white mustache, who was familiar because I'd met him last night at Ted Rand's party: the former judge, now acting as Rand's counsel.

A small mental wheel started turning. Could Cavanaugh have told Jensen to ax me because he didn't like me? Or because I was getting nosy in Standish? I tossed those ideas; in that direction lay the twisty, fevered road to John Carvalho's puzzle palace. Coincidence worked better. The old judge liked golf. Still, the implied link between state committees and land development and local affairs was interesting.

"Fred, do you believe it's possible for a private citizen—let's say a powerful developer—to influence decisions on Beacon Hill?"

"Duh. If you're doing that kind of advanced theoretical thinking, you've got too much time on your hands. *That's* why we need to get you some marketing exposure."

When Meecham had gone, I opened my bottom desk drawer and took out the office bottle and noted how the contents sloshed a little with my shaking hand. I set the bottle down. I reached past the Smith & Wesson and drew out the fat yellow envelope. It had been a while, so I sometimes forgot how fat it was. But I never forgot what was inside. Call it morbid fascination. I unwound the string seal and lifted the flap, but I didn't take out the contents. I poured two fingers of Wild Turkey and capped the bottle and put it away. Then I put the drink away—in a quick swallow. I still didn't open the envelope. I knew every document in there, from press clippings to the transcript of the probable-cause hearing to the final ruling—violation of Massachusetts General Laws chapter 268-A, section seventeen—inked by then Lieutenant (now Captain) Francis X. Droney, informing me that I was permanently relieved of my duties as a sworn officer on the city police force.

"Taking a bribe" is how the hash translates. A city councilman was shaking down developers, who were clamoring to renovate some of the old real estate downtown, but he was slick, and no one had been able to catch him. Working with the state cops, we set up a sting. I was tapped to carry the payoff, paired with a statie wired to catch the transaction on Memorex. But before anything could happen, someone shot him in the head. I was left with the bag of money. The shooter was dead, and although the statie didn't die, any corroborating account of my version of the night's events did. The statie is a fine, friendly fellow who plays shuffleboard in Tampa now year-round, and the only time I ever see him—last summer, for the city golf tournament, as a matter of fact—he smiles and shakes my hand and is convinced he knows me from somewhere.

Nothing ever smelled right about that night. Not the fact that somebody had obviously tipped off the city councilman and set up an out-of-town lead-pusher (who, not so sadly, ended up silent, as only the dead truly are), nor that the statie's wire wasn't there, or even that the receipt for the cop money I was alleged to have taken later vanished from an evidence lockup. But I wasn't around long enough for a detailed investigation. After a hearing and due process I was let go. I kept every scrap of paper I could find on the case; it became my clock spring for a time—and Lauren finally gave up. I didn't blame her. It's lonely being on the outside of another person's obsessions. I put the case in a bottom drawer because it wasn't paying any bills. I thought about it still, though it didn't burn as bright as it once did. Maybe it was just a reflex. Some people clip coupons. The former city councilman is in the state machine now—you know him. The aforementioned Mr. Cavanaugh. Maybe you vote for him, I don't know. I do know he supports raising your taxes and his salary. He's a liberal conservative or vice versa, a John Bircher with an ACLU card. He's been bought and sold more times than a Washington Street hooker and hasn't had a clever thought in a decade. I send him a Christmas card every year. I sign it "Sincerely Yours" and my name. Maybe some cousin on patronage cans it after she shakes the envelope and a check doesn't fall out. Maybe Cavanaugh actually sees the card and his memory's about as sharp as the ex–state cop's (Cavanaugh's got to be sixty-something now) and he figures

I'm just another Jack looking to get my snout in the trough. Maybe it's my delusion that he remembers and has one more little toss in the wee hours of a restless night and imagines a footstep on the stairs. But I think he knows we've got unfinished business.

At the time, my course had seemed clear enough. I was Gary Cooper in *The Fountainhead*: Stand on principle, don't waver, and in the final reel you're awarded the skyscraper contract and you get Patricia Neal. Alas, the badge was history, and so was Lauren. I put the envelope away but not the bottle.

Two more fingers, one more swallow.

The Lowell police blotter for the night of August 12, 1968, shows that Jack Kerouac was arrested for being publicly inebriated. In the line for occupation, the booking officer had jotted "writer." I thought about the city's pull on Jack. He'd gone elsewhere and had been lionized, but periodically he came home, and the past caught up with him. Just over a year after that bust he was dead.

I was thinking about Lauren and about why she had left me, and I realized the fault was my own. She'd have stayed if we could have gone away and started anew someplace else, but I wouldn't leave. Somehow time had a hold on me. It occurred to me now that in her leaving, in going to Florida after her own plans to remarry had fallen apart with the death of Joel Castle, she had taken a risk. I hadn't. I'd stuck. For the first time, I saw clearly that fear had stymied me. I could rationalize all day, all week, forever, that a fisherman needed to know his water to work it with any success. But where was it written I had to stay in the PI business, noble seeker of truth? I could have become a dozen other things (don't ask me to name them), but I hadn't. Could I still?

I knew she wasn't remarried. And she'd kept my name.

I began to feel better. I poured another knock of bourbon. I could call her, see where things stood. Then I could, if I wanted, announce my retirement, undergo the ticker-tape farewell that the city would insist upon, get on a plane and go to her if she'd still take me. Hell, I'd beg. Forget what Charley Moscowitz said about the Sunshine State; I could learn to love it. Jack Kerouac's name was on a highway sign finally, and he was in line for having his handsome Canuck face on a postage stamp; I could get my ex-wife back. I rolled over my Selectric and was typing my report when the phone rang.

"Alex?" Paula Jensen sounded a little breathless. "I'm glad you're there. Ross called me after you two met."

"Do you prefer the functional résumé or the results résumé? Or should I post it on Monster-dot-com?" At her silence, I gave up the routine. "I'm preparing my report. I'll have it to you in the morn—"

"Oh, Alex, I'm sorry. I think he felt he had to do it. I think he felt pressured."

The hum of the typewriter was distracting me. I snapped it off. "By whom?"

"It's just a wife's intuition. I told you, I get these inklings."

"Pressured by his firm?"

"I don't know. Someone powerful."

I gave it a beat. "Does Ross know Senator Cavanaugh?"

"Personally? I don't think so. Ross is Republican."

"What about a former judge who practices law now?"

"I don't know. I only know that I had my dream again, the one where I wake up and feel someone is dead—and I still don't know who it is. I do know that Chief Delcastro has prom——to make a real eff——to locate Shelly. I'm sorry, Al, I tried to make a br——" She was on a car phone. ". . . wanted to personal——thank—" The signal was breaking up like old ceramic tile, taking her away.

What did you say to that? I said, "You're welcome," and hoped she got it.

I cradled the phone and looked at Jensen's check. It wasn't chicken feed. I could still get to the bank before it closed and nest the money in my account, but I didn't move. I was feeling instinctively that there was some underlying organization to everything. Okay, it was concocted of gut feelings and fragments of what I'd been learning in my seemingly scattershot approach to the whole investigation—and maybe toss in a jigger of Wild Turkey for inspiration, and a whisper of fear—but it was there. I couldn't escape the feeling that somebody—Jensen?—had straight-armed me. Which was Jensen's call, if he was the one; he was paying me. And Delcastro wore the badge and was sworn to uphold the law in Standish; he could push me out to the fringes of the case and take over the center. But I also couldn't shake the nagging idea that the fringes were all there would ever be, that the heart would go unprobed because he had too many other things to do.

So, why should I care? I'd been paid; I was well out of it. I didn't need pushy attorneys or small-town cops. I didn't need ghosts, from my own or anyone else's past. I didn't need a suntan for that matter, either. Or an attractive suburban woman friend who seemed to have everything but was starting to wonder why it wasn't enough.

But what about a sixteen-year-old girl who had vanished?

That was the whisper of fear, and the thing I couldn't argue myself out of, and waking up tomorrow with a hangover the size of Tewksbury wasn't going to help. Suppose one day I picked up a milk carton and saw Michelle Nickerson staring at me and realized that, way back, when I might've had a chance to help her, I'd salved my conscience with money and let myself be scared away? I buried the bottle.

I was pulling on my jacket when the phone rang. It would be Paula, calling back to say that Delcastro had found Michelle, or that Jensen had come to his senses and wanted me back on the job, or that she'd come to hers and she loved him with all her heart.

The voice was a child's. "Mister?" it said.

"Hi. Who is this?"

"You helped me fix my bike."

"Katie?" A shimmer of unease went from her voice and down my spine.

"Can you fix something else?"

I was gripping the phone too tight. "Katie, what's wrong?"

"I just got home from camp, and my mom's not—" She broke off. "She's pulling into the driveway now, but I just got a phone call. It was only for like a few seconds, but I know who it was. It was my sister."

25

I got back to Standish in an hour, which is a lot easier to say than to do. The whole way, I was thinking about my thirty-second phone conversation with Katie Jensen telling me of her even shorter call from her stepsister and what Katie had asked me: *"Can you fix something else?"* Her mom had come on the phone in a moment, and with Paula serving as intermediary, we learned that the call had come in around seven-thirty. It had been brief—as though Michelle hadn't had much time to talk, Katie thought. She'd asked for Paula or Ross, but neither was there at the moment, so she'd spoken with her kid sister. "She said she was okay," Katie reported, "but she sounded like . . . scared. She didn't say it, but I heard it."

When I pressed, Katie revealed that Michelle might've been on drugs or drunk. I was still holding the phone in a white-knuckled clutch. "Do you have any idea where she was?"

"Uh-uh. But I kept hearing something in the background."

"What was it?"

"Now I know," the eight-year-old said. "Waves. I was hearing the sea."

"Good. Now, Katie, this part's important. Did she hang up or did someone else hang up the phone?"

"No . . . I think the signal faded. That makes a difference, doesn't it?"

I told Paula I was on my way to Standish. Neither of us mentioned that I was no longer working for the Jensens.

Before I left, I slid open the bottom drawer where I kept the Smith & Wesson K38 Masterpiece. It was the off-duty rod I'd had when I was with the cops. I hadn't upgraded when everyone else went to Glocks, because by then I no longer had a city's budget cushioning the expense. Eight hundred bucks for a handgun was too rich for me. As the sign said, always out-manned, always outgunned. Which is why I left the .38 where it was whenever I could, which was most of the time—pecking into property-tax rolls didn't require much firepower beyond Tums and Preparation-H. I took the gun out, along with a belt holster and some extra rounds, and stashed everything in my car trunk.

It was dusk when I got to the Standish police station and found Delcastro waiting. Paula Jensen had called and told him about the phone call and said that I was on the way.

"This is strictly a police matter," he said, "I hope you've got that straight. I've got officers combing the town, especially areas along the beach."

"What about the call itself? Can it be traced?"

"Doubtful. Mrs. Jensen said it was from out of her area, according to her caller ID. It could've been anywhere. She could be on the road west. Isn't that where Nickerson's from now?"

"I don't believe the sea sounds were the Pacific."

"If it *was* sea sounds. We're going on the suppositions of an eight-year-old."

"Who devours word sandwiches."

"What?"

"I trust her," I said. "And why go looking for another ocean when you've got all this ocean here?" I sighed. He sensed my frustration. He sounded confident, and I had no choice but to go along. "The other day you told me that Nickerson had once been arrested here," I said. "What was the story?"

"I told you that?"

"First time we met."

He scratched at the blue shadow of his whiskers. "It goes back. There was a call; someone was trespassing over on Shawmut. Turned out it was Nickerson. He was poking around in a tide pool that was on private property. He didn't want to leave. He would've got off with a warning, but it was a complaint call, and he seemed pretty keyed up. I think we held him overnight."

"Keyed up how?"

"I don't know. Boozed, maybe."

"Who lodged the complaint?"

"For Christ's sake, it was a long time ago. Details are fuzzy."

"Could it have been Ted Rand? He had a place out there, didn't he?"

Delcastro looked to be trying to remember but shook his head. "I couldn't even tell you if it was. It's unlikely. Anyway, charges were dropped next day. So if you're thinking that Nickerson has a criminal past here, I didn't mean to imply it. Now, so there's no further misunderstanding, this is a police matter. If we get to where we need help with a search party, you're welcome to join—as a volunteer. Meanwhile, the best way you can help is to stand back and let us do what we're paid to do."

I saw no reason to reopen a turf war with him. He had his way of doing things, and I wasn't going to get anywhere locking horns with him. He certainly knew the town better than I ever would. I told him how he could reach me if he had to and said I'd stay in touch.

I drove out to the marina where Van Owen kept his boat. I saw lights aboard the *Goofy Foot* as I parked, and I could hear music coming from the cabin; it had a sixties sound, but I couldn't name it. I hailed him from the slip, and after a moment the volume went down and he appeared in the hatchway, dressed in bathing trunks and a T-shirt. "What's going on?" he asked when he identified me.

"We need to talk."

He appeared to think about it, then invited me aboard. From the cabin came a drift of marijuana smoke. "I'm kind of busy at the moment," he said.

"I can smell."

He turned down the music. "So what is it?"

"I have to know more."

"You know everything you've got a need to know. Trust me, there's nothing else that's related to what you're doing."

"That seems to be everyone's line." I told him about my conversations with Ross Jensen and with Delcastro, holding off on Michelle's phone call for now.

"Well, there you go, then. There's nothing you have to do but wait. Drink?" I declined. "You'll forgive me if I have one."

I followed him into the cabin. He went forward into the tiny galley. I looked again at the photograph of him and Teddy Rand and Ginny Carvalho in her cheerleader uniform. He returned with a can of beer. "Tell me, the time you spoke to Nickerson on the phone," I said, "did he say anything about his business? Or about his daughter?"

"You're not on the case anymore, remember? Nickerson said he wanted a surfboard. He said that he'd be here this month. That was it, period."

"Did he give you any reason for his visit after all these years?"

"We didn't swap nostalgic tales of yore or impart the secrets of our respective successes in life. Sure you don't want a pop?"

"Could he have come back to square something, set some old misstep to right?"

"Man, you're like a bulldog with a rag. I'll settle for his squaring with me for the board, though what the hell? It won't go to waste. Now, how about something a little mellower." He set his beer can down and started to shuffle through a stack of CDs.

I was getting no place with him. I picked up the photo of him on the big wave in Fiji, examined it a moment, then held it up for his view. "What do you see?" I asked.

He took the photo from me and set it back on the table with an exaggerated patience, and went back to his music search. I said, "I'm glad you asked. It's a subtle and penetrating question, Rasmussen, suggestive of a quick mind. I see a guy still doing it—not enjoying the ride much, but—"

"Knock it off."

"—too scared to get off. Too beaten down by—"

He turned fast, upsetting the beer can, which fell to the carpet and started to foam. "Shut up! You think you can come in here, a place you don't know squat about, and start waltzing around stirring things up?"

"Waltzing makes me sound a lot more graceful than I am."

"Well, people have got to live here, man. *I've* got to live here." He slammed a fist onto the table so hard, the photograph flipped off and the glass cracked. "So why don't you go the hell back where you're from, before I make you!"

"I've got things to do first," I said.

"You're not listening. You're not going to do anything, except haul ass." With the heat and the sour air and my baiting, I should've seen it coming. I didn't. His body hit me with the force of a sleep sofa. I had an instant's understanding of how he'd come by his nickname, and then I was down and he was atop me.

Standing, I'd have been a match for him; down here, though, I could barely move to free my arms. He punched me, but we were so close, the blow had little force. Even so, it sparked stars in my head. I couldn't lie there and wait for a light show. Jamming my heels against the wall, I hipped hard and rolled him off. He crashed against the chair, and it was my turn now. I hit him twice in his stomach. It was like hitting a padded safe door. He grabbed a fistful of my shirt and shoved me.

We battled this way for another minute, too close to be doing real damage, wearing each other down. Finally, we silently seemed to agree to a truce. We rose and sank into the facing chairs, breathing hard.

"What the hell was that?" he said.

"An advertisement for why women should be running things. Is that offer of a beer still good?"

He roused himself and fetched a couple of cans. I drank half mine in a swallow and let out a belch. It seemed fitting after all that machismo. We scratched our armpits in silence a moment. "Tell me, you didn't talk to anyone about getting me off the case, did you?" I asked.

"What?"

"Okay. I didn't think so."

I filled him in on the phone call from Michelle, which had

brought me back to Standish. "So she may be here," he said.

"The police are out looking.

"And Ben Nickerson?"

"I don't know. There's something going on in this town that I haven't got a good feeling about. But I don't know enough about the place."

He pondered this a moment, then drained his beer can. "Okay, Rasmussen. You don't learn the easy way." He ducked into a little forward berth and came back and tossed me a pair of swim trunks. "Those'll fit. I'll get my truck and meet you on the pier in a few minutes."

26

I offered to drive, but he insisted. I wasn't sure about his mental clarity, or my own, for that matter, but at least it was my own, more than I could say about the swim trunks that fit me like a pup tent. I'd kept my shirt on for some dignity. We rode in silence for a time, before he drew into a rocky area amid some low dunes. Ahead was a fence with a locked gate and a sign like one I'd seen last night when I'd been with John Carvalho.

KEEP OUT
per order
SELECTMEN TOWN OF STANDISH

Time and weather, however, had effaced a couple of letters, so the bottom line now read ELECTMEN OWN STANDISH. Van Owen kicked sand at the sign. "A bit of truth in that."

I followed him up a low dune to where we could see land and water beyond. "Out there's Shawmut Point—the place I told you about, where TJ and I drank Scotch one winter night and contemplated our futures. It used to be a summer colony, old wood-frame places."

A thought came to me. "Could that be were Michelle Nickerson called from?"

"Unlikely—there isn't much out there anymore. The old houses were grandfathered in, but restrictions on waterfront building made it near to impossible to upgrade them. After a while, it was too much hassle to own a house here. The big motivator though was the nuke plant across the water—you can just make out the top of it there. One by one, a bank acting for a conservation trust bought up the houses and bulldozed them. There were a few holdouts, old-money families that hadn't used the places in decades but who went on paying taxes—you get old Yankees' backs up, they dig in like surf clams and can't be moved."

"So what happened?" I asked, getting a sudden inkling of meaning that stretched beyond what I knew.

"If memory serves—which, by all rights, it should not—one place was trashed by unknown parties, another caught fire. Owners got the idea and eventually sold, and before you could say 'property rights,' it was illegal to be out here. Delcastro will likely check it out, but it takes a four-wheel drive and deflated tires to get anywhere."

I thought of Iva Rand's remarking that her husband owned Standish. "Was either the bank or the trust named Ted Rand?"

He looked at me. "In some form or other. Now he's gotten around DEQE regs and is building an exclusive compound of homes, along with a seven-hundred-acre golf course. I'm told that's sizable. I know golf like you know surfing."

"And golf, too."

Van Owen was gazing at the dark landmass and the water cupping it, aglitter in the light of a rising moon. "Egrets used to nest out there. Horseshoe crabs would mate in the tidal cove."

"Thanks for the history lesson," I said. "What's your point?"

"Hang on; class isn't out yet. Come on." Back at the truck he pulled a surfboard out of the bed, leaned it against the truck and hauled out a second board. "Never been on one of these, right?"

"And I hope you're not suggesting I start now."

He tossed me a wet-suit top. "Use that. When we get out there you'll be glad for the extra warmth."

"Did you hear what I just said?"

"There's no other way to get where we're going."

When I had the wet-suit top on, we carried the surfboards down and set them in the water. "We're sheltered by the jetty," he said, "there won't be any waves. Just do what I do."

We paddled out. "Tell me the part again about all the sharks being on shore," I said.

"Most of them, anyway."

Too late, I realized I hadn't removed my wristwatch—though for the money I'd paid for it, it ought to be more waterproof than a duck. After several minutes of effort, Van Owen paused ahead and sat up on his board, which sank a little under him, nose up. I tried to do the same, but the board was so wobbly I almost fell off. I stuck to lying on my stomach. "I hope this isn't our destination."

"Not yet. Look." He pointed to a noticeable dark line in the water, some distance out from where we were. "That's where the brackish water running out of the tidal rivers meets the cold salt water. There's a lot of stirred-up plant life in it, and that attracts the baitfish, which draws mackerel and blues, and then the big hungry stripers come, all teeth and testosterone—or whatever the fish equivalent is."

I drew my hands up onto the deck of the board.

"Nickerson first clued me to what's really going on out here, underneath. He knew the food chains."

Some of them, I thought but didn't say. Lying there in the dark on the board, maybe I could imagine that narrow and separate darkness where we each finally lay, but there wasn't time for metaphysics, and I hoped Van Owen wasn't in the mood for stoned-soul maundering. I was eager to be back on dry land, back to finding Michelle. He pointed again. "That blinking light out there on the end of the jetty? That's where we're going."

My arms were as rubbery as the wetsuit by the time we drew the boards in close to the sloped side of the jetty. Van Owen dismounted and waded through the rockweed to the nearest boulder. He guided me in, and I scrambled up. The tide was outgoing, so we left the boards propped against the rocks and climbed to the top.

The jetty was built of enormous cut-granite slabs. In the moonlight I could see that the top was broad and flat, the spaces filled with smaller stones and gravel. Once upon a time it had been paved, but the asphalt was corroded and littered with broken crab shells. Weeds sprouted from the cracks. There was the blinker at the far end, but the moon was our chief source of light. We started to walk in the opposite direction, toward the town center, where the Storm Warning restaurant stood in the distance.

Barefoot, we moved over the rocks carefully, and finally Van Owen stopped. Looking down, I saw the charcoal remains of burned wood. Queen Anne's lace and goldenrod sprouted among what appeared to be hard pools of something that shone, as if volcanic activity had sent magma to the surface and it had frozen with time. I stooped and ran a hand over one of them.

"Melted fiberglass," he said.

Something caught my eye, and I pushed aside pieces of charred wood and broken glass to reveal a section of concrete. It was the slab upon which the structure had stood. Painted on it was a design like the one I'd seen on the surfboards at the big shop and on the plank of charred board that hung there. Ride a Legend. I looked at Van Owen.

He squatted, too. "It was my logo. An old fish shack sat here before I took it over for the surf shop. There was a bait shop down that way." He pointed farther out.

I'd gotten a version of it from Fran Albright at the restaurant: the same day, I suddenly realized, that I'd seen a man standing out here on the jetty—Red Dog.

"The two shops were zoned okay because they'd been there a long time, but they were pretty ragged—'rustic,' I guess, if you get into that sort of thing. But the town didn't want an eyesore. Rand offered to buy them. The couple that ran the bait shop were glad to take the money and get out of the business. I wanted to stick."

"Not the most commercial spot," I said.

"It was a place where I could have some peace, not bug anyone, and if they wanted to come out, they made the hike."

It was an attitude that Charley Moscowitz liked for his used-firearms business, but you didn't make the Forbes 500 with it. "What happened?"

"I said no, thanks, to the buyout offer, and that should've ended it. Then the town decides that without both structures out here, the rules changed, no more zoning protection. They threatened to take it by eminent domain, which would've given me less than Rand was paying. Except, one night, before *anything* could happen, the place caught fire. You know what fiberglass burns like?" He stood and scaled a chip of burned wood into the water.

"Wasn't there any insurance? Or protest?"

"No. 'Bad wiring' was the official verdict." He shrugged. "It could've been, for all I know. I should've taken Rand's offer."

"It seems like he'd be a man it's hard to say no to."

"He does good work for the town; he's on this board of trustees and that advisory committee. Can't argue with that. He's a player. He's good for progress."

"With more strings than Percy Faith. Does he own Vin Delcastro?"

"Nah. Delcastro's a proud guy, his own man—but there's no question someone like Rand gets special considerations. One of the 'elect.' Anyway, I can't kick. When the sports supermarket opened up, he told me I could run the surfing department if I wanted. He lets me shape some custom boards, too."

My mind was churning with the possibilities in all this, but I wanted to keep it clear for Michelle Nickerson's sake. I shut up, and we turned and wandered farther out the reach, toward the blinking red and green lights at the end. Van Owen seemed drawn, and I tagged along. The water was calm under its bright polish of moonlight. In the near distance, a sleek motorboat rumbled by, a low pale shape that foamed the dark sea, picking up momentum and noise as it went, until it was just a high-speed growling bound for open water.

"Sorry for before," Red Dog said. "On the boat. What you said . . . I guess maybe it got a little too close to reality. Living here has its different sides."

"Like anywhere."

"I reckon. But one constant for me is the sea. It makes me feel— I don't know . . . young. And at the same time reminds me of how much of my life I've used up, wasted."

"There are other beaches, other towns."

"I grew up here. But Standish can get to you sometimes."

"Not according to Mitzi Dineen and the local booster club."

"They're part of the problem."

The speedboat's wake slapped the rocks at our feet, splashing us, sending a flock of nesting birds squawking into the air just ahead of us. "Nautical couch potatoes. Power required, brains optional," Van Owen complained. "A few years back, there was this shark panic—people went out with deer rifles, shooting everything that swam. They got dolphins, a sunfish, a rare leatherback turtle—hell, they finally even got a shark. The heroes came in towing it like that old guy in Hemingway and hoisted it onto the town pier to pose with the monster. It was a basking shark. A totally harmless vegetarian." He shook his head. "What makes people do it?"

"What makes two grown men roll around punching each other?"

"We solved that one already. This . . . I don't know. Do they hate wildness in any form because deep down they fear it? They get a chain saw, and first thing they do is take down every tree in sight. They rationalize—the leaves clog my gutters, a limb might fall on the house—but they don't know most of those trees would outlast the houses they shade. They worry about coyotes, which are natural there, coming in and snatching their cute pets, which aren't. They want nature they can push around. They hang out a bird feeder to get the little chickadees but don't mind that their cat eats its weight in songbirds in a month's time. Ah, hell, I'm whistling in the wind."

"Somebody's got to," I said, "the wind gets lonely."

His brow wrinkled. "You're an odd character, Rasmussen. I'm still trying to figure you out."

"That's where I'm at, too. Like how come, if TJ was your best friend, you've never gone to see him?"

As we'd been talking, I heard the powerboat returning, its snarl growing. It was moving faster than it had been going out. Van Owen was a step or two ahead of me, moving back to where we'd left the surfboards. I turned and saw the white water as the boat cut a sharp turn, not thirty yards from the end of the jetty, and then I saw the outline of a man in the open cockpit, and for a second I thought he was reaching to brace on the windshield.

"Get down!" I shouted.

Van Owen swiveled in surprise. I actually reached to shove him, but he was nimble and jumped down the inner slope of the jetty. I was slower going down, too conscious of the rocks. A gunshot cracked, and something passed over my head at high velocity. I shoved my face into seaweed.

The boat didn't come back for a second pass. I thrust up my head and watched it turn in an outward arc, flashing its underside, then roar seaward. Van Owen scrambled back to the top of the jetty. "Assholes!" he yelled. But the boat was already fading. He turned to me. "You okay?"

My heart throbbed with adrenaline, and barnacles had shredded my palms, but I didn't appear to have any extra holes. I picked seaweed off my face. "Who was it?"

"The kind of idiots I'm talking about."

In the distance, the roar of the engine still sounded, but dwindling, slipping slowly under the cover of the night. "Yeah?"

"You got another theory?" he challenged.

"A warning?"

He frowned. "You mean somebody telling you not to be talking to me?"

"Or vice versa."

We considered reporting the shooting but decided to let the police concentrate on locating the Nickersons. Van Owen said he'd probe the incident on his own. I fetched my things from his boat and said good night. At the beach house, I took my .38 inside and put it in a kitchen drawer, underneath some dish towels. I telephoned the police, not caring that I was being a pest. There was no word yet on Michelle. As I hung up, I remembered my question that, in the excitement aboard the *Goofy Foot*, had gone unanswered.

27

I hadn't been to Brockton in years, and here I was for the second time in as many days. I got only a little lost but soon found the VA hospital. It was going on nine-fifty. I had no idea what the visiting hours were. The visitors' lot was mostly empty, dotted with pools of coppery light. I took along the copy of Ben Nickerson's high school yearbook, thinking it might come in handy, and headed for the lobby, passing folks wearing post–bedside-visit looks of relief coming out. When I asked at the information desk about hours, the kindly old volunteer's face got as long as Joe Camel's. "They end at ten," he said. "You better hurry."

I found the elevators and rode to the fourth floor, where I oriented myself and headed for Wing C, room 406. As I passed a nurses' station, trying to move by unnoticed, or at least unobtrusively, a broad-shouldered nurse called out to me. "Sir, can I help you?" It was delivered like a sentry's challenge.

Tentatively, I lifted *The Torch*. "I wanted to drop this off for a patient. It's his class yearbook. I thought it might cheer him up."

"Which patient, sir?" She looked a bit like a sentry, at that.

I told her. She glanced at one of the other nurses, who pushed up out of a desk chair and joined her at the counter. "Who told you you could do this?" This nurse was a petite thing, but she sounded just as forceful.

"I wasn't aware anyone had to authorize it. It's still visiting hours."

"This is a private ward," the broad-shouldered nurse said, not bothering with "sir" now. They had smoked out an invader in the smoothly functioning routine of their ward, and they were having none of it.

"But a public hospital, no?"

"You can't be here," said the short one. "You can leave the book with us."

I gave them my disarming smile. "It's a personal keepsake. I'll only be a minute." I'd come this far; I knew now it would be the only chance I got, and all at once I felt a need to see Teddy Rand.

"That makes no difference. You've got to leave right now, sir."

She was a charmer. "Can I stay if I lay off the stewed prunes?"

The petite nurse gave me some thin, menacing mouth action, then spun on her heels and marched off quickstep on a mission. Broad-shoulders reached for a phone.

I hurried along the hall, scanning the numbers above the doors. Two-thirds of the way down, 406 stood open. I glanced back before entering. At the far end of the corridor, the petite nurse was talking with a black orderly, pointing in my direction, saying something I could only see in pantomime.

The room was a double, but the bed closest to the door was unoccupied. The other bed, near the window, had a man in it. He was on his back, hooked up to monitors and IV drips. My first thought was that he was asleep, or even comatose, but as I went nearer I realized he was awake. His head didn't move, but his eyes rolled my way. His face had not changed a lot from the photos I'd seen. The clean jaw and the bright eyes remained, though admittedly they were gaunt. The body, though, which lay under just a sheet, belonged to a different man. Trauma, inactivity, and time had wasted it. The shoulders and arms, which weren't covered by the sheet, lay slack and stick-thin, the muscle bulk gone. I stepped near the bed, and his eyes moved with me—the only part of him that *could* move, I realized.

"Teddy Rand?" I said.

He gave no response, but his eyes held mine, and suddenly I felt exposed by them. Why was I here? What had I imagined I would accomplish by coming? I hadn't brought well-wishes or flowers or hope. I was an utter stranger to him. I had only a book under my arm. The book.

I stepped nearer, so that the blue eyes were full on mine. I said, "I'm Alex Rasmussen. I'm an acquaintance of Red Dog's." I told it then, in quick, streamlined fashion, no time for a back-story, and he didn't need it. Ben Nickerson and his daughter were the centerpiece. I took out the photograph of Michelle to show him—obviously he had never seen her, but I wanted it to go with my tale. He looked at it, but there was no change in his eyes that I could detect. From the corridor outside, I heard a doctor being paged with that controlled urgency of a crisis situation. I held up the yearbook, so that Teddy Rand's eyes could see the title embossed in black on the pale gray cover—*The Torch*.

I flipped pages to the picture of Teddy himself and showed him that. No reaction. I bypassed Van Owen's portrait and went straight for the sports section, to the shot of the two of them as football heroes. Nothing. I paged backward to Nickerson's portrait. Same. I was dealing a losing hand. In the hallway, I heard a mutter of voices, and the quick patter of footsteps on rubber tile, moving this way. Desperate, I flipped through the big shiny pages one last time, fumbling past strangers in the hairdos and garb of twenty years ago. I found what I was after.

Teddy Rand looked at it. It wasn't one of the senior portraits, because she had been a junior that year; but she was in the sports section, and as head cheerleader, Ginny Carvalho was featured alone, standing in her short pleated skirt and letter jacket, her pom-poms held out, smiling.

In Rand's face there was nothing, no visible change. I closed the yearbook. And right then, at the corner of his eye, I saw a tear form and roll down his cheek. He moved his glance to mine. Suddenly, it seemed deep with meaning. I laid my hand on his thin arm.

"All right, what is going on here?" someone demanded from the door.

He was a squat man with a large face, and more jowl than a Saint Bernard, and a voice trying to be firm. A stethoscope protruded from the breast pocket of his white coat, stitched on to which was the name I'd heard being paged moments ago. Dr. Joffrey. "You have no business here!" he said.

"I think you're wrong," I said, not sure what I meant.

"No, *you* are!" The stethoscope jiggled like a rubber squid. "Security is on their way."

Behind him, someone said quietly, "That's okay, Doctor. I know this gentleman." It was Ted Rand.

Looking uncertain but relieved, Joffrey retreated. Rand stayed in the doorway, not looking toward his son. "Can we take this outside, Mr. Rasmussen?" he said with half the volume Joffrey had used, and twice the force.

Clasping the yearbook, I glanced once more at Teddy Rand, then I stepped past the empty outer bed and followed Ted Rand into the corridor. The broad-shouldered nurse and the black orderly were standing by. "We tried to prevent him, sir," the orderly said.

"Thank you, William."

"Anytime, Mr. Rand. I'll just ride downstairs with you."

The man did, and the three of us rode the elevator in silent descent. I didn't know if the orderly saw his role as lending physical protection or moral support. He and Rand exchanged good nights in the lobby. When Rand and I stepped outside, three other men were waiting.

I didn't know who they were: men from the Point Pines work crew, I judged from their general appearances. One was young, with a bodybuilder's size. The other two were somewhere between my age and Rand's, of medium size, but with the kind of leathery toughness that a life of pick-and-shovel work bestows. They fell into place around me, like an escort, and we headed for the parking lot.

A gray pickup truck and a green Lincoln flanked my car. At a signal from Rand, one of the older men asked me to lift my arms. I did, and he patted me down. The other one took the yearbook and the Polaroid snapshot Van Owen had given me and handed them to Rand, who looked at both briefly and reached through the open window of his car and dropped them on the seat. Still speaking quietly, he said, "What were you doing?"

"Trying to find someone."

"In the hospital?"

"I showed your son his high school yearbook. I'm still looking for Nickerson."

"That's his daughter in the Polaroid?"

"Michelle, yes."

"Well, that still doesn't explain what you were doing here." A thought crept into my mind: Had Rand been the one who'd talked to Ross Jensen about dropping me? But why? How? "But that isn't important right now," said Rand. "What you don't understand is that my son isn't to be disturbed. Ever."

"I see that now. I wasn't fully aware of his condition. I'm sorry."

"It's a little late for that. It's already happened, hasn't it?"

I sifted that for hidden meanings. Rand stepped back, his face wrathful in the sodium light from overhead. "You don't seem to know what you've gotten yourself into," he said.

He turned and climbed into the Lincoln and drove away. I looked to the young bodybuilder, standing to my right. As Rand and I had been talking, the man had slowly been wrapping an elastic bandage around his hand. He flexed his hand several times. I wasted a second wondering why. I saw the blow coming and just managed to twist aside. His fist hit my car window with enough impact to spiderweb the safety glass. The man grunted in pain. I bulldozed my fist into his stomach. A flurry of short punches hit me in the lower back. His companions got into it. One poked stiff fingers under my bottom rib. I fought, even connected with a jaw or two, but I might as well have been swinging a fistful of cotton candy for all the effect it had. Hands spun me around and shoved my head against my car roof: once, twice. Quickly, the older two got hold of my arms and turned me back. I felt their strength, pinning me. It didn't last long.

The next thing I knew, I was on the ground. Something wet splashed onto me. I thought I heard more crunching of glass, and another sound, a faint exhalation, like the life being let out of something. Maybe it was me. Maybe I'd been stabbed. I heard a vehicle start up, then a louder crash close by and a tinkle of breaking glass.

I lay in a curl on the asphalt. After a while another vehicle roared to life and lurched off with a squeal of tires.

I don't know how long I lay there. Sights and sounds were blurry and mostly dark, as if a wire had come loose and wasn't making a clean connection. I thought about getting to my feet, which meant I had to find them first. They were down the block. When I rounded them up and got them under me, I levered my way to a standing position with the aid of my car. I leaned against the passenger-side door, winded from the effort, and rested. I could hear the white noise of Brockton around me, but it sounded distant, unimportant. Crumbs of safety glass lay around my feet like bright little pebbles. The Probe's front end was pushed against the steel light pole, which told me what the crash had been. The tire that I could see was flat. I'd have to get out the spare and the jack.

First, though, I had to learn to walk. I took a step. My legs were rolled gym towels and rubber snakes. I knew what ninety was going to be like, with knees that wouldn't lock and a shuffling gait and aches in places I didn't like hurting in. My pants were wet. God. I wondered if I'd brought my bedpan. After a few days I got around to the driver side, noting en route that the other front tire was flat too. Keys. Keys? I patted myself down twice. No keys.

I got through the big automatic doors and into the hospital lobby. No one paid me any mind; they'd seen and smelled it all too many times before. Someone may have asked me if I had medical insurance. I ignored them if they did. I pushed open the door to the first bathroom I came to and winced at the fluorescent glare. I braced myself on a sink, hoping it didn't come off the wall with my weight. When it didn't, and I didn't fall, and I had managed to keep my stomach down, I bent over. They were those faucets you press down and water gushes for all of two seconds. Cupping my hands under the flow before it quit took some practice, but finally I splashed a few drops of water on my face. I swished some in my mouth and spat it out pink and checked my teeth, which didn't tell me much. Finally I used the mirror above the basin. I wanted to tell the stranger to step aside and let me look, but he was a gruesome SOB and scared me. One of his eyes was swollen almost shut, his nostrils had a crust of blood, and his lips were rubber hoses. He stank of booze. I was going to tell the lousy lowlife to move it, or I'd move it for him, when behind him in the mirror I noticed something else: a dispenser for sanitary napkins. I turned to see a row of neat little enclosed stalls, not a trough in sight. I took a step toward the door and fell, banging the floor against my head. As I lay with my eyes shut, my cheek against the cool terrazzo, I heard a woman's voice saying something, asking a question, I think. I tried to say, "Shh," but I'm not sure it came out. I may have heard the flutter of angel's wings. Then, nothing.

28

Movement coaxed me up from a groggy pit. I was on my back, gliding along fast and without effort under honeycombs of light, and someone was softly tingling harp strings in my ear. An angel in rustling white, with chocolate-brown skin, said, "Dr. Marshmallow is on tonight." Her words had a Jamaican flavor.

"Who?" I managed.

"Dr. Marshall, in the ER." I was on a stretcher being wheeled into an emergency examining room. The angel wore a nurse's cap on her crisp dark hair. "He's good. He's a mumbler of the natural board of wacky actors and anorexic gymnasts," she assured me. "So you just hang on, Mr. Rafmataffin. Is that your name? It's what your carnation says." She patted my shoulder. "Have you got any equestrians?"

I floated away on cloud nine.

29

"Surf's up, Dog."

I blinked my eyes open to shimmering red and yellow and turquoise blue. It was a Hawaiian shirt with a likeness of Red Dog Van Owen inside. I was dreaming.

"It's fine with me. Keep on, if you want."

"What?"

"Dreaming," he said.

I *didn't* want. My dream had been about nautical drive-by shootings. I struggled and sat up and saw that I was on a recovery gurney in the hospital corridor. Van Owen stood nearby. "Where're my things?" I asked.

Fifteen minutes later, we were rolling east in his truck. The air was chilly, and I couldn't seem to get warm. Each jounce on the worn-down shocks reminded me of where I'd been, though not fully why. "Your car was towed," he said. "Front end's pretty messed up. You've got two flats."

"Dammit, they were only flat on the bottom."

"You can let the garage know what you want to do. I know the owner; he won't rip you off too bad. Mind if I smoke?"

Cold or carcinogens? It wasn't much of a choice, but one outcome was more immediate. "Just keep the window closed," I said. "I'm freezing."

He left the cigarettes alone. "It's probably a reaction. That ER doc wasn't happy about you leaving."

"I wasn't crazy about his bedside manner."

Actually, except for a few bandages and some swelling and scrapes on my face, the rearview mirror didn't reveal any signs of major damage. Inside, though, my jaw hurt at the hinges, and my voice seemed to hiss with serpents.

"I'm going back and forth," Van Owen said, "between feeling like shit for taking you there in the first place and telling myself you'd have gone anyway. What the hell did you have in mind?"

"You know what happened?" I asked with effort.

"Some of it."

"Let yourself off the hook. You warned me. And I lost your photograph."

"I'm not nostalgic like I once was."

"What stinks?"

"Your eighty-proof clothes. The cop was very interested in you at first. Your car hit that light pole in the parking lot pretty good. You remember that?"

I shook my head. "But I wasn't drinking."

"I know. You passed a breath test, so you weren't charged with anything. Yet."

I had a vague recollection of notebooks and stern faces. "How'd you get into it?"

"The cop, Ferry, phoned me. Look, I know you're itching to share your excellent adventure, but I don't want to hear any more of it right now, you mind? Listening to you is making my head ache."

Fine with me. My central processing unit still felt like jellied consommé; but I needed to know what I'd already revealed. Van Owen said, "You told me that after you left my place you went to see TJ, and his old man showed."

I nodded. "Do the cops know that?"

"No. The emergency room nurse kept them at bay, insisted you were a patient and they could talk to you later. She was pretty feisty. They cleared out."

Good. I had no interest in sharing the truth with them; not now, anyway.

"If you'd listened to me and let it alone, you could've avoided all this. Anyhow, the doctor said you should rest—and you're going to. He shot you up with something."

"Where are we headed?"

"Save it. Someone's waiting for you."

I glanced over, even started to ask "Who?" but my jaw hurt so much I kept it shut. The night rolled by outside, dizzying me with lights. Soon the wonders of pharmaceutical alchemy took over.

It was daylight when I cranked open my eyes. I was in the bed in the beach house, with a heap of soft wool blankets layered up to my chin. I tried to sit and groaned, so I lay back. Someone came in on quiet feet from the next room. "You're awake." It was Paula Jensen. "How do you feel?" she asked with gentle concern.

"Except for my head, stomach, and back, I'm good. Groggy."

"That's the Demerol wearing off." She sat on the edge of the bed and put a cool hand on my forehead for a moment. "The doctor gave you a prescription for more if you need it."

Something came to me. I pushed up on an elbow. "Is Michelle . . . ?"

"I haven't heard anything."

I eased back. "How are you holding up?"

"I'm maintaining. Barely. Everything that can is being done. But forget me for the moment." Her eyes were a tender blue force. "Rest." She made it sound tempting.

"How did I get here?"

"Chet Van Owen contacted me. He said he thought you were working for me. I asked him to bring you here if you were up to it, and I drove straight down. Katie's at my sister's."

"How'd Van Owen find out what happened again?"

I had a hazy notion we'd been through this together already;

some of it sounded familiar, but I wasn't sure. "A police officer called him. Officer Ferry. After Van Owen dropped you off, I put you in a hot bath because you were shivering so. I gave up trying to get you into pajamas and just buried you in blankets. You don't remember?"

I shook my head. Naked with an attractive woman and it was gone. I was living the wrong life. "What time is it?"

"Just after nine. You really should rest."

"I did."

"Maybe we should get you to a doctor . . ."

"No—I'm feeling better."

She didn't look convinced. "Would you like some breakfast, at least?"

"Is there coffee?"

While she went to make it, I got up. In the mirror I could see some bruising on my shoulders and ribs, and knew there would be more to come. There was an abrasion on my right cheekbone, as if I'd skidded on a rough surface. Rand's men had worked me over pretty carefully, though: nothing I couldn't have gotten drunkenly ramming a lamppost. It didn't feel as if any irreplaceable parts were broken. I patted my face with water, brushed my hair and teeth, and put on the fresh clothes I'd brought from Lowell. Making it downstairs was only a minor labor, and seeing Paula Jensen pouring coffee made me feel almost new. She looked as if she'd spent a restless night; she was pale, though her hair was brushed and shining, and in the kitchen sunlight she projected strength.

"How do you take it?" she asked.

"Black."

"I mean the punishment." I could smell her minty toothpaste as she stood at my side and set down a cup of coffee. "I brought along some physician's samples of Relafen—it's a nonsteroidal anti-inflammatory, if you need it. It isn't contraindicated with the Demerol."

"Just coffee, for now. You know something about this?"

"Only what Chet Van Owen was able to tell me."

"About medicine, I mean."

A smile and a touch of color returned; we were synched into

alternating conversations. "I was going to be a nurse," she said. "Actually started the training program." She warmed my cup and slid into the breakfast nook across from me with a steaming cup of her own. There was something almost domestic in it. "Stop me if the tale is all too familiar." But I was happy to listen. She told me about her first year, what it had been like, before she switched her major to English and met Ben Nickerson. "I had this idea I wanted to work on the SS *Hope*."

"And if troubles came, you'd walk across the water to solve them."

Her laugh was a dose of medicine. "You knew me, huh?"

"I was going to save the world in my own way."

"By being an investigator?"

"That just sort of happened. I started out in a uniform."

"You were a soldier?"

"And then a cop."

"That makes sense."

"Every ex-cop thinks he's a born sleuth."

"That's where you got your skills."

"Such as they are. Ouch." The hot coffee made me wince.

We went on talking for a few moments—revisiting the past, commenting on the nice day outside—avoiding what was pressingly obvious to each of us: that her daughter was still missing and might be in real danger. I drained my cup and set it down. "Time to put the aforementioned skills to work."

"Are you really up to this?"

I'd have much preferred to go on sitting there with another round of coffee and our funny conversation, but I needed to get moving or I wouldn't. I pushed to my feet. The room didn't spin too much. But a thought came to me. "Remember that dream you told me about?"

"When I woke up and said, 'He's dead'?"

"That one. Is there anything else you remember about it?"

"Only that it seemed real—and it scares me. Why?"

"Just curious."

"I don't want to have it anymore."

I patted her arm, then put my jacket on. She retrieved my watch and wallet from atop the refrigerator. It was almost 10 A.M. "By the way," she said, "you have no car." I'd forgotten that little detail. "Use mine. I insisted that you be brought back into the investigation. Ross didn't argue. I'll stay here for now; Shel may try to call again." I took the keys. I went to the drawer and got my .38. I could have waited until Paula was out of the room, but I figured we all needed the occasional jolt of reality to make our best judgments. I'd had mine last night. She looked at it with nervous fascination as I snapped the holster onto my belt. "Is that a good idea?" she asked. "A gun?"

"It's rarely the best idea. Sometimes it's called for."

"And this is one of those times?"

I drew on my coat to conceal the .38. "I can't say for sure, Paula. It might be."

She didn't look happy with it, but she didn't argue. Either she trusted me or had decided I was too pigheaded to argue with. "Are we doing the right thing? I don't like the idea of you getting hurt."

"Let's fast-track that into law."

"I'm serious, Alex."

She had stepped close. I took her hands in mine and looked in her eyes. There were tears gathering in them, and fear being held at bay. Gently, I kissed her forehead. "That's how I want you to be. And extra careful. I'm going to be now, too. I wasn't before. Understood?"

She nodded. I released my grip, but she held on. I could feel a pull there in the short intervening space between us. "Does anyone else know you're here?" I asked.

"Only Ross and my sister. And Van Owen."

"All right. Keep the phone handy. I'll call as soon as I can."

She nodded, her eyes bright. "God bless," she said.

As I got in the Blazer, adjusting the seat for legroom, I glanced at the mirror. What had fooled Paula Jensen so as to offer me her total trust? Some harsh words for the man reflected there rose in my mind, but I let them go. Maybe it was a time for compassion. Besides, I sensed the most vague outlines of an idea trying to take shape. The headache didn't help it to form, but I had to hope the idea would come on its own if it had any real substance.

30

In the municipal building I passed the big pointing hand. Chief Delcastro wasn't in, but Officer Ferry was, looking as clean and crisp as ever. I told him thanks for what he had done. "You don't look *too* bad," he said. "Of course, I don't know what's under the bandage. What did you do, doze off?"

"I must've," I lied. "The long hours add up."

"Tell me about it. We're pulling double shifts till further notice."

"Which is why I'm here. Does that hot computer of yours contain arrest records?"

"Everything going back five years. We can deep-dive 'em in a minute."

"What about before that?"

"Hmm. What are you looking for?"

"Delcastro told me that Ben Nickerson had once been arrested in town."

"Do you know when that was?"

"Sixteen, eighteen years ago? I'm guessing. For trespassing."

"We have paper files. But it might take a while."

"How long?"

He glanced at the wall clock. "I could get to it later today? Say, by three?"

"That'd be great. I'll pay for your time."

"No, sir. If this is a legitimate request, it's part of my job."

I assured him it was legit all right and thanked him again.

The tide was low in Harwell's Cove, the river reduced to a green channel that snaked between grassy banks. As I went down the slanting gangway to the *Goofy Foot*, Red Dog was standing by the outer rail with his back to me, working a lazy stream of water across the deck with a hose. "Ahoy," I called. "Permission to board?"

When he turned, I had the momentary impression that I'd made a mistake. But it was Van Owen, all right. The Hawaiian shirt and paint-speckled chinos confirmed it, but beneath the visor of a long-billed fisherman's hat he was wearing, his face looked like undercooked hamburger. One cheek was eggplant-purple, the eye swollen to a slit. I winced in sympathetic pain. "What happened?"

He grinned with puffy lips, and I saw a gap at the side where a tooth had been. He choked off the hose, which gasped and went dry. "Want to swap war stories?" he mumbled and motioned me aboard.

"You know mine."

He coiled the hose and set it aside. "After I dropped you off last night, I went out to the Beachcomber to see if the Nickerson girl might be there. She wasn't. I came back here and was sitting on deck smoking a blunt, thinking, when Shanley came by."

"Mirror Shades?"

"He must've spotted me cruising the club and trailed me back. He had me for violating drug laws."

"For puffing a weed on your own boat?"

"Well . . . I might've lit up before I got here." He shrugged. "Then there was air pollution, and corrupting youth—smoke could've wafted clean back to the kids and they might've forgotten acid and Ecstasy long enough to get a contact high. Oh, yeah," he added, "there was a little matter of resisting arrest. I guess what went down at the VA hospital had me feeling a little feisty. I landed a few before the nightstick tipped the balance."

"Assaulting an officer? Smart."

"Yeah, well . . . they call it dope for a reason. I was looking for a tooth around here someplace, but I guess it's gone. I'm released on personal recognizance."

"How do you feel?"

"Very funny."

"I didn't intend for the trouble to spill all over you."

"Ahh, it was time. That's what I was sitting here thinking about last night. If I'd squared with you sooner, we might've both been better off. I should've told you to stay away from TJ. Kid turn up yet?"

"No. And your telling me about TJ probably wouldn't have mattered. I get in my own way a lot. I came out to say thanks. Sorry, too. You find that tooth, don't forget to put it under your pillow— get *some*thing out of this." I turned to go.

"Rasmussen," he called after me, "you bound anyplace special?"

By rights I should have let him be, and he the same. He had chores to do and so did I. Beyond a pleasant dinner, little good had come of our getting together. But in an odd way I had the idea that we were each trying to make something right. "What's on your mind?"

We took the Blazer; he said the four-wheel was better suited for our ride. We drove back roads out to the site where construction for Point Pines was going on. Several large estate homes were completed, with the shells of several more in progress, sited at discreet distances from one another on the rolling land. They made the houses in Ross and Paula Jensen's neighborhood seem cheesy and small.

"This used to be woodland, with some old homes before Ted Rand got it."

I nodded. "I spoke with Mrs. Rand."

"Iva?" It got a prolonged glance. "You get around. How is she?"

"On the half-sober, half-looped scale? Half, I'd say."

He nodded. "It's too bad. She was a nice woman when I was growing up. She made the best Toll House cookies. I felt more at home there than at my own house—never mind that I had the teenage hots for her."

I didn't reveal her current opinion of him. "She said that Rand owns the town. I gather this is what she meant?"

"Wait, it gets better."

We drove farther east, the land leveling into the coastal plain, and soon we came to the sand road that John Carvalho and I had been on, or one like it. A cable ran across the entrance, and beyond it was a sign that said FUTURE HOME OF POINT PINES GOLF COURSE. And now I understood why Red Dog had wanted to take the Blazer. At his direction, I switched to four-wheel drive, and we went around the gate. "In another year or so," he said, "the only way I'll get out here is carrying somebody's golf bag."

We rode over gently rolling land, beyond which were dunes and beyond that, though I couldn't see it yet, the Atlantic. I shook my head. "How did Rand come to sit so high on the gravy train?"

"Luck, partly, I guess. He's smart, and he works hard."

"A lot of people living in three-room apartments do, too."

Van Owen pointed. "Across the way is the nuke plant. Word got around that in twenty years, folks living out here would be glowing in the dark. A total crock, of course, but you get enough people thinking something and it might as well be true. Most sold and are living in Florida now, soaking up solar radiation. A few petitioned the government to close the plant, which wasn't going to happen. The trust I mentioned grabbed the lots as they came up for sale."

"How far under the document pile would I have to dig to find Rand's name?"

"Deep. Pull over behind that cluster of scrub pine."

We got out. I could hear the sound of heavy equipment in the distance, moving earth around. We climbed a low sandy berm to where we could see workers using the diesel equipment. As we watched, an open Jeep drove up to the workers, and a man got out and started talking to them, pointing, as if he was giving instructions.

We walked along a rough trail behind the thicket of pines, slow going in the deep sand.

"Any idea what all this is worth?" Van Owen asked rhetorically. "There was talk at one point about it being protected as a wildlife preserve. It got to a committee on Beacon Hill."

Where good ideas vanish like planes over the Bermuda Triangle, usually after they've dropped their payload. "No one complains anymore?"

His swollen lips shaped a sour grin. "It's a done deal. There've been a few beefs. One of the workers questioned some of the quality controls on the job and prompted an OSHA audit. Inspectors found fault, but it got cleaned up, or someone got paid off. The poor bastard who'd come forward—I've heard that someone put a cinder block on his chest and wanted him to take back his complaint. He wouldn't, and each time he exhaled, another block was added. He's lucky he can still draw breath. He ended up with brain damage."

"Was it investigated?"

"Industrial accident."

"Is Rand involved in this stuff?"

"Personally? I doubt it. He may not even know. Like I said, he doesn't have to be involved, really. And I wouldn't be a bit surprised if the jokers you danced with last night are out there."

"Working?"

He nodded.

We got past the cluster of pines. Suddenly, I realized that the group of workers was gone, and then I saw they'd piled into the Jeep and were coming our way. Evidently they'd seen us.

"Uh-oh," Van Owens said "Busted!"

There were five of them. My memory was fresh with the beating I'd already taken. I thought about the Smith & Wesson on my belt, but this wasn't the time for it. "When all else fails," I said, "run!"

We galumphed back down the trail—which is the only thing you can do in soft sand—and ran for the Blazer. "I'll drive!" Red Dog yelled.

"Keys are in it."

We piled in, and he got the truck going so quickly my door

banged shut before I was seated. I fumbled for the seat belt and got it on, though it wasn't going to be much protection if they caught us. Van Owen kept the pedal down as he zoomed over the hilly ground. He knew the terrain. At several points I thought we would roll, but we didn't. He didn't slow for the gate. He spun up into the sand, nearly capsizing us, but we tipped back to all four wheels, which caught traction, and we gunned through. When I looked back, I saw that we were alone.

31

The door to unit 3-B at the Sea Chimes was closed this time, so I knocked. I heard the padded approach of footsteps and saw the peephole darken. The door opened. Iva Rand's eyes did, too. "What happened to you? You look awful."

"May I come in?"

She gave me a skeptical look that said no-yes, eyed the paper bag in my hand and then stepped back passively. She had on another sweat suit, a shiny lavender nylon this time. The nail polish on her bare toes matched.

"Did you bring highballs?" she asked. "That's how it goes, doesn't it? Get the lady drunk, maybe make a pass, and she spills the dark secrets?"

"In bad novels," I said. "Anyway, it's a bit early."

"Or late."

I opened the paper bag and took out two coffees in Styrofoam and set them on the coffee table, along with packets of sugar and plastic thimbles of half-and-half. She looked disappointed. "You should've stuck with the cheap novel." But she took a cup anyway and pried off the lid. We sat on the antique love seats. On the table

I saw several old issues of *Silver Screen* and *Photoplay*, one of them open, where she'd apparently been reading it.

"I thought those passed on with William Holden," I said.

"I found them at a yard sale. I confess a longing for the glamour of yesteryear—and all those corny ads for bust-enlarging crème. I was always tempted to try some, but then I worried that rubbing it on I'd end up with hands the size of fielders' mitts."

"Use Latex gloves."

"Thanks, I'll send for the crème today." We both grinned, and I saw again the pretty woman she'd been.

Hoping the convivial mood would last, I said, "Mrs. Rand, Ben Nickerson and his daughter are still missing, but the girl made a call from down this way last night."

She shrugged. "I don't know why you came here. You think I have answers."

"Do you?"

"What is this—a game? You tell me your secrets, I'll tell you mine?"

"I'm just trying to put something together," I said.

"Well, lots of luck. I've got enough troubles of my own, and you appear to have yours."

"Ben Nickerson's trouble may be a lot more serious."

"I want to be left the hell alone, goddammit."

"Garbo did that first," I said, "and better."

Her face tightened. "All right, mister, that does it! You turn around and march yourself right out of here!"

I felt a flare of anger. It was impossible to communicate with this abrasive, self-pitying woman. I drew a breath. "Look, if there's been a crime committed, or the suggestion of one, you can be questioned as a material witness. That'll mean a trip over to Plymouth Superior Court. I don't know how that'll play with your lost-lady routine, but I'd think it'd be easier to talk to me here."

"Why should I? You're no cop."

I sighed. "No, and I'm not your enemy, Mrs. Rand."

She didn't appear convinced, but she refrained from comment. She went over to the sideboard and picked up a decanter and poured herself a knock. Wanting to access her before she hit overload, I said, "Did your husband mention running into Ben Nickerson a few days ago?"

A dark look flitted across her face. "No, I don't think so."

"Did he say he had a business appointment with anyone? Perhaps to meet at the beach?"

"He doesn't make me party to his work. Never has."

"You told me he was talking to someone about the old Surf ballroom."

"To a broker, certainly not to Ben Nickerson. Nickerson doesn't own anything around here."

"You said your husband owns Standish. That's quite a project he's got going out there on Shawmut Point."

"Is it?"

"I'm impressed that he's been able to pull it off."

"Then be impressed. I never said he wasn't smart."

"I mean, with environmental restrictions, and the sheer cost of coastal land . . ."

"Point Pines is his brainchild; he's never really shared it with me. I don't know much about it—or especially care, for that matter. I once cared about everything he did. His dreams were my dreams, but that hasn't been true for many years. Now, if there's nothing more . . ."

I was drilling but wasn't having any luck. "What changed that?" I asked. "Your son's accident?"

Her eyes snapped wide, then almost immediately narrowed. "You shut up!"

I'd struck a nerve. I backed off. "How about a woman named Jillian Kearns? Has your husband ever brought her up?"

"What is this with asking me questions about him and young women?"

"How do you know she's young?"

She sneered. "That's the only kind Randy is interested in. Have you met his charming miss from Takes-ass?"

Her anger was rising again. To stave it off, I said, "A doughnut would go good with this coffee right now, but I'll settle for something sneaky in it."

It was a language she understood. She brought over the dwindling decanter. I held up my cup, and she poured and set the decanter down on one of her movie magazines. We fell back on ritual and touched the drinks, my paper cup to her glass. "To the stars of yesteryear," I said.

"The past—which can stay right the hell where it is."

But I wasn't sure it could. Maybe alcohol and caffeine would help my head, though I honestly couldn't see how. Mainly, I needed a reason to stay a little longer, to try to draw the hermit crab from its shell. I moved over to the large picture window. Beyond, far out at sea, sunlight and clouds moved restlessly on the surface of the water. Closer to shore, the wind was blowing spume off the waves like pale sparks. I turned. "I visited your son."

I braced for reaction—perhaps even attack—but it didn't come. She sat unmoving, staring at nothing. In the stillness, I could hear the growl of a motorcycle along the beach strip.

"He's an impressive young man," I said, "even lying in the VA hospital bed."

She gauged me a moment with questing eyes. Her surprise earlier at my battle scars said she probably hadn't known of my visit, and now I was sure. It was one more secret Rand had chosen not to share with her. "Why is TJ there?" I asked.

She moved a shoulder. "Where else? He needs constant care."

"Your husband could afford private nurses at home. The surroundings would be more cheerful."

She went on looking at me, saying nothing. It was similar to the reaction Van Owen had had. And now I had to wonder: Was it possible that in everyone's mind, because Rand had willed it so, TJ was dead? She took a cigarette from a cloisonné box on the table, and I used the table lighter and applied flame to the tip. She drew in smoke and then sat back, her legs curled beneath her, her cigarette pointed at the ceiling.

"He was the most beautiful little boy. And he stayed that way, year after year—not little, he grew; he was a wonderful athlete—but happy, well-adjusted, good at school." Her voice had lost some of its raspy edge. "I'd wanted to have more children, but it . . . didn't work out. Do you have children?"

"No."

She nodded. "If I was destined only to have the one, I couldn't have had a better child. And then . . ." She fell silent.

I thought about the photograph I'd looked at in Rand's den, of Iva clutching her infant son. "Chet Van Owen told me he was different after he got home from the service."

She frowned, but she began to talk again. "I used to think that Teddy came back from the service with that post-traumatic thing. But I realize it was probably something he'd been feeling before, which is why he chose the military in the first place, instead of college, as his father and I had wanted. I think that his . . . achievements, the kudos, weren't all that satisfying to him. He used to say he wanted to make connection with people, and I wonder now if somehow those things got in the way. But it's true, when he came home from the Marines he . . . was depressed." As she talked, she'd absently begun to round ashes off her cigarette, giving it a point.

"Had he found out about Ginny Carvalho?"

Her gaze came up quickly: dark and sharp. "What do you know about her?"

"She was your son's girlfriend. She drowned while he was away."

"You seem to be quite a student of Standish's history."

"People seem to want to share it. Bits and pieces. I'm lost. I need help."

"From me?"

"If possible."

"Well, that's got nothing to do with anything. Nothing. And I'm dropping it."

She squashed out her cigarette and picked up her drink. I said, "One story I heard was that the Carvalho girl was promiscuous." There was no finesse to my fishing; I was chumming now, casting bait wherever I could. "That she was with some high school guys the night she died."

She waved a hand in sharp dismissal. "That never panned out. It was a drowning, plain and simple."

"Was there an investigation?"

"I don't know."

"How about an autopsy?"

"How would I know that?" She hesitated. "I only know Vin never found evidence of any foul play."

I blinked. "Vin Delcastro?"

"Who do you think I mean?"

Under the bandage, my head throbbed. "He was police chief back then?"

She looked at me, as if astonished by my density. "He was twenty-some years old. How could he be chief? He was a rookie patrolman. He's the one who found the body."

32

Andy Royce, the real estate agent, was sitting at a desk reading a book by Tony Robbins. He hadn't gotten very far in it yet apparently, because when he saw me he didn't hop to his feet and gush optimism. He had already tagged me as a perpetual window-shopper. "Hi, there," he said blandly.

"I believe you're the man with the commercial solutions," I said.

Now he pulled himself out of his chair and came over.

"You're the listing agent for the old Surf ballroom at Nantasket Beach," I said.

"Boy, you're running on a tank of bum luck, fella." His head-shake was all sympathy. "That place was on the market two years, and I finally just moved it the day before yesterday."

"Really? I missed again, huh? Who finally bought it?"

"Leased it, actually. Ted Rand did. He took it for twelve months."

"Is he planning to bring back disco?"

"Down the road, who knows? He'll make it a gold mine, what-ever he does. For now he was just eager to get the keys. He said something about storage."

I made gentle stabs with a few more questions, but he wasn't in the know. "What can you tell me about the Cape Way Motor Lodge?" I asked.

"If you can afford better, don't stay there. It used to be popular, oh, twenty years ago, when people liked the idea of housekeeping cottages. It had a bunch of little units folks could come and stay in for cheap. But the highway yanked most of the traffic off that old road, and when John Carvalho took it over, he let things go. He's a bit of an odd duck, John."

"None of the personality of Ted Rand," I said.

"Not by a mile." Ditto for Andy Royce's sense of irony. "But you want to hear a funny thing? Guess who that property used to belong to."

"Rand?"

"He let Carvalho take it cheap." Royce grinned and shook his head in wonder. "Now there's a man with his finger on the pulse. Point Pines is going to make him richer than God. We'll all benefit. Property values are gonna go over the moon. Now, if you're interested in a business opportunity in town, I've got a dry cleaner's that's coming up for sale. And a landscaping service."

I told him I'd think about it and be in touch. "What happened to your head?" he finally asked.

"A little fender bender. No one else hurt." Starting out, I had a thought. "Curiosity. Did Carvalho buy the motel *before* his daughter died?"

Andy Royce thought for a moment. "After is how I remember it."

My headache, at least, had settled into a dull ache by the time I got out to the Cape Way Motor Lodge. The neon sign was winking away in the hot daylight like a weak pulsar in a lonely galaxy, and I understood for the first time Van Owen's line about the place that time forgot. In back of the motel building I saw Carvalho's old wagon, but the white Toyota was gone, but as I'd hoped it would be. Fran Albright was a lovely and dutiful daughter, but overprotective of her father. A grown man had to able to make his own mistakes.

I went to the door of their small Cape and knocked. To my left, beyond a wooden fence, I saw the dog rear its head. Then, without so much as a snuffle or a bark, it lunged. I knew it was chained, but even so I took a reflexive step backward. "Down, Gruff!" I ordered, and to my surprised relief it obeyed. "Nice, Gruff," I cooed.

I knocked again. I put my face to the door pane and peered inside. The floor-to-ceiling stacks of yellowing newspapers seemed almost to teeter inward over an angular passageway, like the stage set of a 1920s German film. I half-expected to see Conrad Veidt come somnambulating from among them wielding a hatchet.

I jumped. Carvalho was standing three feet to my right. He'd come up without a sound, astonishing for a man of his bulk. I smelled him, though: an effluence of sweat, sour clothing, and bottled fear. His small eyes looked hostile. In one hand he held a galvanized bucket full of soapy water and a scrub brush. His other hand gripped the .44 Python at his side.

"I'm just here to talk," I said.

"Don't have the time for it."

"A few minutes are all I need."

"I've got nothing for you."

A droplet of sweat crawl down my temple. Around us, small dragonflies flitted in the heavy air, the thin bright blue ones that we used to call darning needles when we were kids. The story was they'd sew your lips together if you told a lie. If true, it was going to be a silent world soon; people had been telling me far too many. "Come on, John," I said, "let's talk."

He didn't oblige as his dog had. He studied me, his round heavy face impassive, small eyes dull. It was an ugly stone of a face. It was hard for me to imagine how he'd ever made pretty daughters. But he had.

"I can call the police," he mumbled.

"I don't think you'd bother. I don't imagine you're a big fan of Vin Delcastro's."

Sometimes a key goes into a lock and nothing happens, and you realize you've made a mistake. But sometimes the lock is old, and the key hasn't been in it for so long it takes time to find the tumblers. Carvalho was silent for a full minute. Longer. He set the bucket down. He didn't put the gun away, but at last he grunted for me to come in. I mopped my face and followed him.

The place was as dim and claustrophobic as the first time I'd been there, shadowed at the margins by the great heaps of newspapers, as if time had been stored there, walled in and completely forgotten. I realized I needed to get him back there. Opting to believe that he wasn't going to shoot me in his own home, I walked ahead and into the nook he used as his headquarters, with its maps and pyramid eyes, its radio and police scanner, and the big cubbyholed desk—a haven for lonely believers. "Just so you know," I said, "I'm carrying." I drew aside my coat to reveal the butt of the Smith in my belt holster, then covered it again. I pulled over a chair and sat. Hesitating at my show of stubbornness, or foolhardiness, he settled heavily into his own chair.

"Talk about what?" he asked, only the faintest spark of curiosity in his eyes.

"Before your daughter drowned in September that year, what was she like?"

His carbuncled face seemed to strain with incredulity. "What does that mean—'what was she like?' What the hell are you sayin'?"

"Had anything changed? Different habits, new friends?"

"I don't know what you're after."

I didn't know either. I was free-falling, totally unsure of where I would land. "Had she gained weight? Lost weight?"

"She took to swimming."

"Swimming?"

"For exercise. She'd taken this notion of being a fashion model. My wife told her she wasn't built for it. She wasn't one of those bony wisps you see in the ads. She was a healthy-sized girl. Athletic and sturdy. She took to swimming and eating healthy."

"And she was swimming the night she drowned," I said.

His face wrinkled like an old tarpaulin. "What else?"

An alternative was that she was partying with a bunch of high school guys, as one story had it. Or was there another alternative?

"Vin Delcastro found her early next morning, didn't he?" I said, going through the details that were still fresh in my mind. Carvalho

217

nodded. "It was after Labor Day," I went on, "when the force would be small, so a young patrolman would've handled everything, right? Including the follow-up investigation."

"So?"

"Was there an inquest?"

"You mean . . . ?"

"For an accidental drowning, wouldn't there have been an autopsy?"

He drew his mouth down in a thin, surprised line. "If so, I never heard."

"You never asked?" The sharpness of my words made him flinch. More gently, I added, "No one ever explained?"

His eyes were pained and vulnerable, and water glistened in the corners. "I was a teacher in the junior high school, part of the community . . . It's hard to speak up, maybe make trouble . . ."

"What kind of trouble? For whom?"

"For me . . . for anyone. I only wanted my girl back." I felt sorrow coming from him, leaking from his pores with his sweat. "She's in the graveyard, and her mother beside her."

I glanced around the cramped space: at the desk with its many drawers, at his filing cabinets. "Would you still have a newspaper that carried the story?"

He shook his head. "I don't want to remember that."

"It might help to."

"No. I don't have anything like that."

And yet he could document each column inch of every crackpot idea ever hatched by the nutboxes who dreamed up the worldwide plot to control us all. I thanked him and rose to go, then realized I still had one question. He listened and frowned. "Ginny never mentioned any Nickerson. Only one she ever talked about was Rand's boy. Seemed like no one existed for her but him. It gave her heartaches when he left town for the service."

Carrying the Python, he trailed me back out through the labyrinth of old paper. I opened the door and stepped out, and nearly kicked over the bucket. Soapy water sloshed over the rim. He drew the screen door closed between us. I said, "I'm sorry I had to bring all this up."

"You'd do well not to come out here again. It's not safe."

"Because?"

"The bigger battle goes on."

Wheels within wheels: the man's circling mind kept returning with paranoid fascination to his hunt for the grand theory that would explain it all. Crazy, I knew, and yet, as I drove away, I couldn't let go of the growing feeling that there was another kind of conspiracy going on right here in this beach town. Seeing the old man hadn't cleared up any mystery, nor told me where Michelle Nickerson was, but it had given me an idea.

33

I stopped at the police station. The missing girl was still my reason for being. Delcastro was off duty, but Ferry was there, crisp and intent despite his long hours. He got up and came to the counter. He had found the arrest report on Ben Nickerson that I'd asked for. "You were right about the time frame. It was nineteen years ago—and it was for trespassing. He was above mean high tide. Landowners are allowed to own down to the high water mark, below that is public land. If he was arrested, it means he was higher up the beach. He insisted he was looking for seashells and marine life. He was held overnight, and then charges were dropped. It seems a bigger case came along, a drowning."

"Who was Nickerson's arresting officer?"

Ferry grinned. "Patrolman Delcastro."

"He was a busy man."

"He certainly was. He was destined to make chief."

I was wasting irony again. I didn't tell him about the dates. Had Nickerson been looking for specimens and found something else? A tentacle of something cold coiled up from my belly. "Was the drowning victim named Ginny Carvalho?"

Ferry looked surprised. "How'd you know that?"

"Was there a coroner's inquest?"

"If so, there's no indication of it here."

"But wouldn't there have been? An accidental death? The state requires it." I tried to remember if that had been true twenty years ago.

"I'm not sure. It seems likely."

"Could you check for me?"

"I should clear it with the chief."

Who would pour cold water on it—or a bucket of smoke. Ferry spread his hands on the counter. "What's this all about, Mr. Rasmussen?"

I hesitated. "In your law enforcement courses, is it all straightforward? Procedures, law, science?"

"Mostly that. I'm taking statistical analysis next term."

"Do any of your instructors ever talk about gut feelings, instincts?"

"Well . . . yeah, sometimes. One of them used to be a Boston PD detective."

I nodded. "In answer to your question, I'm not really sure what this is about. But again, could you check on the autopsy for me?"

He hesitated, fingered his sparse blond mustache, and then went over to a filing cabinet. He looked for a few moments, opening several drawers. He stepped back shaking his head. "There's no trace of it here. In fact, there's nothing on that drowning incident at all."

Paula was at the beach house. I told her that I needed to go to Lowell, and she asked to go along if I could drop her at her home. I made a quick phone call, then we locked up and left. It was just after 1 P.M. On the ride, I filled her in on some of what I'd been doing; I didn't trouble her with all the stuff that seemed extraneous to finding Michelle. When we got to Apple Valley, she said she could arrange to use Ross's car, and told me to hang on to the Blazer for as long as I needed it. Before she got out, she hesitated a moment, then gave me a hug. I hugged her back. It seemed to be something we both needed. On the way over to the city, I got Ed St. Onge on my cell phone.

"What's going on down there in Quaintville?" he asked.

I didn't have the inclination to tell it all, or the luxury of time. Maybe some of the Ted Rand shorthand was in order. "Do you know John Milton's *Paradise Lost*—the part about man's fall from grace?"

He grumbled. "You know I don't, for Christ's sake. John Milton." I could tell the taste of the words was making his face pucker. "You sound like one of those phony library-shelf detectives, where the guy's a working stiff who goes around quoting Shakespeare and all these literary illusions."

"*All*usions," I said.

"Who cares? The world doesn't run because of people like that. It runs because people in crummy offices, with tired feet and driving cheap cars, go out and find answers that add up, and are ready to *do* something about them." He sputtered to silence. After a tentative pause, he said, "What about Milton?"

So much for shorthand. "Who?" I told him I might need another favor.

"I'm in the market for a few myself."

"I know," I said. "I owe you."

"That's money in the bank."

"If I need you to, I want you to call the police chief in Standish and vouch for me."

"And say what?"

"You'll know."

"And if he asks how you left the job?"

"Talk to him cop to cop."

"You overestimate this fraternal network idea. Assuming I was disposed to say a good word, what makes you think people in one jurisdiction talk to people in another any more than sanitation workers do? Or school secretaries?"

"I guess it's the existential nature of the work. Riding out there on point all the time does things to people, bonds their souls."

"You've got to quit watching TV cop shows."

"I just need him to believe I'm not some flake. Maybe it'll keep him from arresting me before I can put this all together."

"And *I'm* your spokesman?"

Ed St. Onge, who could spot an out-of-date registration on a license tag at forty yards on a rainy night but missed the bigger meanings of life. He grunted but said he'd make the call if I needed it—but it would have to be soon; he and his wife were leaving tomorrow to visit their daughter in New Mexico. I gave him the Standish PD number in the event. Before I could end the call, he asked, "You know the one about the raccoon that got across both sides of a divided highway?"

"What?"

"True story. This raccoon managed to scamper across both sides, eight lanes. Only, on the far side was a chain-link fence. And that's where he ended up, dead."

"Is that a homily of some sort?" I asked.

"Hardly. You've got to watch that last fence."

Woody Allen kept me covered with his carved-soap gun. Beyond the door I heard the scrape of a police lock being dragged aside, a fitting noise amid the wrecking yards and the restless prowling of mean dogs. Charley Moscowitz opened the door, finger-combing his damp pompadour. He was dressed in fresh jeans and a white shirt. "What happened to you?"

I realized he meant my face, more than my being late. "Genetics, environment, I'm not sure."

He didn't chase it. He shut and locked the door behind me. "I was expecting you earlier. I've got a date."

"Sorry, I was an hour away when I called you, not counting a few detours."

"When Hitchcock was making *Lifeboat,* he told Max Steiner he didn't want music. 'They're in a lifeboat,' Hitchcock said, 'where's the music coming from?' Steiner says, 'You tell me where the cameras are coming from, I'll tell you where the music is coming from.' " Everyone had stories for me today. I didn't press him on his point.

"Okay," he went on, "I called some people I know on the South Shore, and one told me a guy came in yesterday and tried to sell him a dark blue Grand Cherokee. No name given, naturally. Anyway, this isn't my thing. You can try yourself. The place is Mandino's, in Scituate." It was the town next to Standish. "Ask for Waxy. Now, this other . . ." He waved me in back and unlocked one of the old cabinets and brought out a shotgun. For a moment I thought he'd fetched the wrong one—the barrel glowed with blueing and the wood shone—but it was the same. He'd rasped away the worm-eaten portions and oiled it, replaced some screws, but the shotgun looked like a genuine antique.

"It'll shoot?" I asked.

"And it won't kick like an Arkansas mule—as long as it's hanging over the fireplace, next to your rocking chair," he added with heavy emphasis. "You getting this?"

"Wouldn't miss it. Got any shells?"

"Serves me right for waxing sentimental." He got a box of twelve-gauge double-O buckshot shells and clumped it on the desk. "How many you want?"

I scooped the box into my jacket pocket, which sank the hem on that side practically to my knees. He gave me a scrutinizing frown. "You know what you're doing, right?"

"Yeah," I lied.

"You got about five yards."

"Come again."

"To take a man down. Anything beyond that, you're out of luck."

I didn't comment. I put a hundred cash down on the work, with the rest on account.

"You ought to wrap that shotgun in something," Charley said.

"Got a violin case handy?"

But he was thinking about keeping body oils off the blued steel, more than concealment. I still had images of a panicked old pizza twirler tumbling into my office with a sandwich bag. Charley got some newspaper, which he used to wrap up the shotgun florist-style, minus the ribbon and little card. I thanked him and carried it out like a bundle of long-stemmed death. Behind me I heard the police lock rattling into place. I put my package in the back of the Blazer, under a Pendleton blanket. Driving away, I reflected on how I would never sell the shotgun to anyone who might use it in the commission of a crime, and yet I would consider using it myself. For menace?

For death? I'd let the opinion editors at the *Globe* grope through the ethical tangles of that. I was at my apartment in fifteen minutes. I got a directory listing for Mandino's Auto Salvage in Scituate and called. The kid I talked to said, "Waxy went out for supper, but he'll be back." I said I'd try later. I removed the bandage on my head and examined the damage. Nothing gray had leaked out, at least. I showered and put on fresh clothes, minus the hardware this time. I swabbed some antiseptic on my wounds, but didn't reapply dressing. Jack Nicholson could walk around through half of *Chinatown* with a gob of bandage on his nose the size of a snowball, but he was Nicholson. I was running out of snappy replies for when people asked me what'd happened.

I looked in the refrigerator a couple of times, but it was a nervous reflex. I still didn't have much appetite, which was just as well, unless I wanted to eat mayonnaise on slabs of moldy Muenster with a can of Blue Ribbon. I put on the TV to catch the six o'clock news. The top story on Channel 4 was the pollen explosion. "If it sneezes, it leads," joshed one of the anchors. The weatherman promised rain later for the South Shore, the Cape, and the islands. I grabbed a light jacket, along with my .38, and headed out.

There was an envelope in my mailbox that hadn't been there when I'd arrived. It was sealed with tape and addressed with just my name. Inside was a four-by-six color photo of a woman sitting at an outdoor table and smiling for the camera. Attached was a note, penned in the same clumsy hand as the address: "Guess whose girlfriend?! Told you we could work together someday." It was from Grady Stinson. I looked at the woman. She was brown-haired, attractive, though not as pretty as Paula Jensen, to my eye, at least, but that wasn't for me to say; neither of them was my woman. Stinson had likely snatched the photo on his nighttime raid of Ross Jensen's office, and now, thinking he was proving his chops, he had laid it on me. He was wrong. I would have torn it up on the spot, but there was no place to put the litter. I slid the photograph into my pocket.

34

Mandino's Auto Salvage was at the rear of a small industrial park, in a corrugated-steel shed. With assorted wrecks scattered in the yard, it was an ad for Mothers Against Drunk Driving. I got out and heard the high-speed shrieking of a rotary saw cutting steel. I wandered over to the big open doors and peered into the dim interior. Someone was hunched over a fender, showers of sparks flaring around him. I didn't see anyone else around, and I didn't want to come up on the guy unawares and have him whirl my way. I waited until he set his saw aside before I went over.

"Is Waxy around?" I called.

He pushed goggles up onto his forehead. "You found him. What can I do for you?"

He wore greasy gray coveralls and an old GI cap turned bill backward. Lank gray hair spilled under the sides of it. With the pale area around his eyes in contrast to his work-stained face, he looked like one of the Beagle Boys in negative. I guessed him to be about fifty. I mentioned Charley Moscowitz, and he nodded. "Yeah, he said you might be in touch. About the Jeep."

"What can you tell me?"

"This guy comes in yesterday morning and asks me how much

I'd give him for a late-model Grand Cherokee. Dark blue, he said. He tried to make it seem like it made all the sense in the world, bringing it in and selling it for scrap. 'How bad is it totaled?' I asked him. Oh, it wasn't totaled at all; it was just that he needed cash fast and didn't want the bother of selling it. Well, that story made about as much sense as freezing Ted Williams, so I asked to see the car and the title. That got him backing and filling the holes in his story, but he said he'd return later with both, and I said fine, we'd talk then."

"Meanwhile, back in the real world . . . Twenty dollars says he didn't leave a name."

"I lose. I can describe him, though. Medium-sized, sort of tough-looking. Younger than you by a few years."

It didn't describe Ben Nickerson, but then I hadn't expected it to. The car fit, though.

"What's your read?" I asked.

He plucked off his goggles and cap and scrubbed at the flattened gray hair. "If it was his own, he could be working a scam to collect on it, but if the title was clean, it'd make more sense to just sell it. If the car was hot, no title, police maybe looking, you run a risk trying to sell it, so you could look for a chop shop. Which this ain't."

"Did you notify the police of his approach?"

"No reason to. If he'd brought the Jeep in and I wasn't convinced, I would've."

I offered him the twenty anyway, but he waved it off. "If Charley ever found out I took money off a friend of his, he'd raise the devil at the next wedding, or funeral." He saw my puzzled look. "Didn't he tell you? We're second cousins or something, about three marriages removed."

As I drove off, I saw the sparks spitting in the shrieking gloom, like meteors on an August night.

I called the Standish police station and asked for Delcastro. He didn't seem angry at hearing my voice, merely resigned, the way cattle get to biting flies. I told him about the Cherokee.

"It doesn't automatically follow that it was Nickerson's," he said.

"No, but it's a big coincidence. And if it is his, it raises the question, what happened to Nickerson?"

"I'll put out a BOL," he said, sounding reluctant. "I've got the California tag number. Anything else?"

I thanked him and we hung up. Not that I really expected a be-on-the-lookout would produce the car. Having failed with Waxy Mandino, whoever had the Jeep could since have found a chop shop, or a crooked used-car dealer, or have it stashed in a garage to cool off. It could be anywhere, or nowhere. I hadn't forgotten where Jillian Kearns's car had ended up.

At the beach house, as I got out of the car, I noticed a dark Lincoln parked in close to the thicket of beach roses. The driver, who evidently had been waiting, got out. In the dusk, I saw it was Rand. I bristled. As he walked toward me, I did a quick scan of the surrounding area, bracing for a flying wedge, but he appeared to be alone. Studying my face, he raised an open palm, I guess to show he came in peace. "I'm sorry about what happened. I overreacted. I do that." His voice was soft, breathy. "It's a failing, I know. There's no excuse for it. None."

What was he expecting, a hug? I stared at him. He had on the Dartmouth sweatshirt and plaid swim trunks, his white hair a froth of curls. "I'll pay your doctor bill, your car repairs. Whatever you need."

"I've got insurance."

"I appreciate that it didn't end up on the police blotter."

"Would it be there long?"

He sighed. "Look, I am sorry, but I felt I needed to make a point. I overdid it, obviously. It's just that there's more going on here than you can possibly know."

"Then why the hell don't you tell me, so folks won't have to keep saying that. So I don't decide to even the score right now."

His laugh was uncertain, almost grateful. "Good, mad I can deal with. I do apologize, and I mean that." And something in the brightness of his eyes made me believe he did. "It's this land development," he went on. "It's ridiculously complicated. It's a wonder anyone ever gets anything built. There's so much regulation and expense . . . and the timing." He flung his hands skyward. "These deals sometimes sit a hair's breadth from disaster you wouldn't believe. I can't afford anything that might queer it."

"Does my visiting your son threaten something?"

"I'm just sensitive where he's concerned. Too sensitive, I suppose."

"Because you've got him in a VA ward instead of private care? Look, the question has occurred to me—it's my nature to wonder about things—but frankly it's none of my concern. I'm sure you have reasons. And probably I was off base going over there. But I'm looking for Michelle Nickerson. That's the only thing on my radar." That and wanting to get in the house and use the bathroom; a long car ride will do that.

"Of course," Rand said. "But if she were here, you'd have found her by now, wouldn't you? Or Vin Delcastro would have. He runs a tight ship."

"So did Captain Bligh." I was thinking about Red Dog's roust over smoking a joint. "Even so, people can slip away. Like you say, any one of us sits a hair's breadth from disaster. Wasn't there a teenage girl who went missing some years ago and was never found?"

His brow crinkled. "That goes back. A runaway, I think. And anyway, it was never confirmed that she actually disappeared in Standish. You think there's a connection?"

"My point is, the police can't know everything. If Michelle Nickerson was here, she may still be around."

"Granted. Or you might be wasting your time."

Time and the Jensens' money. But my time wasn't important; only Michelle Nickerson's was—and what might be happening to it. "If I'm going to give up looking here, I need a convincing reason why—and that's what I don't have. I've got no stake in interfering in any deal of yours," I said. "But right now, I've got to use the bathroom or I'm going to be tap dancing."

He chuckled. "Go, go."

When I went back out, Rand was waiting for me on the deck, facing the sea, where dark clouds were hastening the coming night. It was the spot where I'd stood when I'd first laid eyes on him, four days ago. "All right," he said. "I'm going to help you. I know lots of people in town, maybe someone's seen the girl. But first I want to swim. If I put things off, I end up not doing them. The ocean is magic when it comes to clearing the mind." I followed him down the steps to the sand. He pulled off the sweatshirt. His torso was sun-browned, his chest covered with woolly gray hair. "You're welcome to join me."

"I still don't have a swimsuit."

"Then, neither do I." He bent and drew off his trunks, dropping them on the sand. In the surrounding darkness I couldn't tell he was naked except for the pale patch where he wasn't tanned. "It's up to you," he said. "You'll do okay—though I have to tell you, muscles don't float. I'll do better, being full of hot air."

"The forecast is for rain," I said.

"It always is." With a chuckle, he waded into the low surf and dived under. He resurfaced a few yards farther out, swept back his hair and started swimming. Not sure why, except that I sensed it was important somehow and should not be put off, I did as he had done. When I'd laid my clothes aside, I headed for the water.

Moving with a lot more style and efficiency than I, Rand continued to stroke outward, foam flashing in his wake. I was soon panting. I worked too hard at things in life to be graceful at most of them, though I usually got to the places I needed to get to. "Will we need passports?" I called.

I changed strokes, and we kept going. After a while, he slowed and turned, waiting for me to reach him. "This is good," he said when I had. "Look." He nodded toward the shore, where the short row of beach houses stood, night-lit in the distance, like scale models in an architect's display. The water was surprisingly warm and buoyant, and I could feel a slow current moving down where my feet hung. I suddenly felt great empathy with the woman in the *Jaws* poster.

"Lord Byron had a deformed foot," Rand said. "What used to be called a clubfoot. Maybe being the wild lover poet was compensation. He liked to swim out into the ocean . . . way, way out, until he was totally exhausted. He'd swim out to his absolute limit, where he couldn't swim another stroke."

I spat some water, listening, wondering if he was going somewhere, or just rhapsodizing. The salt stung the cuts on my face, but it helped keep my mind off the tiny core of fear I'd always felt in deep water. I tried not to imagine how deep it might be.

"Ah, but then he had the life-or-death challenge of getting back to shore." Rand paddled around to face me. "I was born poor, come from a long line of it. That was *my* limiting factor."

"You went to Dartmouth?"

"God, no. They were recruiting my son pretty heavily. I wish he'd gone. Me, I'm a humble man."

"Who reads Byron and quotes 'Dover Beach,' " I said.

He drew a dripping hand from the water and gestured toward the dark sweep of Shawmut Point off to the left. " 'Ah, love, let us be true to one another! For the world which seems to lie before us like a land of dreams, so various, so beautiful, so new.' Thanks for reminding me." He laughed.

"Of what?"

"That's all mine," he said, with a note of half-surprise. "Not literally. Some of it is. But I possess it in my imagination. I've envisioned what it can become and have taken steps to see it happen."

"I heard something about it," I said.

"Understand, not everyone's happy with the idea. I'd like them to be, of course. I try to spread things around and make it work for everyone. But I can't worry too much about folks who choose not to see it that way. The fact is, anytime a person makes something happen in this world, he's going to acquire enemies."

"You must have your share. I know I do."

His eyes twinkled with reflected starlight. "My good friend the judge told me you'd made some in the legislative ranks. I told the judge that probably just meant you've got character."

I found it interesting that I'd been a subject of conversation between busy men, but I was more interested in Ted Rand. "What about *your* enemies?" I asked.

"Well . . . there'll be some attempts to block me. Obscure zoning laws are bound to come up. Or EPA rules no one's ever noticed before. Hell, we found some old bones, and people wanted to shut me down." He gave a bark of amazed laughter. "But the bones are safely housed in a Native American collection now, and maybe the state will approve a casino soon—God knows it'd spur the economy—and most people are happy."

Rand cleared water from his eyes. "I've learned not to rely on anyone but myself. Most people, when they push past their limits, get into trouble. They sink." Like Ben Nickerson? I wondered. "I'm prepared for obstacles. They're like the traps on a golf course. I expect them, *relish* them. They add zest and challenge to the game, and when you overcome them, the satisfaction is high. You see, I've got a vision for Standish."

"I guess you're not a strong adherent of the old one-man/one-vote concept."

"Oh, absolutely. A wonderful notion. But votes aren't what make things happen. Power is, and power always flows from money."

It sounded like an anthem for good old-fashioned buccaneer capitalism. Money and power—and progress—was the charge that arced between the two poles . . . a circuitry of golf links and shops and big homes on the point, which sparked with the electricity of wealth and the cool green promise of more. Certainly, I had no interest in stopping him. Puffing with the exertion of treading water, I said, "How do you propose to find Michelle Nickerson?"

"We'll put some resources into it. Chief Delcastro will handle it."

"That's what Michelle's stepfather said when he told me he didn't need me."

"Well, the fact is, my attorney knows the senior partners at his firm. I had him talk to them, to convince Mr. Jensen it was a matter better handled here. He wanted discretion, and frankly so does Standish. I told the police I could add some resources."

A thought occurred to me. "Is that what you and Delcastro were talking about the other night?" At his questioning look, I said, "I saw you in the alley across from the gas station."

I thought he grimaced, but if so, it was only for an instant and then gone. "Whatever we need to do to find the girl," he declared, "we will. When we get ashore, we'll make a plan."

"I'm ready to go."

"Tarry awhile. This'll clear our heads." He rolled onto his back and floated, gazing up. With the clouds billowing in from the horizon, the sky seemed as deep and dark as the ocean around us. I didn't feel that calm and kept treading water. Off to the right, in the distance, I saw a sweep of bright light, which I took to be the lighthouse where I'd met with Jillian. Farther off, in the other direction, was a dark hump with winking lights atop it. It was the Pilgrim nuclear power plant, as John Carvalho and Red Dog had pointed out to me. Even so, I was disoriented and was huffing a little from the effort of keeping afloat.

"Rand," I called.

With his ears submerged, he didn't hear me. I splashed a little water his way. He raised his head. "Ready?" I said.

His hair was pasted to his head like a gleaming white helmet. Our hands collided briefly as we trod water. Our breathing fell into rhythm, mine more labored than his. "I like deep water," he said. "It's mysterious. It must be like that being a private detective. Right below us, under the surface, there could be all kinds of things going on that we never realize."

I didn't try to one-line or second-guess him. I was conserving breath.

"Well done," he said. "Let's go."

I set out for shore. The water was smooth, undulating in slow swells. After I'd swum awhile, I paused and caught my breath. We were halfway back, a hundred or so yards to go. Rand drew alongside. As I set out again, something cracked against my skull. Lights sparked in my vision. I turned and he was on me, climbing me like a tree, driving me under. I tried to wrestle him off, but he held on. Strength is reversed in the water. Mine worked against me, my efforts pushing me deeper. Desperately, I thrust my chin up and gobbled air. His face was a foot from my own, his eyes fixed and strange, then I went under again. He got something around my neck, a cord of some kind, and I realized it was a long frond of kelp, the rock anchor of which he'd used to whack me.

He held on, twisting the tough seaweed rope. I tried to tug it free, but I needed my hands to get my head above water. I could hear his harsh breathing. I could smell the faint aroma of iodine. Then sound faded. My vision grew smoky, and far back in my brain lights flickered, like sparks from the cutting torch in Waxy Mandino's garage, then they, too, began to fade.

35

I saw one chance. It was an outside shot with long odds that wouldn't allow a replay. I willed myself to go limp and began to sink. Rand came with me, still holding the kelp, and I realized I'd blown it and he was going to make sure. Too dizzy to struggle, I went down. Then, abruptly, he let go.

Cold currents brought me around. I opened my eyes. Darkness. No Rand. I heard my final breath wobble to the surface in a string of bubbles. Clawing loose the cord around my throat, I kicked and followed them.

I broke surface and gulped water and sweet air. I had a sudden panic, sure that Rand was waiting for me. But the sea rolled dark and empty on all sides. My stomach already churned with water, but my lungs couldn't get enough of the air. They filled with it, again and again, and I bobbed there under the night sky in my exultation. I was alive. After a few minutes, I labored toward the shore, which seemed impossibly far away. I was an exhausted but happy man when I got my feet down onto the rough bottom again.

Rand's clothes were gone. I gathered up mine; then, shivering, on wobbly legs, I went up to the beach house. The Lincoln was gone, too. I got my jacket and my .38 from the car. I wanted to kill him. I went inside and put on lights. Maybe Delcastro should have been my first call, but I called Ed St. Onge. He wasn't in; no, the clerk didn't know where he was. I left no message. I poured a knock from the bottle in the cupboard and drank it down, then I climbed into a hot shower, but it was a long while before I got the chill out of my bones. The fear in my mind didn't fade at all.

I dressed and put on coffee. As I was about to call Delcastro, there was a knock on the front door. I shoved my gun into the waistband of my slacks and moved on stealthy feet. I left off the outside light. Leaning back, I peered through one of the sidelight windows. A woman stood out there. She had turned to look away, so her back was to me, and for an instant I thought it was Paula, but then she turned back, and I recognized Iva Rand. I saw no one else, though it was pretty dark out there. Deciding that she and Rand were an unlikely duo, I opened the door.

"You're getting to be a bad habit," she said. "Do you know that?"

"Whose?"

"Okay, I came to you this time. Sue me."

"Are you alone?"

"Yeah, like Greta Garbo."

I invited her in. I turned on a table lamp in the living room. She saw the butt of the .38 in my belt and frowned. I put it away in the counter drawer. "Do you want coffee?"

"God, no."

She didn't want to sit either, but I sat and reluctantly she did, too. She got a cigarette and had it lit before I could find a match. Her eyes were tired, and I had the thought that she was waiting for me to offer her a drink, but I didn't. I still recollected the image that Van Owen had given me, of the decent person she could be when she wasn't half-pickled.

"I've been doing some thinking," she began. "I don't like to, but you've forced it on me. Anyway . . . maybe I contributed to TJ's depression when I sent him a letter telling him about the Carvalho girl." She pondered, her forehead wrinkling. "I wrote him the truth, okay? The harsh, naked truth. A wife knows."

"A wife."

"Right you are, Mr. Detective. Are you sniffing out the clues now, putting the puzzle pieces together finally? I did."

"Wait . . . you're talking about your husband?"

"Hurrah for you. Do you want to go get your big gun now?"

"My head's slow today. I don't—"

"Well, let me be less abstract. In Teddy's military absence, old Randy was doing his patriotic part, too. We were living two doors down from here at the time." She meant the place where her mother-in-law was housed now. "One day I felt restless, so I took a ride out to our house on Shawmut Point. I saw our little aluminum skiff pulled up by the house. We usually kept it here. Maybe that alerted me to something. I went into the house quietly, and—" She broke off, her face drawing inward, as if in self-protection. After a moment she went on. "I came upon them together, going at it like a pair of dogs in rut in the upstairs bedroom, our old brass bed clanging away. They didn't see or hear me—or care, obviously."

Even now, all these years later, the pain of her discovery seemed to etch itself into her words, like acid on copperplate. Her look was stricken. I was searching for clarity. I didn't know if it was my near drowning or the lingering cranial vibrations of the beating I'd taken, but my brain was processing sluggishly. "What did you do?"

"I didn't hang around to listen to sweet nothings over postcoital cigarettes, I can damn sure tell you that." She looked around. "Have you got something to drink?"

"No," I lied.

She knocked ashes into a clamshell ashtray on the coffee table. "Randy used to keep an old army forty-five out there, for shooting rats. I went and got it. I'd never held a gun in my life, but it felt right . . . heavy and self-assured, no doubts about itself. You must know all about that, Mr. Detective. I held it and thought about everything . . . or tried to. My head was full of confusion. And then . . ." Her face tightened around her cigarette, and I saw once more the attractive woman she had been, and probably never would be again. She whiffed smoke to one side. "I put the stupid, lying gun back and got the hell out of there. It's what you should do, too."

"Did you ever confront him?"

"With what? Do you think he'd care? A girl more than half his age must've felt like quite a trophy. Did you hear me?"

"Did they continue the affair?"

"How should I know?"

"I thought a wife did."

She sighed. "For a while. Then it stopped, I think. I don't know why. I just sensed it did. She must've been the one to end it. Though, maybe it dawned on him he was only the second string."

Something dawned on me now, too. "So you wrote to Teddy and told him what you knew."

She turned back. Red-rimmed, her dark eyes burned like coals. I could feel their bitter heat. "He was across the world," I said, "and you told him his father was bedding his girlfriend, shacking up with his prom queen?"

She picked up the ashtray, and I thought she was going to throw it at me, but she ground out her cigarette. "Let me tell you something, mister. When you're going down in deep water, you don't start wondering about anyone else. *Anyone!*"

"No," I said, gripped by her choice of metaphor. "You don't."

"You bastard."

I didn't bother to explain I wasn't being judgmental, because suddenly things were clearer. I knew why Ginny Carvalho had to drown. And perhaps understood why Teddy Rand had grown reckless. As a gesture of kindness—or maybe perversity—I got the bottle of Beefeater and poured her some. She didn't call me on my lie. She got rid of the drink fast. "Later, I was in a way to see how the girl was a victim in her own fashion. She hung around town, kind of aimless. I heard she decided she wanted to become a fashion model, took some mail-order course. She may have gotten hooked on diet pills. I'd see her walking around town, looking lost."

"How long after you'd found them together was this?"

"Four or five months, I don't know. And now, I'm tired." She rose. She was wobbly on the wedge heels of her espadrilles.

"Can I give you a lift?"

"Why?" She looked defiant. "I'm going to go over and see my mother-in-law. I owe her a visit. She'll tell me about her kidney stone for the hundredth time and play her foggy memories of her important son and her lost grandson, and we'll both fall asleep to reruns on the television."

I walked her outside. The weatherman had called it right. A drizzle was falling, making a nimbus around the streetlights on the dead-end stretch of road. The sea was in the air. "Thank you for coming," I told her.

"I don't envy you," she said evenly.

I nodded. As she was walking away, something else occurred to me. "Mrs. Rand. You said your husband was looking at the Surf ballroom. Did he say why?"

"I couldn't care less. Maybe he wants to twist the night away with teenyboppers." She started to turn, then stopped. "I do hope you find the girl. Good luck."

"You, too. You know, it's none of my business, but all your stories don't have to come from *Photoplay* and a bottle."

"What's that mean?"

I shook my head. "I saw a picture of you—a pretty woman with a son she loved and wanted to protect. I could be all wet—hell, I am—but maybe he could still use some of that."

She held my gaze a moment and then turned and trudged toward her destination. Doc Rasmussen, Mother's little helper. Don't take my word for it, ask Paula Jensen. I went inside, shut off the coffee maker, and got a flashlight, my jacket, and my gun.

36

Saltwater and freshwater don't really mix. Nantasket Avenue was mostly deserted in the rain. I saw a few cars parked along the seawall with men behind the wheel, reading the *Herald* or checking scratch tickets, finding reasons not to go home. The rain wasn't much, just enough to dampen the hot pavement, stirring old smells, quickening some part of me that was always in childhood, running barefoot as the first drops fell. It would have been a nice place to be now. I drove a short distance past the old Surf ballroom to an unlighted stretch of the road and stopped. I shut off the Blazer and sat, letting myself become part of the landscape. Diagonally across Nantasket Avenue was a rooming house where a potbellied old man in Bermuda shorts and an undershirt sat in a chair under the overhang, playing solitaire on a lap tray. For some reason, I thought of Grady Stinson and the Ritz Manor. It was the kind of place where people went to die, and it reminded me that I was getting older. I didn't have a retirement nest at the beach, or anyplace else, for that matter. But I couldn't dwell on it now. I was working for a day wage, and so far I was only partway toward earning it. Assuring myself that no one else was around, I got out and locked the Chevy. I climbed over the seawall, dropped to the damp sand, and started back toward the past.

Along with the small flashlight and my gun, I had a screwdriver in the pocket of my jacket. I thought of officer Ferry, with the welter of paraphernalia on his belt, and realized that was how we all began, shedding as we went, till we pared the tools of our trades down to an essential few. I'd like to have added a shovel.

The rain made the sand sticky and had chased the lovers away, so that the beach belonged only to the seagulls and to me. The tide was on its way out. I approached the abandoned nightclub from the side that faced the ocean. Padlocks still secured the double doors, and weathered particleboard was in place over what had been the big picture windows. There was no sign that Rand had made any move here at all. Not yet, anyway; or maybe that was how he wanted it to appear. Or maybe I was wasting my time. Part of me hoped that I was, because an image of what might be hidden here had begun to darken my mind. Then I saw the rib marks of heavy tire treads in the damp sand, where some kind of vehicle had recently drawn up close to the building. They seemed too big for a pickup or an SUV, but I couldn't determine what they belonged to. The tide had washed them away farther down.

In close to the building, I examined the latticework of boards nailed across the foundation windows. I bent close and shone the flashlight through a crack, into the gloom, but there wasn't much to see besides the dull gleam of broken glass. The air had a tang of corroding stucco and urine. At my back, the small, receding waves made a low hissing.

According to Andy Royce, this place had sat on the market for years; then, just days ago, Ted Rand had taken a lease. Why? With his energies focused so on Point Pines, why bother with this? I knelt and wriggled my fingers in behind one of the boards, took hold of it, and tugged. The board resisted awhile, but it had been put up to keep out the elements and the errant beach bum, not a determined man. With a groan and a *skreek,* one end pulled loose. I levered it off and set it on the sand, nails down, and shone the light in again.

Between the concrete foundation and the overhead floor joists, the crawl space had been partly filled with sifting sand. A section of the sand in front of where I knelt had been plowed away, as if something rigid and heavy had been dragged through it. My heart beat faster. Farther in, in the gloom, lay a long wooden box.

I killed the flashlight. Hastily, I pulled off more boards, until there was a space large enough to slip through on hands and knees. I hesitated a moment, then went in. I crawled through the damp, cold sand, using the light to scan the area. The crate was about four feet long, sturdily constructed of wood and fitted with heavy hinges, a hasp, and a padlock. With my pulse hammering hard, I knelt before it. As I ran my hand along the top, I saw beyond it were two smaller crates, equally solid in their design. Sweat was oozing from my brow from my labors, and from the churn of dread in my chest. The boxes hadn't been there long; the wood and the hardware were new. More interesting, stenciled on the ends of each box was MASSACHUSETTS STATE POLICE.

I took out the screwdriver, but I realized that the screws were Phillips head. Ever ingenious, I inserted the blade of the screwdriver under the corner of the hasp and levered. The plate didn't budge. I exerted more force. The screwdriver snapped in half. Outside, a seagull laughed. But actually, the bird gave me an idea. I squatted beside one of the two smaller boxes, got my arms around it, and lifted. The weight surprised me; it felt like a hundred pounds. In the low space, I couldn't stand erect. I angled the box and dropped it corner-first onto a bare patch of cement. The wood creaked. It was a method I'd seen gulls use with hard-shelled clams. I got the box up again. The third time, the top of the box split with a cracking noise. With eager hands, I pulled away the broken boards and shone the flashlight inside.

The dull gleam of steel in rectangular and cylindrical shapes came back at me.

Guns.

There were dozens of them, pistols and revolvers. Some were partially dismantled, but it wouldn't take much to get most of them working again. I tried to imagine what they were doing here.

I heard some fast, hard breathing and shut off the light. I crab-walked over to the opening I'd made. A dog was out there, its nose down, sniffing back and forth, moving my way. I froze. Then I heard a whistle, followed by a distant voice. The dog lifted a hind leg quickly against the foundation, then swung around and loped off into the drizzle. I went back to my discovery.

None of the weapons was new. My guess was that they had been confiscated, perhaps by local jurisdictions, which had turned them over to the state police, who would've sent them to the state crime lab to be checked for connection to any crimes. If the weapons cleared, they were boxed and prepared for disposal. Back in earlier days, they were dropped in the harbor; though that was before we realized that in cleaning up our own neighborhoods we were trashing the fishes'. Now guns were shipped west, melted down, the metal recycled to some further use, maybe to make little replica muskets to give out at NRA banquets. Only I had the feeling that this time someone had altered their destiny in order to put them back into circulation. Perhaps in my town or yours.

The question was, Who? And how did this relate to Michelle Nickerson? And what the hell was I doing here, if it didn't?

Some people passing by not far from the building drew my attention. I watched them as they moved on past, oblivious to the old ballroom. When they'd gone, I did one more quick scan of the crawl space, still looking for what I didn't want to find. Satisfied, I slipped back outside through the opening. The rain had thinned but was still falling. I put the boards back in place as best I could, hammering them into place with my hands. I ought to have done the same with the lid of the box, but it wouldn't have fooled anyone. Anyway, my cover-up didn't need to be too good. The police were only going to take the crates away as soon as I called and told them. Check that—as soon as I told someone I could trust.

In the Chevy I used my cell phone. Ed St. Onge answered this time. "I'm packing," he said. "For New Mexico." He made a low whistle when I told him what I'd found.

"There must be fifty or more in the one crate. I didn't open the other two, but I don't think they hold pruning hooks and plowshares. The longer box looks like it could be rifles, submachine guns, maybe."

"What about the missing girl? No sign of her?"

"No."

"It adds up," St. Onge murmured.

"What does?"

"Guns. Inner-city buyback programs in Springfield and Worcester put together their semiannual haul. Only it disappeared from a state police lockup last weekend. We got a bulletin."

"I think this Rand is behind it."

"Is he involved in what you're after?"

"It's looking like it. I'm just not sure how. He tried to kill me tonight." I told him about the swim.

St. Onge swore. "You fell for his story?"

"It was convincing at the time."

"And he left you out there."

"He thinks I'm swimming with the fishes."

"Damn. Where are you now?"

"Going back to Standish."

"And the hardware?"

"Where I found it."

"Bad idea. You need to get hold of the state police."

Ironically, as he said it, a cruiser went past in the gray rain, a local. My impulse was to draw farther down in the seat. With the taillights fading in my rearview, I said, "I don't know if that's a good idea."

"Tell me why the hell not! All of a sudden you're the best judge of ideas?"

No, but I was possessed suddenly with a foreboding, like a cloud hanging darkly in the distance. An unexpectedly pregnant girl would be a problem for an ambitious man, older and married and with a reputation to uphold. How might he have handled it? Sometime after Ginny Carvalho drowned, Rand had deeded the old motel to her father. Payment? A hush fund? Had he pressed the local police to cover up the inquest? I said, "You don't understand, Ed."

"The hell I don't. You want me to call the staties?"

"No. No, don't." I was practically whispering now, a constriction of paranoia making my throat tight. I wasn't the one who had voted for cell phones over the old accordion-door pay booths, but

I hammered down the door lock and felt slightly better there inside the two tons of steel.

"It's a matter for the cops to handle," he insisted.

"I think there may be problems with that."

"You care to be specific?"

"I'd rather not just now. Let's just say there may be some conflicts of interest."

"Whose? Yours?"

"Rand golfs with the governor. He *owns* Standish. And probably some of the local cops, too; maybe even some of the state police. I can't. I can't call anyone until I know for sure—he might have Michelle."

He mulled that a moment. "Then the state should definitely step in. Goddammit, there are mechanisms for that."

As there were to keep illegal guns off the streets, wildlife habitats out of the hands of developers, and kids safe from monsters. I said, "Maybe they can appoint a blue-ribbon panel that'll investigate for a year or so and forward a list of recommendations to a grievance board that can schedule public hearings . . . A splendid idea, there's only one problem. Time. His hand's been forced. If what I fear is going to happen *does,* it'll be soon. Today."

"All the more reason. Let's call ATF."

He wasn't getting it; nor was I. There was sense in what St. Onge was telling me; he wasn't stupid—the government was a big potent machine that could get things done, but you didn't kick-start it to life. It was a Rube Goldberg device. You had to overcome the friction of special interests and crooked politicians, the inertia of an indifferent public. And St. Onge didn't know Ted Rand—*I* didn't really know him—but I did know he was powerful, and cagey, and maybe crazy, too. In the past half hour, an idea had been growing in my head, a bad cancer of an idea—Rand and Ginny Carvalho, the two of them out skinny-dipping, and maybe she'd decided things had gone much too far between them and was calling it off. Or maybe she wanted to write to Teddy and confess to him what was going on. But it was one further thought that rattled me all out of proportion to the others. "If he's got Michelle Nickerson and he got word that I'm on to him—"

"He thinks you're dead!"

"—if he got word," I repeated, "and I think he may already have it—no one will ever see the kid again."

That took a bite out of Ed's certainty. "He's that cold?"

I thought of Van Owen's story about the cinder blocks. "He's warm and fuzzy, and people take him for what he seems—hell, I did—and he'll swim with you and smile into your eyes, he'll give you moonlight and poetry. He's smooth as a silk stocking, and if he feels he needs to, he'll wind the stocking around your throat and kill you." I didn't tell Ed what Rand had done to his wife and his own son. There wasn't time to reckon adequately with the villainy of it, and it would have made me too angry. All at once, I didn't want to be angry. I wanted to be smart, and rational, and ice-cold. "Do what you have to," I said. "I'm going back."

"Hold on, Raz, is that the best way?"

"Give me another," I said, and I meant it. I didn't like the idea one bit. The town gave me the major creeps, and I was a total outsider, but time was ticking away and I couldn't think of an alternative. I paused, allowing a moment for Ed, with his intelligence, to come up with a game-saving plan that I simply hadn't thought of. But he was silent, and when the WELCOME TO STANDISH sign floated by in the wet dark, I said, "I'm going to talk with Delcastro. Maybe he's straight, maybe not—my gut feeling is he's okay—but either way, it's his turf. He needs to know. I'll take him over and show him the guns."

St. Onge sighed. "Be very careful."

"You be careful in Mexico."

"New Mexico." He sounded listless.

"Yeah. Watch the tourist traps."

37

Standish was wet and gleaming. As I passed shops and houses, heading south, a beach ball rolled along, pushed by the wind. It bounced and floated across the road, moving like something in a dream. The few people I saw out appeared subdued. Rain didn't work in a place like this the way it could in Lowell, where it felt as if it belonged. There it made the buildings look like the hulks of ships that have sunk and are moldering away, made the streets grayer, turned the soot to ink. Here, I imagined that the rain would soon end, and a rainbow would appear and the colors would gleam that much brighter. But I passed a raccoon that lay at the side of the road, sodden and gas-bellied and dead, and I gave up that that notion. With a shudder I thought of St. Onge's story.

At the edge of the soon-to-be Point Pines golf course, I churned the Chevy in close to the gate and parked and got out. For a moment, I shut my eyes and tipped my face up, welcoming the rain, and put my imagination to work.

While his two more rugged classmates went off to be marines, Ben Nickerson had stayed behind to become a marine biologist, in time to meet a lively coed named Paula and marry her and go west and have a child. But before that, one night on a little beachcombing walk, what if he'd had the blind bad luck to witness something he shouldn't have seen? What? Ted Rand and Ginny Carvalho going out for a moonlight swim? Or Rand coming out of the water alone, looking agitated and furtive? Maybe he had gone back later, looking, and had been reported trespassing and taken in. Maybe he'd told the arresting officer—a young Vin Delcastro—what he'd been doing there, and maybe he'd been let go with a warning to keep his nose clean and his mouth shut. Maybe one day he'd realized that a deal had been cut—his freedom for his silence. Only he wouldn't make the link until years later, when the motivation of a failing business got old wheels turning and he connected the discovery of Ginny Carvalho's body with what he'd spotted a few days prior.

This was my wheel turning, and maybe I was way off. But the timing more or less fit, as did the fact that Ben Nickerson, reading the local paper that he had delivered to him in California each week, couldn't have missed all the hoopla about Rand's Point Pines success. So maybe he'd set up a meeting with Rand and made his pitch: Nickerson's silence again—for a price. What would Rand do, take him out to swim and drown him? No, Nickerson wouldn't have gone along with it; only I was that dumb. Rand would've been calm and reasonable, said, "Let's talk," and Nickerson would've agreed, careful to take along a gun when he went. Maybe earlier he'd dropped his daughter at the movies and promised to pick her up, except he hadn't been able to. And poor Jillian Kearns had the bad fortune of looking for love and had bad timing. Was it possible even that had been set up? Her "chance" meeting with Nickerson as Rand's way of keeping tabs on what Ben might be trying to do? I didn't like that part; I wouldn't believe that Jillian had been conniving. More likely she was just a talker, and Rand might have worried that she was talking to a nosy PI and so had to be silenced.

Was I blowing a solo as warped and wiggy as old man Carvalho's? I might as well, if I didn't have something more concrete than paranoia to back it. I wiped rain from my face, walked over to the gate, and put my eyes to work.

The land had been graded and turfed, and it sloped away in long drives and sweeping fairways, skirted around sand traps and roughs of scrub oak and pine, and eased toward eighteen holes as deep and as soft as cash drawers. Red Dog had said it was seven hundred acres. Was Nickerson buried out there somewhere? Maybe turning up his vehicle would provide an answer—if it wasn't already a cube of rusting steel. But time was ticking away. Michelle Nickerson had been alive to make a phone call last night. I prayed she still was. Any chance I had of finding her had to start with selling Vin Delcastro that I had something solid. The young desk officer I got on the phone told me that the chief was on the job, Ferry, too—out by the lighthouse, she thought.

I could have taken it easier on the curves. The officer had asked if I wanted her to relay a message, but I hadn't. Delcastro's knowing I was looking for him would only put his ruff up. I wanted an element of surprise. Ahead, I could see the lighthouse, sending its warning out into the rainy dark. As I neared, I came upon a pair of police cars. A speed trap, probably. One cruiser had its lights going, and there was an officer standing alongside it, wearing a rain jacket. I drew up and stopped. It was Ferry. His face had taken on a sharper cast than ever before, alternately shadowed and then washed with blue and white lights from his rooftop strobes. For the first time, he didn't look like just a boy playing dress-up. I climbed out.

"What's the occasion?" I called.

Ferry seemed to have glued his shoes to the ground. He was whey-faced. He looked at me, though I had the distinct feeling I wasn't registering. I glanced toward the second cruiser. No lights going on that one. I looked back at Ferry for an explanation, but he said nothing. The very act of standing seemed to be taxing his reserves. I gave the second cruiser another look and walked toward it. The small number "I" painted on the side confirmed that it was Delcastro's car. The chief was at the wheel. I went nearer, and as I did, I heard a crunch and looked down to see that I was stepping on broken glass. I glanced back at Ferry, who was watching me, but he gave me no sign.

Delcastro, too, ignored me when I tapped on his side window. He sat with his head resting on the brace pad. I'd seen it often enough in Lowell, beat officers catnapping behind a mill building. His mouth even hung open as theirs sometimes did. I leaned close to peer through the rain-streaked glass.

The backup I'd hoped for was null and void. He wasn't sawing logs. In the steady wash of light from the other cruiser's headlights, I saw that blood had run down onto the front of Delcastro's uniform shirt. There was a gaping wound beneath his chin, and his cheeks looked swollen. He wore a freshly laundered uniform, one with several decorations on it. He'd hooked on his aviators, and donned his cap. He needn't have, of course. With fluids and gristle and bone debris, with sphincters letting go, and flesh lumping and going gray, he wasn't going to pass any inspection.

The bullet's impact had jarred the aviators askew and addled his cap in the process of boring a hole through the soft tissues of his mouth, through the firewall of bone, into the serious business the bullet was designed for, and ultimately had passed through the back window of the cruiser, taking out a small web of safety glass, which I'd stepped on. His eyes were open in a confused expression of surprise and recognition. He'd been dead before the blast would've faded from the air. *If a gun went off in a parked car, and there was no one around to hear it . . . ?*

I felt a spin of nausea, a wrench of remorse. Delcastro had tried to straight-arm me, but then I'd crowded him a little bit, too. He hadn't been a bad guy. Probably he'd made mistakes, but he'd made them early and had found a way to live with them and keep some honor. It was what cops did when they got protective about a town they liked, especially a town with secrets they felt a need to protect. And every town and city had them: secrets and torn cops. The average citizen never saw it, but it was there, and the knowing wasn't always an easy knowledge. I'd kidded Ed St. Onge about it, but there was a brotherhood—and now a sisterhood, too—of cops. Peace officers whenever they could be, but sometimes they had to adopt other means. And I grasped that, as well. When you were sworn and wore the badge and the sidearm, you became different from other people; you were someone working out there on the edge on a thin sliver of nerves and courage and training, burdened by the perpetual misunderstanding of everyone else and your own flawed understanding of things around you. You wore death on your hip, and you were sometimes asked to make split-second decisions that saved lives or took lives away, also. Scrap the hype and the masturbatory bullshit fantasy of power, and there really was a thin blue line.

The Ford's doors were locked. At the scrape of boots on wet gravel, I stepped back.

"I've called it in," Ferry said, clearing his throat to take the hoarseness out of his voice. It didn't want to go. "He was shot."

"Yeah," I said.

He dropped to his hands and knees, and I had the idea that he was going to vomit, or pray. But he was moving his fingertips around on the wet gravel and the broken glass, like a man reading Braille. "What are you doing?"

"Searching for spent casings. Whoever did this stood about here."

"Hey," I said softly, "come on." I reached to help him up, but he shook me off and rose on his own.

"I want the shooter! Look there." He pointed to a large round hole in the glass.

"I think you'll find that's an exit hole."

He stared at me in accusation and then horror. "But the door's locked and . . ." He moaned. I almost thought he was going to lean on me for support—he was so close I could smell his English Leather. After a moment, he seemed to pull himself partway together.

"I don't know how you want to run it," I said. "Your dispatcher is going to put this out. The press is going to pick it up PDQ, and there's no way it'll play as anything but what it is. You with me?"

He stared but did not speak.

"You'd be stupid to try," I said. "You can maybe come up with a statement that'll make things easier for his family, the town, whatever. Not so easy on you, maybe. Unless I'm wrong, Delcastro was probably a pretty good boss, with a solid résumé of public service."

Ferry stood slack-jawed and hollow-eyed. Nothing in his textbooks and seminars had readied him for this, or ever could. "Have you got a key?" I asked.

"Key?"

"For his car." He fished one out of a pouch on his belt. I unlocked and opened the door. The gun was in Delcastro's hand, which hung at his side, a 9-mm or 10-mm, shiny with blood. Blood had snaked down under his shirtsleeve and ran in a maroon thread across his stiffening fingers. Touching nothing inside, I glanced around for a note, perhaps a hastily torn page from a pocket notebook. I drew the door wider. Ferry saw and took the view numbly for a moment, though it more or less cinched that the wound was self-inflicted. "Cato, falling on his sword," I murmured.

"What?" It wasn't worth a replay. He cleared his throat again, but the hoarseness had settled in to stay. "Why?"

Was he being dense? Then I realized he was looking for a bigger answer. I thought: Read it yourself. Delcastro is telling us now. Not in words, but there, in the fresh uniform, the cap, the medals. Even in the choice of setting perhaps, a beacon sending a lonely message out into darkness. It bespoke a sense of pride that he'd seen eroded. Delcastro tried to work a compromise with his integrity, and maybe he'd finessed it to fit, but then Nickerson had come to town, and I'd come around asking questions, nosing into things that didn't want disturbing, and in the end Delcastro hadn't been able to hang on.

Unlike a Grady Stinson, who would whine and blame others till his final old-age breath and still be clueless, Delcastro had kept a personal and professional honor. But there is no acid so corrosive as our fallen estimation of our once-good name. No slow slide down into the lush life for him, no excuses, and no note—not here, at least. There might be something elsewhere, a loving word for his family, or for the citizens of his town, whose welfare and safety he'd always had in mind and who probably took him for granted, never thinking to question him or ask how *he* was doing, really doing, deep down, because cops were not thought to be vulnerable in the way other people are. But he'd succumbed to temptation: a temptation that had come from only one hand, and I knew whose. I could blame myself—hell, there was blame to go around—but I saw a hand pointing as directly as the hand on the stairway at the town hall, or the bloody hand there in the car. I confirmed with Ferry that backup was indeed on the way, then I started toward my car.

"Mr. Rasmussen?"

He looked lost there in the pin-wheeling lights with his raincoat and his polished boots. "What . . ." He cleared his throat. "What do I do now?"

"You're doing it. Some flares by that curve might be a good idea. Secure the scene, and hang on until backup arrives." Which wouldn't be long; I could hear already the impressive whine of a fast-approaching siren. "Good luck."

"Sir?"

I turned again.

"That information you asked me to check . . . the autopsy report—I found it."

Our gazes locked a moment, and I saw his almost imperceptible nod and I knew that he was going to be okay—different from yesterday, when he'd been five years younger—but okay. The jitters were steadying.

"What does it say?"

He nodded toward his cruiser. "It's on the front seat."

It was in a large envelope, which I took to my vehicle and opened. It didn't take long to read, but then I didn't have to read far before one sentence grabbed me. For a moment, I stared at it with a growing sense of understanding, then I put the report back into the envelope and set it aside. The past was unraveling faster than I'd imagined it might. I'd been a lot younger yesterday, too. It was the looming present, however, that I had to concern myself with now.

38

At Nantasket Beach I parked half a block beyond the old Surf ballroom. Farther back, some of the arcades and juice joints were hopping, but this area was dark now, and deserted, as I'd hoped. The wet street was eerily still as I got out. I took the sawed-off shotgun out of the Blazer and shucked off its jacket of old newspapers. I dug a fistful of shells out of the box I'd got from Charley Moscowitz and loaded two into the breech and put the rest in my pocket. I had my .38 in its snap-on holster, and I had a flashlight. Carrying the old shotgun like a talisman, I climbed over the seawall to the sand and went down the beach. The tide was a long way out, the ocean visible only in pale lines frothing almost noiselessly in the rainy darkness.

I checked to see that the crates were still where they'd been. They were undisturbed. I set myself up in the shadows at the side of the building, out of the chill mist as best I could, and squatted against the wall and waited. I didn't know exactly what I was waiting for. Somehow it seemed an alternative to *acting,* and maybe that's why I was there, though something told me that Delcastro's final act had links that tied to here in some way and that energies were in motion. Except for the occasional swish of a car going past on the road, invisible from where I was, things were quiet. And cold. I drew my coat closer to me. Midsummer, and I was cold.

A mistake. That's what I realized after ten minutes. I was in the wrong place. And this thought brought relief. I was out of harm's way. My heart began to pump slower. The rain was thinning, too. I actually felt warmer. It was time to get the authorities involved.

Then I heard the low thrum of an engine. I craned a look toward the road, but it was empty. I realized then that the sound was coming from the ocean. I listened, but it stayed out there, in the darkness. A fishing boat?

I jumped when a voice called my name. I jerked around to see a figure in dark clothing move from the shadows of the seawall, not ten feet away. "Alex," he repeated. It was Ed St. Onge. He hurried over and hunkered down beside me.

"This isn't New Mexico," I said in lieu of something more revealing. I wanted to hug him. "How'd you know I'd be here?"

"I didn't. I guess I wanted to check out those guns for myself."

"I'm not sorry to see you."

"I've got enough murders back in Lowell to worry about," he grumbled. "Like I'm eager to go hunting out of town for more."

"Who said anything about murder?"

"Good, let's keep it that way. I'm glad you're alive." He had on what looked like an army and navy store raincoat. He was staring at the dilapidated building at our backs, with its graffiti and chalky stucco facade. "When you mentioned the name on the phone, it didn't click. I thought this place was history years ago." There was wonderment in his voice. "I heard Bobby Vee sing 'Blue Velvet' here."

"Vinton," I said.

"What?"

"Bobby Vinton sang 'Blue Velvet.' "

"Who's Bobby Vee?"

"He sang 'Take Good Care of My Baby.' "

He went back to recalling. "On a warm night, the doors would be open in front here. Often as not, somebody'd bite a knuckle sandwich and spit blood from a fat lip. A few kids would drink too much warm Schlitz and puke in the sand, and the local make-out king would get to third base with the local falsie queen in the front seat of his dad's station wagon and go home feeling like he'd been jocked."

"Thanks for the memories," I said.

"It's a whole crazy other world now." He shook his head, clearing it. "I called your man Delcastro, he wasn't in."

I told him what had gone down. His face creased into grim lines, and his eyes probed mine. "I think he caught a whiff of pending trouble," I said.

"Was he on the take?"

"I don't think he was palming cash. Gifts to the department in the form of the equipment and cars would've made it a lot easier to take, but the end result, yeah. I think Delcastro was beholden to Ted Rand. I think he obstructed an unexplained drowning investigation years ago. Maybe he intimidated a witness. It sat in the way of acting now."

"I'm liking all this less and less."

"Yeah. When's the cavalry supposed to show?"

"He's here." I gawked at him. "I didn't call ATF," he said. "You made the point pretty well."

"I was going to tell you the same."

"What are friends for?" He nodded at the sawed-off propped beside me. "Aren't you going to introduce us?"

The gun was as illegal as it could get. He could've busted me on the spot and sent me up. I winced. "I didn't know what I might run into."

"Neither did I." From the folds of the raincoat he pulled a riot gun.

It was a great comeback, and I let him enjoy it. Then I said, "Is that from the LPD armory?"

"Shh."

"But you're not official."

"My shield and ID are in my desk drawer back in that city where this widow maker belongs. Where you and I belong," he said emphatically.

I relaxed a little more. "Then let's make this easy. Let's go in and get those crates, and you can deliver them to ATF on your way home."

He nodded. We started forward, and just then, someone emerged from the shadows by the seawall farther down to the left, jogging toward the water. He evidently hadn't seen us. He stopped some fifty feet down the beach and blinked a flashlight at the ocean twice. The motor, which I'd heard earlier and which had faded into an almost inaudible hum, revved up, and lights came on a short distance offshore. Something in the pattern of the lights was familiar . . . and then I knew why. It was the same pattern I'd seen on the beach in front of the rental house two nights ago in the fog, lights that had vanished before I could tell where they came from.

"What the hell . . ." St. Onge whispered beside me.

A craft was emerging from the surf, coming right up onto the beach, like some sea monster from Japanese television. I realized suddenly that it was an amphibious duck. The only place you saw them anymore was rolling through Boston, full of tourists. But this wasn't here for a tour. It growled up the incline on knobby oversized tires, lights glaring, and drew to a stop where the man with the flashlight stood. I could hear voices, but I couldn't make out words. Then the man with the flashlight swung it toward the abandoned building with a quick jab, and the duck chugged our way.

I shifted position and felt St. Onge do the same at my side. Through the glare of lights it was impossible to know who or how many were on the duck. It stopped ten feet from the back of the Surf, and the headlights died. Two men jumped down to join the man on the beach. Both of the newcomers were carrying assault weapons—fun little numbers that looked like TEC-9s.

"For the record, it's not cops," St. Onge whispered. "I checked."

Maybe I'd hoped it was, hoped that this could all be explained and make sense and turn out okay.

The man with the light blinked it again, and the duck backed off a distance to become just a dark shape in the spectral mist. The three men hurried toward the rear of the building. Soon we could hear the chirp of boards being popped loose. They came off a lot easier than they had for me.

I kept scanning the scene, trying to determine if there was a teenage girl with them, maybe still in the duck. I was wondering if this was a gunrunning and kidnap ring of some kind. I didn't know how many people were still aboard; there had to be at least one. We had only the advantage of surprise. The man with the light held it on the corroding stucco wall as one of the others yanked at a final board, which squawked feebly, as if tired of keeping its secret, and let go. The men stared into the black hole a moment, evidently debating who got to play tunnel rat.

"Recognize any of them?" St. Onge whispered.

Yeah, white males between the ages of twenty and sixty. I shook my head. The two with the TEC-9s slung them and crawled into the opening. The man with the light stayed outside, playing the beam into the hole. The amphib stood by, rumbling in the fog. St. Onge nudged me. "One more thing." He handed me a pair of heavy latex gloves, the kind that evidence techs wore, along with practically everyone else in these days of contamination paranoia. But germs were last on his list of worries. "In case someone wants to scrape together a trail later."

The gloves made tiny squeaks of protest as I pulled at them, then they encased my hands like new skin. In a moment, the two men emerged, grunting with effort as they dragged out the first crate. The outside man lowered his weapon to give them a hand. I was suddenly thinking about what I'd told Van Owen, how inertia sometimes settled around you like wet sand, and when a time came to take action, you no longer could. It was my show. I stood up and flashed my light in their direction and shouted, *"Police! Freeze!"*

There were probably a half dozen better ways to handle it. I'm sure that the textbooks they study in the criminal justice programs at universities had recommended approaches. Mine might appear as a little sidebar: the bad example. But textbooks are rarely written by people who ever have to do what they write about. And I didn't know what the hell else to say. I did know that if that's *all* I said, you might as well tag our toes and put us in cold storage right now. I was aware of St. Onge darting to his left, away from me, perhaps wanting to give an illusion of numbers. I killed the flashlight, not eager to be a ready target from the duck, and stepped nearer so as to make the double-bore twelve-gauge visible. "You're surrounded," I shouted. "Don't move."

The man with the light swung it toward the duck, slashing it in a signal. Suddenly, the amphib's headlights came up, like klieg lights blistering a stage. I flung my arm up to block the glare, but even so I felt my night vision shrivel. A silhouette with a TEC-9 started back into the hole under the Surf. Ed's riot gun barked, and the man went down headfirst. I could make out the other two scrambling for their weapons. Dropping the flashlight, I dived toward the seawall, rolling as I hit the sand. Their assault weapons went *pop-pop-pop* and chips of concrete flew.

The duck's motor gunned, and the vehicle came churning up the slope of beach like an ungainly sea monster, flinging damp sand from its knuckled tires. I could just make out a man standing behind the low windshield holding a rifle. A thin red laser beam cut across the stucco wall, seeking out, then finding, St. Onge, who crouched near the building. I drew the .38 and sent fire toward the duck. The vehicle swiveled abruptly, like a Tonka Toy in the grip of a heavy-handed kid in a sandbox, and closed on me fast. I saw the laser streak out like an angry finger, zipping across the seawall at my back.

New technology has its place, but so does old. I snatched up the sawed-off. It was from 1928, and who knew but what the barrels would peel back like bananas, but I didn't ponder it long. The staccato popping of the assault weapons was firecrackers; the shotgun's boom was dynamite. One blast knocked the duck's windscreen apart about where I imagined a driver to be. The second blast earned a scream. The assault rifles on the ground fired a burst, then fell silent. In the dark, I saw two men dart for the craft and get behind it as St. Onge fired his riot gun in a quick series of blasts whose sound alone would've quelled a Third World rebellion. I heard the rounds thunk into heavy wood and whine off steel. One of the men flopped in the sand and lay still. I knocked down a second, who got up again and scrambled up into the duck. As Ed reloaded, the duck started to grind toward him.

I fumbled two more shells into the sawed-off.

The duck was coming right at St. Onge. I raised the shotgun and fired. It kicked at me like an angry horse. The man who'd leaped

aboard levitated, was flung sideways, and rolled off the vehicle, but
his foot must've snagged. He was dragged bouncing along the hard
sand. Whoever was inside didn't notice or didn't care. The vehicle
swerved and St. Onge was clear. But as it passed him, someone inside shot him in the chest, and he went down. I ran toward him,
firing the last round. The craft swung in a tight arc, its tires throwing sand, ribbing the beach with the tread tracks I'd noticed earlier,
and rolled toward the water. The way the man flopped, I knew his
bones were broken into pieces. At the water's edge, the body hit a
piece of driftwood or a large rock, gave a final bounce, and was
flung aside.

I got to St. Onge. He was facedown on the sand, his arms curled
under him as if he'd brought them together to cover his wound,
which I couldn't see. He lay still. I dropped to my knees beside him.
I called his name and got no reply. I debated for just one second,
then I rolled him carefully over. He felt limp as a sack of sand. The
front of his coat was ripped and wet. Feeling helpless all at once, I
looked up the beach toward the road, wondering what to do. I could
hear only the diminishing chug of the amphib.

St. Onge coughed. With a moan, he sat up.

I grabbed him. "I thought you were—"

"Aren't I?" He gazed around. "*Some*thing hit me."

But there was no blood. A round had evidently lodged in the
thick leather of his shoulder harness, and another had ripped his
coat's shoulder, but he wasn't hurt.

With vast relief, I helped him up. He wobbled a little as he tried
to walk, but then he caught on. We checked the two men on the
sand; they weren't as lucky. St. Onge looked at me. "Either one of
them your guy?"

They were strangers. The third man rolled in the surf—a few
feet in, a few feet out—but he wasn't Ted Rand either. I got my
feet wet hauling him above the reach of the waves.

"You okay?" St. Onge asked.

My knees were gimpy. "Yeah."

"Me too."

It wasn't the whole truth for either of us, but it was a start.

The Sand Bar was only slightly busier than the first time I'd been there. The yin/yang philosopher looked up as we went in. If I thought he had answers to fill my needs right then, I'd have been glad to listen, but what I really needed was a drink. Maybe a chug-fest was in order. Ed and I moved to a table in a far corner. My shoes made squelching sounds. If we had been official, SOP would've required that forms be filled out, ballistics checked on all the weapons used, probably some kind of posttraumatic-stress counseling, and a full internal investigation. If we were official. Instead, we'd gathered up our weapons. I found the flashlight mashed flat. We dragged the crates of weapons back into the space where they'd been to get them out of sight. I didn't think anyone would be coming back for them tonight. We peeled off the latex gloves and stashed our own weapons in the trunks of our vehicles.

The bartender came over. "I remember you," he said. "Olde Mr. Boston." He grinned.

"Yeah."

"You look pale. You ought to get some rays."

"A couple drinks will have to do for now." I glanced at St. Onge.

"V.O. double and a Bud," he said.

"Two," I said.

"That'll work also," agreed the barman.

When he'd gone to get them, I said, "Maybe I should've just let them take the guns."

"They were selling death in the streets. They weren't going to lie down."

"I could have walked away when I found the boxes. It wasn't what I was after. I didn't have to call you."

"How would you calculate the body count then? Not here, not today, but you can bet it'd be high." He held out a hand, palm down, and I saw it tremble. "But we put some bad guys out of business."

"A few permanently."

He nodded grimly. "But we also clipped whoever in the staties made this possible. He won't be able to hide. Unless he's shark food already, his ass is grass. He'll get pinched."

But Rand was smoke. Grab your metaphor. And maybe I'd blown everything. Maybe Rand had killed Michelle Nickerson when he'd killed her father—*had* them killed. No, I wedged that thought away. Why would he kill her? She was no threat. But I didn't know. I didn't have her.

"Here you be, gentleman." We took the drinks. The barman slid a glance at St. Onge, and then leaned toward me. "Don't tell me it's not a flat earth, brother. One day we all of us reach that horizon and go over into the void. In the meantime, do good where you can. I thought about what you asked me when you were in before. I recognized him."

I stared, then got it. "The guy Jillian was with when you saw her last?"

"Uh-huh. I must've blocked it out, like a defense mechanism against reliving pain."

I glanced at St. Onge, who was concentrating on his drink, then back. "What pain are you talking about?"

"The humiliation of playing against Point Pines—it's like a conspiracy against every other team in the league. They crush us every time. The guy plays for them." He set the drinks tray on the table and lifted a framed photograph from it. "Here he is here, the son of a bitch—getting an MVP award."

St. Onge kept out of it. I scanned the photo he had removed from the wall behind the bar—it was an end-of-season banquet, all right, and Ted Rand was there at the table with his players. "This guy here?" I said, touching the picture glass.

"That's him."

I was confused. It wasn't Ben Nickerson. "You're sure he's the one she was with a few nights before her crash?"

"A few *nights*? I'm talking a few hours. He left with Jilly that same night."

I stared again at Mr. Softball, at his sturdy, suntanned face, with its shaggy hair, and I recognized him even without the mirror shades.

39

I drove out to the Old Cape Road, through the lonely slack-water places, and in the stillness the old Surf ballroom seemed far behind. St. Onge had looked questioningly at me when the bartender took his photograph back, but I didn't offer an explanation of what the cryptic exchange had meant, and Ed didn't ask. He had already shoved his neck way out. "I've got to get back to Standish," I told him. "Can you handle things here?"

"An anonymous pay-phone call to the local heat is the extent of my involvement, then I'm out. I still haven't packed for vacation."

He cut off my thanks with a wave. I left money for the drinks, and a five-dollar tip. So the cop named Shanley was the softball player who'd approached Jillian Kearns in the parking lot of the Cliff House and who'd been with her after she and I had parted at the lighthouse. That was interesting, but what it might signify would have to wait. Something else was beginning to knock at the back of my mind as I got in the Blazer. "Like a conspiracy against us," the barman had said. He'd been speaking metaphorically, about a softball dynasty, but it reminded me of something I hadn't given any thought to until now.

Of course, maybe it was just goofy foot.

There was no one in the motel office, so I went around to the small house in back. The rain had stopped. I glanced at the dog pen and saw that Gruff was gone. After a minute of my knocking, Fran Albright came to the door looking puzzled. "Hi," she said.

"Is your father here?"

"I don't know where he is. I just got home a while ago." She glanced past me. "Is it still raining?"

"It stopped."

"He went out this afternoon. I'm a little surprised he's still out." I was, too, given his fear of spy satellites and phantom helicopters. Fran was looking closely at me, her brow knit. "Is something wrong, Mr. Rasmussen?"

Wrong? Things were as wrong as they could be. People were dead, and I'd helped some of them get that way. Time wasn't on my side, and now I was entertaining wiggy notions of how her father's idea of a grand conspiracy might in fact have a basis right here in this town. I stepped nearer to her there in the door, wanting to form some intimacy between us. "Fran . . . did you know that your sister was pregnant when she drowned?"

She blinked several times. "What?"

"It was in the autopsy report. Three months."

"But that's . . . impossible. She . . . she . . ." Fran broke off, gaping at me from her doorstep. "You've actually seen this report?"

"Yes. Your parents must have seen it, too."

"My God. She never . . . They . . ."

She was reeling with the revelations, unable to pick up a cohesive thread. I let out a breath, not sure what else to say. The tiny housekeeping cottages in back were as dark as ever, obscured by the jungle of sumac growing around them. "Do you have any idea where your father is?"

She shook her head blankly. She stepped outside and moved closer to me, as if feeling a sudden need for companionship. I was reluctant to leave her. I lifted my chin in the direction of the cottages, just to shift the subject. "How long since those have been used?"

She squinted toward the units, as if she'd lost track of their existence. "Years and years. Dad let them go while I was living in Colorado. Too much upkeep and not much demand."

I nodded. "I've got to go. Will you be okay?"

"Years ago, it was the way families traveled. Rent a little place for a week, and move in. This time of year, folks would sit in front and talk—there was no air-conditioning, just the sea air. Kids played in the yard because it was safe, there was no traffic . . . it was nice," she said quietly, and for a moment I wished with all my might that the world could be rolled back to that simpler time. But it couldn't. I started for the Blazer.

"Ginny and I would play flashlight tag with the kids, and blindman's bluff," Fran went on in a quickened voice, moving with me. "Now people on vacation want conveniences, and children play at video arcades. These places are totally forgotten, like those games we played as kids."

I had the Blazer's door open and was about to get in, but I stopped. "I thought your father got this place much later?"

"Dad was a schoolteacher when we were little, but summers he and Mom managed the motel for Mr. Rand. Dad bought it only later, after—" She broke off.

"After your sister drowned."

She looked at me quizzically, which was probably the way I was looking at her. I looked again at the cottages. "Do you have a flashlight?" I said. "I seem to have lost mine."

Together we walked back toward the cottages. What had been the parking area was just crumbled paving, the pine needles and gravel making soft sounds under our feet. A sway-backed picnic table stood rotting nearby. There were nine cottages, arranged in a semicircle in a grove of sumac and second-growth pines that dripped with the recent rain. The last two cottages were almost completely overrun with honeysuckle. "Forgotten" was what Fran had called them, as Van Owen had called the road out here. It seemed as if Standish's collective memory was faulty; it had forgotten a lot.

The cottages had once been white with green shutters, but time had painted everything in shades of gray, and now the night added dark tones. The roofs sagged with the load of years. Shutters hung crookedly on rusted hinges. I could see bird nests in the broken window screens. There were padlocks on the doors. Stepping forward through a surf of damp leaves, I shone the light into the first building and saw only emptiness. I glanced toward the other cottages.

"What is it, Mr. Rasmussen?" Fran Albright asked at my back, her voice with a little underlay of tension now. "Is there something you're looking for?"

Was it history? Explanations? Understanding? I didn't know. Honeysuckle gave its fragrance to the wet air.

The second cottage was the same as the first, and the third, too. In the next cottage, the light beam roved across old mattresses stacked on their sides like vertical slices of moldy bread, the striped ticking had split open in places, stuffing protruding. Farther in was the suggestion of stored furniture: dim angles and bulky shapes. The door was dry-rotted, and the hasp and lock were rusted. The screws pulled out as I applied pressure to the panel, and the door *rawked* open. I looked over my shoulder at Fran Albright. For a beat of edgy silence, our eyes met; then I pushed the door wider and stepped inside. She stayed with me.

Motes of dust drifted in the flashlight beam, and an odor of mildew filled my nostrils. A strand of sticky web stretched against my cheek, then snapped. I brushed it aside and stepped farther in, pushing past the image of some jaunty Jolly Roger of a spider hurrying down the broken strand, eager to sink fangs into whatever had invaded its fine and private place. Beyond the stacked mattresses, the beam found a rounded contour that gleamed dully. It was the corner of an old steel bed frame. I sidestepped nearer and saw an old gray blanket, humped with folds and wrinkles. As I reached for it, my scalp gave an odd, premonitory tingle. I lifted a corner.

Beside me, Fran Albright drew a sharp breath and clapped her hands to her cheeks. Then I saw it, too. Under the old blanket, tied with a faded red bandanna, was a dark mass of what could have been hair. Fran's eyes were wide, agleam in the faint peripheral glow of the flashlight. Motioning her to stay back, I drew the blanket all the way off.

She screamed. She cupped her hands over her mouth, as if to cut it off, but it came anyway, a shrill cry ending in a strangled gasp. *"Oh my God!"* She turned, bumped into one of the mattresses, sending up a plume of dust, and fled.

Her screams had sliced across my nerves like a serrated knife. I wanted to go, too, but I stepped closer to the old bed and shone the light. I felt as if I was studying one of those projective images, where you sometimes have to look and look before you finally see the dual image of a young woman and an old hag. I saw it now, a body— actually, skeletal remains. Most of the flesh was gone. The clothing had fared somewhat better, as had the hair, and I judged from these that the body was that of a girl. She was hunched in an almost fetal posture, as if she'd wanted to give herself comfort. I forced myself to squat by the mattress and look more closely.

The remains had been here a long while. Exposed to heat and cold and time, they had become mummified. What was left had a dark, sinewy texture, shiny like old greased leather. The fingers were claws. I saw no sign of jewelry or a handbag or other personal effects. I scanned the surrounding area, quickly looking for anything that might help me make sense of what we'd found. Then I turned and went outside to Fran Albright.

She clutched her hands before her as if she were about to pray. Seeing me, she gave an odd little laugh, then she moaned. "Oh, my God, don't let this be happening. Oh, please, God, no." She seemed to be on the brink of hysteria.

I put an arm around her. She bucked, as if she wanted to run, but she didn't. After a moment, she pushed her face against my chest, and I held her. When she'd steadied a bit, she stepped back. "What . . . what is that?" she asked, her voice throbbing. "It's not the . . ."

"No. I think it's a runaway girl who vanished years ago. A hitch-hiker." I didn't go into details. That would be for the ME and the police to establish. I took Fran Albright's hand, which was cold as death, and led her farther away.

It wasn't the same mild summer night we'd left. The pine trees were menacing shapes, dark and spiky, that crowded near. Something foul had erased the honeysuckle sweetness. Wet brambles clawed at our clothing, and the silence was spooky with threat.

"Does . . . does my father know it's here?"

"I don't know," I said. But I was pretty sure I did. I led her back to her house and we went inside. "Where does your father keep his guns?"

She led me to a cabinet in another room. The door was locked, but she got a key and opened it. John Carvalho had himself a regular little arsenal: several deer rifles, an assortment of handguns, even a powerful-looking hunting bow. The Colt Python that he had taken with him the last time was missing. In one of the drawers below, I found boxes of ammunition, including .38s, and I reloaded the Smith & Wesson. Wordlessly, she watched. When I'd stashed an extra handful of rounds in my pocket and put the box away, I said, "Your father has scanners, here and in his car. Does he monitor police radio traffic?"

"Sometimes. He's kind of . . . afraid of police."

I nodded. "I've got to leave for a while, Fran." Her eyes went round with fright. "I'm going to try to prevent anything worse from happening," I said, hearing the hollowness of my words. I considered taking her with me, but I knew it would only add risk that I couldn't afford. "I don't think you're in danger, but I want you to telephone the police and get someone to come out here as soon as they can make it."

"Can't you do it?"

"It's best if I don't."

"Who should I talk to?"

"Anyone you get. They're dealing with other things right now, but be persistent. Tell them we may have found a girl who disappeared in town six years ago."

"That must've been when I was in Colorado. I don't remember it."

"They will. Can you handle it?"

She didn't seem quite sure. I took her hands in both of mine and held them, trying to put some warmth in them. "Make the call, Fran," I said gently. "I'll wait." She was motionless for a moment, uncomprehending, I feared, but then she nodded and went into the kitchen. I watched her move among the high stacks of old newspapers and magazines, as if she were fading into the past. I listened until I heard her speaking to the police, then I left and hurried toward the Blazer.

40

I tried to retrace the route that John Carvalho had driven in his heap two nights ago. I wasn't sure of the way, but I felt I was on the right track, my instincts honed sharp by adrenaline, and before long I came upon the old barn set back from the road, and I drew in. Leaving the headlights on, I got out. Bats fluttered through the air above the tilted cupola. Ahead stood the boat on a cradle; with the wind moving in the high grass, it appeared to be underway in a rolling sea. In the glow of the headlights, I walked along the path and came to the sand road that led out to Shawmut Point. The cable was down and I could make out dry tire grooves in the damp sand, where a vehicle had recently passed.

Back in the Blazer, I engaged the four-wheel drive and shut off the lights. Between the expanses of clearing night sky, sand, and ocean, there was enough visibility to maneuver by, and as I did, my mind's eye kept panning back to the human remains lying in the cottage, scanning it for something I might have seen but not noticed. It was one of the cop skills I'd once possessed.

Soon, ahead of me in the gloom, I could make out a row of houses, including one that Rand had owned, which would shortly be torn down to make way for the final phase of Point Pines. I tried for a moment to imagine this place as it must once have existed, pristine, with a margin of low trees and long stretches of dunes and empty beach. Off to one side was Carvalho's old station wagon. It hadn't needed a hidden kill switch to bring it to a halt. I could see that the wheels were sunk to the hubs in the soft sand. I got out and went over to the car. It was empty and unlocked. I opened it. The interior held the aromas of dog and the old man's fear. I glanced around. I tried the glove box, but it was locked, or jammed. Using my key, I pried the edge down enough to get a hold and I yanked the lid open. Inside, among old maps and papers was a cell phone. I was surprised; it didn't seem like technology Carvalho would trust. I pressed the power button, but it was dead. And now I was pretty sure why Paula Jensen's calls to her daughter had never reached her. I slid the phone into my pocket.

From beyond the row of houses, I could hear the sound of the surf rolling against the slope of outer beach. I was sick of the ocean. I wanted a desert, a barren land without people and problems. I approached the last house, which sat slightly apart from the others.

It was like finally seeing a place that you've only heard about in stories. It was the scene of TJ's and Red Dog's dark night of decision, where they'd played an adult game with booze and a gun, and pushed friendship to its limit. And it was the scene of harsh discovery for Iva Rand, where betrayal had slapped her in the face. There were probably a host of other memories, fond ones, of family and closeness and fun, and some bad ones, too, but I didn't know them. The house was unimpressive, in need of the TLC an occupying family would give it, but its family had moved on to other things and were scattered now, and the house was doomed to destruction to make way for bigger things. It was a small drab structure; the only splash of color was a cluster of old lobster buoys, which hung beside the door, like a corsage on a gray dress, though under starlight even they didn't offer much. I was ten feet from it when the door opened.

Gruff lunged out, tugging John Carvalho, who held the dog on a chain leash. In his other hand was the Python. He was holding it up, peering over the barrel of it at me. I raised my hands, the way

I had when old Vito had come into my office with the sawed-off. Had that been only a few days ago? It felt far longer. Carvalho stopped where he stood.

He was a massive, humped presence in his old work clothes, his large dog taut on its leash. "I could've killed you at any point coming in here," he said, his hoarse voice cracking.

"You didn't, and that's good. It tells a lot."

I was near enough to see large loops of perspiration darkening the shirt fabric under his arms. His forehead was clenched in tight furrows. I was trying to read what went on behind them, there within the vortexes of his dread and paranoia. Was there sickness? The kind that would lead to the torture and murder of a child? I tried to void the image of the body in the cottage, though it didn't want to go away. "I'm not here to hurt you," I said. "Or anyone. Put the gun down." I slid a glance at the dog, which stood rock-still, its eyes locked on me. I drew a slow breath and went nearer.

"Stop!"

From the other side of the low rise just beyond the house, the waves beat monotonously against the shore. "Let me take the girl," I said.

Carvalho's small, dark eyes showed no comprehension.

"She's here, isn't she?"

"What're you talking about?"

"She made a cell-phone call to her mother." Still he didn't move; so I applied whatever pressure a lie might bear. "I traced the call to here."

He shook his head firmly, and all of a sudden, I had my doubts. I even felt sympathy for him: his daughter had been taken from him, and it had cost him his wife. He'd been paid off with bad real estate and worse promises. "We can talk about this," I said.

"Why? You seem to have the answers." His voice sounded on the verge of a wail.

"I was slow in putting it together. I should've picked up on it when you first told me about the cameras at the nuke plant—that's not your only fear about being out here, is it? You've worried Rand might be watching you. You didn't want to be found out."

He hooked a thick forearm across his brow, mopping sweat.

"Come on," I said. "All this is negotiable."

"That's the trouble with the world. Everything is. Sentences for criminals, tax rates for the superrich, even grades for students . . . it's why I left teaching. Nothing's clear or sure anymore."

"It never was, Mr. Carvalho. Some people have just tried to convince us it was. But it's a lie."

"It's how they *want* it to be," he said with sweaty desperation. "I thought you were one of the smarter ones, who understood it. I tried to explain it to you."

I knew his riffs—eyes in the sky, Jews in Hollywood, Arabs running the gas pumps, alien encampments on the dark side of the moon . . . and an unholy high command pulling all the puppet strings. Or there was Rand, who owned Standish. They were simpler scenarios of the constant struggle of the good with the bad, courage with cowardice, all going on right inside our own selves. "Think," I said. "You haven't physically hurt anyone yet. Have you? Michelle Nickerson made a phone call last night. On this phone." I drew out the cellular unit I'd taken from his car. Sweat was streaming from my brow.

"You're not making sense," he mumbled.

"Tell me about the girl in the cottage behind your motel. The hitchhiker."

His eyes widened for an instant. He heaved a breath and seemed to recoil at the idea of my having found out, or at something else churning inside him. "When did you . . ." His voice almost broke.

"Just tonight," I said. "Fran knows, too. The police have been called."

Now he did moan. "She . . . I—I didn't hurt her. She walked into the office off the road one day. She'd been thumbing, she told me, and someone picked her up. The driver said he'd take her where she wanted to go, but instead he drove her to someplace and . . ." I could see his Adam's apple bobble in his thick throat. "Then he . . . kicked her out of his car, in the woods. When she came to the motel, she was scared to death. I let her stay in the cabin."

"You didn't go to the police, though. Or a hospital."

"She didn't want that. No. She was sick, and scared, so I let her stay a few days—we had those old cabins no one was using. I didn't know then it was drugs making her so sick."

"She overdosed?"

"I was so afraid. There were reports then that she was missing. She'd run away because her father was bad to her, she said. I gave her a place to stay. I . . . I didn't know. She stayed out there awhile and I . . . I didn't find her right away. I got very scared."

He looked it now, too: capable of rash and unreasoned action. I was scared, as well. "If true," I said, forcing myself to stay calm, "you've got nothing to worry about. Do you know who it was who picked her up?"

He shook his head.

"She didn't describe the person? Or a car?"

He shook his head again, as though stubbornly resistant to the idea that he might know.

"What about where he took her?"

"It sounded like someplace . . . remote."

"Out here?" I asked. "Perhaps as Ginny had been?"

He drew a harsh breath and seemed ready to explode, whether in tears or violent rage, I didn't know. "All right," I said. "All right. That's past. We have to talk about now. About Michelle Nickerson."

For a moment he didn't move. My fear had begun to gather. Then he backed up slowly and stepped inside the door, drawing the dog with him. As he turned from me for an instant, I drew my gun. I had the idea that stopping him would take considerable force. I didn't want to have to apply it—but I had to face the reality that I might be out of choices. I clutched the .38 by my side.

He left the dog inside. After just a moment, a young woman emerged, with Carvalho behind her, still holding his weapon. My heartbeat quickened. I knew who she was; not that she looked like any photograph I had of her—she looked haggard. She was older than the pictures, too. Her hair, once dyed black, was matted and showing its lighter roots. Her gothic garb had been exchanged for a pair of shapeless overalls and a Cape Cod sweatshirt that looked lived in.

"Michelle—it's going to be okay," I called, wanting it to be so.

Carvalho gripped her upper arm in one hand and pointed the Python at me with the other. It was as if the grand conspiracy he had feared in his soul, and thrilled to, had corroded the very structure of his world. Sweat was pouring off him. He glanced quickly skyward, then toward the light blinking feebly atop the Pilgrim nuclear plant across the bay to his right. He seemed disoriented.

"I'm not the Commission," I said, hoping he was capable of discernment. "But if this goes bad, the Tri-Lateralists win." I was talking to him in the terms of his delusions, but maybe it was the best chance any of us had of not ending up dead.

In the distance, a siren wailed. Carvalho glanced up in panic, and for an odd instant I was back in my office the day when Vito, the old pizza man, had come in holding a shotgun. A police car was coming out along the strand, not in sight yet, and there was time aplenty for this to go bad. Keeping the Python on me, Carvalho gave the girl a light shove. "Run!" She stumbled a few steps sideways, and stopped. She seemed to be coming out of a stupor. She blinked at him. "Go!" he croaked. She did, moving away from us in a run. I felt relief.

"You did right," I told Carvalho.

He suddenly looked startled and lifted the gun.

"Don't!" I yelled, though the word seemed to come like saltwater taffy, stretched out and torturously slow.

He paid me no attention, may not even have heard me over the distant hiss of surf. He started toward me, the weapon raised.

Growing up, I had watched Roy Rogers shoot the gun from an outlaw's hand at twenty yards. It was easy in TV-Land, and no one ever had to die.

"Stop right there," I shouted—another line for the textbook.

He lumbered forward. I lifted the .38 and fired. The shot went way wide, as I'd meant it to. Inside the house, the dog was barking furiously, throwing itself against a window. "Hands high!" I yelled at Carvalho (I was on a roll), but he didn't obey me this time either. I fired wide again.

He got the idea finally. He got down on his knees and laid the Python on the sand.

"Good," I said.

His eyes found mine and brightened for a moment; then he lay down sideways. I waded through the sand to him. I could see a dark froth on his lips and a quick-spreading stain on the front of his shirt. What? I'd missed him both times. Then, slowly, his eyes dimmed— perhaps in peace, as though in witness of something radiant and true—or perhaps they were seeing the storied descent of a human soul through circle after circle of hell. I gaped. I'd purposely missed, and yet he was dead. In the house, the dog was leaping at the window.

41

I'd been right. I *had* missed Carvalho. As I'd missed whatever muffled sound Ted Rand's gun had made behind me. He held a shiny automatic, the barrel lengthened by a suppressor. Carvalho's Python had been ridiculous, too, but at least he'd had the mitt for it. This looked too big and powerful for Rand's small hand. Still, he had been able to find the trigger just fine. He glanced at me and then walked over to Carvalho, who lay on his side, his lower legs bent, his face on the sand. "Poor deluded fool," murmured Rand.

He could've been talking about me. I looked up at the approaching sounds of people. One of them was Michelle Nickerson. The other was the cop, Shanley—Mirror Shades. He had them on now. Otherwise, he was dressed for night, in dark civilian clothing, and he was holding on to Michelle's arm. Her gaze went to the body sprawled on the sand, and her free hand came to her mouth, but she made no sound.

"I'll take that," Rand said to me, nodding at the .38. I hesitated and then handed it over.

"Are you all right?" I asked the girl.

She paid no attention. Her expression was one of dull horror.

"Leave her and go get the boat," Rand told Shanley. "Hurry."

Shanley glanced at us and then released the girl's arm. When she didn't move, he turned and jogged off over the dune.

Rand looked at Michelle Nickerson, but he didn't seem interested in her. For her part, she was oblivious to both of us. In the distance, though closer now, came the rising, falling sounds of sirens. Covering us with his shiny gun, Rand said, "Come on. We're taking a ride," and ushered us in the direction Shanley had gone.

"I'll go," I said. "Let her stay. Her parents may be in one of those cars."

Rand shook his head. "We all go."

"Why?" I said. "You didn't kidnap her."

"Keep moving."

"She's got nothing to do with your plans. Carvalho took you, didn't he, Michelle?" She glanced at me for the first time, but she didn't speak. I said, "Maybe he heard a police dispatch that had you walking along the road at night, and he wanted to take you in. Did he hurt you?"

She blinked and shook her head slowly. "He . . . he said I'd be safe out here. He thought something had happened to my dad. I . . . want to go home."

I looked at Rand. "Let her go."

"Can't. You're right—I didn't even know about her until you came to town asking questions. My business was with Ben. But she's fallen into it now. So have you. Move."

I was trying to find an approach to convince him it was useless to flee, that the gunrunning was out in the open now and he'd be tagged for it, and for killing Nickerson, and John Carvalho, too. But I wasn't going to be able to persuade him. Rand wasn't a person who spooked easily: he finagled and bought and soft-talked; he offered Faustian bargains, and when those weren't enough, he rode roughshod over anything or anyone foolish enough to be in his way. He burned out resisters, as he had Chet Van Owen, only to turn around and give him a job. He drowned a girl and deeded her father a worthless motel. He ransacked Indian graves, then built a museum for the bones. He was tough and sweet and as remorseless as a great white shark. He hadn't had anything to do with Michelle's disappearance, but that wasn't important to him now.

We heard a boat approaching, and Rand ushered us down a slope to where we could see the skiff coming ashore. Shanley gunned it in close, tilted the outboard motor, and ran the bow onto the beach. Rand motioned us toward it. "Let her go," I pleaded once more. "She can't do anything to stop you."

Rand pointed his gun at me. "Neither can you."

It was a punky old aluminum skiff with a newish outboard motor, no running lights. I saw a life jacket and some cushions. "Put on the jacket," I told Michelle as we sat on the middle seat. Rand didn't object. With zombie movements, she drew it on, snapped the buckles. Rand shoved the boat back out and jumped in and sat facing us. Shanley got the motor going and came about. "Head for the channel," Rand ordered. "That green light's our bearing."

Shanley gave the motor full throttle and we moved out quickly. I felt the skiff's flimsiness as it began to bang against the small waves. The motor was newer, but I wondered if it was the boat that Red Dog and Teddy Rand had gone out in with whiskey and a gun all those years ago to weigh their futures. It was part of my need to put all the pieces into a whole, even when they were of small consequence by now. Away from the shelter that Shawmut afforded, the wind spanked at us and the swells grew.

"The person who picked up that runaway girl," I said to Rand, "was it you?"

He looked at me with an expression of hatred. I had my answer. He waved the gun impatiently. "Keep quiet." I was forced to grip the seat as we bounced over swells. Back on the land, the flicker of lights signaled the approach of several vehicles moving through the scrub oaks, heading for the point, like a small cortege. I hoped that Fran Carvalho wasn't with them.

And with that thought, I realized how Rand and Shanley had come to be here. The cop had taken Fran's call at the station and pumped her for details about her dad's being gone. I turned slightly to look back at Shanley as he worked the outboard motor, gazing at me, *through* me. Who could tell with the glasses?

Rand crouched in the bow looking seaward, and I realized he had no intention of letting us go. Why would he? We were tools, possibly useful as bargaining chips, but ultimately he would kill us.

Or get Shanley to do it, the way I figured he'd gotten the cop to secure Jillian Kearns's silence.

Far out toward the horizon, I saw a boat. It was low and pale, and moving in our direction. Was that our destination? Was it coming for Rand? As it moved nearer, I recognized it as the boat that Van Owen and I had seen from the jetty, the boat from which someone had fired a warning shot at us. Rand shifted position, as if getting read to stand and hail it. Then, off to starboard, at the edge of my vision, something else caught my eye. A dark moving line. At first I thought it might be a second boat, but then I realized it was the churn of swift, rising water where the outflowing bay water and the cold incoming tide met. Where the blues feed, Red Dog had told me, and the stripers, and sometimes the sharks.

I realized the cruiser would spot us in a minute if it hadn't already, and then, who knew? I glanced at Michelle Nickerson, and she seemed to be aware of the boat, too. Hoping the motion was imperceptible, I angled my body slightly toward the rear. We were just reaching the outer rim of the swift water. Shanley throttled down as we edged into the current. I glanced back at him and saw the green flicker of the channel marker in the lenses of his glasses. I lunged at him. He tried to avoid me, giving the throttle an unintended twist as he did. The motor roared, and the boat lurched. I hit him hard in the face with one hand and with the other grabbed for the control. In front, Rand half-rose and swung his gun around. Michelle threw herself to the floor. Rand fired, and I saw the mirror sunglasses shatter, blown apart by the round that hit Shanley in the face. He flopped back against the motor housing like a broken doll. Michelle screamed. I just managed to turn the motor, and swung the boat sharply. Rand stumbled to catch his balance. The skiff took a wave broadside.

I had hoped the rising water would just be enough to upset things, to shift the power ratio, but I underestimated the current. The wave flipped the skiff up into the air and capsized us. As I broke the surface, something crashed against my neck and shoulders, and I went down.

42

In the dark ocean I didn't know which direction was up. Muted sounds came to me, and I kicked myself in their direction.

Michelle was already afloat when I came up ten feet away. The skiff was bottom up but going nose down. The shrilly whining motor chopped the air, burning itself out. I looked around for Rand, but I didn't see him.

The water was rougher than it had looked from the boat. I glanced around again for Rand. He'd bested me last time, nearly drowned me, but I hoped that without the element of surprise working for him, I could hold my own. I needed to give the girl a chance to get to land. I yelled to her to swim hard for shore. To my relief, she started to.

With my fear growing by the moment, I scanned the dark hills of water around me. I did a three-sixty. Rand wasn't there. Had he swum farther out, toward the powerboat? I no longer even heard the other boat. A thought grabbed me with an icy jaw. He'd gone after Michelle. He was a strong, quick swimmer; he could have already reached her. I bobbed on the next rising crest, and this time I saw no one.

I labored in the direction where I'd last seen Michelle, my heart hammering at my ribs, my head woozy with panic. But soon I could see her: she was alone, moving slowly shoreward.

I didn't waste precious breath trying to call to her. I followed.

After a very long time, I felt my feet touch bottom. Michelle was already wading ashore. There were cops on the beach, and Paula and Ross Jensen, too. Paula ran splashing right into the shallows to Michelle, and then Ross did, too, and the three of them hugged each other in a tight circle. I could hear both women sobbing with relief. I angled away and let them be. I waded ashore farther down and stood by, dripping on the sand, scanning the dark water for whatever might be there. In no time at all I was ringed by cops.

43

One morning on my way to my office I stopped by the city library and picked up a volume of Matthew Arnold's poems. I found "Dover Beach" easily enough. Ted Rand had known it by heart, all right, but when he'd talked about that dreamworld that lay before him, he hadn't recited the final lines. Arnold wrote that it:

> Hath really neither joy, nor love, not light,
> Nor certitude, nor peace, nor help for pain;
> And we are here as on a darkling plain
> Swept with confused alarms of struggle and flight,
> Where ignorant armies clash by night.

I read the poem through a couple times.

"Is this what you do up here all day? No wonder you stay so pale."

I looked up from the volume. I didn't need to see the dazzle of parrots and tropical flowers on his shirt to recognize the speaker. Red Dog Van Owen stood in the doorway looking weathered and salted and reasonably happy. "I wanted to see if this place really exists," he said.

"Satisfied?"

"Just as ratty as I'd imagined. I like it."

I rose to shake his hand, but he grabbed me in a grizzly hug and thudded my back. He smelled of the ocean and cigarettes. I got him seated in the client chair.

"You heard about them finding Ben?"

I had. His body had turned up under the golf course.

"What do you think happened to Rand?" he asked. "Think he got away?"

"I don't know. The water was pretty rough that night. On the other hand, he was a swimmer. Though I have to imagine that if he did get ashore, people are going to find him."

He nodded. "I visited Iva. She didn't want to see me at first, accused me of wanting to drink her booze, but I told her I wasn't taking any shit. We got to it. I let her know how it was from my angle, said I'd always thought she was a good mom to TJ. She ended up hugging me and crying."

"She's a tough shell over a tender lady."

"Yeah. She's not too sorry about Rand. She's been going over to the hospital to visit TJ. She said she'd reach me if there's any change."

"Is that likely?"

He chewed it a moment. "I guess I still think of him running a football on October afternoons."

"It's a good thing to remember."

He went over to the window and peered out onto brick walls and flat rooftops and chimneys. He watched a flock of pigeons wheel past. "How can you live so far from the water?"

"We've got six miles of canals and a big river two hundred yards out that window. You couldn't toss a rock across it on your best day. Supposedly it's got Atlantic salmon in it, and it empties into the ocean a day's walk east of here. That's water enough for me."

"I guess people can get used to anything."

"I guess, but there's a difference between choosing and just settling. This is a choice."

He turned, nodding. "I used to think Standish was, but it got too small . . . has been for a long time; I just didn't see it. Or maybe

I did and I didn't have the nerve to do anything about it."

"A hermit crab moves when it's time. Standish seems as good a place as any."

"Life goes on. They're looking for a new police chief." He raised his eyebrows.

"I don't look good in a blue baseball cap. A fedora's more my style."

"Yeah. I saw Mitzi Dineen running around like crazy doing her thing. And the high school looks like it'll have a decent football team for the first time in years."

"How's Fran Albright doing?"

"Fran's good. She sold that white elephant. Somebody wanted the land. They'll knock the buildings down. She's going to open a little coffee nook in town."

"As long as she charges the cops, she should do okay."

We went on for a few minutes, but he was growing restless, with Atlantic Casualty right behind. He picked up one of my cards and put it in his pocket. "Take a bunch," I said, "hand them out to everyone you see."

I walked him downstairs. We stood in the shadows of buildings, amid the scurry of passersby and the noise and fumes of traffic, and he looked around, checking out my city.

"And what about Standish's fabled surfer dude?" I asked. "Notice I saved him for last?"

"I'll be heading west in a few days. California, for a start. I'm looking for something different."

"A beach without footprints? You'll find it."

He lifted his head in a silent laugh. He didn't look so certain, but he seemed adjusted to trying. We shook hands. "If I do," he said, "I'll let you know; you can come visit. I'll teach you how to hang ten."

I couldn't cap it and didn't try. The image of that was too ludicrous to imagine.

August sunshine fell through the canopy of a clear afternoon sky, painting all the old buildings on Market Street in dusty hues. I stood outside the Ale House, waiting, when I saw a deep red Porsche Boxter pull up in front. Paula Jensen got out of the passenger side, and the car rumbled off. She was wearing a flower-print summer dress that showed her suntanned shoulders, and she moved with that coltish grace I'd seen the first time I'd met her. Spotting me, she smiled, and I reached to shake her hand, which she ignored and gave me a warm hug and a kiss. I think I glowed.

"Was that Ross?" I asked.

"He's going to find a parking spot. He'll join us."

"New car?"

"A gift to himself. His firm won that case." It had been in the papers, along with all the news about how Michelle Nickerson had been found safe, apparently sheltered against her will by a deluded man who'd believed her to be in danger. Part of his delusion, it was suggested, may have grown out of his loss of his own daughter in a drowning accident years ago and a misplaced desire to protect the young: "Holden Caulfield syndrome" a psychologist was quoted as saying. "Unfortunately, we can't stay long," Paula said. "Ross is meeting a client at the Red Sox game tonight, and I've got to get back for the kids."

"How are they?"

"They're just great." She smiled and met my eyes with clear sincerity. We went inside and caught up quickly.

"Ross's big case is over, thank God. I'm hoping we can do some family things. I'm sure once he relaxes . . ." But she wasn't sure; I heard it in her voice now, as I had when she'd phoned to say let's all get together for an afternoon bite.

I told the hostess our party was almost complete, and she seated us in a booth by the window overlooking the narrow cobblestoned street beyond a window box full of flowers.

"And how are you, Alex?" Paula asked.

"Curbside seats when I request them. Geraniums. I'm a king in my realm."

"Is that all I'm going to get out of you?"

Her gaze was steady, inquiring. It was customary, in my experience, for people to forget your name when you'd finished a job for them. They came to you in a time of turmoil, when they were at their weakest, and afterward they wanted only to forget. I respected that Paula had called and insisted that we all get together, but now I almost wished she hadn't. Or that I had begged off. "I'm okay," I said. "Busy, too."

She watched me, her blue eyes asparkle, examining me as if looking for something she'd misplaced or lost. Abruptly, she glanced outside, and I realized she was looking to see if her husband was coming. He was walking up the block, neat in a tan summer-weight sport coat and dark slacks. Paula reached and took my hand and gripped it. "I know I don't need to tell you again," she said, "but I'm so grateful for what you did. What I do want to say, or try to is that . . . in ways you may not know, you saved my life."

A hundred lines rose in my mind, where I left them. I gave her hand a squeeze and then let go. In a minute Ross appeared, loping over like a big grinning schoolboy. I shook his hand, and we did the man car-talk thing for a moment. He said they could only stay for a drink because . . .

"I explained," Paula said, and we all laughed, and the talk slipped back to the level where everyone operated most of the time. When our drinks arrived, Paula excused herself to go to the ladies' room. I stood, and seeing me do it, Ross shuffled to his feet, too. When she'd gone, Ross reached into his coat pocket and took out an envelope and handed it to me. For a moment, I thought it might be Red Sox tickets, but I saw several crisp new bills with 100s on the corners. I put the envelope down.

"You guys paid me already."

"Take it." He pushed it toward me. "From me."

"No, I can't. You've already been generous."

"You got answers. Call it a bonus. I got a little windfall myself."

I smiled; I liked an understatement, too. "Thank you, Ross, but it's not necessary."

"Give it to a charity, then." His tone was insistent. When I didn't take it, his eyes narrowed. "What's your problem?"

I tried to lighten it with a little laugh. "Maybe we should be drinking Fog Cutters. Paula sent me a check. It cleared. It's in my bank account already. I'm satisfied."

"Are you?"

"I don't follow you," I said.

"I doubt she really knows what you accomplished. I have a better appreciation of these things."

"Because you're a man? And she's only a woman?"

"What?"

"Nothing."

"No, what did you mean? What's going on?"

Stow it, Rasmussen, I told myself, or you're going to regret it. Be graceful, take the money; pay off your old parking tickets with it. But I didn't listen. I reached into my inside jacket pocket and took out the photograph, the one that Grady Stinson had given me, and handed it over. Ross looked at it a moment, and I had the thought that I'd been wrong, that he would ask me who the woman was and where I got the photo. But then I saw him redden slightly. He ripped it in half and then again and put the pieces into his pocket. "That's over," he said. "It has been for a while. It was a mistake."

He puffed a breath and sat back, his gaze drifting away to something only he saw. I glanced outside. The Porsche was parked a little way down, in a no-standing zone, as bright as a fire truck, not a cop in sight. Neither of us spoke for a sluggish moment. Then he asked, "Did Paula give you that?"

"No. As far as I know she never saw it." He went on staring at me. I said, "What's the point?"

"What?"

"The object, the goal—the raison d'être?"

"You mind telling me what the hell you're talking about?"

"Is it to become a partner in the firm? Blankety Blank and Jensen."

"You think that's small change?"

"No, but in the end, what've you got? A win-loss record? A tally of how much money you've made for your clients, for the firm? What's the net? How much you jack up the other guy?"

His hand clenched. "You put a sock in it right now, pal! Or I will!"

I was holding my beer glass way too tight. "I'm saying that when they log your name in the book of hours, the only testament you, or anyone, has got is the pride and the passion in what you've left behind. Doesn't matter if it's the azaleas, or wooden decoys you carved, or the afghan you knitted. It can be a book of poems, or your own good name. But it can't be just about money, or sitting in the best seats." He'd started to draw away; I actually reached and clasped his coat sleeve. "You won't *miss* anything. I sat at Fenway that October night in '75—along with the two million other folks who swear they were there—when Carlton Fisk danced his clout fair in the twelfth, and the miracle kids took Cincinnati to game seven."

He pulled his arm free. His face looked as hot as his new car. "Your alleged point being?"

"If I'd never seen another game, I wouldn't have missed a thing. The Sox will take you close but will always trounce your heart, because they know your love's unconditional. But who cares? Good arms give out, toys break. The river flows, as a philosopher bartender I know might say. Your girls won't be eight and sixteen forever."

Jensen's lean jaw locked. His hand on the table was a fist. If he was going to hit me, this was the moment. I waited. He didn't swing. "What the hell do you know about it?" he hissed. "Have you got children? Huh? You don't even have a wife anymore, do you."

I glanced outside and felt the last of my anger cooking away, and realized that the one I was angry at most was me. I lifted my glass and took a drink and set the glass down carefully in the wet ring it had made on the plank table. "You're right," I said. "Forget it."

44

"Did you see it yet?"

Fred Meecham stood in my office doorway, waving the mail, including the day's edition of the *Sun*. "Page nine," he said.

I'd expected page one. "Local PI Is Hero" or some such. News had come through that a body found on a Cape Cod beach had proved to be Ted Rand's. But I looked at where Meecham was pointing, and there was my paid ad, "Alex Rasmussen Investigations," right under an ad that read "Say Good-Bye to Unwanted Hair Forever."

"Well?" he said, grinning expectantly.

"Some people *want* hair. Couldn't it be put up for adoption or something?"

"And with the press you've gotten for closing that missing kid case?" he went on, jived on his own excitement. "You got the answers you needed. Your capital will definitely rise." He laid the paper on my desk, along with the junk mail, and split, leaving me to my joy.

I didn't have to tell him that every answer raised new questions. Okay, Ted Rand had become lower man on the food chain and had gone to his separate doom, but how was Iva Rand? And TJ? Would they be all right? I didn't know. I did know that Nickerson's company had been sold to pay off his debts, and that Rand's had gone into receivership, its large assets frozen. I guess I was rich in comparison. I knew that Point Pines was on indefinite hold, the legal and real estate wrangling likely to take years to sort out as the lawyers pulled sad, serious faces and shouldered the burden. I knew that at the state house, bugs would be scurrying, as they always will when someone rolls over a rotten log and lets the blaze of daylight in, and some of them would be looking for work come November, but others, the quickest, would squirm to cover and live and breed for another time.

What would happen to Michelle Nickerson and to Fran Albright and to Officer Ferry? I didn't know that either. I did know that there are monsters in the world. I knew that all of us are sometimes fated to go around the wheel for another turn or two, hoping to get something right that so far we'd only gotten wrong. I was on that line, ahead of quite a few others. But that was metaphysics, not anything you could take to the bank. I was tired. I'd been beaten, chased, shot at, damn near drowned. I'd come within a whisker of losing my life, my license, and my self-respect. I was sore. I needed a rest. I went through the mail: the same stuff that turns up in your mailbox and that gets the same response. There was a flyer from a writing/correspondence school that wanted me to tell children's stories for lucrative markets. Would anyone be interested in the tale of a sixteen-year-old child whom a bunch of grown-ups had very nearly lost. I balled up that idea and tossed it away fast. The letter I was waiting for, the one granting me immunity from financial worries and future woe wasn't there. There was a postcard from Vancouver.

"*Dear Alex,*" Paula had written, "*Canada is friendly and beautiful. We may drive down the coast to San Francisco. Ross has extended his vacation. Can you believe it? Kids are great. Happy August. Fondly, Paula, Ross, Michelle and Katie.*" A PS in another handwriting, which I recognized as Ross Jensen's, read "*Dawn rising slowly over Marble Head. Thanks.*"

Seemed everyone was going someplace, I thought as I locked up the office at lunchtime. Maybe that's what I needed to do: take a vacation. Yeah, maybe that's just what I'd do. I went by Tony's Pizza, but the sign on the door read "See You in September," so I went down the block to a sandwich counter. I sat on a stool in the window and watched the traffic passing and people walking by. I gazed at the sunlight on old brick, which was like beauty itself. But underneath the surface, I knew, there were people in bad trouble who didn't always know where to turn. I'd hold off on the vacation for now. Maybe when the leaves flew or when the frost came . . .

For Rand, all had become spoiled, because he'd been the spoiler. No amount of money could ever change that. Sure, there was ample cause to grow weary of the stupid violence, the frauds and the tricksters and the bent men, the lost women, the sad, tired streets, and the bitter aftertaste of human travail, but still and all, it was a pretty good old world, no denying, where sometimes dreams came true. I had another cup of coffee, and when I figured I'd given enough time for folks to read the newspaper and see my ad, I went back. The lobby of my building was musty and welcoming.